MISBEHAVING
UNDER THE
Mistletoe

MISBEHAVING
UNDER THE
Mistletoe

Heidi   Charlotte   Nina
RICE   **PHILLIPS**   **HARRINGTON**

MILLS & BOON

Published in Great Britain 2014
by Mills & Boon, an imprint of Harlequin (UK) Limited,
Eton House, 18-24 Paradise Road, Richmond, Surrey, TW9 1SR

MISBEHAVING UNDER THE MISTLETOE
© 2014 Harlequin Books S.A.

On the First Night of Christmas... © 2011 Heidi Rice
Secrets of the Rich & Famous © 2012 Charlotte Phillips
Truth-Or-Date.com © 2012 Nina Harrington

ISBN: 978-0-263-25039-8

013-1114

ON THE FIRST
NIGHT OF CHRISTMAS...

HEIDI RICE

Heidi Rice was born and bred and still lives in London. She has two sons who love to bicker, a wonderful husband who, luckily for everyone, has loads of patience, and a supportive and ever-growing British/French/Irish/American family. As much as Heidi adores London, she also loves America, and every two years or so she and her best friend leave hubby and kids behind and *Thelma and Louise* it across the States for a couple of weeks (although they always leave out the driving off a cliff bit). She's been a film buff since her early teens and a romance junkie for almost as long. She indulged her first love by being a film reviewer for ten years. Then a few years ago she decided to spice up her life by writing romance. Discovering the fantastic sisterhood of romance writers (both published and unpublished) in Britain and America made it a wild and wonderful journey to her first Mills & Boon® novel. Heidi loves to hear from readers—you can e-mail her at heidi@heidi-rice.com, or visit her website, www.heidi-rice.com.

To my Mum and Dad,
for so many wonderful Christmas memories

CHAPTER ONE

IF ONLY my love life were as perfect as Selfridges at Christmas.

Cassie Fitzgerald let out a wistful sigh as she gazed at the explosion of festive bling in the iconic London store's window display. The Sugar Plum Fairy sparkled flirtatiously on the shoulder of a hunky mannequin dressed in a dinner suit, silver snowflake lights making her tiny wings twinkle. Cassie's heart lifted. Selfridges' Christmas window dressing never let you down. It always captured the hope and expectation of the season of goodwill so beautifully. And okay, maybe her love life wasn't perfect—in fact, it was non-existent—but that was still a big improvement on last year.

A frown creased Cassie's brow as she recalled the Christmas wish she'd made the year before while standing in front of Selfridges—involving Lance, her boyfriend of three years, and a proposal of marriage.

She wrinkled her nose in disgust, the frozen air making it tingle, as her mind conjured up the image of Lance and Tracy McGellan getting up close and pornographic on the sofa in Cassie's flat a month after Valentine's Day. A month after Cassie had accepted that wished-for proposal.

Colour hit her cheeks as she remembered her shock and disbelief, swiftly followed by the shame of her own idiocy.

What on earth had possessed her to agree to marry a deadbeat like Lance?

As Christmas wishes went, it was one of her worst. Right up there with wishing for a pair of inline skates when she was eight—which had resulted in a broken wrist and four hours in Accident and Emergency on Christmas Day. Marriage to Lance would have been worse, but in her typically romantic fashion she'd overlooked all his shortcomings, determined to convince herself that he was The One.

Cassie hunched her shoulders against the brisk winter wind. From now on she was going to stop looking at life through rose-tinted glasses...because all it did was blind her to reality. And she wasn't making a Christmas wish this year, because it might come true.

It would be a shame not to have anyone to wake up with this Christmas morning—and she'd been in a funk about it for days. She adored bounding out of bed, brewing a pot of spiced apple tea and then savouring the presents artfully arranged under the tree. Having to do all that alone wasn't quite the same.

But as her best friend Nessa had pointed out, Cassie was better off doing it alone than with Lance the Loser. Cassie huddled in her coat. Absorbing the bright sparkle of Sugar Plum and her beau, she let the thought of her lucky escape from Lance strengthen her resolve.

'What you need is a candy man—to give your girly bits a wake-up call. Then you wouldn't need another deadbeat boyfriend.'

Cassie's lips edged up as she recalled Nessa's use-him-then-lose-him advice when they'd chatted on the phone that morning. Sometimes she really wished she could be as pragmatic about sex as Nessa. If she could just take sex a little less seriously, maybe she could have some fun without getting tangled up with creeps like Lance.

Bidding goodbye to Sugar Plum, Cassie jostled her way to Bond Street tube. Frantic shoppers herded in and out of the shops along Oxford Street on a mission to buy all those essential last-minute items that would make their Christmas complete. Stopping at the kerb as the traffic barrelled past on one of the cross streets, Cassie squeezed her eyes shut and fantasised about her candy man. Hot, hunky and devoted to making her feel fabulous, he would be magically gone by the New Year—so she'd never have to spend time picking his socks up off the bathroom floor, or washing the dirty dishes he left piled in the sink, or persuading herself she was in love with him.

Her erogenous zones zinged pleasantly for the first time in months.

She opened her eyes as the roar of a car engine interrupted the warm, fuzzy glow. Then shrieked as a wall of freezing water slammed into her. The elderly gentleman next to her muttered, 'Damn inconsiderate,' as a puddle the size of the Atlantic sluiced back into the gutter, and a sleek black car sped past.

Cassie gasped. The warm, fuzzy glow replaced by ice-cold shock. 'What the…!'

The driver hadn't even stopped. What a prize jerk.

Flinging her bag over her shoulder, she turned to glare at the vehicle, which had braked at the crossing ten feet away. Her fingers curled into tight fists at her sides.

Normally, she would have let the matter pass. Normally, she would have chalked the drenching up to bad luck and assumed the driver hadn't meant to splash her. But as she stood there, the other shoppers edging past her and gawping at the huge wet patch on her favourite coat as if she had a contagious disease, she felt something new and liberating surging up her torso.

Whether he'd meant to do it or not, she was soaked. And she wasn't going to just stand by and take whatever life had to throw at her any more.

Dodging through the crowd, she drew level and rapped on the passenger window. 'Hey, Ebenezer.'

The tinted glass slid down with an electric hum. She blinked, the zing tingling back to life as a man peered out from the shadows on the driver's side. Dark hair swept back from a broodingly handsome face accented by a strong jaw and hollow, raw-boned cheeks. She felt the odd jolt of recognition as the scent of new leather wafted out of the car. Did she know him?

'What's the problem?' he demanded.

Clammy water dripped down inside Cassie's boots and kick-started her tongue—and her indignation.

'You're the problem. Look what you did to me.' She held up her arms to show him the extent of the damage, ruthlessly silencing the zing. He might have a striking face, but his manners sucked.

He swore softly. 'Are you sure that was me?'

The blare of a car horn had Cassie glancing at the lights. Green. 'Of course, I'm sure.'

The horn blared again. Longer and angrier this time.

'I can't stop here.' He straightened back into the shadows and Cassie saw his hand grasp the gear shift.

No way, pal. You are not driving off and leaving me in a puddle on the pavement.

Yanking the heavy door open, she launched herself into the passenger seat.

'Hey!' he said as she slammed the door behind her. 'What the hell do you—?'

'Just drive, Sir Galahad.' She pinned him with her best disgusted look. 'We can discuss your crummy behaviour when you find somewhere to stop.'

His dark brows drew down, the piercing emerald of his irises glittering with annoyance.

'Fine.' He slapped up the indicator, shifted into First. 'But don't drip on the upholstery. This is a rental.'

The car purred to life, and a blast of heat wrapped around Cassie, engulfing her in the subtle aroma of man and leather—and wet velvet. Her heart careered into her throat as the flicker of Selfridges' fairy lights disappeared from her peripheral vision—and the surge of adrenaline that had propelled her into the car smacked head first into her survival instinct.

She was sitting in a complete stranger's car being driven to who knew where—which probably rated a perfect ten on the 'too stupid to live' scale.

'Actually, forget it.' She grasped the door handle.

The driver pulled to a stop at a loading bay. 'So it wasn't me after all.'

Cassie's fingers stilled on the handle at the accusatory tone and her common sense dissolved in a haze of outrage. 'It was definitely you.' She glared at him over the gear shift. 'Don't you know it's Christmas? Show a bit of respect for the season and stop being such a jerk.'

Typical. When Cassie Fitzgerald is on the hunt for a candy man, what does she get? A candy man with a crappy attitude.

Jacob Ryan cranked up the handbrake, slung his arm over the steering wheel and stared at the furious pixie in his passenger seat whose wide violet eyes were shooting daggers at him.

How the hell did I end up with Santa's insane little helper in my car?

As if it weren't bad enough that Helen had manoeuvred him into accepting an invitation to her 'little soirée' tonight, now he had a mad woman in his rented Mercedes. A mad woman who was dripping all over the custom-finished leather upholstery.

He'd never been a fan of the season to be jolly, but this was getting ridiculous.

The sight of the filthy splatter on her coat, though, had the tiniest prickle of guilt surfacing. The car *had* hit a rut in the road.

Hoisting his butt off the seat, he tugged his wallet out of his back pocket. Okay, maybe he had been the culprit. He'd been so aggravated by Helen's petulant demands, he hadn't been paying attention.

'How much?' he asked. A hundred ought to cover it.

Her full Cupid's bow mouth flattened into a grim line and the daggers sharpened. 'I don't want your money,' she announced. 'That's not what this is about.'

Yeah, right.

He counted five crisp twenty-pound notes out of his wallet and presented them to her. 'Here you go. Merry Christmas.'

She gave the money a cursory glance, and the line of her lips twisted into a sneer. 'I told you. I don't want your money, Ebenezer.'

The sarcastic name grated, but then she tightened her arms under her breasts, and his gaze dipped—distracted by the creamy flesh exposed by the wide V in the lapels of her coat.

Hell, is she naked under that thing?

The wayward thought came out of nowhere, and sent a blast of heat somewhere he definitely didn't need it.

'What I want is an apology,' she demanded.

He tore his eyes away from her breasts. 'Huh?'

'An apology? You do know what that is, right?' she said, as if he had an IQ in single figures.

He shook his head, struggling to stem the immature fantasy. Of course she wasn't naked under the coat. Not unless she was a lap dancer. And he doubted that. Given her big doe eyes and the helping of Christmas whimsy she'd dealt him, the picture of her getting sweaty tenners folded into a G-string didn't fit, despite that eye-popping cleavage.

He stuffed the money back into the wallet and dumped it on the dash.

'I apologise,' he said curtly, deciding to humour her.

He didn't usually bother with apologies. Especially to women. Because he'd discovered from experience they didn't count for much. But these were extenuating circumstances. He needed to get her out of the car before that glimpse of cleavage melted the rest of his brain cells and he did something really daft. Like hitting on a crazy lady.

'That's it? That's the best you can do?' She twisted in her seat—all the better to glare at him, he suspected—but the movement made her breasts press against the confines of her coat and threaten to spill out. His mouth went dry.

'I'm going to have to spend an hour on the tube,' she ranted. 'Then get hypothermia walking across the park. And you can't come up with a better—'

'Look, Pollyanna,' he interrupted, the heat tying his gut in knots as he breathed in a lungful of her scent. Cinnamon and cloves and orange. 'I've offered you money and you don't want it,' he ranted right back when she remained silent. 'I apologised and you don't want that, either. Short of sawing off my right arm and gift-wrapping it I don't know what else I'm supposed to do to make amends.'

Her mouth closed and her delicately arched eyebrows launched up her forehead into the soft brown curls that haloed around her head.

That had certainly shut her up. Although he wasn't quite sure what he'd said that had put the shell-shocked look on her face. The unusual colour of her eyes had darkened to a vivid turquoise and all the pigment had leached out of her cheeks.

She covered her mouth with her fingers. 'Jace the Ace.'

The words were muffled, but distinctive enough to make him tense. 'How do you know my name?' he asked, although no one had called him by that particular nickname for four-

teen years. Not since he'd been kicked out of school when he
was seventeen. The minute the thought registered, another
more disturbing one hit him—and the insistent throbbing in
his groin increased.

Damn it. That had to be it. What other explanation was
there for his instant response to her?

She hadn't replied, so he forced himself to ask the obvious next question.

'Have I slept with you?'

He doesn't remember me. Thank you, God.

Cassie tried to speak, but her tongue was too numb to
form coherent words. Not all that surprising given that the
punch of recognition had hit her squarely in the solar plexus
and expelled all the air from her lungs. She shook her head.
'No,' she whispered.

'I *definitely* didn't sleep with you?' he asked as the un-
flinching emerald gaze that had broken a thousand female
hearts at Hillsdown Road Secondary School searched her
face.

She nodded.

His shoulders relaxed and she heard him mutter, 'Good to
know.'

No wonder she hadn't recognised him straight away. The
Jacob Ryan she remembered had been a boy. A tall, troubled
and heart-stoppingly handsome boy, who at seventeen had
been the perfect mix of dashing and dangerous to a girl of
thirteen with an overactive imagination and hyperactive hormones.

They hadn't slept together. In fact, they'd never even
kissed. She'd been four years younger than him, and when
you were at school that might as well have been a fifty-year
age difference. But she'd had a wealth of immature romantic

fantasies about him—like every other girl in her year—which were now playing havoc with her heartbeat.

She shifted in her seat, feeling disorientated and a little light-headed, the damp velvet of her coat like a straightjacket.

Her stomach muscles clenched and released. Exactly as they always had all those years ago, if she'd spied him brooding in the dinner hall, or at the bus shelter busy ignoring all the girls giggling around him... Or during what had come to be known in the annals of Cassie's teenage years as The Ultimate Humiliation. The excruciating moment when she'd disturbed him and head girl Jenny Kelty snogging on the back stairwell.

Cassie's nipples tightened painfully, the impossibly erotic picture they'd made entwined on the dimly lit staircase still astonishingly fresh.

She'd been anchored to the spot, her thigh muscles dissolving as she gawped. His hand had been under Jenny's blouse, his stroking fingers visible beneath the billowing white cotton. Cassie had watched transfixed, her teeth digging into her lip, as his other hand had skimmed to Jenny's waist then moulded her bottom, grinding her against him. Then he'd raised his head and nipped at Jenny's bottom lip. And Cassie had felt her own lip tingle.

As Jenny had groaned and writhed, warmth had flooded through Cassie's system and her strangled gasp had slipped out without warning.

Jace Ryan's sure steady gaze had locked on her face. She'd been trapped, like a deer about to be mown down by a juggernaut. Frozen in terror as reaction skidded up her spine.

But instead of looking angry at the interruption, he had curved his sensual lips into a confidential grin. As if they shared a secret joke that only they understood.

She'd grinned back, opened her mouth to say something, anything.

Then Jenny had spotted her standing there like an idiot and screeched, 'What are you smiling at, you silly cow? Get lost.'

Hot humiliation had blazed through her entire body and she'd scrambled back down the stairs so fast she'd nearly broken her neck. The pounding of blood in her ears far too loud to hear the words Jace shouted after her as she ran.

He turned back to her now, tapped his thumb on the steering wheel. 'So what's your name?'

'Cassie Fitzgerald.'

His forehead furrowed. 'I don't remember anyone called—'

'That's a relief,' she interrupted, praying his memory loss lasted a lifetime. 'That chartreuse blazer was not a good look for me.'

He chuckled. The low rumble of amusement did funny things to her thigh muscles. 'Look, why don't we start over?' he said, his eyes darkening as his gaze rose to the top of her head, then settled back on her face. 'I've got a suite at The Chesterton. Why don't you come back with me? We can get your coat dry-cleaned.' Reaching forward, he tucked a curl behind her ear. 'It's the least I can do for an old school chum.'

They hadn't been chums. Not even close.

'I'm not sure that's a good idea,' she murmured, trying not to pander to the thrum of awareness that pulsed against her cheek where his finger had touched.

Jace Ryan had been dangerous to a woman's peace of mind at seventeen. He was probably deadly now.

He sent her a conspiratorial wink. 'Good is overrated.'

Cassie's pulse sped up, then slowed to a sluggish crawl— and she completely forgot about not pandering to the thrum. 'Is bad better, then?'

He smiled, the penetrating green gaze sweeping over her— and the thrum went haywire.

'In my experience—' his eyes met hers '—bad is not only

better, it's also a lot more fun.' He glanced over his shoulder to check the traffic. 'So how about it?' he asked as the car pulled away from the kerb. 'You want to come back to the hotel and we can raid the mini-bar together while I get your coat cleaned?'

'Okay,' she replied, before she had a chance to think better of it. 'If you're sure it's not too much bother?'

He sent her an easy grin. 'Not at all.'

Crossing her arms, Cassie pressed down on her treacherous boobs, which were still throbbing at the memory of Jace Ryan on that stairwell a million years ago, and studied his profile in the glimmer of the passing streetlights.

Maturity suited him: the light tan, the hint of five o'clock shadow, the thick waves of dark hair, the little lines at the corners of his eyes and the once angry red scar that had faded to a thin white line slashing rakishly across his left eyebrow. He'd grown into those brooding heartthrob features, his hollow cheeks defined to create a dramatic sweep of planes and angles. And from the powerful physique stretching the expertly tailored suit as he shifted gears, he'd also grown into his lanky build.

Cassie huddled in her seat as the powerful car accelerated onto Park Lane. The majestic twenty-foot spruce under Marble Arch glided past, its red and gold star-shaped lights glittering festively in the early winter dusk.

He'd asked her if he'd slept with her—which meant either he suffered from amnesia, or he'd slept with so many women in his time, he couldn't remember the details. Recalling the never-ending string of girlfriends he'd had at Hillsdown Road, Cassie would take a wild guess it was the latter.

Jace Ryan was the sort of guy no sensible woman would ever want to have a relationship with. But as she watched him drive his flashy car with practised efficiency, sexual attraction rippled across her nerve-endings and the thrum of awareness peaked.

Jace Ryan might be a dead loss in the relationship department, but could he be the ultimate candy man? Because as coincidences went, this one was kind of hard to ignore.

She eased out an unsteady breath.

And did she have a sweet enough tooth—and enough guts—to risk taking a lick?

CHAPTER TWO

THAT would be a no, then, came the answer as Cassie peered out the windshield of Jace's car. Evergreen garlands of holly and trailing ivy shimmered with a thousand tiny lights on the ornate stone and gold frontage of the luxury hotel.

When Jace had mentioned The Chesterton she hadn't pictured him having a suite at this art deco palace on Park Lane. The vision of her scurrying into its rarefied elegance in her soiled coat and muddy biker boots plunged her ridiculous candy man fantasy into cold hard reality.

He had offered to get her coat cleaned. He had not offered to perk up her Christmas with prurient sexual favours. And he wasn't likely to when she looked such a fright.

Jace skirted the hood of the car and took the front steps two at a time. He tossed the car keys to a doorman, whose gold-braided green livery and matching top hat weren't doing a thing for Cassie's anxiety levels.

What on earth had she been thinking when she'd accepted his invitation? She felt as if she were thirteen again, getting caught staring at something she shouldn't on that stairwell.

She slid down in the deep bucket seat as the doorman approached the car. Swinging the door open with a slight bow, he sent her a courteous smile.

'It's a pleasure to welcome you to The Chesterton, Ms Fitzgerald.' He held out a hand. 'Mr Ryan has requested we collect your dry-cleaning as soon as you are settled in his suite.'

Cassie stepped out of the car, but studiously avoided letting her coat touch the poor man. Like he wanted mud all over his nice clean uniform. Jace waited at the hotel's revolving doors, looking confident and relaxed and completely at ease in the exclusive surroundings.

She wrapped her arms round her waist as she mounted the steps towards him.

Candy man or not, Jace Ryan was way too much for her to handle. He'd probably known more about seduction when he was seventeen than she ever would. The thrum of awareness that had arched between them had been nothing more than the echo of an old crush. Which she'd grown out of years ago.

She touched his arm before he could direct her through the revolving doors into the lobby.

'Is there a back entrance?' she asked, dropping her hand as her fingers connected with the solid strength beneath the blue silk of his suit.

His lips twitched. 'I wouldn't know. Why?'

'I'm all wet.' Hadn't he noticed she looked like something the cat had dragged through a puddle?

His gaze wandered over her, and the back of her neck burned. 'Your coat took the worst of it. Just take it off.'

She slipped off the wet coat and bunched it in her hands, the blush climbing into her cheeks.

A rueful smile curved his lips and she thought he whispered, 'Pity.'

'Sorry?' Was it her imagination or was there a twinkle of mischief in his eyes?

'Nothing,' he murmured, but the twinkle didn't dim one bit.

The simple sapphire tunic skimmed the top of her thighs and was one of her favourites of Nessa's designs, but the short sleeves and plunging neckline meant wearing it without a coat was a good way to get hypothermia in December. The fragile, bias-cut fabric moulded to her figure as the wind brushed against her skin and made her shiver. She clamped her teeth together to stop them chattering and jumped when his warm palm settled on the small of her back.

'Here.' He shrugged out of his jacket and draped the garment over her shoulders. 'I'll take that.' He lifted her coat out of her arms.

She gripped the lapels of his jacket, the tailored silk dwarfing her as he placed his hand on her hip and led her through the revolving doors into the marble lobby. The fragrance of the roses, freshly cut pine boughs and cinnamon sticks arranged in giant urns by the reception desk greeted them, but did nothing to mask the scent of soap and man that clung to his jacket.

'Wait here.'

Crossing to the desk, he handed over her coat to one of the uniformed receptionists, who took the wet garment without showing a hint of surprise, then sent Cassie an efficient smile. As if it were perfectly normal for half-dressed women to track mud over their foyer.

Cassie tried to look invisible in Jace's jacket as he led her through an ornately furnished lounge accented by deep-seated sofas in tartan upholstery, polished mahogany occasional tables and wrought-iron planters overflowing with winter flora. A scattering of perfectly dressed people sipped afternoon tea from delicate china cups and watched her pass.

Fabulous. She felt like Cinderella arriving at the ball in her rags.

When they stepped into the lift, she eased back against the panelling, still clinging to the jacket. 'This place is seriously posh.'

He huffed out a laugh. 'Don't let them intimidate you.

They're just rich, they're not royalty. Or at least most of them aren't.'

'Fabulous,' she said wryly.

He chuckled again, shoving one hand into his pocket as he stabbed the top button on the display panel. She tried not to notice the way the movement made the linen of his shirt tighten across one broad shoulder.

His gaze took a leisurely trip down to her biker boots and back again as the lift whisked through the floors. She clamped down on the sudden wish to have him like what he saw.

Been there, done that, got the battered ego to prove it.

But when his eyes lifted to her face at last, the beat of anticipation still throbbed in her ears.

'Money doesn't buy you class,' he said. 'I ought to know.'

Sympathy welled and lodged in her throat, the blunt statement reminding her of the angry boy he'd once been. No one had ever found out that much about him at Hillsdown Road, his air of mystery only tantalising his army of admirers more. But one thing she did know was that he'd come from a 'bad home', because she'd overheard Ms Tremall, the head of the sixth form, talking about him to the headmaster, Mr Gates.

'You've got more than enough class to go round now,' she said passionately, the injustice of the teacher's whispered comments surging back. Like all the rest of the school staff, Tremall and Gates had condemned him because of his background and never given him the benefit of the doubt.

His eyebrow arched at her rabble-rousing tone. 'It's not class. It's money,' he said, with more than a hint of irony. 'But I find it does the job just as well.'

The relaxed statement made her feel foolish. Who exactly did she think she was defending here? He certainly wasn't that troubled boy any more. In fact, from his exceedingly posh digs, he was most likely a millionaire. She shook the thought off. Probably best not to go there given her already thriving inferiority complex.

The lift bell pinged and the doors slid back to reveal a marble lobby area only slightly less palatial than the one downstairs.

Here too, a tall vase filled with dark red lilies gave the carved stone and gilded plasterwork a Christmas glow. Using his key card to open a mahogany door, he stood back as she walked into a vaulted hallway that led into a suite of rooms.

Cassie came to an abrupt halt, dismayed by the deep-pile carpeting that led down the corridor into what looked like a large living room.

'Is there a problem?' he asked, lifting the jacket off her shoulders.

'I should take off my boots.' Mud would not look good on all that magnolia.

'Go ahead.' He slung the jacket over a chair. 'I'll call Housekeeping and get them polished while your coat's cooking.'

'That's... Thanks,' she said, embarrassed.

She hopped on one leg to unzip one of the boots, only to jerk upright when he placed his hand on her waist.

'Hold on to my shoulder,' he said casually enough, but as his eyes connected with hers the awareness that prickled up her spine reminded her of that dark school hallway a lifetime ago. Except this time those long, strong fingers held her, and not Jenny Kelty.

'Thanks,' she mumbled, her heartbeat battering her ribcage like a sledgehammer.

She touched his shoulder blade for balance, only to have her insides tilt alarmingly as the muscled sinews tensed beneath her fingers.

He kept his hand on her waist as she struggled with the

boots. But once she'd yanked them off and pulled away from his touch, she realised she had another problem.

'You might want to lose those too,' he mentioned, apparently reading her mind as he examined the wet leggings. 'They're soaked.'

'Right.' She hesitated. The problem was, without her leggings, she'd only have the butt-skimming tunic on. She did a quick mental check. Had she put on her much-prized silk high-leg panties with the lace trim this morning, or had she opted for the usual cheap cotton passion-killers?

The instant the dilemma registered, she yanked herself back to reality.

For pity's sake, Cass. It doesn't matter what knickers you're wearing.

The state of her undies had no bearing whatsoever on this situation. She was here to get her coat cleaned. Nothing more. Bending down, she wiggled out of the leggings and then shoved them under her arm.

'You warm enough?' he asked.

Gripping the hem of the tunic, she yanked it down, goose pimples rising on her bare thighs as her toes curled into the downy-soft carpeting.

'Fine, thanks,' she murmured, noticing the tiny dimple winking in one hard, chiselled cheek. That he found her predicament amusing only confirmed how ludicrous that moment of vanity had been. He wasn't remotely interested in her. Or her knickers.

'Make yourself comfortable in the lounge.' He indicated the large living area as the dimple deepened. 'While I get these sent down.' He picked up her boots, then reached for the leggings under her arm.

She forced herself to relax so he could take them. 'Oh— Okay.' She cleared her throat when the words came out on a squeak. 'Thanks, I will.'

'Help yourself to a drink.' To her dismay he didn't turn, but seemed to be waiting for her to move first. 'They're in the cabinet under the flat-screen.'

She opened her mouth to say thanks for the millionth time, then thought better of it. He'd probably got the message loud and clear by now. Bobbing her head, she forced herself to move. But as she headed towards the lounge, her footsteps silenced by the carpet, she strained to hear him walk away. When silence reined, she couldn't help hoping that if anything was peeping out from under her tunic, it involved crimson lace and not utilitarian white cotton.

Jace spotted the flash of white cotton and the pulse of heat tugged low in his abdomen.

Something about the plain, simple underwear only made the sight more erotic. For a small woman, she certainly had a lot of leg. Slim and well toned, the soft skin of her thighs and calves flushed a delightful shade of pink, making the bright white of her panties all the more striking.

What made his lust a little weird, though, was that he'd remembered her. When those big blue eyes had lifted to his face a moment ago, the flashback had been so strong, he'd known instantly it wasn't a mistake. Or a trick of his libido.

She was the kid who had once disturbed him and one of his girlfriends on the back stairwell at school. He couldn't remember the girlfriend's name, couldn't even picture her face. All he really remembered about her was that she'd been more than willing and she hadn't had much of a sense of humour, which was why he'd dropped her like a stone after she'd shouted at the child watching them and scared her off.

But he could see Cassie Fitzgerald clearly enough. He'd been kicked out of school two days later, and the memory had quickly become buried amid all the crap he'd had to deal with when he'd been expelled.

But the image of her heart-shaped face came back to him now with surprising clarity.

She'd been young, way too young for him and not conventionally pretty. Those bewitching eyes had been too large for her face and her wide lips at the time had seemed too full. He hadn't fancied her, not in the least. She had been a baby. But something about the way she'd been watching him had struck a chord. Those big eyes of hers had grown huge in her face, and he'd felt as if she could see right into his soul, but, unlike everyone else, she hadn't been judging him. He'd smiled, because she'd looked so shocked, and it had been funny, but also because, for a second, he'd forgotten to feel jaded and angry and resentful, forgotten even his burning quest to get Miss No-Name's bra off and instead had felt like a kid again himself.

Unfortunately, as Cassie Fitzgerald disappeared into the lounge and the flash of white cotton disappeared with her, she wasn't making him feel like a kid any more. Not now that little girl had grown up—and into her unusual beauty.

Squeezing the damp fabric of her leggings in his fist, he lifted them to his nose, breathed in the sultry, Christmassy scent of cinnamon and oranges, only slightly masked by the earthy smell of rain-water, that had got to him in the car—and realised he was in serious trouble.

The impromptu decision to invite her to his suite had seemed like a good idea at the time. He had an hour to kill before he had to turn up at Helen's soirée and convince her once and for all to leave him alone, and he didn't want to think about what a pain in the backside that was going to be. Cassie would provide a welcome distraction. Plus getting her coat cleaned had solved the mystery of what it was she did or did not have on under it.

But he hadn't expected her to be quite this distracting. Her skittishness as soon as they'd arrived at the hotel had intrigued him. And the way she'd defended him in the lift had surprised the hell out of him—and reminded him of that kid on the stairwell. But what was distracting him a whole lot more was the sight of her lush, curvaceous figure in that dress, which was roughly the size of a place mat, and the resulting shot of arousal currently pounding like a sore tooth in his groin.

Not only was he going to find it next to impossible to keep his hands off her for the forty minutes the receptionist had said it would take to clean her clothing.

He was fast losing the will to even try.

Which was annoying. Mindless, meaningless sex had lost its appeal a long time ago—and he didn't seduce women he'd only just met any more.

Only problem was, right now, he couldn't for the life of him remember why.

Cassie stood by the wall of panelled glass, spellbound as she gazed out over the wraparound roof terrace and the dark expanse of Hyde Park below, the fairground lights of the Winter Wonderland shimmering playfully in the distance. She sipped from the glass of Merlot she'd poured herself to ease her dry throat, then placed it on a smooth walnut coffee table. She must be careful not to drink it all. Not only was it still barely six o'clock, but she'd forgotten to ask her host how long her clothes would take—so she didn't know how long she would be required to keep her wits about her. She'd always been a very cheap drunk. And on the evidence of her recent knicker meltdown, dulling her wits with alcohol could well lead to more candy man fantasies. Which was the last thing she needed if she didn't want to make this more awkward than it already was. Better to stay sober and sensible.

Swivelling round, she took in the full grandeur of Jace Ryan's hotel suite. Then released a staggered breath. This was the penthouse suite—the lofty view of Hyde Park nothing short of spectacular. The lounge area alone was considerably larger than her entire flat. She set aside her apprehension about spending time in his company as curiosity about him burned. How had the angry youth from a 'bad home' who'd been summarily expelled from their bog-standard comprehensive fourteen short years ago ended up affording the best suite in one of London's best hotels? Had he robbed a bank or something?

'Right, we're all set.' The man in question strolled into the room and dumped his key card on the coffee table next to her glass of wine. Even in the tailored trousers and linen shirt, he could easily be a bank robber, Cassie thought. He certainly had that confident, dangerous edge that made him seem capable of anything.

He delved into the bar and came up with a bottle of imported Italian beer. 'Do you need a top-up?' he asked, nodding towards her glass as he twisted off the bottle cap.

He'd rolled up his shirt sleeves, revealing forearms roped with muscle as he took a long slug of the beer.

'No, thanks,' she said. A couple of sips would definitely have to be her limit. 'Do you know how long the dry-cleaning will take?'

He shrugged. 'About forty minutes,' he said, sinking into one of the leather sofas. 'Take a seat.' He signalled the cushions next to him with his bottle, then kicked off his loafers and propped his stockinged feet on the table. 'You might as well get comfortable.'

Not likely, given that the sight of him lounging on his sofa was making her pulse pound like a timpani drum. He looked like a male supermodel, for goodness' sake, with those long, leanly muscled legs displayed in perfectly creased trousers, the rugged shadow of stubble on his chin, and his dark hair sexily mussed.

Forget candy man... Jace Ryan was an entire sweetshop.

She sat gingerly on the sofa opposite him, not about to risk getting too close to all that industrial-strength testosterone. Swooning would not be good.

Her tunic rose up her thighs and she hastily shifted onto her bottom, tucking her legs up under her to hide any hint of plain white cotton from view. If he looked like a supermodel, she looked like a banner ad for dull and boring.

She tore her eyes away from the intensity of his gaze, which seemed to have zeroed in on her face.

'How did you do it?' she asked, struggling to think of a safe topic for small talk.

'Do what?'

The puzzled reply had her realising the gaucheness of the question. 'I just wondered how you...' She trailed off, wishing she'd never asked. Was he embarrassed by his past? She doubted it. Sitting in the midst of the luxury he'd earned, he looked perfectly at home. Even so, she didn't want to pry.

'How did I manage to afford all this?' he prompted.

She debated trying to pretend she'd been asking something else, but had to give up on the idea. She couldn't think of an alternative interpretation. And even if she could, the steady, knowing look in his eyes suggested he already knew exactly what she'd been referring to.

She nodded, and took one more sip of wine, strictly for Dutch courage purposes.

He tilted his head to one side, as if considering his answer. 'I discovered I had a talent for design.' He paused for less than a heartbeat, but she heard the hesitation. 'Or rather my parole officer discovered I had a talent for design.'

'Your parole officer?' she asked, startled. He *had* robbed a bank.

'Relax.' He grinned, the light in his eyes twinkling again. 'It's all right. I'm not an ex-con.'

'I didn't think you were,' she lied.

'He was a young-offenders liaison officer. The school pressed charges. After they expelled me.'

'But that's ridiculous. The drawings were hilarious.' She could still remember the reason he'd been expelled. And the pinpoint accuracy of the staff caricatures he'd graffiti'd all over the back wall of the new gym in DayGlo spray paint.

'Gates never did have a sense of humour.' Jace shrugged. 'And it worked out fine for me.' Again she heard the slight hesitation. 'I got to move into a bedsit and onto an art foundation course—thanks to the officer assigned to my case, who actually believed I could be rehabilitated.'

'But you didn't need rehabilitating. You just needed someone to believe in you.'

His lips quirked in an indulgent smile. 'You really are Pollyanna, aren't you?'

'It's not that, it's just...' *What?* 'You didn't deserve to be treated so harshly. It was only a bit of fun.'

He placed his bottle on the table. 'It was criminal damage. And it wasn't the first time. So of course I deserved it.' The smile stayed in place, as if it didn't matter in the slightest. 'But that's more than enough about me.' He took his feet off the table, leaned forward and rested his elbows on his knees. 'Let's talk about you. You're much more interesting.'

'Me?' She pressed her hand to her chest. Was he kidding? 'Believe me, I'm not as interesting as you.'

'I'll be the judge of that.' He lifted his beer, held it poised at his mouth and studied her with an intensity that made her breath catch. 'So is Cassie short for Cassandra?' He took a swig and her eyes dipped involuntarily to the sensual line of his lips. He lowered the bottle. 'Apollo's paramour,' he murmured. 'Gifted with the power of prophecy but forever cursed not to be believed.'

Cassie trembled, the rough cadence of his voice sending

little shivers of excitement over her skin. She gave a breathless laugh, her gaze darting back to his face. 'If only it were that exciting.'

His lips edged into a seductive smile. 'It's not exciting. Cassandra's story is tragic.'

Not from where I'm sitting.

Cassie smiled despite the tension that crackled in the air. Was he trying to melt her into a puddle of lust? Or was that just wishful thinking on her part? 'Cassie's short for Cassidy.'

His eyebrow rose a fraction. 'Cassidy?'

'As in David Cassidy,' Cassie added, her grin spreading as his eyebrow arched upwards. 'The seventies teen idol. Unfortunately my mum was a huge fan. And I've been suffering ever since.'

How fitting that her mum had given her a name as unsexy as her knickers.

'Mind you, it could have been worse,' she continued, amused by his obvious surprise. 'Thank God she wasn't a Donny Osmond fan or I would have been saddled with Ossie.'

His laugh rumbled out, low and rough and setting off the little shivers again. 'I like Cassidy. It's unusual. Which suits you.'

She tipped her glass up in a toast. 'Yup, that's me, very unusual.' *If only.* 'Unlike you. Who's so totally run of the mill,' she added, unable to resist fluttering her eyelashes.

Instead of looking appalled at her heavy-handed attempt at flirtation, he clinked his bottle against her glass. 'You are unusual,' he said. 'Why don't you believe me?'

She took another hasty sip. The rich, heady wine flowed down her throat and wrapped around her chest like a winter quilt.

She let her gaze wander over to the blue spruce expertly decorated with glass baubles and ribbon bows in the corner. Jace Ryan might be a lot more man than she felt capable of handling. But where was the harm in enjoying his company? At least for as long as it took to clean her coat.

'How exactly am I unusual?' she asked, knowing it wasn't true, but happy to have him try to persuade her.

He placed his beer bottle on the coffee table and stood up. Lifting her hand from her lap, he wrapped his long fingers around it and gave a soft tug to pull her off the sofa. 'Stand up, so we can examine the evidence.'

She did as she was told, the appreciative gleam as his gaze roamed over her shocking her into silence.

'Your eyes are a really unusual colour. I noticed that as soon as you jumped into my car. Even though you were ruining the upholstery and calling me a jerk.'

'I only called you a jerk because you were being a jerk,' she pointed out in her defence.

He placed his hands on her hips. 'Stop ruining the mood.'

'What mood?' she asked, standing so close to him now, she could see the gold flecks in his irises.

The buckle on his belt brushed against her tummy and the little shivers became shock waves, shuddering down to the place between her thighs.

'The mood I'm trying to create' he said, a lock of dark hair flopping over his brow. 'So I can kiss you.'

Her gaze dipped to his mouth, those sensual lips that had once devoured Jenny temptingly close. 'You want to kiss me?' she said on a ragged breath.

He pressed his thumb to her bottom lip, the touch making it tingle. 'I must be seriously losing my touch. Isn't it obvious?'

'But we've only just met,' she whispered, not sure how to respond to his teasing. Did he seriously plan to kiss her? And why the heck was she arguing with him about it?

He wrapped his hand round her waist, pulled her flush

against him. 'Not true,' he remarked, his lips only centimetres from hers. 'We've known each other since school.'

'But you don't remember me.'

'Sure I do.' His warm breath feathered against her cheek. 'You're the little voyeur on the stairwell.'

She tensed and drew back. 'You remember? But how?'

'I told you, those eyes are very unusual.' His lips curved, in that same offhand grin that had captivated her over a decade ago. And suddenly, she understood. This wasn't a seduction. He was making fun of her.

She placed her hands on his chest, stumbled back, the sweet, heady buzz of flirtation and arousal replaced by embarrassment. 'I should go.'

He caught her elbow as she stepped back. 'Hey? What's the rush all of a sudden?'

'I just…I have to go,' she mumbled, pulling her arm free.

'Don't be ridiculous—your coat isn't back yet.'

She tugged down the hem of her tunic, feeling hideously exposed.

'I'll wait downstairs, in the lobby.' It would be mortifying in her bare feet, but what could be more mortifying than simpering all over a guy who was secretly laughing at her?

She crossed the living room, holding her head up.

'Hang on a minute. You're being absurd. What exactly are you so upset about?'

The frustrated words stopped her dead. She swung round.

He stood by his walnut coffee table, looking like a poster boy for original sin and the humiliation coalesced in her stomach into a hot ball of resentment.

'I know I'm absurd,' she said, and watched his brow crease in a puzzled frown. 'I had a massive crush on you. Which was my own stupid fault. I admit it.' She walked back and poked him in the chest. 'But that doesn't give you the right to make fun of me. Now or then.'

He grasped her finger, the green of his irises darkening to a stormy emerald. 'I'm not making fun of you. And I didn't then.'

'Yes, you did.' She tugged her finger free, not liking the way his touch had set off those silly shivers again. 'I heard you and Jenny Kelty laughing at me.' Not that it mattered now, but it was the principle of the thing. She had gone over that encounter a thousand times in her mind in the months that followed. And felt more and more mortified every time. Why had she stood there like a lemon? Why had she smiled at him? But she could see now, she hadn't been the only one at fault. They shouldn't have laughed at her.

'Who the hell is Jenny Kelty?' he asked.

'Unbelievable,' she said, exasperated. 'Don't you remember any of the girls you slept with back then either?'

'It was a long time ago.' He shoved his fingers through his hair, the movement jerky and a lot less relaxed than before. 'And whatever her name was, I didn't sleep with her. You put a stop to that.'

'Well, good,' she said, righteous indignation framing each word. 'I'm glad I saved Jenny from becoming yet another notch on your bedpost.'

'You didn't save Jenny. She saved herself. Once I found out what a cow she was, my interest in her cooled considerably.'

Jenny *had* been a cow, and every girl foolish enough to cross her had known it, but Cassie was still startled by the vehemence in the statement.

'So what changed your mind about Jenny?' She threw the words back at him. 'Did she refuse to snog you?'

His eyebrows rose another notch at the sarcastic tone. And Cassie felt power surge through her veins as if she had been plugged into a nuclear reactor.

Finally she, Cassie Fitzgerald, was standing up for herself.

And not letting her rose-tinted glasses blind her to the truth. She wasn't dumb little Cassie who had caught her fiancée on the couch with his lover and was too stupid to see it coming. Or naive little Cassie who felt pathetically grateful just because a sexy guy had said her eyes were an unusual colour and that he wanted to kiss her. She was bold, brash, powerful Cassie, prepared to fight for the respect and consideration she deserved.

'She didn't refuse to snog me,' he said easily. 'I refused to snog her. After she shouted at you and scared the hell out of you.'

'I—' The tirade she'd planned cut off. 'After she what?'

'I don't like bullies and I told her so.' He slung a hand into the pocket of his trousers. 'She got the hump and stomped off. And I was glad to see the back of her.'

'But you…' That couldn't be right. That wasn't how she remembered the incident at all. 'But you were laughing at me, too. I heard you.' Hadn't she?

He shrugged. 'I very much doubt that, as I didn't find her behaviour remotely funny.'

'But I thought…' Cassie trailed off, the power surge deflating inside her like a popped party balloon. 'I misunderstood.'

He'd stood up for her. The knowledge should have pleased her. But it didn't. It only made her feel more idiotic.

How come she'd instantly assumed he hadn't stood up for her? Why had her self-esteem been so low? Even then? And why on earth had she flown off the handle like that about a minor incident that had happened years ago? And meant absolutely nothing?

He probably thought she was a complete nutjob.

She risked a glance at him. But instead of looking concerned at the state of her mental health, he looked amused, that damn sexy grin bringing out the dimple in his cheek.

'Now we've cleared that up,' he said, 'why don't you sit back down and finish your wine?'

Wine was probably the last thing she needed, but doing what he suggested seemed easier than getting into a debate about what a complete twit she'd made of herself.

She perched on the edge of the sofa and lifted the glass to her lips, another even more dismal thought occurring to her. He really had been planning to kiss her. But there was no chance he'd want to kiss her now.

Nice one, Cass.

He picked up his bottle and saluted her. 'So let's talk about that massive crush.'

She sucked in a surprised breath at the bold statement, inhaled wine instead of air and choked.

CHAPTER THREE

JACE rose and stepped over the coffee table as his guest coughed and sputtered. Settling beside her, he gave her a hefty pat on the back. 'Take a breath.'

The coughing stopped as Cassie drew air into her lungs and cast a wary look over her shoulder. She shuddered as he ran his palm up her back, exploring the delicate bumps of her spine beneath the skimpy dress.

Either she was the most fascinating woman he'd ever met or she was totally nuts, but either way she was proving to be one hell of a diversion. And her little temper tantrum had only intrigued him more.

He'd never met anyone before whose every emotion was so plainly written on their face.

He'd been accused of worse things in his time...most of which he had actually done, so, rather than feeling aggrieved at her accusations, he was oddly flattered that moment on the stairwell had mattered to her so much. And quietly astonished to discover at least one incident from his teenage years when he'd actually done the right thing. Given that his schooldays had sped past in a maelstrom of bad behaviour and even worse choices, that was no small feat.

'The wine went down the wrong way,' she said, straightening away from his touch.

He plucked a tissue out of the dispenser on the coffee table, and handed it to her. 'Now about that massive crush?'

She sent him a quelling look, but the pretty little flags of colour that appeared in her cheeks contradicted it. 'I don't think your ego needs that kind of validation,' she said so cautiously, his lips twitched.

'Probably not.' He settled back, stretched his arms across the sofa cushions, and noted that she was now perched so precariously on the edge of her seat it was a wonder she hadn't toppled onto the floor. He was used to women throwing themselves at him, so the fact that he found her wariness refreshing was probably a bit perverse. 'But I've got to admit I'm fascinated. Weren't you a little young to have a massive crush on me?'

'I was thirteen,' she said, the tantalising sparkle of annoyance returning to her eyes.

'Oh, right. Thirteen. An old woman, then,' he teased.

'I was in love.' She frowned slightly, reconsidering the implications of the statement. 'Or at least I thought I was. At the time.'

'Is that a cryptic way of saying you haven't got a massive crush on me any more?'

Her stern expression cracked a little. 'You covered me in dirty water, then tried to deny it. Do I look like a masochist?'

Leaning forward, he skimmed a knuckle down her cheek. 'For the record, it was an accident. And I did eventually see the error of my ways.'

Her gaze skittered away, but this time she didn't shift out of reach. 'Tell me something,' she said softly. 'Do you try to kiss every woman you meet?'

He smiled. Nuts or not, her candour was captivating. 'The answer is no.' Sitting up, he nudged the riotous curls of chestnut hair over her shoulder. 'Not *every* woman.'

Her gaze came back to his and her throaty chuckle made

reaction coil in his gut. 'You must have kissed quite a few, though, if you can't remember who they are.'

He stifled a groan. Busted. 'What can I say? I had a misspent youth.'

He'd been reckless and easily bored as a teenager and had found it far too convenient to seduce women and then forget about them. Not something he was all that proud of now. But he'd eventually realised, like most hormonally charged boys when they became men, that quality was much more rewarding than quantity. And that women deserved to be savoured. And Cassie Fitzgerald was fast becoming a woman he definitely planned to savour. The only problem was, he didn't want to rush her and risk scaring her off.

'If it's any consolation...' he looped his finger in one of her curls, watched the silky hair spring back against her cheek '...I can guarantee you, I pay a lot more attention now.'

Her tongue flicked out to moisten her lips and he felt the jolt right down to his toes.

'We could always give it another go,' she said, a tentative smile lifting one corner of that lush mouth. 'If you want.'

'That sounds like a plan,' he murmured.

Caressing her nape, he threaded his fingers through the tendrils of hair then slanted his lips across hers. He wasn't going to wait for a second invitation.

Cassie braced her palms against his chest as his mouth captured hers. His lips were firm, hot, demanding. His pectoral muscles flexed beneath his shirt as he angled his head to deepen the kiss.

Heat scalded the pit of her stomach and radiated out, sizzling and tingling across her skin. He raised his other hand, massaged her scalp to hold her in place. She gasped as reaction raced through her, and his tongue thrust into her mouth, exploring in intimate strokes.

She clung on, poised over him as they sank into the sofa cushions—and desire spiralled and twisted inside her. It had been so long since she'd had a chance to feel a man's heat, his mouth on hers, the hardness of his chest pressing into her breasts. And she certainly didn't remember a kiss ever feeling this incredible.

He lifted her head, nipped her bottom lip as he stared into her eyes. His hands cradled her cheeks, his quick smile making the pulse of desire settle lower.

'Thanks, I enjoyed that,' he said, his voice husky. 'It's been a while.'

'For me too,' she said, although she didn't believe him. Anyone who kissed as well as he did had to practise regularly. 'I've wanted to do that ever since I saw you kiss Jenny.'

He stroked her cheek, pressed his thumb into her bottom lip. 'Have you really?'

She sat up. Why had she told him that? Talk about sad.

He skimmed his palm up her bare leg. 'So did I live up to expectations?'

She nodded, not wanting to divulge exactly how strongly the simple kiss had affected her. It would only make her look more sad and pathetic.

'Unfortunately I have an engagement...' He lifted his hand to glance at his wristwatch. 'In about half an hour. Otherwise we could take this further.'

'That's okay.' She should have been relieved. He was letting her down gently. But she didn't feel relieved, she felt disappointed. What had he meant by 'take this further'? How much further?

He shifted, his hand resting back on her thigh, stroking lazily. 'You could wait here until I get back,' he said, the heavy-lidded gaze as arousing as the feel of his rough palm on her skin. 'Although you might get bored.' His fingers slipped under the hem of her tunic, and she shuddered. He laughed. 'And I wouldn't want that.'

Bored? How could she be bored when her body felt as if it were about to explode? 'I don't underst—'

'Or you could come with me,' he interrupted.

Her breath gushed out. She tried to concentrate on what he was saying but it was next to impossible as the tips of his fingers drew lazy circles on her leg. Her sex throbbed, ached, begging for him to move higher still and stroke her there.

'Where to?' she heard herself ask as she tried to keep up her end of the conversation.

'The Blue Tower Restaurant,' he murmured, mentioning London's newest hot spot. His thumb traced the edge of her panties, then dipped underneath and her breath sawed out in a ragged pant.

Her hands fell to his shoulders, and she dug her fingers into the ridge of muscle, scared she was going to fall off the sofa. His green eyes watched her, the lids at half mast.

'I don't...' She swayed towards him. What was happening? What were they talking about? Her skin flushed hot, then cold, then hot again.

His tongue licked at her lips, then he cupped her head, his mouth taking hers in another mind-numbing kiss. Her heavy breasts flattened against the solid wall of his chest, the nipples squeezing into rigid, arching peaks.

'Say yes, Cassie,' he murmured as his fingers eased under the gusset of her panties and plunged.

'Yes.' The single word burst out of her mouth.

'God, you're so wet.' He circled and rubbed her swollen flesh, pushed inside her, his thumb pressing against her clitoris. 'You feel incredible.'

She straddled him, her knees digging into the sofa, her arms wrapping around his shoulders as his fingers continued to drive her into a frenzy. She couldn't talk, couldn't think, couldn't breathe. All thought, all feeling concentrated on the nub of pleasure between her legs. The rigid length of him, confined by his clothing, nudged the inside of her thigh—and she rubbed herself against him, yearning to have him deep inside her.

Her head dropped back and she moaned, heat soaring up her body. 'Please, don't stop.'

His strained laugh brushed against her cheek. 'I'm not going to stop.'

And he didn't, as the spasms of an unstoppable climax eddied up from her toes, coursed through her body and collided in her sex.

'Let go, Cassie. Come for me.'

The orgasm roared through her, exploding into a billion glittering sparks like a firework display on Bonfire Night. She heard someone cry out as the wave of pleasure crashed over her. Someone who sounded a lot like her but was thousands of miles away.

Then she buried her face in his neck, dazed and delirious, and whispered, 'Candy man.'

CHAPTER FOUR

'WHAT did you call me?' At Jace's gruff chuckle, Cassie stiffened and rose to see the teasing grin on his face.

Had she just said that out loud?

'It sounded like candy man,' he added.

'Did it?' She hedged, pressing her palms to the heat in her cheeks.

He laughed. 'Interesting,' he murmured, the smile more than a little smug. 'What does it mean?'

She climbed off his lap, adjusted her clothing, struggling to think straight while noticing the impressive bulge in his trousers. She smoothed the tunic down. 'It means, that was…' She halted, her face flushing. How did you thank a guy for giving you the most incredible orgasm of your life? She'd never come that quickly before, or with such intensity. And certainly not with a man she hadn't been in a relationship with. 'It means, that was amazing. So thanks,' she said, opting for honesty while her endorphins were still high on the afterglow.

He stretched out his arms across the back of the sofa. 'The pleasure's all mine.'

'I'm sorry, you didn't…' Her gaze snagged on his obvious state of arousal, and she wondered if she should offer to do something for him in return. It seemed only fair. 'Would you like me…?'

He tucked a finger under her chin, lifted her gaze to his. 'It's okay, Cassie. I'm not fifteen any more. I can wait.' He placed a quick kiss on her nose, before standing up. 'In fact, unfortunately, we're both going to have to wait, we're already fashionably late.'

'Late? Late for what?'

Instead of answering, he took her hands in his, and hauled her off the sofa. 'If you want to go do whatever it is girls do while they hog the bathroom, go ahead.' He placed his hand on her bottom and gave her a proprietary pat. 'It's that way.'

'Yes, but...where are we going?' she asked, trying to maintain a little sanity. Why had the invitation turned the afterglow into a giddy rush of pleasure?

He settled his hands on her shoulders, swept her hair back and kissed her neck. 'The Blue Tower. With me. This evening.'

When had she agreed to that? 'But I...' She trailed off, unable to concentrate on anything but his lips nuzzling the sensitive skin under her ear—and the darts of sensation shivering down her spine.

The doorbell buzzed and he nipped her ear lobe. 'That'll be your clothes. Don't take too long—we don't want to be too fashionable.' So saying, he strode out of the room.

Locating her bag under the coffee table, Cassie dashed off to the bathroom he'd indicated. She knew when she was being railroaded. But right now she didn't care. She needed time to think.

Once inside the lavish marble bathroom, she flung her bag on the vanity and studied herself in the mirror that covered one wall.

She hardly recognised herself.

Her hair sprung out in all directions, the unruly curls spilling out of the topknot she'd swept it up in that morning. Her cheeks were flushed a vivid red, her lips puffy and swollen, and her pupils so dilated her blue eyes were almost black. She touched her fingertips to the raw spot beneath her bottom lip. And she had whisker burn on her chin.

She looked like a woman who had been well and truly satisfied. She huffed out a breath. Probably because she had been. But she needed to take stock and think clearly now.

Or at least try to think clearly with her brain still addled from the endorphin rush and her core still throbbing from Jace Ryan's exceptionally skilled caresses.

Unwrapping a bar of the fragrant vanilla soap in a basket on the vanity, she washed her hands and face, then doused her cheeks in cold water. After patting herself dry with one of the hotel's monogrammed towels and finger-combing her hair, she examined her face again. She still looked dazed and dishevelled, but at least the colour in her cheeks had subsided from a vivid magenta to a pale rose. And her pupils had shrunk enough so she didn't look as if she were on crack.

Okay, so what had happened out there? She simply wasn't that into sex. Not that she was frigid or anything. She liked sex well enough. The sensible, comforting, predictable kind with a man she knew well and cared about and respected. Even if it later turned out he didn't deserve it. A line formed on her brow in the mirror. However, she did not do the hot, wild, knock-you-for-six kind of sex with a man who was a virtual stranger.

But there was no denying she'd done just that with Jace Ryan.

One minute they'd been talking, then they'd been kissing and then she'd been begging him to bring her to the most earth-shattering orgasm of her life. Another line appeared on her brow. And he had.

How had he known just how to touch her, and where? How had he known so instinctively just what she needed when she didn't know herself? She'd only had two serious boyfriends in her life. Two men whom she'd become sexually intimate with before she'd leapt into Jace Ryan's car this afternoon. She'd known both of them for weeks, months even, before she'd ever considered taking things to the next stage. But even after forming proper committed relationships with them, even after convincing herself she was in love with them, neither of them had ever been able to make her lose her mind as Jace had with a simple touch. In fact, Lance and David, her college boyfriend, had both complained at one time or another that she thought too much during sex, that she wasn't spontaneous enough.

She swallowed heavily, her throat dry. She hadn't merely been spontaneous on Jace's sofa. She'd come close to spontaneously combusting.

And she hadn't been thinking either. In fact, she'd been doing the opposite. Jace had offered to get her coat cleaned, and, less than an hour after walking into his hotel suite, she'd been straddling his thighs and writhing under his touch like a woman possessed. What had happened to her smart, safe, sensible, measured approach to sex and intimacy?

Opening her bag on the vanity, she rummaged for her phone. Unlocking the keypad, she scrolled down to Nessa's name.

What she needed now was some expert advice. Until Nessa had finally admitted that their old school friend Terrence was the love of her life, she'd had an enviably straightforward attitude to men and sex. Nessa knew how to handle a candy man, because, to hear Nessa tell it, she'd had more than her fair share of them.

There was little doubt that Jace Ryan was a candy man. But now she'd identified him, Cassie didn't have a clue what to do with him. Should she do what her hormones were begging her to do? Go out with him this evening so they could finish what they'd started later tonight? Or should she do what her head was telling her and run a mile? Not just from him but from the wild woman who had inhabited her body?

Nessa owed her, she thought as she pressed Dial and listened to the phone ring. It was Nessa's fault she was in this ridiculous situation. If she had kept her advice to herself, Cassie would never have had that moment of recklessness and accepted Jace's invitation in the first place—and ended up having an out-of-body experience on his sofa.

'It's Ness. What's up?' Her friend's familiar greeting had the tension in Cassie's shoulders easing.

'Ness, it's me,' she whispered into the phone. 'I'm in trouble.'

'What kind of trouble?' Nessa replied, her voice instantly direct and focused, reminding Cassie why Nessa was the perfect person to turn to in a crisis.

'Do you remember Jacob Ryan? From school?'

There was a slight pause on the line, then Nessa gave an appreciative purr. 'Oh, yeah. Jace the Ace. That boy's tight white buns looked so fine in black jeans, they occupy a real special place in my school memories. Why?'

'I met him. Tonight. I'm in his bathroom at The Chesterton. And we just had…well, not exactly sex, but nearly sex on his sofa.'

'Define nearly sex?' Nessa said, apparently completely unfazed by Cassie's confession.

'I had an orgasm. A really amazing orgasm,' Cassie blurted out, not quite comfortable discussing the mechanics. 'But he didn't.'

'That's not nearly sex, honey.' Nessa's deep, satisfied laugh echoed down the phone line. 'So little Cassie finally found herself a candy man. I always knew that boy looked fine for a reason.'

'Don't you dare mention that stupid candy-man thing again. I'm in trouble. And you've got to get me out of it.'

'Sounds like good trouble to me.'

'He's asked me to go out with him. Tonight,' Cassie continued, deciding to ignore Nessa's observation. 'To some do at the Blue Tower.' Her lips pursed. Some do that she knew nothing about, because he'd been deliberately cagey with details. 'On the understanding that when we get back, we'll take this further.' She swallowed as her stomach did a back flip. 'A lot further.'

'And you don't want to go further?' Nessa asked.

'It's not that I don't want to.' She did want to—the warm, liquid pull in the pit of her tummy was pretty incriminating on that score. 'I just don't know if I should. I've never had a one-night stand before. And what if he wants more than a one-night stand? I'm not ready for another relationship. Especially not with a guy who—'

'Cass, stop right there. You're overthinking this thing. The question is, did he give you a good time?'

'Yes, but—'

'But nothing,' Nessa interrupted. 'You had a good time. Next question. Is he pressuring you to do the same for him? 'Cos you shouldn't feel beholden.'

Did she feel pressured? Beholden? He'd bulldozed her into agreeing to go to the trendy restaurant, but he'd seemed remarkably relaxed about the sex part of the equation. Even though he'd been fully erect, he hadn't insisted she do anything about it. Her stomach somersaulted at the thought of that long, thick ridge stretching the loose pleats in his trousers. The truth was, if he had insisted, he wouldn't have had to insist very hard.

'No, I guess not.'

'Fine. So what exactly is the problem here? He's given you an amazing orgasm, there's the promise of more and he isn't making you do a thing you don't want to.'

'You don't understand. The problem's not him. It's me. I

don't know what got into me. One minute he was kissing me and the next I was… I lost control. It was like I couldn't stop myself. And it happened so fast. I've never felt like that before. It was scary.'

Nessa's low chuckle didn't do a thing to calm Cassie's nerves. 'Welcome to the club.'

'What club?'

'The Really Amazing Sex Club. It's way past time you got your membership.'

'But how can it have been really amazing when he's a stranger?'

'Because sometimes it's just about the sex,' Nessa said bluntly. 'You've got the urge, he's got the urge. You're both young, free and single and the chemistry's hot. Sometimes it doesn't have to be about anything more than that.'

The loud rap on the door had Cassie juggling the phone.

'Cassie, your time's up.' She heard his low voice through the door and it set off a whole new set of tingles.

'That's him now,' she hissed into the phone. 'Just a sec,' she shouted back. 'I'm doing my make-up.'

'I've got your clothes.'

She whipped the phone behind her back as the door opened. He'd changed out of his suit into a black sweater with a crew neck and dark blue jeans, his tall, broad-shouldered frame filling the doorway. He'd also shaved. Without the five o'clock shadow the line of his jaw looked clean and sharp and the dimple in his cheek more pronounced. His damp hair swept back from his forehead, and the dark waves glistened in the overhead light as he placed her folded coat on the vanity unit with a small bag bearing the logo of an exclusive boutique. 'Your coat. The boots are outside. They couldn't launder the leggings in time so I ordered a replacement.' His smile widened as his gaze inched down her bare legs. 'The car will be here in five.'

'Wait,' she said as he turned to leave. 'How dressy is this do? And whose do is it? Will they mind if I come? I haven't been invited.'

A sensual smile spread across his lips that had her fingers tightening on the phone. '*I'm* inviting you.' Reaching forward, he brushed his thumb across her chin, pressed a quick, sizzling kiss to her lips. She breathed in the clean scent of soap and the spicy hint of aftershave as he raised his head and the pull in her tummy became a yank. 'And you're dressy enough.'

She released the breath as he walked out of the room. Only once the door had closed did she realise he hadn't answered a single one of her questions.

She heard the crackle of Nessa's voice, lifted the phone to her ear.

'I think I just agreed to go,' she murmured, terror and excitement churning in her gut.

Nessa gave a jubilant whoop. 'Don't sound so worried, honey. All you've got to do now is relax, enjoy, flirt your heart out and let your candy man introduce you to all the club's member benefits.'

After bidding Nessa goodbye, Cassie disconnected the phone and shoved it back in her bag.

She dug her emergency make-up out, and counted to ten to stop herself from hyperventilating as she took the top off her liquid eyeliner.

Relax. Enjoy. Flirt. She could do that. How hard could it be?

But as she hastily lined her bottom lid with black kohl her fingers were trembling so hard, she nearly poked her eye out.

CHAPTER FIVE

CASSIE focused on evening out her breathing as the chauffeur-driven car pulled away from the kerb and the lights of The Chesterton blurred behind them. Going out on the town with a devastatingly sexy guy to one of London's hottest night-spots was exactly what she needed to dynamite herself out of her pre-Christmas funk. And getting to do it in serious style was not going to intimidate her.

She shouldn't over-analyse this situation and second-guess her behaviour. Her confidence had taken a huge knock when she'd walked in on Lance and Tracy. He hadn't been faithful to her, and she'd thought she'd moved on. But the truth was a tiny part of her had always blamed herself. She hadn't done enough, been exciting enough to keep him interested. And that nasty little seed had festered ever since, making her doubt herself. Tonight would be about getting that part of herself back. And moving on in body as well as spirit.

A warm palm came to rest on her leg. Jace rubbed his thumb across her kneecap and she trembled, the heat seeping through the luxury silk he'd ordered to replace her wet leggings.

'We won't stay long. There's no need to be nervous.'

His dark gaze devoured her, the promise in his eyes so compelling nervous energy turned into the sharp tug of sexual arousal.

'I'm not nervous,' she said and realised she wasn't. Not about going to this event with him anyway. It would give her a little time to prepare herself for what was going to happen later. And getting to know a bit more about the man she was planning to have her first and probably only wild fling with might not be a bad thing.

Added to that, she enjoyed social situations, meeting new people. And getting the chance to see Jace with his friends intrigued her. At school, he'd always been a loner despite the never-ending stream of girlfriends—unlike most of the other kids, he hadn't belonged to any specific clique, he'd never turned up for any after-school clubs or events and he hadn't participated in any of the sports teams. She suspected seeing how different he was now from that misfit boy would be another revelation.

'Whose party is it?' Assuming it was a party.

He lifted his hand off her leg, tucked one of the curls behind her ear as he hitched his shoulder in a lazy shrug. 'Just an associate. She's the reason I'm in London. And believe me, if she hadn't insisted on meeting up tonight, we wouldn't be here.' He leaned across the seat and kissed the side of her neck. Her pulse galloped against her skin. 'I can think of a few other things I'd much rather be doing,' he murmured. He took a deep breath in. 'You smell delicious.'

She.

Cassie's mind seized on the word as she struggled not to get sidetracked by the feel of his lips tracing across her collarbone. The man had seriously talented lips. 'Who is she?'

'Hmm?' he said nonchalantly, his hand moving to her waist.

'Are you involved with her?' She forced the question out, felt the shimmer of regret when his lips stopped nuzzling.

She couldn't see his expression clearly in the dim light of the car, her heart beating hard in her chest as she waited for a reply. She should have asked this question sooner. A lot sooner. She knew that she was young, free and single, as Nessa had put it. But she'd got so carried away with her own fantasies, she hadn't stopped to check if he was. She knew what kind of a guy he was where women were concerned. He hadn't exactly disguised it. She had no right to feel disappointed. But still the thought that he might be attached made her stomach turn over.

He touched her cheek, ran his thumb down to her chin. 'Exactly how much of a jerk do you think I am?'

The question sounded amused, but underneath she detected an edge. The breath she hadn't realised she was holding gushed out. She told herself the relief was purely physical. Having psyched herself up to enjoy tonight, it would be devastating to have the prize whisked away at the last minute.

'It's not that...' She wasn't judging him. She didn't have the right to judge him. This was just a one-night deal. For both of them. But even so, she would never allow herself to hurt another woman the way she'd been hurt. The way her mother had been hurt. 'It's just, I want to be sure you're not in a relationship. I wouldn't feel right sleeping with someone else's boyfriend.'

Jace stiffened at the question. He hated being asked about his personal life.

But this was his own stupid fault. He could hardly blame her for wanting to know more about him. He'd rushed things, indulged himself and this was the inevitable result.

He hadn't planned to get so carried away earlier. Had only planned to kiss her, but once he'd tasted her, she'd been so delicious, her response so artlessly seductive, he'd been consumed by the desire to taste more, like a starving man at a banquet, desperate to tuck in. The sound of her shocked little sighs as he'd stroked her thigh, the weight of her plump breasts pillowed against his chest, and the sultry Christmas scent of her hair had been so damned erotic he'd been rock hard in seconds. She'd been slick and wet and ready for him and the feel of her contracting around his fingers had nearly made him come in his pants. He'd had to use every last ounce of his control not to rip her clothes off and bury himself deep inside her. All thoughts of Helen's stupid party and the reasons why he'd flown three and a half thousand miles across the Atlantic had shot right out of his head. The desire to stay in the suite and spend the time devouring Cassie Fitzgerald instead had been all but irresistible. Which was exactly why he'd resisted it.

He should have won an Oscar for the performance he'd given, pretending he wasn't as affected as he looked. But he'd forced himself to hold back. Because he'd learned from experience that losing control and rushing into sex was never a good idea. He didn't do that any more and—once he'd managed to get his blood pressure back out of the danger zone—he'd remembered why.

Taking her to Helen's party for an hour had presented the perfect way to curb his lust without risking her running off. And seeing Helen again would bring him face to face with all the reasons why he couldn't afford to let his guard down with any woman—even one as apparently guileless as Cassie.

Given all of that, it shouldn't matter that she'd assumed the worst of him. He'd stopped caring about other people's opinions when he was a boy—when he'd figured out that it really made no difference what he did, they would always think the worst. But even Helen's constant and completely unfounded accusations of infidelity hadn't bothered him as much as the disappointment and resignation he could see in Cassie's wide blue eyes.

He didn't know Cassie and he didn't want to know her other than in a purely physical sense. The only connection they shared was a live-wire sexual chemistry that would soon burn out, once they'd both had their fill of each other. But even so, he couldn't quite deny the knot of tension in his shoulders.

'I'm not in a relationship,' he replied, struggling to keep his voice casual. 'And I wouldn't be trying to seduce you if I were.'

'I'm sorry,' she whispered. 'I didn't mean to imply...' she cleared her throat '...that you weren't honourable.'

The earnest statement was so sincere, he laughed, the tension dissolving as quickly as it had come. Settling his other hand on her waist, he dragged her closer. The movement tightened the seat belt under her breast and drew his gaze down to the enticing swell of her cleavage.

'Cassie, the one thing I've never been is honourable.' He pressed his face into her hair, let his lips linger on the fluttering pulse beneath her ear. 'If you had any idea how I plan to take advantage of you later tonight, you'd know exactly how dishonourable I am.'

She gave a husky little laugh that had his insides twisting into knots of a different kind. She tilted her head back; her bright gaze met his. 'I don't remember agreeing to come back with you tonight.'

'Yeah, but you will,' he said, his confidence returning full force as he saw her tongue dart out to wet her bottom lip. His palm rode down the curve of her hip, then snuck under her coat to caress the top of her thigh. 'How about I remind you how persuasive I can be?'

She grabbed his wrist, brought it firmly back to her waist. 'Let's not,' she said, her lips tilting in a nervous smile. 'We wouldn't want to shock the chauffeur.'

He lifted his hand to cup her cheek. 'Wouldn't we?'

She wiggled her eyebrows at him playfully. 'Not while he's driving.'

As if on cue, the screen slid down and the man in question spoke. 'We've arrived at the restaurant, Mr Ryan.'

'That was quick.' *Too damn quick.*

'Traffic was surprisingly light tonight, sir,' the driver replied.

Releasing the catch on Cassie's seat belt, Jace took her hand in his. 'Don't bother to get out, Dave,' he said through the partition.

Opening the car door, he stepped out, tugging Cassie out behind him.

'See you back here in an hour,' he said to the chauffeur as he closed the car door. An hour should be more than sufficient to calm himself down and make sure he was completely in control of this situation before he jumped Cassie again.

Cassie shivered as the car accelerated away. Sliding his palms under the opening of her coat, he placed a quick kiss on her forehead below her hairline. He wasn't risking going anywhere near her lips again until they had some privacy. 'Let's get this over with.'

Taking her hand firmly in his, he strode towards the entrance to the restaurant, impatience in every stride as he listened to the tap of her boot heels against the paving stones.

Taking a time-out to slow things down had been the smart thing to do, but right now, with a whole hour ahead of him before he could get her naked, he couldn't help wishing he'd been a lot more stupid.

Erotic anticipation rippled through Cassie's system as she stepped out into the lobby of the Tower's eighth floor. Her skin felt tight and itchy, and her pulse pounded against her throat like a metronome as Jace's masculine scent teased her nostrils, and his rough palm squeezed hers. Tonight would be an adventure that she intended to enjoy. For once she wasn't going to worry about tomorrow, she was going to concentrate on now.

Relax. Enjoy.

She repeated Nessa's mantra in her head. Then let out a staggered breath as Jace led her into a panoramic rooftop bar, its sleek lines and streamlined elegance reminding her of a vintage thirties ocean liner. Strobes of blue fluorescent light reflected off the forty-foot bar's steel panelling and illuminated a crowd dressed in everything from exclusive ball gowns and designer suits to artfully ripped denim. The loud buzz of conversation and the clink of glasses were only partially masked by the backing beat of drums and bass-guitar riffs coming from a live band at the far end of the room. Cassie's astonished gaze riveted on the wall of glass to her left, which framed a breathtaking view of the Thames' North Bank and the City of London beyond. The majesty of St Paul's Cathedral dome spotlit in the frosty twilight broke up the geometric shapes of the City's glaringly modern financial district.

Cassie hesitated, her fingers flexing in Jace's hand. 'Wow, no wonder this place is so popular.'

His grip tightened. 'Yeah,' he said, not sounding very impressed. 'Helen always knew how to throw a party.'

'Who's Helen?' she asked. But before she got a reply, Jace stiffened beside her. His jaw clenched as a tall woman in floating red silk made her way through the crowd towards them. The woman's figure was so thin and delicate, her collarbone stood out against the wispy straps of her gown. Either she was a supermodel or she had an eating disorder. Cassie opted for the former as she glided closer, deciding that her striking face, all high cheekbones, almond eyes and collagen-stung lips, could easily have graced the cover of a fashion magazine.

Dropping Cassie's hand, Jace placed his palm on her hip

to anchor her to his side. And she heard him swear under his breath.

'Hello, lover boy,' the woman said breathlessly as she drew level, her six-inch heels bringing her almost eye-level with Jace, and making Cassie feel like a midget. 'Long time, no see.' A cloud of expensive perfume engulfed Cassie as the woman leaned into him and pressed postbox-red lips to his. Her mouth lingered on his a moment too long for the kiss to be mistaken for platonic. Cassie wondered if she'd just become invisible.

Jace grasped the women's waist, deliberately setting her away from him. 'Where the hell is Bryan?' he asked, his tone frigid.

'That's for me to know and for you to find out,' she said, batting her eyelids as spots of colour appeared on her angular cheekbones.

'I didn't come all this way to play games, Helen,' he replied, his voice low with annoyance.

So this was Helen.

The woman's long eyelashes dipped in a bashful gesture that seemed out of keeping with the bold flirtation of a moment before and she gave a breathless little laugh. 'Don't be such a spoilsport.' She touched a perfectly manicured nail to Jace's chest. 'I have good news. I have some friends here tonight you must meet. I've whetted their appetite already and they're gagging to hear more about Artisan so they can invest.'

Catching her finger, Jace lowered it. 'You of all people know I'm not looking for new investment.'

She flicked her fingers in a dismissive gesture. 'Stop being difficult—you're not going to sell Artisan. I know how much the company means to you. I'm the one who watched you sweat blood over it.'

'It served its purpose,' he replied flatly. 'I don't get sentimental about business, any more than I get sentimental about the past.'

The chill in his voice sent a shiver of alarm up Cassie's spine. Who was this woman? And why did the familiarity between them remind her unpleasantly of the time when Lance had laughingly introduced her to his 'work colleague' Tracy at their New Year's Eve party last year?

She knew she didn't have any claim on Jace, this was just a casual date with the promise of wild sex for dessert, but that didn't make the uncomfortable feeling go away. She cleared her throat, loudly, and Helen's head whipped round.

The woman stared blankly at her as if she were noticing her for the first time, but made no move to introduce herself. Hostility rolled off her in waves, but there was something else there, a flicker of sadness and distress, that made Cassie wish she could disappear for real.

'Why don't I go get us a drink?' Cassie directed the question at Jace. Whatever was between these two, she was pretty sure she'd be better off not knowing what it was.

'We'll get one together,' he replied. 'I'll catch you later, Helen.'

But as he took Cassie's hand and went to sidestep their host she simply stepped the same way, blocking his path. 'What's the matter, Jace?' she said, her raised voice turning several heads by the bar. 'Does it make you uncomfortable introducing your little tart to your wife?'

He swore viciously as shock and disbelief made blood pound in Cassie's ears.

His wife?

Seeing the other guests staring at her, Cassie felt the blood pump into her cheeks. Jace said something, his voice low with temper, but she couldn't make out the words, the buzzing in her ears deafening her. Pulling her hand out of his, she rushed out of the bar and didn't look back.

She covered her mouth with her hand as reaction set in.

Oh, God, she was going to throw up.

So much for her fabulous adventure, she thought as she stabbed the lift button with frantic fingers. She should have seen it coming. Cassie Fitzgerald decided to have a wild fling and she ended up flinging herself straight into the arms of a married man. It would be ironic, if the guilt and embarrassment and the stupid sense of betrayal tumbling about in the pit of her stomach weren't making her gag.

'Hold up, Cassie.' A large hand wrapped around her forearm and whisked her round. 'Where the hell are you going?'

'Home.'

'Helen's not my wife,' he countered. 'We've been divorced for over five years now and separated a great deal longer. And up until about ten seconds ago I thought she'd be here with her new fiancé, so I didn't anticipate having to deal with this rubbish.'

The dispassionate explanation went some way to dispelling the nausea, but did nothing for the heat burning in her cheeks. 'Thanks for letting me know that,' she said, using sarcasm to mask the stupid sting of tears. What on earth was she so upset about? His relationship with his ex-wife really had nothing to do with her. 'It might have been nice if you'd told me a little sooner, though. Like when I asked about her in the car.'

'I'm not interested in talking about her or our marriage,' he said, as if withholding such a vital piece of information was perfectly reasonable.

'I specifically asked you if you were involved with her. And you didn't say a word.'

She stared at the lift display panel as if her life depended on it. She didn't want to look at him. And where the heck was the lift? It needed to get here before she did something really idiotic like bursting into tears. For some reason her emotions had been too close to the surface all night. Ever since she'd leapt into his car like a crazy lady—and then come apart on his sofa.

'Because there's nothing to say,' he huffed. 'I was never involved with her. Not in any real sense. Our marriage lasted exactly six months and I've regretted it ever since. The fact that she's delusional and insists on pretending there's still something between us is not my problem.' His thumb and forefinger gripped her chin and he directed her gaze back to his. 'Do you think you could look at me while you're having your snit?'

'This is not a snit.'

To her astonishment his lip curved up at one corner. 'It looks like one to me.'

'Excuse me, but you weren't the one who got called a little tart in front of three hundred people.'

The other corner curved up. 'I'm sure it was only two hundred and fifty,' he replied, his eyes now smiling too.

He placed a hand on her shoulder. She shrugged it off.

'Now, Cassie,' he said, amusement lightening his voice as he threaded his fingers into the fine hair at her nape. 'You're not looking on the bright side here.'

'What bright side?' she snapped, trying very hard not to be charmed by that sensual smile and the caressing touch. It wasn't fair. She'd been humiliated. Branded a tart by a woman she didn't even know. And he seemed to think it was a joke. She wasn't about to humour him.

Following her into the lift, he pressed the ground-floor button then placed his hands on either side of her head, caging her against the wall. 'The bright side is, we get to leave straight away. A whole hour earlier than planned.'

She braced her palms against his chest, but her arms felt heavy, sluggish, the coil of desire unravelling at an alarming speed and sapping her ability to push him away.

'You don't seriously think it's still game on for tonight, do you?' she said, trying for indignant but getting breathless instead.

He leaned down to suckle the pulse point in her neck. 'Uh-huh.'

'Well, you're wrong,' she sputtered, but her head dropped back, instinctively giving him better access.

His gaze, dark and intent, fixed on hers as he let one hand drop to snake under her coat and grip her waist. 'You're a terrible liar, you know.' He pulled her flush against him, all trace of amusement gone. 'Now tell me again you don't want me and I'll take you home.'

The gruff invitation and the feel of his rigid arousal pressing into her stomach made the words catch in her throat. She couldn't say it, because she did want him. And he was right, she'd never been a good liar.

She wanted him more than anything she'd ever wanted. Like a child in a sweet shop, offered the chance to grab as many delights as she could handle.

'It's not good to have everything you want,' she mumbled, mesmerised by the golden flecks that gilded the vivid green of his irises.

His thumb brushed across her nipple and she groaned, the aching tension that shot straight to her sex making resistance futile. 'It will be tonight,' he said.

The lift doors opened onto the ground-floor lobby and he eased back. Stepping out, he drew her with him, then dug into the back pocket of his jeans.

He flipped his phone open and dialled without taking his eyes off her. 'We're ready now, Dave. How soon can you get here?'

His lips tipped up as he listened to the reply. 'We'll be waiting.'

'How long is it going to take him?' she asked, her teeth

tugging on her lip. She might as well stop pretending that she wasn't going to jump him as soon as they got back to his suite. Because she wasn't fooling anyone, least of all herself.

It didn't matter that he hadn't told her about his ex-wife. It didn't even matter that the woman had called her a tart. All that mattered now was that the chemistry was hotter than molten lava—and she couldn't wait any longer to feel it erupt.

'Too damn long,' he said as the chauffeur-driven car squealed to a halt at the kerb.

CHAPTER SIX

'READY for your candy now?' Jace growled, his voice husky with lust and humour as he kicked the door of the suite shut.

Cassie giggled, adrenaline and desire coursing through her veins. Her back hit the lobby wall with a soft thud, the hard lines of his body flattening her breasts and making her belly throb.

'Yes, please,' she flirted back, sinking her fingers into the silky waves of his hair.

Don't think, just feel. And enjoy. Although relaxing was out of the question, seeing as she was about to explode.

They'd kissed and touched on the ride home, stoking the need to fever pitch, but through their clothes the caresses had been as frustrating as they were exciting.

He fastened his lips on her neck, his hands parting the flaps of her coat. The caress roamed over her hips, tugged up her tunic to settle on her behind. He dragged her towards him, grinding the hard bulge in his jeans against the swell of her stomach. 'You've got too many clothes on.'

Cassie ran her hands inside his leather jacket. Lifting the hem of his sweater, she finally touched bare skin. 'So do you,' she moaned.

Her fingertips explored the soft line of hair over washboard-lean abs, the warm skin like velvet over steel.

He shuddered, huffed out a laugh and stepped back. 'Let's remedy the situation.'

Shrugging off his jacket, he threw it on the floor. Then reached for her coat. She twisted to help him pull it off. Crossing his arms, he grasped his sweater and struggled out of it.

As he tossed the light jumper away Cassie stared, transfixed, at broad shoulders, beautifully defined pectoral muscles and the curls of dark hair that stood out in tufts under his arms, outlined flat brown nipples and then trailed down to bisect the ridges of his six pack and arrow beneath the buckle of his belt.

Her breath backed up in her lungs. That was one seriously gorgeous chest.

She watched him toe off one of his boots, then bend down to hop on one leg while yanking it off.

What was she doing? She should get naked too. She kicked off her own boots, then grasped the hem of her tunic just as his second boot hit the floor.

He grabbed her wrist, stopping her before she had raised the tunic past her midriff. 'No.'

She let go, the boldness fading. 'What's the matter?' Didn't he want her naked?

He swore softly, grunted the single word, 'Bedroom,' then started hauling her down the corridor.

He shoved open the door into a large, luxuriously furnished room with an enormous king-sized bed in the centre. Releasing her, he crossed to the bedside table, rummaged around for a second and then flung a cellophane-wrapped box onto the gold bedspread.

'Condoms,' he said unnecessarily. 'I figured I should locate them before I lost the ability to think.'

She smiled, ridiculously pleased to see he was as eager as she was. But when she went to take off her tunic again, he shot back across the room and took both her wrists in his, holding her hands manacled to her side.

'No. Wait.' He touched his forehead to hers, pressed his lips to her temple. 'There's no rush.' He breathed in her scent, eased out a steady breath. 'Let me do it.'

'Okay,' she said, surprised to feel an odd catch in her chest.

Taking the bottom of the tunic in his hands, he lifted it gently over her head, tossed it over his shoulder.

She sucked in a breath as the green of his eyes turned to a shining emerald. His dark gaze roamed over her, touching her skin like a physical caress, burning a trail of fire from her cheeks, to her breasts, blazing into her sex and sizzling right down to her toes.

He slid his thumbs and forefingers under the straps of her simple cotton bra, then tugged them off her shoulders. Her breasts became heavy, the nipples swelling into hard peaks as he peeled the cups down, exposing her to his gaze.

The dark arousal flared. 'Damn,' he murmured. 'You're perfect.'

The little catch in her chest clutched at her heart. No one had ever thought she was perfect before. Let alone said so.

Reaching around her waist, he drew her closer. His lips buzzed her shoulder where the strap had left a red mark as he released the catch on her bra. He dragged it free, flung that away too.

His eyes met hers as he cradled the weight in his palms, circled her nipples with his thumbs. Then he bent to fasten his lips on one aching peak.

Cassie threaded her fingers into the hair at the side of his head, and arched into his mouth, the hot, wet suction sending her senses into overdrive. He suckled strongly, drawing her into his mouth, then pulling back to flick his tongue over the tip, massaging and teasing her other breast with his fingers.

A sob escaped as she writhed. It wasn't just his fingers

that were talented, it seemed. She'd never realised she was so sensitive there. The raw nerves pulsated as moisture flooded between her thighs.

The pressure built and intensified at her core as sparks of fire originated in her nipples, fanned out across her breasts, then darted down to her centre. She shut her eyes, her legs like wet noodles as he transferred his mouth to her other breast.

He stopped the devastating caresses briefly to tear off her tights and panties, then as his mouth returned to her pounding breasts he flattened his palm against her stomach, pressed the heel of his hand onto her aching centre, then delved into the curls at the apex of her thighs.

He circled for several agonising seconds, then flicked his finger over the heart of her. She cried out, bucked against his palm, the sparks triggering an explosion of need that reared up and crashed through her as he continued to rub the swollen nub. She dug her nails into his shoulders, braced herself as her legs gave out and the final waves of pleasure drained her body, leaving her as limp as a rag doll.

He gave a strained laugh, and bent down to lift her onto his shoulder. 'Come on, Cassidy,' he said, his hand patting her bare buttocks. 'Time for bed.'

Her stomach rode the ridge of his shoulder blade as he strode across the room and dropped her on the mattress. She watched in a daze as he kicked off his jeans and boxers and climbed onto the bed.

Shock reverberated through her, widening her eyes and slicing through the haze of afterglow, as she stared at the massive erection that prodded her thigh when he settled beside her.

As if in a dream, she reached out and touched her nail to the tip. It bobbed towards her, as if it had a life of its own.

'You're perfect too,' she whispered. A strange combination of euphoria and excitement tightened like a vice around her heart. And for the first time ever she let instinct take over, the heady endorphins of her recent climax making her yearn to give him the same pleasure he had given her.

She trailed her finger down the line of hair on his belly, then wrapped her hand around the solid length of his erection. It felt hard and smooth against her palm. But it wasn't enough, not nearly enough. She pushed at his shoulders until he lay on his back. He thrust his fingers into her hair, as she ran a trail of kisses across his magnificent chest.

His fingers flexed, massaging her scalp, as she inched lower, sliding her tongue over his six pack, licking at the ridge of his belly button, then delving within. The muscles of his flat belly tensed as she encountered the powerful erection at last. Darting her tongue out, she licked up the length of him like an ice lolly, then took the swollen head between her lips.

He swore, shuddered, then, cradling her cheeks in his palms, yanked her off him as he jerked into a sitting position.

Colour flooded into her cheeks as she scrambled back onto her knees. She'd done it wrong. 'Sorry, you don't like that?' she said, the euphoria fading as inadequacy flooded in.

Lance had always told her what to do, had hated it when she took the lead. Why was she so rubbish at sex?

He gave a strained laugh, then reached for her. 'Are you kidding? I love it,' he said, sliding his palm over her shoulder to pull her closer. 'But we'll have to save it for later or I'm not going to last long enough to get inside you.'

'Oh, I see,' she said, feeling gauche and yet ridiculously relieved. She hadn't done it wrong after all.

Shifting over, he reached for the condoms. Tearing the cellophane, he dumped the contents out on the bedspread. He grabbed one of the packages and fumbled with it. 'Someone ought to tell the manufacturers they use too much packaging,' he grumbled, finally ripping it with his teeth.

As he flipped out the rubber she took his wrist. 'Do you

mind if I do it?' she asked, the urge to touch him again over-whelming.

'Do I mind?' His eyebrow rose a fraction. 'Of course not.' He smiled and passed it to her. 'Be my guest.'

Lying back on the bedspread, he crossed his arms behind his head, and watched her with heavy-lidded eyes, the desire in them so palpable her heart pounded against her ribcage.

Holding the slick contraceptive in her fingers as if she were handling nitroglycerine, she gave a faltering sigh, anticipation and trepidation colliding to make her heart beat double time. Her eyes feasted on the beauty of his body, wisps of dark hair highlighting the masculine planes of sleek muscles and lean sinews. Then her heart throbbed right into her throat as she focused on the magnificent evidence of how much he wanted her. He was all hers for tonight, and she didn't want to muck it up. She didn't want this to be going-through-the-motions sex, or, worse, bad sex. Just this once she wanted what Nessa had promised her. She wanted really amazing sex.

'Cassidy, I hate to rush you,' he said, jerking her out of her stupor. 'But if you keep looking at me like that, I'm not going to be responsible for my actions.'

The sensual threat made her smile.

Do not overthink this.

She rolled the lubricated latex down the thick length with careful fingers, confidence surging through her as he sucked in a shaky breath and the muscles of his abdomen quivered.

Taking her by the shoulders, he swivelled round, so that she would be lying beneath him. But she reared up. 'Could I be on top?'

He gave a tense laugh. 'Absolutely,' he said, then framed her face with his hands. 'I'm always happy to oblige a woman who knows what she wants.'

He rolled to reverse their positions, then skimmed his hands down to cradle her bottom as she kneeled over him, lifting her above the enormous erection. 'Climb aboard, candy girl.'

She laughed, the compliment burning away the last of her inhibitions in a rush of pure unadulterated pleasure. Directing the powerful shaft to her entrance, she lowered herself onto him.

He was big, bigger than she had expected, and her bottom lip caught on her teeth as she tightened around him. She tried to force her hips down, but the pleasure dimmed, the penetration too full, the stretched feeling unbearable.

'I can't do it.'

'Shh, relax,' he crooned. 'Take it slowly. You're tensing up.' He lifted her, sat up, deftly adjusting their positions so that his lips could fasten on her breasts while seeking fingers touched her core. The hot suction of his mouth, the clever caresses had pleasure returning in a rush. She sobbed as she began to move, her hips undulating to relieve the pressure, then sinking down farther to let it build again. Instinctive, basic, she gloried in the ability to control the penetration, throwing her head back, and clasping his shoulders.

'That's it, Cassie.' He lifted his head from her breast, his fingers continuing to circle her clitoris as his other arm banded around her bottom, urging her into a devastating rhythm. 'You've got it, sweetheart. Once more. You're almost there.'

She plunged down, the encouragement spurring her on, and took him in to the hilt at last.

The huge erection bumped her cervix and touched a place deep inside, the waves of pleasure quickly swelling into an uncontrollable torrent.

His ragged breathing rasped in her ears as she rode him frantically, driving them both to completion. The contractions held her body in a vicelike grip for what seemed like an eternity and she cried out, revelling in the sheer joy of the wild ride. He shouted out his release as she tumbled into the abyss, shattering into a billion quivering shards of light.

She fell forward, knocking him back, their sweat-slicked bodies collapsing onto the bed.

He hugged her, holding her on top, his deep, satisfied laugh brushing against her ear lobe. 'Cassie, that was…' he paused, his hands stroking her back, the still-huge erection pulsing inside her '…amazing.'

Her heart flipped over, afterglow turning into the sweet glow of triumph. 'No, it wasn't,' she said, a wonderfully smug smile curving her lips. 'It was *really* amazing.'

He brushed her hair back from her face, the confidential smile on his lips reminding her of the secret joke they had once shared on a stairwell. 'Yeah, really amazing,' he said, and her heart soared.

CHAPTER SEVEN

'Wake up, sweet cheeks. Dinner's here.'

Cassie's eyes fluttered open to find Jace sitting on the edge of the bed, gently stroking her cheek with the palm of his hand. He wore one of the hotel's monogrammed robes, but the wisps of chest hair revealed in the V of pristine white towelling had sensation shimmering across her skin. Heat rode up her neck as she felt the unfamiliar tenderness between her thighs—and the recollection of what he'd done to her, of what they'd done to each other, came flooding back.

'I fell asleep?' she asked, her voice groggy and confused. All she could remember was lying curled in his arms, feeling sated and better about herself than she had felt in a long time, her bottom butting his softening erection and his hands resting on her belly.

'We both did,' he said, his thumb running down her neck and over her collarbone, then slipping beneath the edge of the fine linen sheet to touch the tender skin of her breasts. 'Really amazing sex will do that to a person.'

She stretched, stifling a yawn, and luxuriated in the feeling of triumph.

It *had* been really amazing. Hadn't it?

But then her nostrils caught the sent of tarragon and roast meat and her stomach grumbled audibly, making the flush spread.

He chuckled. 'Unfortunately, really amazing sex also makes you ravenous.'

She lifted up on her elbows as he stood and walked across the room.

'I ordered us some fancy French chicken dish to keep our strength up,' he said as he lifted another monogrammed robe off an armchair.

A quick grin lifted her lips. He wanted her to keep her strength up. That sounded promising.

He returned with the fluffy white robe, held it up for her. 'But you have to put this on first, or I'm liable to start ravishing you instead of the food.'

She pushed back the sheet, and made herself hop out of bed, concentrating on her hunger to stave off the silly spurt of shyness about her nakedness. Which was patently ridiculous given what they'd been doing before she drifted off.

'What time is it?' she asked, shoving her hands into the sleeves.

He wrapped the robe around her, tying the belt from behind and then hugged her round the waist. His nose nudged the top of her head. 'Nearly eleven.'

She'd been asleep for *three* hours!

She pulled out of his embrace, swung round, dismayed and desperately disappointed.

Would he expect her to go home? She had no idea what the etiquette for one-night stands was, but she had a feeling staying until the morning might be awkward.

He frowned. 'Damn, you're a vegetarian, right?'

'No, I...'

He took her chin, his brow creasing. 'Then what's the matter?'

She swallowed. She might as well ask. She had a right to ask. 'What are we going to do *after* dinner?'

'*After* dinner,' he said, his lips quirking. 'Well, now.'

Gripping her hips, he tugged her easily towards him. 'After dinner, I figured we could try out the whirlpool tub in the master bathroom. Considering the rates this place charges, I haven't made nearly enough use of it. And then—' he wiggled his eyebrows comically '—I thought lots more really amazing sex wouldn't go amiss.' The teasing expression sobered a little. 'If you're not too sore, that is,' he added. 'You weren't kidding when you said it had been a while for you, were you?'

The thrill of arousal rushed through her, tempered by the little clutch in her chest at the concern in his eyes. She'd always thought of him as being dangerous. And he was. Even more so now she knew how devasting he was in bed. But how could she have guessed that he would also be such a considerate lover?

'I'm not sore,' she said, deciding to ignore his probing question. She certainly didn't intend to tell him how long it had been. Or why.

She placed her palms on his bare chest, felt the thunder of his heartbeat matching hers. 'But you may still have to persuade me,' she teased, twirling one of her fingers in his chest hair, the fine art of flirtation and temptation coming as naturally as breathing.

He laughed, taking her finger and bringing it to his lips. 'Don't worry, I intend to.' He gave it a nip, then groaned as his stomach growled loudly. 'But first we better eat. We're likely to need it. For stamina.'

She let all the deliciously dangerous thoughts of what the night ahead might hold drown out any doubts as he led her into the suite's living room. But her steps faltered, her bare feet sinking into the silk rug, when she saw the ornate table laid with gilt-edged china plates covered with silver domes, a bottle of champagne chilling in an ice-bucket and a single tapered candle illuminating the table with the help of the fire glowing in the open hearth. Her heartbeat slowed at the romantic scene, but she quashed the sentiment as he held out her chair for her.

She propped her elbows on the table and forced herself not to overthink things as she admired his darkly handsome face in the flickering light.

He was only hers for one night. That was all she wanted. One night of really amazing sex, which she wasn't going to ruin—as she had so many times before—with misguided hopes of romance.

'*Voilà!*' He whisked the dome covering her plate with a flourish. 'Tuck in.'

Taking a sighing breath of the delicious scent rising from the plate, she lifted the heavy silver knife and fork, intending to do just that.

Jace watched Cassie lick the creamy tarragon sauce off her lower lip and felt the now familiar heat pulse in his groin. Diverting his attention to his own plate, he sliced into the succulent chicken breast, let the rich aroma of butter and herbs go some way to dispelling the spicy scent of her that seemed to have invaded his senses.

Problem was, he wasn't just hungry for food. He took a swallow of the delicious dish. And controlling his appetite for Cassie Fitzgerald was proving to be more of a challenge than he had anticipated.

After waking up with her curled in his arms, he'd lain awake for twenty minutes. Torturing himself with the feel of her plump breasts rising and falling against his forearm, her soft buttocks pillowed against his reinvigorated erection, and recalled their lovemaking in every exquisite, excruciating detail.

He pictured her gorgeous breasts after he'd taken off her bra. The large, rosy nipples rigid with arousal as he teased the swollen tips with his teeth. Then her pale cheeks flushed with colour, her lips slightly parted, the harsh sobs of her orgasm as his fingers sank into the wet heat at her core. Her limp body draped over his shoulder. And at last, the incredible feel of her full lips caressing his erect flesh.

He'd never seen a more erotic sight, and had been forced to stop her before he went off like a rocket. But he'd instantly regretted it when she'd lurched away, the desire and excitement in her eyes snuffed out by regret and panic.

He'd never met a woman who was so effortlessly seductive, who could turn him inside out with lust without doing much more than breathing and yet was so unsure of herself.

Some guy had clearly done a number on her. That could be the only answer. And as he'd listened to her sleep and resisted the urge to wake her up and ravish her all over again, he'd felt his curiosity—and his anger—grow.

He'd struggled to get a grip on both before he did something idiotic. So he'd eased her out of his arms, and climbed out of bed to arrange dinner.

While he'd run a bath in the enormous whirlpool tub, then sat in the lounge waiting for their meal to arrive, he'd contemplated exactly how he was going to play things for the rest of the night, and had come to a few important conclusions.

Cassie Fitzgerald was sweet and sexy and just what he needed after his dry spell. He'd spent far too many months recently sweating over the direction of his business and more specifically figuring out the best way to cut the last of his ties to his ex-wife—and his sex life had suffered as a result.

Maybe he wasn't anywhere near as prolific as he had been in his teens, but he wasn't a man who dealt all that well with months of abstinence. His explosive, uncontrolled reaction to Cassie in the first place was evidence of that.

That Cassie was the complete antithesis of the women he usually chose to date, who were as jaded as he was in the sack, was the only reason why he found her so captivating—and so refreshing. But making an issue of it by satisfying his curiosity about her past wasn't an option. It had been quite a while since he'd had a one-night stand, but he knew that mixing sex with intimacy was always a mistake.

This trip was about correcting the mistakes of his past, his marriage being the biggest one of all; getting involved with anyone would kind of defeat the purpose of the whole enterprise.

He planned to enjoy this evening, and he wanted Cassie to enjoy it too. From her fragile confidence and her touchingly insecure reactions when they made love, he suspected she hadn't got to enjoy sex nearly as much as she should have in the past. And maybe it was arrogant of him, but while he'd never professed to know what women wanted emotionally—and didn't intend to find out—he'd made it his life's work to know what they enjoyed in bed.

Cassie's sexual liberation was a little project that he was more than happy to dedicate himself to. Especially as Cassie seemed so receptive to the idea. Anything else wasn't going to happen. So he wasn't about to risk encouraging her to think this was more by asking her personal questions.

But as he took a pensive sip of his champagne and Cassie's eyes met his he noticed the potent mix of desire and reticence in their depths and couldn't quite ignore the thorn digging into his side.

Setting his glass down, he reached across the table and anchored the errant curl of hair that had fallen across Cassie's cheek back behind her ear.

'How's the food?' he asked.

'Delicious,' she said, and his gut tightened right up again.

He'd always had a bad habit, he thought wryly, of finding the forbidden irresistible. That was why he'd spent a night redecorating the school gym at seventeen and ended up getting arrested. And it was also why he'd been unable to resist sleeping with his main investor's daughter years later, and got trapped in a marriage of convenience that had caused him no end of headaches. He thought he'd learned to curb the impulse to do something he knew he would later regret.

But as Cassie's gaze flicked back to her plate the dangerous impulse took charge of his tongue and he heard himself saying, 'Correct me if I'm wrong, Cassidy, but I got the impression earlier that you're not a veteran of really amazing sex?'

Cassie jerked her chin up, stunned by the perceptive question. And what it might mean. Why had he asked that? And how did he know? Was her lack of proficiency that obvious?

She pushed out a laugh. 'Why would you think that?' she scoffed, deciding to bluff. Unfortunately, the colour charging into her cheeks wasn't exactly playing along.

He pushed his plate aside, the quizzical smile he sent her making the colour charge faster. 'There's no need to be embarrassed,' he said, not just calling her bluff, but trampling all over it. 'I'm surprised, that's all.' Placing his hands behind his head, he stretched back as he studied her, making the chair creak and the robe fall open revealing a tantalising glimpse of those mouth-watering abdominal muscles.

She reached for her champagne flute, trying not to follow the line of hair bisecting his abs, which she now knew arrowed down to something even more enticing.

'You're a beautiful woman, with an extremely passionate nature,' he said, his voice so low she was sure she could feel it reverberating across some of the tender places he'd explored so thoroughly earlier in the evening. 'I just wondered why you haven't indulged it more?'

She gulped and put the glass down, grateful that she hadn't taken a sip of the champagne yet.

An extremely passionate nature! Had he actually said that? About her?

She was both stunned and flattered by his assessment, and her heart squeezed a little. It had never been her fault that first David then Lance couldn't remain faithful, and now she had indisputable proof. Jace Ryan, who was a much more talented man than either of them would ever be, found her beautiful and extremely passionate.

She felt both vindicated and empowered by the thought, and her recently activated flirt gene flickered back to life. 'Because, of course, you'd be an expert on that,' she teased, determined to steer the conversation away from anything too personal. She certainly didn't plan to talk about her past relationships with men, because that would ruin the nice little buzz from his compliment.

One dark brow lifted. 'An expert on what?'

'Indulging an extremely passionate nature.'

He huffed out a laugh. 'Guilty as charged.' Tilting his chair forward, he stood up. Taking her hands in his, he tugged her out of the chair. 'But I definitely think your extremely passionate nature needs a lot more indulgence. And tonight I'm more than happy to sacrifice myself for the cause.'

Her pulse points pounded.

How easy would it have been for her to start tumbling into love with a man as overpowering as Jace Ryan last Christmas, with a lot less encouragement than really amazing sex and a few casual compliments? But luckily now she was much more pragmatic. He didn't know anything about her or her past, so he couldn't possibly know how much this night meant to her.

And she had no intention of letting him find out.

'That's very noble of you,' she whispered cheekily, glad to have deflected his questioning so easily.

He gave the tie on her robe a slow tug, until it released, the flaps falling open. His rough palms brushed around her waist and cupped her bare bottom. 'I thought so,' he said, a mischievous gleam in his eyes as moisture flooded between her thighs.

He pushed the robe off her shoulders and she gave a soft gasp as it dropped to the floor. Then yelped as he lifted her into his arms.

'Time for your next lesson,' he said as he carried her into the bathroom. 'Really amazing sex in a whirlpool tub.'

She clasped her arms round his neck and clung on, laughing while her senses stampeded into overdrive—the tight squeeze in her heart drowned out by the frantic beat of arousal and the loud splash as he dumped her into warm scented water.

CHAPTER EIGHT

'I'M GOING to be stuck in London on business until New Year's Day,' Jace's voice murmured in Cassie's ear, his soap-slicked hands cupping her heavy breasts and lazily teasing the nipples with his thumbs. 'Have you got any plans for the Christmas period?'

A little shocked by the renewed jolt of heat, and a lot more shocked by the casual enquiry, Cassie shifted in his lap, feeling the heavy arousal nestled between her legs, and her heart leapt into her throat.

After they'd soaped each other into a frenzy, he'd insisted she sit on the edge of the huge tub so he could take her into his mouth. She'd never felt anything so exquisite in her life before, the rough, expert play of his tongue on her sensitised clitoris quickly becoming more than she could bear. But when she'd come down from the intense high, the look of satisfaction on his face had made her feel ever so slightly vulnerable.

She was feeling a lot more vulnerable now.

'Why do you ask?' And why had her heart just rocketed into her throat at his question? He couldn't be suggesting what she thought he was suggesting? Could he? That they should extend their one-night fling?

He rubbed his palms over the rigid peaks and chuckled when a moan slipped out. 'Because I want more time to play with you while I'm here. One night isn't going to be enough.'

There it was again, the smug tone of voice—and the bump of her heart in her throat.

'The water's getting cold,' she said, levering herself out of his lap.

But before she could climb out, his large hands bracketed her hips, holding her in place. 'Why didn't you answer my question?' he said as she glanced over her shoulder.

He didn't look hurt or offended. Why would he? But even so she couldn't quite bring herself to give him a straight answer. The desire to say yes to his suggestion was so powerful, she knew it had to be a bad idea.

She wasn't the naive little twit she'd been for the first twenty-seven years of her life. She'd turned a corner in the last ten months and she would never go back to that. Believing all the empty promises her father had told her as a child, only to be left devastated when he never lived up to any of them. Or falling for David at art college, only to be told she wasn't what he was looking for. Or, worst of all, accepting a proposal from a man who, during the whole three years he'd bunked at her flat while he was 'between jobs', she now suspected had never been faithful to her.

But while she knew she had finally learned her lesson with Lance—that men were about as reliable as the electrical appliances you bought from a door-to-door salesman—she wasn't at all happy about the way her heart was leaping about in her chest. Just as it had done all those years ago when her father had rung up from Tokyo or Rome or San Francisco to tell her he'd definitely see her that weekend... Or when Lance had got down on one knee on the tiny balcony of her flat on Valentine's Day and asked her to marry him...

She wasn't a sucker any more, but was she completely cured? And did she really want to put her new, cynical self to the test with a man like Jace? Especially at Christmas time, when losing your grip on reality was practically a requirement of the season?

Crossing her arms over her bare breasts, she wriggled out of his grip and stepped out of the tub.

'Hey, come back here. You haven't given me an answer,' he said.

Grabbing a large fluffy white towel from the neatly folded pile on the vanity, she wrapped it round her dripping body.

'Why don't we talk about it later?' she offered. 'I'm not sure what I'm doing over the next week or so,' she added, glad she sounded so blasé when she didn't feel blasé. She secured the towel over her breasts and glanced back, fluttering her eyelashes for all she was worth. 'And I thought you promised me more really amazing sex?' she said, deciding that flirtation was the best defence.

She heard the splash as he followed her out of the tub. And gulped as she watched him in the mirror, her eyes devouring the sight of his naked body, glistening wet. His arm reached over her to grab another towel.

'Are you trying to distract me?' he murmured against her hair as she watched his reflection hook the towel around his waist.

'Is it working?' she asked, tilting her head to see the hot look on his face.

His hands circled her waist, tugged her back against his chest. 'What do you think?'

Arousal charged through her system as the feel of something hard and insistent butted against her bottom through the layers of towelling. 'Yes,' she murmured.

Turning her in his arms, he gripped the top of her towel in his fist. 'You know, you're a much badder girl than I gave you credit for.'

'Bad is more fun, remember,' she quipped back. 'You said so yourself.'

'So I did.' He pressed his lips to hers, distracting her, while he loosened her towel with a quick tug. 'But from now on there are rules.'

'Rules?' She grasped the fist he had on her towel with both hands as the knot slipped. 'What rules?'

'For starters—' he manacled her wrists in one hand, lifted her fingers to his lips, forcing her to let go of his fist, then whipped her towel off with the other '—I want you naked.'

'Oh,' she said, the blush spreading up her neck at the wicked grin on his face as her towel dropped to her feet. 'Well, fine,' she said, wrestling her hands free from his grasp. 'But I happen to believe in women's rights.' She slid her hands under his towel and yanked it free. 'Which means the same goes for you.'

He laughed, not remotely embarrassed by the powerful erection standing up against his belly. 'Good thing I happen to be a firm believer in women's rights,' he said playfully, then grabbed her and hoisted her onto his shoulder. She shrieked, kicked, giggled, but didn't struggle too hard, distracted somewhat by the upsidedown view of a very nice male behind.

'Or you'd be in serious trouble now,' he finished as he marched her into the bedroom. Tossing her onto the bed, he climbed up after her, the wicked gleam in his eye so full of purpose she wondered if she ought to make a run for it.

His hand gripped her ankle and he dragged her beneath him before she could make up her mind. 'But I'm still going to want an answer.' Cupping her hips, he cradled the thick erection against her belly. 'Eventually.'

'I'll give you an answer later.' She ran her hands over his broad shoulders, let her fingers caress the strong column of his neck and fist in the hair at his nape as he sheathed himself efficiently with the condom.

Much later.

She couldn't think about his suggestion now, couldn't let it ruin the rush of excitement tingling along her skin.

He grasped her hips, and she lifted up, taking his mouth in a seeking kiss. He eased into her as his tongue thrust, the penetration so deep it took her breath away. Pleasure blind-sided her as he rocked in short, sharp, devastating thrusts. She built to peak with startling speed, the fanciful leap of her heartbeat, the questions racing in her head, lost in the roar of ecstasy.

'About the next week or so.' Jace brushed the flat of his hand over the curve of her bottom, struggling to focus his mind and sound nonchalant while his body was still humming. 'What's your answer?'

'Hmm?' Her soft breasts snuggled against his side as her nose pressed into his neck and her hand rested against his chest.

He hoped to hell she couldn't feel the way his heart was battering his ribs.

'I want to do more of this.' He turned his head, placed a kiss on her forehead. 'How about you?' he finished, a little surprised he was having to press the point.

Why hadn't she already leapt at the chance to have an affair with him?

Suggesting it had seemed like little more than a formality in the bath, given the way she'd responded to him so far. Damn it, she'd nearly passed out when he'd put his mouth on her—and watching her come apart like that had been exquisitely arousing. But instead of agreeing to the suggestion, she'd been instantly evasive, just like when he'd asked her about her past over dinner. And he'd had to face the unthinkable prospect that she might say no.

He wasn't so arrogant as to believe every woman wanted to jump into bed with him, but the sexual chemistry between them was explosive. Any fool could see that. She wanted him all right. She wanted him a lot. So why had she refused to give him a straight answer? Was there some problem he wasn't seeing? And why had the thought that there was a problem piqued his curiosity about her even more? Usually if a woman put up any resistance he backed off instantly. But with her he couldn't seem to let it go.

It had been a long time since he'd been stupid enough to let his sex drive dictate his actions. But even knowing he should probably back off, he knew he wasn't going to.

He had close to two weeks in London to meet a series of European buyers and deal with his ex-wife's solicitors—so he could sell Artisan and finally shove the skeletons of his past back in the closet they had lurched out of and forget about them for good.

For a man who had spent the last fourteen years of his life working eighteen- to twenty-hour days—and playing pretty hard in the hours that were left—the next thirteen days spread out before him like a long, slow canter into extreme boredom. The fact that it was Christmas wasn't a big help either.

He wasn't a fan of the festive season. All that false bon-homie and conspicuous consumption got on his nerves—and having to endure it in the place he'd struggled so hard to get out of was going to add a nice thick layer of irritability to his aversion. Sure, the five-star luxury of The Chesterton was a far cry from the cramped council flat in Shepherd's Bush where he'd grown up—which was the main reason he'd booked the best suite here, the difference proving to him just how far he'd come from that unhappy troublesome kid—but he'd left this city for a reason, and being forced back here by Helen and her recent interference in the company hadn't improved his disposition one bit.

Until Cassie had leapt into his car with an indignant scowl

on her cute face and those deliciously full breasts spilling out of her drenched coat.

He gripped her waist and jostled her slightly. 'So, Cassidy, what's it to be?' he murmured into her hair, her enticing cinnamon scent made even more tempting mixed with the fresh scent of the hotel's vanilla soap. He imagined all the fun they could have together as he waited for her to reply, ready to do some serious persuasion if she didn't give him the answer he wanted.

The next two weeks would be the opposite of boring with Cassie in his bed. So he wasn't about to let her give him some lame excuse. A grin split his features, and luckily she happened to be uniquely susceptible to his powers of persuasion.

Having taken a moment to mull that satisfying fact over in his head, he tilted his chin down to peer into her face. And the smug smile vanished.

Her eyelashes touched the flushed skin of her cheeks while the steady murmur of her breathing brushed against his collarbone.

He cursed under his breath. *Unreal.* She'd only gone and fallen fast asleep on him.

CHAPTER NINE

SEDUCTIVE, intensely erotic images swirled in Cassie's head as she drifted out of a dream-filled sleep. Her eyelids fluttered open and the fierce tug of arousal pulsing in her sex intensified as she became aware of the muscular forearm banded under her breasts. Deep, even breathing brushed the top of her head and a warm body pressed against her back.

Jace.

She blinked at the thin winter sunlight gilding the opulent furnishings of his hotel suite and shifted slightly, the tenderness between her thighs so acute it was almost as if he were still lodged inside her. A hot flush swept through her as the erotic images from her dream recurred in vivid detail. And she realised they weren't dreams at all, but memories.

She tensed as Jace's sleep-roughened murmur made the hair on the back of her neck prickle. His arm tightened briefly under her breasts and then relaxed back into sleep.

Waiting a minute to make sure he was completely asleep, she took a moment to enjoy the feel of being wrapped so securely in his embrace.

A wistful smile curled her lips. So Jace Ryan was a snuggler? Who would have thought it?

Dispelling the thought and the tightening in her chest that accompanied it, she scooted over in incremental movements, then gingerly lifted his arm from around her waist and placed it behind her.

He grunted, and she sucked in a breath, praying he wouldn't wake up.

Then he flopped over onto his back, taking the sheet with him, and she let out the breath she'd been holding. She twisted round, then hesitated, momentarily mesmerised by the handsome face thrown into sharp relief by the morning sunlight peeking through the room's heavy velvet curtains. With his jaw shadowed by morning stubble, the thick locks of hair falling across his brow and that magnificent body bare right down to the springy curls of hair that peeked above the sheet draped low on his hips, it took Cassie a moment to catch her breath.

He had to be the most beautiful man she'd ever seen. And he'd been all hers for the wildest night of her life. She forced herself to look away and climb off the bed as carefully as possible so as not to wake him.

The night was over now and she needed to go home. He'd asked her about extending their fling, and as much as she yearned to wake him up and accept the offer she wasn't going to. She couldn't take the risk. While she might want to believe she could be smart and sensible about a brief fling with Jace and just concentrate on enjoying lots of really amazing sex for the next week or so, she didn't entirely trust herself. Those silly clutches in her heartbeat, last night and this morning, were proof that her delusional tendencies hadn't quite died the death she'd hoped in the last nine months... And she wasn't ready yet to tempt fate with someone as devastating as Jace Ryan.

It was cowardly and fairly pathetic, but she could live with that. What she couldn't live with was the thought of making a fool of herself all over again with yet another man who had nothing to offer her. Her brow creased as the pulse of aware-ness rippled across her nerve endings.

Well, apart from lots of really amazing sex, that is.

She gathered up her tunic and underwear from the other side of the room, determined not to give in to the tempting thought. But she couldn't quite resist returning to the bedside to study him while he slept as she slipped on her clothing.

As she sat in the chair by the bed, and rolled on the luxury silk tights he'd bought her, it occurred to her that, unlike the other men she'd known, Jace didn't look any more vulner-able in sleep than he did when he was awake.

Was that part of his allure? she wondered. Was that the quality that had made him so irresistible last night but made her so wary of him in the cold light of morning? That, unlike her, he seemed so sure of himself? So controlled? Even in the throes of lovemaking, at the height of passion, he hadn't lost the commanding, almost ruthless self-confidence of some-one who knew exactly what he wanted out of life. And was more than prepared to do whatever he had to do to get it.

Standing up, she smoothed damp palms down the beaded tunic, then leant over the bed and pressed the lightest of kisses to the rough stubble on his cheek. The tantalising musk of vanilla soap and man filled her senses.

'Goodbye, Jace,' she whispered.

Then she turned and hurried from the room, trying excep-tionally hard not to think about missing out on the sexiest, most exhilarating Christmas of her entire life. Or the painful ache under her breastbone that she refused to interpret.

She'd done the smart, sensible thing. She was now offi-cially a grown-up.

Cassie's ink pen jolted as the doorbell buzzed, sending a thick black line slashing through the Sugar Plum Fairy's nose and ruining two hours' work.

She cursed and dropped the pen into the cup she kept at the side of her drawing easel. It was her own stupid fault. She shouldn't have attempted to design her Christmas cards today. She'd been jumpy ever since she'd got back from the West End, her hormones refusing to settle down despite all her best efforts.

The doorbell buzzed again. Wiping her hands with a wash-cloth, she got up and walked from her bedroom, through the tiny living room to the front door, ruthlessly quashing the hope that it might be Jace. He didn't even know where she lived. And anyway, she didn't want to see him; the endorphin withdrawal he'd caused was quite hard enough to deal with without the added stimulation of seeing him again.

Unlocking the deadbolt, she pulled the door open.

'Hey there, what's up?' Nessa grinned, holding up a grease-spotted bag from the bakery downstairs. 'I brought apple Danish to bribe you into talking about your new man over morning coffee.' She breezed past Cassie into the flat, her extensions arranged in corkscrew curls that bobbed around her shoulders as she waltzed into the kitchen.

Cassie stifled a groan. She loved Nessa like a sister. But the last thing she needed right now was to have to relive her wild night with Jace.

'He's not my new man,' she grumbled. Or not any more. She followed Nessa into the snug galley kitchen. 'And anyway it's nearly lunchtime,' she moaned, attempting to redirect the conversation. 'Pastries will spoil our appetite.' Not to mention apply several extra pounds to her hips, which she probably didn't need. A vision of Jace's ex-wife with her skeletal supermodel figure popped into Cassie's head.

Correction, which she *definitely* didn't need.

Bending to grab Cassie's coffee jar out of the fridge, Nessa gave a rich chuckle. 'You're very grumpy this morning.' She straightened, shooting Cassie a knowing smile and not looking redirected in the least. 'Couldn't be because you didn't get enough sleep last night?' She wiggled her eyebrows before ladling coffee into the cafetière. 'Now could it?'

Cassie sighed and gave up. She knew Nessa. They'd been best friends since their first day at Hillsdown Road when Nessa had got a detention for talking back to the teacher, and Cassie had got one too for giggling at Nessa's antics.

Nessa loved to share and discuss. She adored girl talk. And she was like a Rottweiler with a T-bone when it came to talking about sex. No way would she let the subject of Cassie's wild night drop until she'd got all the juicy details.

'Fine, all right.' Cassie grabbed the kettle, held it over the sink and wrenched on the tap. 'You got me. I did the wild thing with Jace Ryan last night.'

Nessa gave a deep chortle. 'I knew it.'

'How?' Cassie asked as she plonked the kettle onto its stand and flicked the switch on. Surely it couldn't be that obvious?

'Well, now, let me see,' Nessa said as her gaze roamed over Cassie's rapidly flushing face. 'Apart from that patch of whisker burn on your chin. There's that dazed look in your eyes that says your girly bits definitely got one heck of a wake-up call last night.'

'I see,' Cassie muttered, not too pleased with the reminder.

Her girly bits weren't doing denial nearly as well as she'd hoped when she'd walked out on Jace that morning. And Nessa's observation was not helping them get with the programme.

'So tell me,' Nessa said, pouring boiling water onto the grounds and infusing the small room with the tempting aroma of fresh coffee. 'Is that boy as mad, bad and dangerous to know as I remember him?'

Cassie lifted the pint bottle out of the fridge, added a splash of milk to the two Drama Queen mugs Nessa had placed on the counter top, and tried not to remember exactly how mad and bad Jace Ryan was in bed. 'He's certainly not a boy any more,' she murmured.

Nessa gave a joyous whoop, arranging the two apple pastries onto a plate. 'Hallelujah and amen to that!' She lifted her coffee, toasted Cassie with the china mug. 'It's about time you got yourself a man who knows what he's doing.' Picking up the plate, she led Cassie into the living room. They settled in their usual seats on the vintage fifties couch. 'So your Christmas is looking up, right? No more worries about missing he who shall not be named,' she hissed in a deliberately theatrical voice, using the nickname she'd coined for Lance, the morning Cassie had run round to her best friend to tell her the sordid details of what she'd discovered Lance and Tracy doing on her vintage couch. 'You got yourself a real man to snuggle up with on Christmas morning now.'

Cassie took a careful sip of her scalding coffee, and glanced over the rim of her mug at Nessa. 'Not exactly,' she said, and braced herself for the inevitable.

Nessa's perfectly plucked brows drew down in a sharp frown and she placed her mug on the coffee table. 'Why not exactly?'

'It was strictly a one-night deal.'

'You mean he doesn't want a repeat performance? Why not? Is there something wrong with him?' Nessa's voice was so full of indignation on Cassie's behalf she almost didn't want to admit the truth. Why not let Jace take the heat instead of her?

Unfortunately, the guilty flush burned in her cheeks before she could even open her mouth. Nessa's brows arrowed down further as suspicion flickered into her eyes.

Why couldn't she even tell a decent white lie? It was pathetic.

'Wait a minute, it's not him.' Nessa pointed an accusatory

finger at her. 'It's you, isn't it? Please tell me you're not still holding a candle to that tool Lance?'

'No, it's nothing like that. It's just...' Cassie hesitated. How did she explain her cowardice to Nessa, who was bolder than anyone she knew? 'Jace suggested continuing our fling, until he leaves on New Year's Day. But I don't want to do that.'

Nessa held up her hand, her eyes narrowing. 'Let me get this straight. The man offered you—' she did a quick calculation on her fingers '—twelve whole days of really amazing fornication. That'll see you right through your Christmas funk. And you turned him *down*?'

Cassie shifted in her seat. She hadn't exactly turned him down. She hadn't even been brave enough to do that. But there was absolutely no need to admit that to Nessa.

'Ness, I'm not ready for something like this.'

'But it's been nine months since you kicked out that no-good, lying—'

'I've slept with exactly two men in my life,' she interrupted, not wanting to hear another of Nessa's tirades against Lance. 'Well, three now,' she revised. 'And I'm not sure I...'

Cassie's fumbling explanation ground to a halt as Nessa sucked her teeth in derision.

'What?' Cassie said. 'Why do you look so fierce?'

'Right this second, I'm visualising what I'd like to do to that little cheater's nuts. This is all *his* fault,' Nessa snarled, sounding as fierce as she looked.

Cassie sighed. 'It's not his fault. Not any more. I got over him months ago.' The truth was it had been remarkably easy to let go of Lance. Once she'd kicked him out of her life it had become distressingly obvious that they had never been that good together. What had been much harder to let go had been all the romantic dreams she'd had of having a settled secure life with a man who loved her. Something her mother had never managed. Cassie had picked Lance for the male lead in her Happy Ever After plan because he'd been convenient and available and had seemed to want the same thing. She'd never looked beneath the surface of their relationship. Had taken the tepid attraction she felt for him, and the yearning to have a real commitment from a man who wouldn't break his promises, and turned their relationship in her mind into something it had never actually been.

'This goes further back than that,' Cassie admitted. 'Lance was just the trigger to make me realise something I've been refusing to admit to myself for years.'

'What's that?' Nessa said, clearly not getting Cassie's rambling explanation. Not all that surprising as she was only just starting to understand it herself.

'Remember how I always fell for my dad's lies too, Ness? Remember how excited I'd be when he said he was taking me to the zoo, or the cinema? I'd build all my hopes up, convinced this time would be different. And then I'd be devastated when he didn't show.'

'It isn't your fault your daddy was a tool too.'

'And David?' Cassie said. 'Remember him? The love of my life in art college who turned out not to be all that interested in me? Can't you see there's a pattern here? That has as much to do with me as them?'

'What pattern?'

'I've always been so gullible. So easily fooled by even the slightest show of affection. It's pathetic.'

Reaching across the coffee table, Nessa covered the hands Cassie had clenched in her lap. 'You're not gullible. You're sweet natured and optimistic. It's not a crime to always think the best of people.'

Cassie met her friend's steady, reassuring gaze. 'It is if you always end up letting yourself get hurt...I just don't want to tempt fate with a guy like Jace Ryan.'

'Damn.' Nessa shook her head. 'That is a shame, when he's so good in bed.'

Cassie sent her friend a weak smile. 'He's *too* good in bed. How can I guarantee I won't start getting more than just sexually attracted to him? I'll overdose on really amazing sex. And before you know it I'll be concocting yet another stupid fantasy that's going to end up biting me on the backside.'

Nessa threw up her hands, looking exasperated. 'Now wait a minute. Who says this couldn't lead to more? Stranger things have happened. Look at me and Terrence. We plain out hated each other at school and now we're engaged to be married.'

Nessa and Terrence hadn't hated each other at all; they'd just been in denial about their attraction for years. Something all their friends had figured out long before they had.

'Now who's the hopeless romantic?' Cassie arched her eyebrow. 'Quite apart from the fact Jace lives in another country.' She hesitated—or at least she had assumed he did, it was one of the many things they hadn't discussed during their all-night sex-fest. 'We're not talking about Terrence. We're talking about Jace the Ace. Do you have any idea how many girlfriends he got through at school? Because I do. He was my first major crush.' In fact he'd been her only crush. Once he'd been kicked out of school, she'd never got so obsessed again, because no one else had ever been able to live up to his perfection in her teenage eyes. 'Every other week, he'd have a new girlfriend hanging on his arm.' And every other week she'd gone through the torments of hell, as only a thirteen-year-old could, because that girl hadn't been her.

What a complete twit she'd been about men. Even then.

Nessa cradled her mug in her palms, scowling slightly. 'All right, I'll admit he may not be long-haul material. He certainly wasn't at school. But people change.'

'He hasn't,' Cassie mumbled, remembering the 'have I slept with you?' remark.

'Maybe. Maybe not. But one thing I do remember,' Nessa countered. 'He was always real careful not to be doing more than one girl at once. He was never a cheater,' she finished pointedly.

'Great!' Cassie puffed out a breath. 'So he's a serial monogamist. So what? He's still far too dangerous a man for me to get involved with at the moment. I'm through having my dreams trampled on...and I've got to take some of the responsibility for that. I've got to be proactive from now on, and make sure I only have realistic dreams.'

'Realistic dreams!' Nessa scoffed. 'Where's the fun in that? That sounds more boring than one of my Aunt Chantelle's Bible-study classes.'

'The fun is,' Cassie said mildly, 'with realistic dreams, you might actually have some hope of them coming true.'

CHAPTER TEN

THE loud buzz of the doorbell cut through the hum of the radio. Cassie's hand jerked and the newly reconstructed Sugar Plum took it on the nose again.

'Oh, for Pete's sake!' She glared at the white card, the intricate design of gossamer wings, willowy body and delicate features ruined a second time.

It had been two hours since Nessa had left and Cassie had set to work recreating her original drawing. After her chat with her best friend, her nerves had finally stopped jitterbugging enough for her to pick up her pen without risking another mishap. And to be honest she had to get this design done today. It was the twenty-first of December tomorrow. She had to get the cards printed this afternoon or she'd risk not getting them in the post in time for Christmas. Something she'd never failed to do before.

The doorbell buzzed longer and louder. Dumping the pen and picking up her washcloth, she marched to her front door. She had lots of friends and neighbours who often popped round to see her unannounced, but this was ridiculous. She'd put a sign on the door after Nessa left so she could draw in peace for the rest of the afternoon, and also because she'd wanted a bit of time to contemplate the revelations she'd finally discovered about herself in the last twenty-four hours.

Her body would always regret having to turn Jace down,

and it would have been wonderful to indulge herself over Christmas, but she was coming to terms with the fact that she'd done the right thing. Now all she had to do was persuade her hormones. And the best way to do that was to stop thinking about what she'd left behind in The Chesterton hotel suite this morning and start concentrating on her Christmas card design. Unfortunately her friends were not playing along.

Slipping the deadbolt lose, she wrenched open the door.

'Can't you read, you…?' Her hormones sprang into a brand new jitterbug as her gaze landed on the tall man standing on her doorstep with his hand braced against the door jamb and his pure green eyes glittering with annoyance.

'Jace? What are you doing here?' she whispered, her breath backing up in her lungs.

He straightened. 'What the hell do you *think* I'm doing here?' He marched past her into the flat, instantly making her tiny living room shrink to shoe-box size.

'I…' Her gaze devoured the broad shoulders accentuated by the black leather bomber jacket, the thick waves of dark brown hair brushed back in untidy furrows from that striking face. She was so shocked to see him. She didn't have a clue what to say. Why had he tracked her down? The bump in her heartbeat, which she had spent the day telling herself she had to ignore, kicked in again.

'You ran out on me!' He thrust his fingers through his hair, and she realised where the furrows had come from. 'I wake up and you're gone. No note. No nothing. How's that for a double standard?' He rested his hands on his waist, sent her an accusatory look. 'Because if a guy does that to a girl, it's considered incredibly tacky.'

He didn't just sound annoyed, she realised. She could hear the low growl of carefully controlled temper vibrating in his voice. And see the muscle clenching in his jaw. Had he been hurt by her silent departure? It didn't seem possible. But at the thought the little bump in her heartbeat took a sudden unexpected leap.

'I had to get home,' she said as guilt made the fine hairs on the back of her neck prickle. 'And you were fast asleep,' she added, struggling not to sound too defensive. She hadn't intended to hurt him. 'I didn't think you would want me to wake you.'

'Oh, come on!' He stepped forward, towering over her, his scowl darkening and the muscle in his jaw twitching. 'We used a whole box of condoms last night. I got so deep inside you that last time I could feel your heart beating. Don't start pretending you didn't know me well enough to at least give me the courtesy of a goodbye.'

The blunt words made heat pulse low in her abdomen. Colour exploded in her cheeks, but not before she realised something crucial. She hadn't hurt him. She'd insulted him. And that was entirely different.

'I'm sorry I left without saying goodbye,' she said carefully, feeling monumentally stupid. After everything she'd said to Nessa today, after everything she'd finally discovered about herself, how could she have been led astray by her romantic nature again so soon? 'I really didn't think you'd be that bothered.'

'Yeah, well, think again,' he snarled, so close now she could smell him, that devastating musk of man and soap. He cupped her head, drew her against him. She gasped, stunned by the unexpected contact, and the fierce arousal in his gaze, and then his mouth was on hers.

He thrust his tongue between her parted lips. Her hands braced against his chest, but instead of shoving him back, as she'd intended, her fingers curled into the soft sweater, the forceful strokes of his tongue igniting the heat at her core, and sending it burning through her system like a forest fire.

When he finally lifted his head, both of them were breathing heavily.

He dropped his hand, looking as shocked as she felt at the instant and violent attraction that had blazed to life in seconds.

Last night had been fun, flirty and intense, but only ever in a sexual sense. Why should a simple kiss feel more intimate?

'I'm sorry,' he murmured, shoving his hands into the pockets of his jacket. 'That was out of order. I guess I was more pissed off than I realised.'

'That's okay,' she said, feeling both stunned and wary. Although it wasn't okay. Not really, but not for the reasons he thought. She'd welcomed the kiss, her body reacting instinctively to it. So how on earth was she going to get her jitterbugging hormones back under control now? And how was she going to persuade herself that she didn't care what she was giving up, when her body would probably never stop reminding her?

'It was rude of me to leave without saying anything,' she whispered.

He propped his butt on the edge of the sofa. Hitched his shoulders as he shoved his fists deeper into his pockets. 'You never gave me an answer.' A crooked smile lifted his lips. 'I guess I'm not used to women doing that. I wasn't expecting you to be gone this morning.'

It was as she suspected. His ego had been dented. Nothing more dramatic than that.

He levered himself off the sofa. 'Let me ask again, the way I should have done when I walked in. Instead of giving you a hard time.'

And a kiss that had nearly blown the top of her head off, Cassie added silently as he took one hand out of his pocket and touched her cheek.

She shivered, the contact as electric as it had been a moment ago, even though he was barely touching her.

He stroked his thumb across her lips. 'How do you feel about hanging out with me, till I go back to New York on New Year's Day?'

'You live in New York?' she said a bit inanely.

'Haven't I mentioned that already?'

She shook her head.

He smiled. 'Seems like we've got some catching up to do. We've kind of done this thing backwards, haven't we?'

What thing? They didn't have a thing, she thought, her panic button tripping again.

'So do I get an answer this time?' he prompted.

But he didn't sound nearly as sure of himself as he had yesterday. The thought made her feel a little less wary of him. That cast-iron control had slipped when he'd kissed her. If only for a moment. And it made him seem a tiny bit less overpowering.

She took a steady breath and opted to tell him the truth. 'My answer is, I'm not sure.'

He tilted his head to one side, rubbed one of her curls between his thumb and forefinger. 'What's not to be sure about?' he asked.

'I don't know you.'

'We'll get to know each other.' His lips curved into a rueful smile. 'As much as I'd like to spend the next ten days making nonstop love to you, even I have my limits. And we'll probably have to eat occasionally. Which means we'll no doubt have to talk to each other.'

She stepped back, tucked her hands into the back pockets of her jeans, impossibly tempted by the chance to get to know him better. But she would have to tell him the rest first.

She met his eyes. 'I got hurt. Nine months ago. When my

last relationship ended. And I don't want to get involved with anyone right now.'

'Involved?' His eyebrows shot up. 'How does ten days of small talk and great sex equal involved?'

'It doesn't,' she corrected quickly. She didn't want him thinking she was a romantic fool. Because she wasn't. Not any more. 'I know it doesn't. Which is a good thing. Because that's definitely not what I want.'

He slipped his hand round her waist, hauled her against him. 'Then there isn't a problem.' He kissed her, lingering on her lips this time, making her sex ache and her breasts swell and tighten. 'Is there?'

Could it really be that simple?

The crooked smile became even more charming. 'You know, Cassidy, you're being a bit of a girl about this.'

'That's possibly because I am a girl,' she pointed out, not sure whether to laugh at the statement or be affronted.

'I know.' He kissed her again. 'And that's a very good point. But why don't I give you a guy's perspective?' he said, as if he were humouring her. 'To help clarify things.'

'Okay,' she said, intrigued to see where this was going.

'The truth is,' he began, 'I'm not the sort of guy anyone gets *involved* with. And for a very good reason. I'm not remotely reliable,' he said, not sounding in the least bit ashamed of his lack of constancy.

'You got involved with your wife, didn't you?' she countered.

He cleared his throat. 'She's my ex-wife. Which sort of proves my point.'

'Fair enough.'

'So as I was saying, before I was so rudely interrupted,' he admonished, his eyes twinkling. 'You don't need to worry about me expecting more from this relationship than you want to give me. Because I can guarantee you. I won't want more than I've asked for, which is—'

'Great sex and small talk,' she finished for him.

'Exactly!' he said as if she were a brilliant student and he the teacher. 'You see, guys are very straightforward. We want what we say on the tin. There is hardly ever a hidden subtext. And there certainly isn't one here.'

'And what does your tin say?' she asked, unable to stifle a grin.

The man was a complete rogue where women were concerned. And while she probably shouldn't find his lack of scruples refreshing, somehow she did. David and Lance had both pretended to be something they weren't. Namely dependable and reliable and in the market for a real relationship when they never had been. While Jace, for all his wicked ways, had been honest about what he wanted. And what he didn't.

Nessa had told her he wasn't a cheater. And she'd been spot on.

He smiled as the desire in his eyes intensified. He pressed against her, the rigid arousal making her hormones do a very happy dance indeed. 'My tin says that I don't get involved.' He sank his fingers into her hair, framing her face. 'But I do have some other fine qualities that we can explore at our leisure for eleven whole days.'

He lowered his head, until his lips hovered over hers. 'What do you say, Cassidy? Are you gonna go for it or not? Ladies' choice.'

As arousal sprinted through her system and her body swayed instinctively into his, Cassie knew she was lost, the promise of pleasure in his eyes, and the feel of the thick ridge outlined against her abdomen, too tempting to resist a second time.

Circling his waist and lifting on tiptoe, she closed the distance and settled her lips on his. The kiss was slow and easy this time, but a smouldering heat built in her belly that quickly threatened to rage out of control.

He pulled back, his ragged breathing matching hers. 'I'll take that as a yes, then?'

She nodded, her tongue too numb to speak—and her mind too dazed with passion to consider refusing. Optimism flooded through her as he bent to devour the pulse point in her neck, then grasped her thigh to hook her leg over his hip. He pushed her back against the wall, ground the heavy weight of his sex into the juncture of her thighs, making moisture release in a rush through the denim of her jeans.

She arched against him, pushing herself into the hardness, desperate to feel it inside her again.

But when the heart bump came this time, the panic didn't follow.

This was about sex. Really amazing sex. And nothing more. She'd examined the pitfalls and knew what they were, so she could guard against them. But she wouldn't even have to.

She'd tried to complicate something that was remarkably simple.

Those telltale bumps in her heartbeat had been caused by the intensity of her arousal, that was all. And she'd panicked. But there was nothing to panic about. And there never had been.

She could have her candy…and eat it too. Because candy was all it was ever meant to be. And she knew that now.

Clasping her hips in his hands, he lifted her. 'Wrap your legs round my waist.'

She did as he demanded, delirious with the sharp, insistent need she no longer had to deny.

He carried into her bedroom, dumped her on the bed, then got to work on the buttons of her jeans.

'At last.' He let out a satisfied sigh as he eased his hands under the waistband, pushed the denims over her hips. 'Let's get this party started.'

And he did.

'Is that the right time?' Jace squinted at the clock on the wall above Cassie's desk. Easing his arm from around her shoulders, he sat upright in her small double bed. 'It can't be two o'clock already.' When he'd come charging out of the hotel an hour ago, determined to give Cassie a roasting for running out on him, he hadn't checked the time. Why hadn't he checked?

'Yes, it is,' Cassie murmured, sitting up beside him, her voice husky as she clutched the duvet to her breasts. 'What's wrong?'

He ruthlessly controlled the surge of heat at the sight of the soft flesh. He knew why he hadn't stopped to check the time. Because he hadn't been able to see past his lust, and the spike of temper that had gripped him when he'd woken up to find Cassie gone.

Damn it all to hell, he needed to focus now. Getting out of the bed, he grabbed his boxers off the floor, tugged them on. 'I have a meeting I was supposed to be at an hour ago.'

'Can you ring them?' she said, sounding concerned. 'Will it be a problem for you?'

He grabbed his trousers, shoved his legs into them, then whipped his sweater off the floor and pulled it over his head. 'I don't have to call. It's not a problem,' he said, knowing it wasn't. Not in a business sense. The buyers would be happy to wait a week to see him, let alone an hour. But that didn't stem his irritation with himself.

When was the last time a woman had distracted him from his business? Even for an hour. Never. Not even during his marriage. It was the thing that had always upset Helen the most. That he insisted on putting the business first.

But he hadn't given a thought to his business commitments today when he'd been showering and then getting The Chesterton's concierge to find out where the cab Cassie had booked at the front desk had taken her.

And while he'd got what he'd wanted—namely Cassie agreeing to be his playmate for the next week or so—he didn't much like the ridiculous way he'd behaved when he got to her flat either. The minute he'd seen her again, the combination of lust and longing and anger had got all tangled up inside him—and he hadn't been able to distinguish them. He'd discovered at an early age the value of keeping your emotions under wraps. And as a teenager, the even greater value of being able to deflect and deny the more destructive ones. Anger was definitely one of those emotions that was better controlled.

But for some damn reason, he hadn't been able to control it today. He needed to get out of Cassie's apartment and get to the meeting. Indulging himself with her was going to be fun over the next week or so. But he needed a little distance now to get this fling in perspective. He'd got what he wanted. And he wasn't going to worry too much about why he'd wanted it so much.

The sound of her sobbing out her release as her sex tightened around him ten minutes ago was all the explanation he needed for that.

'I'll have to dash,' he said, sitting on the edge of the bed to pull on his socks and boots. Having a little time out would be good for both of them. His smile edged up as his heartbeat calmed. Especially as they had well over a week of really amazing sex ahead of them.

He twisted round, laid his hand on her knee. 'Why don't you pack a bag? I'll send a car over and see you at the hotel for dinner.'

'Pack a bag?' Her brows lowered in a puzzled frown. 'Why do I need to pack a bag?'

He sent her a level look, tried not to overreact to the genuine look of confusion. 'Because you're moving in till New Year's Day, remember?'

Her teeth tugged on her bottom lip. 'But I—'

He silenced her by pressing a finger to her lips. 'Cassie, it's easier this way.' He made an effort to lighten his voice, add a little of the charm that he was so famous for. The charm that had pretty much deserted him once already today. 'They have room service. And a much bigger bed.'

Her cheeks pinkened prettily. 'I suppose you're right,' she said, still sounding unsure.

'I know I'm right.' Then he pushed his advantage. 'Just out of interest, how many flings like this have you had?' he asked.

She looked down, the pink in her cheeks turning to a vivid red. 'None,' she said.

He quashed the odd tightening in his chest, which made no sense at all. Why should he care if she'd done this before or not? He'd had plenty of flings; in fact, that was pretty much all he'd ever had. Even during his marriage, he'd never cared about Helen's past sex life. So he didn't get to care whether Cassie had done this before or not. But still her inexperience, and the comment she'd made about the end of her previous relationship, bothered him in a way he couldn't quite figure out.

He lifted her chin with his finger. 'Then you'll have to take it from me that I know how these things work. And really amazing sex is a lot easier with room service.' And in an anonymous location, where no one's personal space was involved, he thought silently.

'Okay, I'll pack a bag,' she said.

He ignored the rush of relief.

It was only because she'd been a harder sell than he would

have expected. But he'd got what he wanted now. All he had to do was enjoy it.

'But I have plans for Christmas Day,' she added. 'And shopping and stuff to do before then.'

'Not a problem,' he said, curving his hand round her neck and pulling her to him for a long, languid kiss that would have to last him till dinnertime. 'I've got business commitments myself.' When he lifted his lips, the blush of embarrassment had turned to the flush of arousal. Just the way he liked it. 'I won't hold you prisoner at The Chesterton.'

She gave a quick, artlessly sexy smile. 'Promise?'

He chuckled. 'See you in a couple of hours.'

But as he strode through the living room, grabbed his jacket off the sofa and then let himself out of the tiny flat he knew it wasn't a promise he was likely to keep. He wasn't going to be letting her out of his sight for the next few days; whatever plans she might have, he'd just have to persuade her to adjust them. He'd speak to his PA after this afternoon's meeting and get her to reschedule the rest of his own commitments until after Christmas.

He'd been denying his libido too long; the way he'd overreacted this morning was proof of that. His sudden inability to control his emotions had all been tied in with his lust. The next few days would be about working that need out of his system. And showing Cassie what he suspected she might have been missing in her sex life too. Once they'd both got what they wanted out of their affair, Cassie wouldn't have any more of an effect on him than all his other flings.

Cassie climbed out of bed as she heard the front door slam behind Jace. And pushed aside the spurt of hurt and disappointment that he'd rushed off so quickly.

What was she upset about? She'd agreed that their liaison

was about great sex. He wasn't making a commitment for anything more than that and neither was she.

And while his suggestion that she come and stay at the hotel—correction, his insistence that she come and stay at the hotel—had made her panic button pop again, she could see now it was the practical solution.

Grabbing her clothes up off the floor, she dropped the duvet and began to get dressed. Not only that, but the hotel suite was beautiful. And it would be much easier to remember this whole thing as some glorious sexual fantasy afterwards if they didn't spend too much time in her flat. Not that it would be a problem. But she didn't want to store up memories of him here. It would seem too much like a proper relationship when it wasn't.

And she'd be free to come and go at her leisure. Which she would definitely have to do. Because while she'd done her usual copious research for all the Christmas presents she had to buy, she hadn't actually got round to buying any yet.

Sitting back at her easel, she lifted up the Sugar Plum Fairy design and scrunched up the card. Then drew out a new card and started drawing. She'd finish her Christmas card design, get Manny at the printing shop round the corner to do a rush job, then post them before she packed up some stuff and went round to The Chesterton later.

There was no big rush, especially as Jace wouldn't even be there.

This was a casual affair. That was how he was treating it, and how she would treat it too. No blowing it out of proportion in any way. And no getting upset about him having to rush off to a business meeting, especially as she had lots of things to rush off and do in the next few days too.

CHAPTER ELEVEN

'It's Sunday!' Cassie stared at the Sunday papers she'd just noticed folded on the coffee table, the spoon of muesli poised in mid-air. 'It can't be.'

Jace glanced up from the plate of Cumberland sausage and eggs he'd been tucking into. 'That's correct. Sunday usually comes right after Saturday.'

Cassie plopped the spoon back into her bowl. 'But Sunday is Christmas Eve.'

'Is it?' Jace said, apparently unconcerned as he sliced into his sausage.

Cassie blinked. Watching him as he chewed the meat, then swallowed, her mind having gone completely blank. How could this have happened? She'd arrived at his hotel suite on the night of the twentieth of December. And now it was the morning of the twenty-fourth!

Which meant, even with her atrocious maths skills, that they'd spent three whole days cocooned in his hotel suite. Ordering in room service and indulging in an orgy of sexual pleasures, fulfilling every prurient fantasy she'd ever had, not to mention a great deal more that she'd never even dreamed of.

'I can't believe it's nearly Christmas Day already,' she murmured, feeling disorientated.

Three whole days. It didn't seem possible she could have

spent all that time doing nothing but making mad, passion-ate love to Jace Ryan.

The small talk he'd promised hadn't really materialised. Not in the way she would have hoped. He'd asked her a lot of questions about her work as an illustrator and she'd learned a little about his web design business, which was clearly very successful. But the few times she'd strayed into more personal territory, he'd clammed up and then distracted her. Mostly with sex. And she had forced herself not to take it personally. And not to push. Revelling instead in the passion he stirred so easily.

He shrugged, sent her a suggestive smile that had the heat pooling low in her abdomen. 'We've been busy.'

Cassie's skin heated as he pierced her with that hungry look again.

Pushing back from the breakfast table, she tightened the tie on her robe. 'I should shower and get dressed. I've got a lot to do today.' Three whole days had gone by in a haze of lust and passion and she hadn't even noticed.

As she went to walk past him he snagged her wrist. 'How about I come in and scrub your back for you?'

She tugged her hand free, dismayed by the way her pulse punched his thumb and her hormones instantly jitterbugged into overdrive as if leaping for joy at the prospect.

They'd made love less than half an hour ago when he'd woken her up to tell her breakfast had arrived, his fingers had started stroking and before she'd known it she'd been rock-eting to orgasm while she was still barely awake. And just like all the other times they'd made love, she'd felt the clutch in her chest, the tightening in her heart muscle as he'd car-ried her into the suite's living room and plopped her down in front of her breakfast. And she'd steadfastly ignored the bump. But even she couldn't ignore the fact any longer that her behaviour was veering out of her control.

If this was all just about sex, why couldn't she seem to get enough of him? And why was the need inside her increasing with each passing day instead of abating?

'I'd better shower alone this morning,' she said, remembering how last morning's shared shower had ended.

'Hey.' He stood up as she turned to go, circled both of her wrists with his fingers to hold her in place. 'What's the matter? You look kind of spooked.'

Spooked was putting it mildly, she realised as she looked into his pure green eyes, and realised she didn't actually know any more about him than she had four days ago. 'I think I'm just getting a little stir crazy,' she said. That had to be it. She simply wasn't used to a physical relationship of this intensity. And it would probably be good to dial it down today. Plus she really did have a lot to do. She had a ton of Christmas presents to buy. 'We haven't left the hotel suite since Wednesday night,' she reasoned.

'True.' He lifted his hands to frame her face, leaned in to give her a quick kiss. 'I guess I haven't kept my promise, have I?' he said sheepishly.

'What promise?'

'Not to keep you a prisoner here.'

She felt herself flush, and her heart clenched again as she sent him a crooked smile. She forced the feeling of elation down. *Don't be daft.* The intensity of the relationship in the last three days had been purely sexual. His desire to spend time with her had no more significance than fulfilling a physical urge. For both of them. And the fact that her body still responded to him with such intensity was proof of that. For goodness' sake, she'd just established the fact that she hadn't got to know him, as she'd planned. And that hadn't just been his doing. She hadn't pressed because she'd been happy with the way things were. Because she'd been determined not to read anything more into their intimacy.

'I've enjoyed it,' she said. 'But I'll have to break out today. I've got a ton of shopping to do.'

His hands trailed down her arms, gripped her wrists for a second then let go.

'I guess that means I'm going to have to let you go for the day,' he said, sounding genuinely disappointed.

'Not necessarily,' she heard herself reply. 'You could always come with me,' she added, before she lost her nerve.

While she totally understood this was about great sex and nothing more, the compelling desire to spend time with him outside the hotel suite was unstoppable.

It would give them the chance to talk properly. And there were so many things she'd become curious about in the last four days. His failed marriage, his past, how the moody boy from a 'bad home' she remembered from school had become such a charismatic and successful man. All things she hadn't had the chance to ask about. Maybe that was why the heart bumps kept getting worse. Because she wanted to know more about him, and the more she didn't know, the more he avoided giving her that information, the more vulnerable she felt.

If he came shopping with her, she'd be able to quiz him without him being able to distract her quite so easily.

She dismissed the niggling little voice that told her she might be straying into dangerous territory. She'd become more sexually intimate with this man than she had with any other man. He knew things about her body that no other man had ever even bothered to discover. How could it be wrong to want to know a bit more about him? It didn't mean she would lose sight of her objectives. They'd already set out exactly what this relationship entailed and what it didn't. And they'd been busy reinforcing that point in the most delicious way possible for three whole days. So where was the harm in satisfying a little of her curiosity about him now?

Jacob Ryan had been a fascinating enigma ever since she'd

had a crush on him at school. He'd always been so taciturn and surly then. And while he had acquired a layer of relaxed easy-going charm as an adult, she couldn't help wondering if traces of that angry boy still existed, or if he had disappeared for good.

Surely this would be the perfect opportunity to dispel her fascination with him once and for all. Because she had an awful feeling that all the great sex they'd been having might have started to reawaken that stupid crush. Which would explain all the heart bumps. And that could not be a good thing.

'Nah, you go ahead,' he said, sitting back down and picking up the paper. 'I'll contact my PA. I should schedule some of those meetings today while you're not here to distract me.'

'But, Jace, that's silly. It's Sunday. And it's Christmas Eve. No one will be able to meet today. And we could have lunch out together.' She hurried on, trying not to sound too eager, the opportunity to have some of her curiosity satisfied suddenly irresistible. 'And don't you have any Christmas shopping to do?'

Jace stared at Cassie and kept his mouth firmly shut, before he did something really daft, like agreeing to go with her. Ever since she'd turned up at the hotel four nights ago, her small wheel-around suitcase in her hand and a shy but eager smile on her face, he hadn't let her out of his sight. In fact, he'd barely let her out of his bed. The plan had been to seduce them both into a coma, overdose on great sex for a few days and get the driving need to have her out of his system. Parts A and B of his plan had worked out great—a bit too great. Because part C had clearly been a dead loss. If not, why would he have the driving urge to stop her going out as soon as she had suggested it?

The woman was becoming an addiction. An addiction that

all the really amazing sex seemed to be making worse, not better.

Luckily he had the perfect excuse not to accept her invitation. He folded the paper, dumped it back on the coffee table. 'Believe me, Cassidy. You don't want me along.'

'Yes, I do,' she said, earnestly. 'Why wouldn't I?'

'Because I hate shopping. I won't be good company.'

'Why do you hate shopping?'

He shrugged; this bit at least was easy. 'There's always crowds of people and too much stuff to choose from and it takes for ever. Before you know it you've lost the will to live over a rack full of suits. I'd rather be kicked in the...' He paused when Cassie winced. 'I'd rather be kicked somewhere a guy definitely does not want to be kicked,' he finished, deciding to spare her the graphic visual.

'What is it about guys and shopping?' she said, exasperation edging her voice. 'It's the eighth wonder of the world if you do it right.'

'I do do it right,' he said flatly. 'I do all my shopping online.'

She didn't just wince this time, she flinched. 'That's awful. How can you buy clothes on a computer? Especially designer ones. You've got to try them on, see how they hang. What the cut's like. You can't tell that from a picture and a list of measurements.'

'If I don't like it, I send it back. Get a refund.'

'Which means standing for hours in a post office queue. Personally, I'd rather take my chances at the shops.'

He sent her a level look. 'I don't do post office queues.'

'How can you send it back if—?'

'Put it this way.' He stopped her in mid-argument. 'One of the reasons I worked so hard to earn my first million was so I could send someone else to queue at the post office.'

She dropped back on her heels, an adorable crease of consternation lining her brow.

'And so I would never have to enter a department store again in this lifetime,' he added forcefully. 'Especially not in the West End on Christmas Eve. It'll be my worst nightmare,' he said, determined to keep that fact front and centre. He didn't do shopping, even with someone as cute and sexy as Cassie.

'No, it won't,' she said, clearly not prepared to be beaten. 'It won't even take that long.'

'How so?'

'I happen to be a champion shopper.'

Yeah, right. Most women didn't even know what that was.

'I'm getting the impression from that sceptical look that you don't believe me,' she said. 'How about I make you a bet that we get everything done in under an hour?'

'How many people do you have to get stuff for?' he asked judiciously.

'Umm.' She curled her plump bottom lip under her teeth as if she were counting up the number in her head. 'Ten. No.' Her eyes met his, the bright light of excitement in them almost tangible. 'Eleven.'

'Eleven presents in under an hour? In the West End? On Christmas Eve? For a woman who loves to shop?' he clarified.

She nodded enthusiastically.

'Not possible.' This had to be the sucker bet to end all sucker bets. 'And what do I get if you don't manage it?'

'Hmm, let me think.' She pressed the tip of her finger to her mouth, then leaned forward and touched his chest. Her nail trailed down over one nipple, across his ribs, down his abs and stopped just short of his belly button where his robe closed. She sent him a coy smile. 'I'm sure I can think of something that you'll enjoy,' she said, her voice husky with provocation.

Despite his recent climax, he could feel himself rising to attention. He wrapped his hand around her finger, lifted it off his belly. The little tease. She was going to pay for that.

'You're on,' he declared. 'But once the hour's up we head straight back here and get naked.'

One hour of shopping seemed like a small price to pay for the fantasies he was already conjuring to go with her sultry smile. And once they were back in the suite, everything would be back where he wanted it.

'You're assuming you're going to win,' she said sweetly. 'But when you don't, when the hour's up, I get to take you to lunch.' The sultry smile became decidedly smug. 'And we get to have a proper conversation. About something other than sex,' she added.

He smiled back. It had been fairly easy to distract her up to now. So even if the unthinkable happened and he lost the bet, that didn't scare him. 'All right, you're on.'

He dragged her into his arms to seal the deal, but she wrestled out of his embrace and tapped a finger to his nose. 'Not so fast, Ryan. No kissing until we're in public.' She lifted her eyebrows. 'I know all your tricks.'

He chuckled as she dashed off to the bathroom. 'Not yet you don't,' he murmured, feeling pretty smug himself. He'd managed to manoeuvre her into only spending an hour away from his bed today.

If this was an addiction, he had the will power to overcome it, once he set his mind to it. He'd overcome much bigger weaknesses to get what he wanted.

But there was no need to go cold turkey. At least not today.

Jace was feeling a lot less smug an hour later as Cassie walked back towards him with her latest purchase clutched in her fist and a triumphant smile on her face.

'What's the tally now?' he muttered.

She held the bag up. 'Jill's present makes eight.'

Jace glanced at his watch and groaned. They were only thirty-five minutes into their shopping marathon, and she'd already got over two-thirds of her stash.

She laughed at his frown. 'Regretting taking me on, Ryan?'

'You're not there yet, sweet cheeks,' he countered, but his confidence about winning the bet was ebbing fast. He slung the three bags of purchases she'd given him to carry over his shoulder. Although, funnily enough, he hadn't been nearly as bored or frustrated as he would have expected. In fact, watching Cassie shop was nothing short of fascinating.

She really was a champion shopper. Unlike with any other woman he'd had the misfortune to shop with, she seemed to know exactly what she wanted and where to get it. She'd attacked Oxford Street with military precision, avoiding the big chain stores, and instead using a string of smaller independent shops and boutiques mostly dotted on the side streets whose merchandise she seemed to have expert knowledge of. She didn't browse, she went straight to the counter and described exactly what she wanted. He'd also noticed that her purchases were incredibly well thought out and individual. If he didn't know better, he could have sworn she'd actually researched this trip.

As they walked out of the chocolaterie and back towards the throbbing activity of Oxford Street he noticed her open her bag and peek at something inside. He'd noticed her doing that a couple of times already. Snagging the leather bag from behind, he whisked it out of her hands and off her shoulder. 'Let's have a look in there.'

'Hey, what are you...?' she yelped.

'What have you got? A secret weapon?' Spotting the piece of paper she'd been reading, he whipped it out of her bag.

'Give that back.' She made a jump for it, but he held the paper easily out of reach.

'Damn, it *is* a secret weapon.' He stared at the handwritten list, which had annotations and notes, hand-drawn maps and several intricate little drawings jotted all over it. The thing was a work of art. She must have spent hours on it. A weird feeling of weightlessness lifted his stomach at the thought that she'd gone to so much trouble. That anyone would go to that much trouble. Over a bunch of Christmas presents.

'What is this?' he asked.

'Give it back. It's my Christmas list,' she said, embarrassment turning her cheeks a bright shade of pink. She looked so damn cute and determined, the weightlessness increased.

'How comes I never knew this about you?' he teased, pushing the sentimental thought to one side. It was a shopping list, for goodness' sake, not the Declaration of Independence or the Magna Carta.

'Knew what?' she said, swiping the list out of his hand when he dropped his arm.

'That you're anal.'

'I am *not* anal,' she declared, stuffing the list back into her bag. 'I'm organised. And where Christmas shopping is concerned, it pays to be organised.'

'I get it.' The drop in his stomach lifted. 'You write the list so you don't overspend, right?' That had to be the reason why she'd gone to all that trouble. It was so long since he'd had to buy on a budget he'd forgotten what it was like.

'No.' She stared at him as if he were witless. 'I go to the trouble of writing a list so I don't get the wrong thing. Getting people the right present takes work and consideration. I know it's a cliché but it really is the thought that counts.'

If that were the case her friends would be rich, he thought, feeling uncomfortable again.

He couldn't quite believe how much time and effort she'd clearly put into the process. This wasn't about being a shopaholic. It was about actually caring about people enough to want to get them something they'd really like. The minute the thought registered, the weightlessness returned and the uncomfortable feeling got worse.

'I like going that extra mile for the people I care about,' she said doggedly. 'Because I know they'll go that extra mile for me.' She looped her arm through his. 'Now stop trying to waste time, we've still got three presents to go and they're the most important.' She headed across Oxford Street, the fairy lights of Selfridges' facade making her hair sparkle. 'And for that we need the big guns.'

As she dragged him into the legendary department store he realised that he'd never cared about anyone enough to want to get them something special for Christmas. And no one had ever really cared that much about him.

And it hadn't bothered him.

Right up until he'd got suckered into going Christmas shopping with Cassie Fitzgerald.

'See, I told you I was a champion shopper,' Cassie said as she pushed onto the bench seat and settled the bags of presents she'd purchased under the dinner table, the sense of accomplishment making her feel more than a little smug.

She folded her arms and waited for Jace to take the seat opposite. She had a lot to be satisfied about. Not only had she got all her shopping done in under an hour, she'd also managed to awaken Jace to the true joys of retail therapy. Despite all his earlier protestations, she thought he'd actually quite enjoyed the experience. She'd asked his opinion so many times that after a while he'd been forced to get involved. And by the time they'd got to Selfridges, instead of the usual monosyllabic answers, they'd had a very useful discussion about the merits of different brands of men's sportswear. She'd wanted to get Nessa's fiancé Terrence something really good to train in, but didn't know a thing about tracksuit brands—what was in at the moment and what wasn't—and Jace had been surprisingly informative. She doubted he would appreciate her pointing that out now though. Because, while it had been touch-and-go for the last ten minutes of her allotted hour, when she'd wasted precious seconds agonising over whether to get Nessa the amethyst pendant or the faux sapphire, Jace had lost the bet. And he didn't seem to be a very good loser.

Jace slid the tray holding the steaming pastrami on rye sandwiches they'd purchased at the counter, and sent her a disgruntled look. 'Don't rub it in, Fitzgerald. If I'd known you were going to cheat, I would never have made the bet.'

'How did I cheat?' she exclaimed, having to fake her outrage, as she was enjoying her victory too much.

'That list.' He sat down and lifted the plates off the tray. 'I didn't know you'd been in training for weeks. If I had...' His voice trailed off.

She grinned. 'Gee, Ryan. Sore loser much?' she teased, unable to resist rubbing it in, just a tad.

His lips tilted up as he slathered mustard on his pastrami. 'Gee, Fitzgerald,' he countered. 'Smug winner much?' He took a bite into the sandwich with relish. 'Damn, that's good,' he said, wiping his mouth with a napkin. 'It tastes like the real thing.'

'It *is* the real thing,' Cassie replied as she sliced into her own sandwich to make the hearty slabs of rye bread a bit more manageable. 'This is Selfridges Food Hall.'

'I know that,' he replied, his voice gruff, but his eyes bright with humour as he took a swig from his bottle of mineral water. 'I've just wasted five minutes of my life debating the merits of Marmite chocolate, remember.'

She gave a light little laugh. 'Stop pretending you weren't severely tempted to buy a bar.'

He sent her a smouldering look that promised retribution at a later date as he took another bite.

'And you should be looking on the bright side,' she added, watching him devour his sandwich. 'Now I've done all my shopping, we can devote some time to doing yours,' she announced, hoping that he hadn't done his already. All the guys she had ever known did the majority of their Christmas shopping at the last second. 'You have a champion shopper at your disposal to help. And I know Selfridges and Oxford Street like the back of my hand. All you have to do is tell me who the person is, what they like and don't like and I'll be able to locate the perfect present within a mile radius, I guarantee it,' she said, her enthusiasm increasing. Seeing whom he bought gifts for would provide a fascinating insight into his private life without her having to probe. 'Really, I should charge for my services,' she finished.

She picked up her sandwich and took a bite as he swallowed the last of his down. He took another swig of his water, swiped the spot of mustard from the corner of his lips, then dumped his napkin on the empty plate, a considering look in her eyes.

'No need,' he said. 'I don't have any shopping.'

She gulped the bite of her sandwich down, trying not to be too disappointed by the news. 'That's a first. I've never met a man who has all his Christmas shopping done before Christmas Eve.'

'I haven't done it already.' He tapped his thumb on the side of his plate. 'I just don't do any.'

'What do you mean you don't do any?' she said, disappointment replaced by shock as her eyes widened. 'What about your family? Your friends? Don't you get them presents?'

He didn't seem fazed by the question, even though the very thought of not buying anything for people you loved was unthinkable to her.

He shrugged, the movement stiff. 'I don't have any family. And my friends know I don't like to receive anything, so they don't expect anything in return.'

'But how do you celebrate Christmas, then?' she asked, shock giving way to astonishment and an odd sense of sadness. She didn't have any family any more either, not since her mother had died. Her father was still alive, but she'd given up on him years ago. Even so she'd filled the gap with a wide circle of friends—and Christmas had always been the perfect time to catch up and enjoy each other's company. She loved the ritual of the season, the sense of love and companionship she shared with the important people in her life. How could you really participate in that without the giving and receiving of gifts? They didn't have to be expensive. She'd splurged this year because she'd had a couple of successful commissions and had begun to make a name for herself as an illustrator. But she could still remember previous years when all she'd been able to afford were home-made stuff or bargain gifts, and she'd still enjoyed doing her Christmas list just as much.

'Simple,' he said, his voice devoid of emotion. 'I don't celebrate Christmas.'

'You don't…' She paused, nonplussed by the blank look on his face.

Of course she knew there were people who hated Christmas, usually for specific reasons. It could be a stressful time, especially when your family life wasn't great. And whatever Ms Tremall had meant all those years ago by a 'bad home' she suspected Jace's family life might have been the opposite of great. But he didn't sound as if he hated Christmas, just as if he were indifferent to it. Which somehow seemed even sadder.

'But you must have celebrated it with your wife?' she asked, her skin flushing a little at the boldness of the question.

She hadn't meant to probe. She knew however curious she

was about his past, she didn't really have the right to ask him personal questions, but instead of clamming up as he had before, he simply leant back in his chair and studied her for a moment.

'We weren't married that long,' he commented. 'You know, if there's something you want to ask me about my marriage, why don't you just ask?'

Her skin heated. Had she been that obvious? Clearly, she had been if the implacable look in his eyes was anything to go by.

But despite feeling exposed, despite knowing she'd been caught asking something that was none of her business, and despite being certain that Jace's offer to ask him about his marriage was disingenuous, the rapid ticks of Cassie's heartbeat rose in her throat and she recalled the look in his ex-wife's face five days ago. And admitted to herself that the naked pain in Helen's gaze had niggled at the back of her mind ever since that day.

'All right, I have got something to ask,' she said softly, forcing the question out before she could stop herself. 'Did you love Helen when you married her?'

CHAPTER TWELVE

'DID I *love* her?' Jace choked out a laugh, and wanted to kick himself for being so stupid.

Why had he opened himself up to this? He always kept things casual with women he slept with, and opening up the can of worms that was his marriage could get a little heavy. He should probably just lie. He'd done it before, because it had been the easy way out.

But somehow the earnestness in Cassie's expression and the gently asked question made him hesitate. And then he really wanted to kick himself, because, however easy or convenient it was, he knew he couldn't lie to her. Which was all wrapped up in watching her spend an hour devoting so much time and energy to getting presents for people he didn't even know. He now knew just how sweet and genuine she really was—which meant it would probably be wise to let her know exactly the kind of man he was.

They had already agreed about the terms of their relationship, and that was great. But he'd seen the way she'd looked at him, knew that he was a first for her when it came to no-strings sex—and he didn't want any confusion about what was really going on here.

'No, I didn't love her,' he admitted flatly, careful not to put any inflection into his voice. The facts spoke for themselves. He watched the look of confusion cross her expressive face.

He could have added in his defence that as far as he was concerned there was no such thing as love. But once you said that, women had a bad habit of trying to persuade you otherwise. Or worse, find out why you thought that. Something he wasn't about to get into. Because if the subject of his marriage was a can of worms he didn't like prising open, the subject of his childhood was a whole barrel of them.

'But if you didn't love her, why did you marry her?' she asked.

The delicious pastrami sandwich he had eaten sat in his stomach like a ball of lead.

He swallowed heavily and looked down at his plate. He probably should have expected the question, but it didn't make it any easier to answer.

'Her father provided the start-up investment for Artisan. He found out I'd been screwing Daddy's little girl and gave me an ultimatum. Either I make an honest woman of her, or he was pulling the finance.' He met her eyes as he said the words. He'd done what he had to do to get out. And okay, he'd made mistakes. Succumbing to Helen's questionable charms being a whopper. But he'd paid the price for his stupidity and his lack of restraint. So why should he feel guilty about it now?

'Basically, I married her for her father's money. And not all that surprisingly, the marriage only lasted six months.'

Cassie didn't look disgusted or even all that judgemental about what he'd told her, but annoyingly he still felt the need to justify his actions. Not something he'd ever done before. 'Luckily, the company was a lot more successful. It was my ticket out and I took it. Whatever I did to get it was worth it.'

'Your ticket out of what?'

'Just out,' he hedged. 'It's an expression,' he added. He definitely wasn't getting into that. 'Anyway, Helen's father died two months ago and left her his shares and his seat on the board of directors. Which is why I'm in London, selling the company.'

'So you don't have to deal with Helen?' she said, making it sound like theirs had been a real marriage.

'Nothing that dramatic. I can handle Helen fine,' he said easily. 'Unfortunately she has a problem handling me. Or rather leaving me alone. And anyway, it was time to let the company go. I was going to expand anyway. I've got more control if I start afresh, with a new board of directors. New designs. My own finance. And I can cut my ties to London for good.'

'Did Helen know?'

'Did Helen know what?'

'That her father had forced you into the marriage?'

'He didn't exactly force me.' He laughed, but heard the bitterness that he thought he'd got over years ago. 'More like persuaded. There were no shotguns involved.' He stretched back against the chair, glad to have steered the conversation away from anything too revealing. 'But to answer your question, yeah, Helen knew,' he said, thinking of the lies Helen had told her father, about how Jace had taken her virginity. 'She was used to having Daddy get her what she wanted,' he continued. No need to tell Cassie exactly how stupid he'd been— and railing against all the wrongs his ex-wife had done him had never been his style. His marriage hadn't meant enough to him to make vilifying Helen all that worthwhile. 'And for some unknown reason, she wanted my ring on her finger.'

'She must have loved you,' Cassie murmured.

He swigged the cool, clear water, astonished by how sincere she sounded. Did people really believe all that rubbish? But he could see by the forthright tilt of her chin, the conviction in her eyes, that she did.

Funny that her gullibility should seem enchanting though, rather than simply naive.

He jerked his shoulder. 'Maybe.' He didn't care either way whether Helen had loved him or not.

What was a little disturbing, though, was realising that he did care what Cassie thought of him now she knew the truth.

'Eat up,' he said, nodding at Cassie's sandwich, which she'd barely touched. He stood up. 'I'll go get us some coffee, then we can grab a cab.'

He wanted to get back to the hotel…where he knew lots of good ways to avoid any more dumb conversations about his past.

Cassie picked at her sandwich and watched Jace walk away.

He stopped at the diner's retro counter, his shoulders stiff and unyielding as he spoke to the waitress. Taking her napkin out of her lap, Cassie folded it neatly over the remains of her meal as confusion made her stomach churn. What she'd learned about Jace and his marriage had killed her appetite completely.

He'd been surprisingly open, answering all her questions despite his statement on their first night that he didn't like talking about it. And now she could see why. Despite his flat, emotionless tone, and the apparent ease with which he'd told her he'd married his wife for her father's money, she couldn't help thinking that what he'd revealed raised a lot more questions than it answered.

He clearly wanted her to believe that money had been his only motivation, but she knew it was a lot more complicated than that. For despite his obvious wealth, he didn't seem like a man who was motivated by money. He didn't even like to shop, for goodness' sake. Which meant that it hadn't been the money, it had been what the money represented—the opportunity to escape—that had really been driving him. So why had he been so desperate to escape? And what had he been so desperate to escape from? So desperate that he'd been prepared to endure a loveless marriage.

He wanted her to believe he was shallow. An opportunist. But she knew from the other things he'd said about the web design business that had been his ticket out that he'd worked extremely hard to make it a success.

As a teenager, she'd conjured up lots of bad-boy fantasies about how all he really needed was someone to love him and support him. Someone like her. All of which had been ridiculous, and had had much more to do with her need to be needed than anything else.

But maybe there was a grain of truth in some of it. Because she could see now that surly disaffected boy hadn't disappeared completely.

He walked back through the tables, carrying a tray laden with her latte and his espresso. With his shoulders slightly hunched and his dark hair falling carelessly across his brow, she suddenly had a vivid picture of him at seventeen, the day he'd come into school with a vicious cut across his brow and a black eye. Everyone had assumed he'd been in a fight.

The rush of tenderness made her stomach lighten and an idea formed in her mind. A wonderful idea that she should have thought of sooner.

'You didn't finish your sandwich,' he said as he placed the coffees on the table.

'I know.' She grasped her handbag, slung it over her shoulder, then took a quick burning sip of the latte. 'I hate to eat and run, but I have to dash. I should take this haul back to my flat and wrap them. My best friend Nessa's doing Christmas lunch tomorrow and everyone will be there.'

He sipped his espresso. 'All right, I'll see you at the hotel later.' It wasn't a question, but she could see the flicker of uncertainty in his eyes and the tenderness wrapped around her heart, warming her more than the latte.

'You want a hand getting all that loot into a cab?' he asked as she gathered up the array of different bags, struggling to hold them all.

'I've got them. I'm an expert at this, remember.' Leaning over him, she gave him a quick kiss.

His hand settled on her waist, and he tugged her closer, turning the kiss from quick to burning in a heartbeat. 'Don't be too long,' he said when he let her go.

As she dashed off past the displays of Japanese noodles and exclusive French wine she could feel him watching her, and a wide grin spread across her face.

Jace Ryan was going to celebrate Christmas this year. Whether he had planned to or not. Because it was way past time he discovered how much he had been missing.

CHAPTER THIRTEEN

'MERRY Christmas, Mr Ryan,' Cassie murmured as she settled onto Jace's lap.

His arms came around her waist and he gave her a hard hug. 'Same goes, Ms Fitzgerald.' He nuzzled her neck, and she felt her pulse leap. They'd just had a leisurely bath together and demolished a huge cooked breakfast. 'What time do you have to be at your friend's house?' he asked.

She drew back. 'Not for a while.'

'Great!' He shifted, stood up with her in his arms, but as he headed to the bedroom she wriggled down.

'Not so fast,' she said breathlessly, anticipation making her heart flutter in her chest. 'I have a surprise for you. In honour of the season.' She'd promised herself she wasn't going to make a big deal of it. But she was still looking forward to seeing his reaction.

'Oh, yeah.' He sent her a suggestive grin and grabbed the tie on her robe. 'That's what I was hoping.'

She slapped his hand away playfully. 'Not that sort of surprise. You really do have a one-track mind.'

'Hey, from the way you jumped me in the whirlpool tub this morning, I'm certainly not the only one.'

She giggled at the mock irritation in his tone as she crossed to the huge spruce tree in the corner of the suite, and the stack of presents for her friends that she'd placed beneath it yesterday evening ready for her trip to Nessa's.

Taking the brightly wrapped parcel and card perched on the top, she carried it back to him. 'Merry Christmas, Jace,' she said, presenting the gift.

Instead of taking it, he pushed his hands into the pockets of his robe, a puzzled frown creasing his brow. 'What's this?' he asked.

'It's a Christmas present,' she said brightly, holding it up. But his hands stayed buried in his pockets, the confused frown becoming more acute as he stared at the present, as if it were an unexploded bomb.

'But I told you, I don't bother with Christmas presents,' he said, his eyes lifting to hers.

She lowered the present, the flutter in her chest turning to a deep pounding beat as she registered the expression on his face. She'd expected him to be surprised. But she'd persuaded herself that the decision to buy the present was simply to thank him for giving her back that part of herself she'd lost. She had to admit now, though, that the decision had also been a little bit of a ploy to jolt him out of his cynicism about Christmas. What she hadn't expected, however, was the dazed shock in his eyes. Seemed she'd given him a bit more than a jolt.

'I didn't get you anything,' he said, his voice hoarse, his stance stiff.

'I know,' she said, emotion gripping her chest at the thought that he would be worried about that. 'I didn't expect you to.' Taking his arm, she lifted his hand out of his pocket, placed the gift in his open palm. 'It's just a token, Jace. To say thank you for everything you've given me over the last week.'

'What have I given you?' he said, the dry note of suspicion strangely defensive.

'Lots of really amazing sex,' she said lightly, but as she saw his stance relax a little she realised he'd given her so much more than that.

Being with him had been exciting and exhilarating; it had liberated her from the mistakes of her past relationships. Instead of worrying about the future, and where things were leading, with him she'd been able to stay in the moment, to enjoy their relationship for what it was with none of the weight of responsibility. And she'd had fun. More fun than she'd ever had before. Christmas had been something she'd been dreading this year, because she was going to be alone on Christmas morning, which would have reminded her a bit too forcefully of her first Christmas without her mother.

The rush of tenderness from the day before intensified. She knew she couldn't tell him any of that. Because it would alter their fling in a way neither of them wanted. But giving him the present seemed like the perfect way to say it without words.

'So thanks for that,' she added saucily. 'Plus you've been paying for all the room service, so I feel I owe you one,' she said.

He gave a rough chuckle, turned the present over in his hands as if he didn't quite know what to do with it. 'I'm not sure if I should feel used or flattered that you're giving me a gift for services rendered.'

'I'd say probably a bit of both.' She gave a light laugh, impossibly pleased that she'd got him to accept the gift. 'Why don't you open it?' she prompted.

He looked up. 'All right.' He sat back down in his chair, then eased off the sticky tape with such care her heart began to hammer her ribcage. It was almost as if he'd never received a gift before. Which was ridiculous, but somehow she couldn't shake the thought as he lifted the emerald-green designer sweater she'd bought the day before and held it up as if it were incredibly precious. The colour matched his eyes and the cashmere was soft enough that it wouldn't irritate his skin if he chose to wear it without a T-shirt.

'Cassie, this is expensive. Too expensive.'

'Do you like it?' she asked, although she didn't need to, she could see the astonished wonder in his face, which she suspected had as much to do with getting the gift as it did with the gift itself.

'You know I do. But I can't—'

'It wasn't that expensive,' she interrupted. 'It certainly didn't cost as much as four days' worth of room-service meals at The Chesterton.' She lifted the card off the table, handed it to him. 'You forgot the card.'

Her pulse sped up as he took it, shaking his head. 'You shouldn't have gone to all this trouble.'

She smiled, glad that she had. Suddenly struck by the realisation that despite his success, and his money and his industrial strength sex appeal, Jace Ryan had never made any meaningful human connections in his life. Not with his so-called friends, not during his short-lived marriage and certainly not with his family... Or he wouldn't have been so completely poleaxed by a simple Christmas gift. As a teenager, she'd always believed in her typically rose-tinted way that what he needed was true love, but maybe all he had really needed was a friend. A proper friend. And she could be that. At least for the short time they were together.

Jace drew the white card out of the envelope and stared at the picture on it while willing the tightening in his chest to go the hell away.

But it didn't go away, it got worse as he studied the expertly drawn caricature of himself standing next to a Christmas tree with piles of shopping bags under it, his bare chest looking like something out of a body-builders magazine while the seductive smile on his face was tinged with wickedness. The words written underneath in an elaborate serif font read:

To Jace, Ex-Bad Boy, Candy Man extraordinaire and Champion Shopper in training!
Merry Christmas, Cassidy x

He huffed out a laugh past the constriction in his throat, so touched by the silly card he felt like an idiot. Who knew the Christmas spirit could be contagious?

He looked up to find her watching him, her face flushed with pleasure. Dropping the card on the table, he shifted round and grasped the tie on her robe. 'Come here, clever clogs,' he said, dragging her towards him until she straddled his lap. She rested her hands on his shoulders, the sweet, impossibly pleased smile on her face making his insides flip over—a strange feeling of lightness and excitement and anticipation swelling right alongside the lust.

'I feel kind of bad,' he said, stroking his thumb across her collarbone, and watching her pulse flutter against her neck, 'that I don't have anything for you in return.'

'That's okay, Jace.' Her eyes went to half mast as his index finger traced the line of her throat then dipped down to explore the tempting display of cleavage revealed by the lapels of her robe. 'Don't you know, it's much better to give than to receive?' she purred, her voice husky with desire.

'Is that so?' He nudged aside her robe, heard the sharp intake of breath as he exposed the fullness of her breast and the swollen nipple to his gaze. 'Then I guess it's my turn to do the giving,' he said before swirling his tongue across the puckered flesh and drawing it into his mouth.

She bucked in his lap, her fingers digging into his shoulders as he feasted on her. But as the blood pounded into his groin, the lump in his throat swelled and he had to push down the tidal wave of regret that he would never be able to give her more than this.

'I shouldn't be here,' Jace grumbled as Cassie stabbed the doorbell on the wall panel for the red-brick block of flats situated next to the shutters of a closed shop. The metal frames of the market stalls stood behind them, making the empty Hoxton Street Market look eerily quiet in the cold afternoon air. 'I wasn't invited.'

'Nessa won't mind,' Cassie replied, glancing over her shoulder, her cheeks pink from the cold. 'Why would she?'

'Because she doesn't know me,' he said, stating the blatantly obvious. And more to the point, he didn't know her.

He still wasn't quite sure how he'd got strong-armed into coming to Cassie's friend's Christmas meal in the first place. One minute he'd been riding on the crest of a wave of endorphins, the heady rush of afterglow tempered by the confusing emotions Cassie had caused by giving him the Christmas gift. And the next he'd been driving through the deserted streets of East London en route to a dinner date with a load of strangers.

He'd had a perfectly good plan to go jogging in Hyde Park, sweat off the room-service meals he'd been devouring in the hotel and then catch up on reading through some of the proposals his PA had emailed him from the various buyers he still hadn't got round to meeting.

He didn't want to be here. So why was he?

'Of course Nessa knows you,' Cassie said matter-of-factly, giving the door a hefty shove when it buzzed. 'She went to Hillsdown Road too.'

'Terrific,' he muttered sarcastically, tension tightening his shoulder blades as he held the door open for Cassie and her sack full of gifts.

'Don't look so worried.' She grinned, patting his cheek. 'You were a legend at Hillsroad.'

'Which is exactly what I'm worried about,' he said grimly as he trudged up the darkened stairwell behind her.

The door on the first-floor landing was painted a glaring shade of yellow with black and green edging. And the pulsing beat of a current funk rap anthem could be heard from inside.

Jace braced himself as the door swung open and a curvaceous black woman wearing a beaded tunic, similar to the one Cassie had had on that first night, came bounding out and flung her arms round Cassie. 'Hey, girl? What's up?'

Cassie dropped the bags and hugged her friend back. 'Happy Chrimbo, Ness. I hope you've got enough turkey for one more?' She stood back, and the woman's lushly made-up eyes landed on Jace.

'Oh, my days, Jace the Ace!' she proclaimed.

Jace winced. He'd never liked that nickname much at school, he was liking it even less now.

'Haven't you grown up nice?' she said and then sent him a cheeky grin that had memory blindsiding him.

He grinned back. 'Damn, Vanessa Douglas,' he said, his shoulders relaxing for the first time since he'd agreed to come. 'The scourge of the lower third.'

She laughed, the sound rich and full, and he recalled how much he'd enjoyed it when they'd ended up in detention together—which with her smart mouth and his aptitude for trouble had been fairly frequently.

'Guilty as charged,' she said, giving him a high five. 'Remember how we made Ms Clavell's life a living hell?'

'The poor woman nearly had a breakdown,' Jace said, amazed to realise he'd now discovered two memories from school that hadn't been at all bad.

'That woman was way too uptight.' Nessa batted the

thought away as she shut the door behind them. 'We just loosened her up a bit.'

She turned to Cassie as they followed her into the flat's cramped hallway and took off their coats. 'And of course I've got enough turkey. The thing's a mutant,' she added, hanging up their coats as the scents of roasting meat and Caribbean spices wafted down the hallway, along with the shouts of raucous conversation and the bass-heavy music. 'Terrence had to cut the legs off to fit it in the oven,' she said, leading them into a surprisingly large open-plan kitchen-diner, which was packed with people who were chatting and chopping and cooking and carousing in that disorderly but choreographed way that old friends did instinctively.

Clapping her hands, Nessa got everyone's attention.

A tall, good-looking, mixed-race guy standing by the stove with an apron on that said 'World's sexiest chef' turned down the speakers on the counter top.

'Okay, folks, Cassie's here and she's brought her new candy man, Jace. So treat him nice.'

Cassie slapped Nessa's arm, blushing profusely as she hissed over the chorus of cheers and wolf whistles from her friends, 'Ness, I can't believe you just said that.'

Jace choked out a laugh, the last of the tension easing out of his shoulders as he got slapped on the back by one of the guys and offered a hearty handshake by another.

So, Vanessa Douglas still had the smartest mouth in London.

'I reckon you've finally found yourself a keeper.'

Cassie glanced over her shoulder, her arms elbow deep in soapy water, the noise from the raucous game of Twister in the living room covering Nessa's murmured comment. The heat hit her neck as she gave what she hoped was a nonchalant shrug.

'You mean Jace?'

'Mmm-hmm.' Nessa slanted her a don't-play-the-innocent-with-me look. 'So what happened to "I'm not ready for too much spectacular sex"?' she teased in a little-girl voice.

Cassie coughed out a laugh and put the washed saucepan on the draining board. 'For goodness' sake, Ness, keep your voice down. After that candy-man comment everyone's going to think I'm a loose woman.'

'Like it isn't already obvious how loose you are,' Nessa said, picking up a tea towel.

Cassie's blush intensified, but her lips quirked at Nessa's typically saucy observation.

She'd had such a good time this afternoon, it was hard to get snippy with her best mate for pointing out the obvious. And in a funny way, the fact that Nessa could tell what a difference her days with Jace had made to her state of well-being reinforced her decision to indulge in her wild fling.

The afternoon had gone better than she could have hoped. And that had been mostly down to Jace. While it had taken a lot of persuasion and quite a bit of trickery to get him to Nessa's, he'd relaxed and enjoyed himself once he was here. Her friends were a close-knit group, having all known each other since they were teenagers, but with his sharp wit and easy-going charm Jace had fitted right in. He'd joined in with their banter, told some entertaining stories about life in New York, wowed everyone with the apps on his phone that were just a small segment of his company's output and had bonded with Nessa's fiancé, Terrence, over the subject of Spurs' chances of making Europe this year.

Funny to think that even after three years of dating Lance, none of her friends had ever hit it off with him nearly as well.

'So what's happening with you two?' Nessa asked, picking up the wet saucepan. 'Seems like you've got off to an excellent start.'

Cassie deposited a frying pan on the sideboard, and quashed the silly pang radiating up her torso. 'It's not the start of anything. It's nothing more than a Christmas fling. He's going back to New York on New Year's Day and that'll be the end of it.'

Nessa shoved the saucepan in a cupboard with a loud clatter. 'That's stupid. Why don't you go over to New York with him for a while? See how things work out? You can draw anywhere.'

'Ness, stop being absurd. Quite apart from the fact that he hasn't invited me.' And he wasn't likely to, she thought as the silly pang got worse. 'I told you, this isn't a relationship. It's just a bit of fun.' Which was all she wanted, she told herself staunchly. But her golden glow from the afternoon faded a little.

'Uh-huh,' Nessa said, scepticism oozing from every pore. 'You wanna know what I think?'

Cassie yanked the plug out and wiped her hands on Nessa's tea towel. 'Not really, but I'm sure you're going to tell me anyway.'

'He can't take his eyes off you, especially when he thinks you aren't looking. And your gaze follows him wherever he goes too. And you buy him a sweater that he wears first chance he gets. Plus you've been having spectacular sex for the last four days without an intermission.' Nessa doggedly counted off the points on her fingers, then slapped her hands on her hips. 'That *is* the start of something. It's the start of something called a relationship.'

Cassie blew out a careful breath, tried to quell the seed of hope that had been budding inside her all day. The seed of hope that wanted to believe that what Nessa was saying was true, when her head already knew it wasn't. 'It's not a relationship. It only looks that way.'

Nessa made a scoffing sound. 'Why do you always sell yourself short like that?'

'I'm not, I'm being realistic.'

Nessa waved the comment away with a flick of her wrist. 'So that's what they call giving up now, is it? Realism.'

'I'm not giving up, it's not like that.' She couldn't let herself hope again. Hope for something that wasn't real. She'd learned that lesson too often to want to learn it again. And worse, she somehow knew that if she let herself dream for something permanent with Jace, the devastation would be that much worse. Because he already meant more to her— in four scant days—than Lance had meant to her after three years. 'You've never had anyone tell you to your face, in the most graphic way possible, that you didn't matter, so you don't know what it's like,' she hit back.

'Maybe not,' Nessa conceded. 'But then I never made the mistake of hitching my dreams to guys that weren't worth the effort either.'

'What's that supposed to mean?' Cassie whispered, shocked by the accusation in her friend's voice. Nessa had been the Rock of Gibraltar throughout her adolescence and her adult life. She was the one who had always been there, picking her up when the men in her life had let her down, or abandoned her, or cheated on her.

Nessa gripped her upper arms, gave her a little shake. 'Don't get all pinched face on me. I'm not saying what Lance did was your fault. You're the one who said that. But what I am saying is why did you ever settle for someone like him in the first place? He was never good enough for you, honey, but you were the only one who couldn't see it. Now you're falling in love with Jace Ryan, a guy who might actually be worthy of you, and you're too scared to even admit it 'cos for some dumb reason you think you're not entitled to be that happy.'

'It's not that...' Her voice trailed off. She wasn't falling in love with Jace; she couldn't be. Her panic button wasn't just tripping now—alarm bells were blaring out at full blast.

'Stop freaking out,' Nessa said, pulling her into a hard hug. 'All I'm saying is, if you decide you want him, don't be scared to fight for him.' She drew back, held Cassie at arm's length, a confident smile spreading across her lips. 'Because it's exactly like they say in that hair ad. You're worth it, honey.'

CHAPTER FOURTEEN

'Who's Lance?' Jace shifted gears too forcefully, making the rental car's engine whine.

'Hmm?' Cassie glanced over from the passenger seat. She'd been subdued since they'd left Nessa's place. But then so had he.

He'd had a good time. The food had been fabulous, and plentiful, and the company even better. But there was something about seeing Cassie with her friends, and getting drawn into their Christmas celebration, that had been kind of unsettling towards the end of the evening. As they'd said their goodbyes, it had occurred to him that he'd never see these people again. And for the first time ever he actually regretted the transient nature of the friendships in his own life.

Not that he was missing anything, he reassured himself. He had friends. Just not people he wanted to depend on, the way Cassie clearly depended on hers. But watching the way she blossomed in their company had been captivating. Gone was the woman who seemed unsure of herself. She had been more confident, more in control—just as she was when they made love.

Or at least she had been, until Terrence had made a passing reference to this guy Lance. Cassie had changed the subject and, after a few knowing looks had passed between her friends, they'd gone along with it. It was obvious they all felt protective towards her. Which had made him wonder what exactly it was they were protecting her from. Then of course he'd had to wonder why he cared.

But even knowing he shouldn't care who Lance was, he hadn't been able to stop the question spilling out.

It was just curiosity. He wanted to know why she'd changed the subject, and why the mention of the guy's name had caused that moment of distress to flash across her face.

'Or Lance the Loser, to give him his full name,' Jace prompted, jerking his gaze from the road to watch her reaction.

A frown line appeared on her brow. 'He's nobody,' she said. 'Not any more.'

His fingers fisted on the steering wheel. So he did have something to do with Cassie. 'But he was someone once,' he said. 'So who was he?'

And what was he to you?

She sighed, turned to look back out of the window as the darkened shops along Kingsland High Road whipped past. 'We were engaged to be married,' she murmured. 'Until I found him doing the bare-butt boogie on my sofa with one of his ex-girlfriends.' She huffed out a little laugh, but there was no humour in it. 'I should have dumped him for being such a cliché, even without the cheating.'

'Is he the relationship that came to a bad end?' he asked, unable to keep the edge out of his voice as his knuckles whitened.

Loser was right. What kind of lowlife did that to a woman? Especially a woman as sweet-natured and generous as Cassie?

'Yes, that would be Lance.' Her affirmation sounded resigned and touched something deep inside him that hadn't been touched in longer than he could remember.

The urge to comfort and reassure came from nowhere.

Reaching across the console, he put his hand on her leg, squeezed. 'He was obviously a total jerk.'

'I know.' She sighed heavily. 'My problem is that I seem to be a magnet for total jerks. Even my dad was a total jerk.'

'Yeah, how's that?' he asked, not sure he really wanted to know the answer. He knew what it was like to be screwed up by a parent. Thinking of Cassie having to go through that wasn't the best way to keep his anger under control.

'He didn't do anything that terrible,' she said carefully. 'I've always been oversensitive about it.'

He doubted that, given the way she'd let Lance the Loser off the hook. 'What did your father do?'

'It's not what he did. It's what he didn't do.'

He waited for her to elaborate.

'My parents got divorced when I was four,' she began. 'He'd found someone else, and started a new family with her. He hurt my mum terribly but she maintained contact with him because she wanted me to have a relationship with him. Only problem was, I don't think he was ever that interested. He felt guilty and obligated, so he went through the motions.' She gave a soft sigh and he felt the pulse of anger beat in his temple.

He'd never considered becoming a father because he knew he wouldn't be any good at it. His own role models had been atrocious and he didn't like to rely on anyone, or have them rely on him. But even he couldn't imagine being uninterested in your own flesh and blood.

'He'd say he was going to take me to do this and that,' Cassie murmured, her voice so quiet he almost couldn't hear it. 'We'd make arrangements, I'd get all excited and then...' She paused. 'Mostly, he didn't show. He'd ring at the last minute with some excuse. And the few times he did show, usually because my mum had pressured him into it, he'd be preoccupied, talking on his mobile, or getting irritated with me if I asked too many questions. He was a busy man and he let me know that he didn't have time for me.'

'Good thing he didn't show up more often,' Jace said forcefully, thinking what a waste of space the guy must have been.

'What?'

He shrugged. 'Sounds like you were well rid of him. Who wants to spend time with a jerk like that.'

'Do you know something? I've never even thought of it like that.' She laughed, but this time the sound had the light tinkle of real amusement. 'But you're right. Whenever he didn't turn up, my mum would take me out instead. We'd go ice-skating or swimming, or one time she took me and Ness to the Open Air Theatre in Regent's Park and we had a great time. She was always more fun than him anyway.'

The genuine pleasure in her voice had the uneasiness prickling up his spine again.

'There you go,' he murmured, lifting his hand off her knee. *Time to back off. You don't get involved, remember?*

'What were your parents like, Jace?' she asked softly.

He flinched. Where had that question come from?

He flipped up the indicator, then gripped the gear shift as he accelerated past St Paul's Cathedral, the silence in the car suddenly deafening.

Cassie listened to the quiet hum of the powerful car's engine and watched Jace's jaw tense.

'Why do you ask?' he said, so evasively her heart pummelled her chest. She should probably let the subject drop, but his defensiveness was so unlike the confident man she had come to know, she didn't want to back down. Had his parents been the thing he had wanted to escape?

'When we were at school, I overheard Ms Tremall saying you came from a bad home,' she said. 'I always wondered what on earth she meant.'

'I guess she meant it wasn't good.' He laughed, the sound brittle. 'But it wasn't that terrible. And it's so long ago now, it doesn't matter.'

Why did she have the feeling it did matter, then? She thought of the unguarded look of surprise and pleasure on his face when he had unwrapped her gift that morning, and realised it mattered a lot.

'How bad was it?'

He looked at her as the car braked at the traffic lights along Fleet Street, his expression carefully blank. The sound of his thumb tapping a rapid tattoo on the steering wheel cut through the evening quiet. 'You know what?' he began, his voice tense. 'How about we skip this conversation?'

Cassie studied the stiff set of his shoulders as he pressed his foot to the accelerator. 'Why do you want to skip it, if it doesn't matter?'

He accelerated as the lights changed, and hitched his shoulders. 'Okay, fine,' he said, his voice clipped. 'If you really want to know, my mum married a guy when I was eight who had a violent temper and didn't make much of an effort to control it.'

Cassie's stomach tensed, the faded scar across his left eyebrow illuminated by the lights of Charing Cross Station. 'He *hit* you?'

'Not too much. I got very good at staying out of his way. And eventually I got big enough to fight back,' he replied, in a tense monotone. 'My mum took the worst of it.'

'Jace,' she whispered, covering the hand he had wrapped around the gear shift. 'I'm so sorry.' Tears pricked the backs of her eyelids at the thought of what he must have witnessed and endured. 'That's hideous.'

He stared at her briefly in the half-light. 'There's nothing to be sorry about. I'm all grown up now and it's over.'

He pulled his hand out from under hers, rested his palm on her knee.

'How about we change the subject—' his hand trailed up her leg '—and concentrate on something a lot more interesting?'

She forced a weak smile to her lips, swallowed the tears down, as the familiar rush of heat sizzled up her thigh where his hand wandered. 'Okay, Mr One-Track Mind,' she joked, trying not to let her wayward emotions overwhelm her.

But as they drove round Trafalgar Square the light flurries of snow framed the giant Norwegian Spruce at its centre and made the view from her window as the car sped past look as picturesque and magical as a Christmas card. Her heart thundered and her mind raced, unable to let go of the image of Jace as a boy and the miserable home life that had been exactly the opposite of a Christmas card.

He didn't need a friend. He needed so much more than that. Something she knew in her heart she could give him. As soon as the thought registered she tried to push it down and bury it deep. But it was already too late.

She turned to look at the man next to her as he negotiated the steady stream of traffic on Piccadilly Circus. She considered the harsh line of his jaw, the dark concentration on his brow and the closed expression on his handsome face that gave so little away even when they were making love—then pushed out a ragged breath.

Nessa was right. She *was* falling for Jace. Or why would she have been so devastated by that brief insight into the horrors he'd suffered as a child? And why would she believe she could fix it?

She pushed her head into the deep bucket seat, listened to the purr of the powerful car and struggled to calm her heart's frantic leaps and pirouettes.

So she was falling for Jace. But what the hell did she do about it?

Should she tell him? Or would that complicate things even more?

'That's it, Cassie. Come for me again,' Jace rasped, sweat popping on his brow, the corded muscles in his arms and neck straining as her hot slick flesh tightened around him. He drove deep, clung onto sanity, the exquisite torture pushing him to the brink. Her eyes glazed over, her body bowed back and the ragged sobs of fulfilment echoed in his ear as he crashed over right behind her.

He drew out slowly, the dull ache in his groin from the intensity of his climax nothing compared to the raw rush of emotion clutching at his chest as she gazed up at him.

Her palm cupped his cheek, her eyes alight with an emotion so pure and elemental a muscle in his jaw clenched. As always her expression was as open and easy to read as a children's picture book.

Don't say it, Cassie.

He placed a kiss on her lips before she could speak. 'That was terrific,' he said, keeping his voice deliberately flippant. 'Merry Christmas, Cassie.'

Shifting off her, he slung his arm round her shoulders, tucked her against his side and braced himself to hear the words he feared she was about to say.

She wouldn't be the first woman to tell him she loved him. He'd seen that look in a woman's eyes dozens of times before. Women often got sentimental after great sex and—after his momentary lapse in the car when he'd told her about his stepfather, and the dumb way he'd reacted to her present, plus the fact that he and Cassie had been having great sex for nearly a week—it was kind of inevitable that someone as romantic as Cassie would fall into the familiar trap. What did surprise him, though, was that he hadn't seen it coming, and he didn't know what the hell he was going to do about it.

She was the first woman he'd ever been scared to hear say it. Because for the first time ever, he knew the usual ploys he used to deal with the dreaded 'I love you' moment wouldn't work.

He couldn't lie, as he usually did. Just repeat the phrase as casually as possible, or simply brush it off and then forget about it. Because Cassie would see right through it. And if he told her the truth, that as far as he was concerned love was just a gimmick that people used to trap each other, she'd be hurt. And he didn't want to hurt her. Not only that, but she might walk out on him. And while he knew it was selfish of him—not to mention arrogant and egotistical—he didn't want her to walk. Not yet. She was good company, she was sexy as hell, and he liked the way she looked at him—with that strange combination of innocence and confidence and understanding. It made him feel lighter, more optimistic than he had in a long time. As if all the mistakes he'd made in his life, all the things he'd done wrong, didn't matter if he was with her.

'Merry Christmas, Jace,' she whispered at last.

Relief washed through him, the lucky escape making him feel like a man who'd just walked away from a firing squad.

She hadn't said it. Thank God.

He frowned. Had he just imagined that look?

The frown deepened. Okay, too much great sex was clearly making him a little nutty too because why should that bother him? This was good news.

He skimmed his hand down her back, felt her lush body curl against him—and shoved down the stupid swell of contentment that followed.

'How about we get out of here tomorrow?' he suggested. 'Go someplace?' There were tons of things they could do in

London. They'd hardly been out of the hotel suite and—while he was going to find it torture keeping his hands off her—he probably needed to reduce the physical intensity for a while. And after Boxing Day he really needed to get stuck into those meetings that he'd been holding off on too.

Today had got way too intense, for a number of reasons. Letting her simple Christmas gift get to him had been bad enough, but then blurting out all that stuff about his childhood and letting the sympathy and compassion shining in her eyes get to him too had only compounded the problem. Cassie had slipped under his guard somehow, and it was a mistake he would have to correct, and fast. They only had six more days before his flight back to New York and by then he was letting her go.

She lifted up, propped her elbows on his chest to look down at him, her full breasts distracting him as they swayed enticingly.

'Mr One-Track Mind isn't seriously suggesting we do something other than sex, is he?'

He choked out a laugh, then grasped her hips and neatly reversed their positions, nestling his hardening erection against her stomach.

'Don't push your luck, Cassidy. Or you may find yourself imprisoned here for another six days.'

Much later, after the storm of passion had passed a second time, Cassie lay awake listening to the steady rise and fall of Jace's breathing and blinked back the foolish tears.

She'd nearly blurted out the words. Nearly declared her feelings earlier. But then she'd seen him flinch, almost as if he knew what she was about to say, and she'd managed to hold back, the frigid chill settling in the pit of her belly.

Just because her heart went out to the boy Jace had once been and she was tumbling into love with the man he had managed to become. Just because she had convinced herself that his life could be richer with her in it, and vice versa, she had to remember that Jace had never asked her for a thing.

And until he did, until he gave her some sign that his feelings had deepened too, she'd be mad to tell him how she felt and risk ruining what little time they had left.

CHAPTER FIFTEEN

'It's time for some candy floss,' Jace announced, gripping Cassie's gloved hand and hauling her through the milling crowd towards the confectionery stand.

'No more food, I'm begging you,' Cassie groaned comically, rubbing her belly. 'We had hot dogs half an hour ago. And my stomach's still in revolt after the Big Dipper.'

'See, I prove my point.' Jace laughed, stopping at the stand. 'Women make rubbish dates at funfairs.'

He ordered a large helping of candy floss from the vendor.

'That is such a load of crap.' Cassie slapped her hands on her hips in mock outrage as he took a huge bite of the giant helping of spun sugar. 'I had my brain scrambled on the Twister, took the Helter Skelter at close to sixty miles per hour and nearly swallowed my own tongue on the Power Tower,' she declared, still shuddering at the memory of plunging a hundred and fifty feet in free fall. 'And I didn't make a single complaint.'

He wrapped one arm around her hips, yanked her close and gave her a sugar-coated kiss. His devastating green eyes twinkled with humour. 'You screamed like a girl in the Haunted House.'

A smile edged her lips, the bud of hope that had been building for days blossoming in her chest at the affection on his face. 'A severed head flew past my ear,' she muttered, trying to sound stern. 'I should get a pass on that.'

He touched his nose to hers, the cold tip sending little shivers of excitement down her spine as the smell of burnt sugar and man engulfed her. 'You didn't hear *me* screaming, did you?' he murmured, his low voice intimate and amused.

She shoved him back, laughing. 'You definitely flinched.'

'A manly flinch is permitted. My ears are still ringing from that scream.'

She cocked her eyebrow. 'So now who's complaining?'

Taking her hand, his fingers closed around hers as he chuckled. 'Not me,' he said. 'I guess you make a pretty good funfair date,' he added magnanimously, swinging their joined hands as they strolled through the thoroughfare of Christmas-themed market stalls at the entrance to the funfair that was set up every year in Hyde Park. 'For a girl,' he finished.

She socked him on the arm, making him laugh. Then shuddered as the brittle winter wind found its way through the bare chestnut trees sheltering the fair and whipped at her hair.

He slung his arm over her shoulder, hugged her against his side as he dumped the last of the candy floss in a rubbish bin. 'How about we head back to the hotel? Get you warmed up.'

She circled his lean waist, leant against him as they strolled out of the park together. But she knew she didn't need warming up, the spark inside her that had ignited days ago now burning like a log fire and giving her a golden glow inside and out.

The last five days had been magical. He'd handled all his business meetings with ruthless efficiency first thing in the mornings, leaving the afternoons and evenings free to play. And play they had.

They'd gone ice-skating at the crowded rink in front of the Natural History Museum. Feasted on fine French wine and steak and *pomme frites* in the stark Mayfair elegance of Quaglino's and on champagne and oysters in the Italian gothic splendour of Bentley's Bar and Grill in Piccadilly. They'd taken long walks with his arm around her shoulders through the frost-bitten parklands of Kensington Gardens. And she'd even managed to drag him to the Boxing Day sales along Oxford Street where he'd endured over an hour of bargain hunting before he'd made her spend almost as long genuflecting over the newest gizmos in the gadget store on Regent Street.

And every night they'd made passionate love in the seclusion of his penthouse suite. Her senses and physical awareness of him were so acute now, all he had to do was look at her with hunger burning in his eyes and she became moist, her body readying itself to indulge in all the pleasure she knew he was about to give her.

She was falling in love and she wasn't scared of her feelings any more.

They hadn't had any more conversations about serious stuff, like her past or his. They hadn't discussed what would happen in two days' time when he returned to New York. And he hadn't said anything specific to her about continuing their affair. But sometimes actions spoke louder than words. The appreciation and affection and approval that shone in his emerald gaze whenever he looked at her. The way he couldn't stop touching her: the hand-holding, the fleeting kisses, the impromptu hugs, the palm brushes down her hair or the knuckles he skimmed across her cheek whenever they were in public. And then there was the way he made love to her, sometimes two or three times a night and often in the morning too, with a power and a passion and an urgency that increased in its intensity with each passing day.

All those things could only mean one thing.

Jace was falling for her too. Although she suspected, given his past relationships with women, he didn't have a clue.

Tomorrow was New Year's Eve and he'd arranged for them to watch the countdown and the fireworks from the balcony of an exclusive nightclub overlooking the Thames.

As his arm tightened around her shoulders, and the garish sights and sounds of the winter funfair faded, she made her own special New Year's resolution. If he didn't say anything by tomorrow night, she would take the initiative.

Nessa had told her she should fight for what she wanted. And she intended to do just that.

She wasn't going to put undue pressure on him and make some lavish declaration of undying love. But why shouldn't she see if they had a future together? It seemed foolish to let what they had slip away, just because both of them were too scared, or too cautious or too clueless about love to admit their feelings for one another went deeper than a Christmas fling.

'Only ten minutes to go, then we can make our getaway,' Jace murmured against Cassie's hair as his hands skimmed over her waist.

He heard her draw in a quick breath, his palms settling on the cool silk covering her hips.

'I don't think so,' she whispered, her eyes connecting with his in the floor-to-ceiling window that looked out over the Thames. The Millennium Wheel stood proud and glaringly modern, spotlit across the choppy water as the anticipation of the well-off crowd rose with each incremental movement on Big Ben's clockface to the right of the terrace. Cassie's lips edged up in a nervous smile. 'We have to see the fireworks. The view from here is incredible.'

'I've got a much better view.' He nuzzled her ear lobe as

he caressed the sensuous silk. 'And I've got some much better fireworks in mind too.'

She giggled, covering his hands with hers, to halt his increasingly insistent caresses. 'Stop it. You didn't pay five hundred pounds a ticket to miss the main event.'

He chuckled. 'Cassidy, as far as I'm concerned, tonight's main event does not involve us being cooped up on a terrace with a hundred other people.'

She turned in his arms, lifted her hands around his neck and sent him a saucy smile. 'Well, you'll just have to be patient. This is our last night together and I want it to be special.'

He tensed slightly, his hands settling on the small of her back. She'd given him the opening he'd been waiting for. He'd been thinking about his options for days, made the final decision that morning. But now he had the chance to say the words he found himself hesitating. Evaluating the situation and the best way to handle it—and her—one last time.

Everything had worked out perfectly in the last few days. He'd had more fun in her company than he could ever remember having with another person. She seemed to understand him in ways no other woman ever had. She was bright, lively and sweetly optimistic and had no need to cling to him. In fact, her lack of expectation had made it possible for him to relax and enjoy himself without fear of having to deal with the suffocating prospect of commitment. Maybe the plan to reduce the physical intensity hadn't quite worked out, given that the instant, insistent need had turned to a constant, growing ache that he had found harder and harder to control. But he wasn't too worried about that any more. Because the 'I love you moment' he'd been dreading hadn't materialised. He'd kept things light and non-committal—even forcing himself to take time out every morning to handle the meetings his PA had rescheduled—and Cassie had gone along with it. She hadn't made any demands, or any requests even. And while part of him had been relieved, as the time drew close for him to leave he'd actually begun to find it a little galling.

Because now he was the one who was going to have to do the asking. But as she looked at him expectantly, her eyes shining with excitement, the compelling look of acceptance on her face, he knew he couldn't hold back any longer.

'About this being our last night.' He paused. 'I was thinking...' His voice trailed off.

Come on, Ryan, spit it out. It's not that big of a deal. If she says no, it won't be the end of the world.

'How busy are you right now, workwise?'

She tilted her head to one side, the shine positively glowing now. 'Why do you ask?'

His hands rode up her sides, tightened. Maybe it wouldn't be the end of the world, but the desire to hear her say yes was still pretty damn acute.

'Why don't you come back with me tomorrow?' he said, as casually as he possibly could. 'For a few days? Or a week. Or even two. I've narrowed down a buyer for the business. I'm planning to finalise the sale tomorrow. So I figured I'd take a break from work when I get home. I can show you around New York. It's an incredible city.'

He clamped his mouth shut, realising with horror he was starting to babble.

For God's sake, shut up, you sound like a boy asking a girl on a first date.

But then a huge smile spread across her face, and the panicked ticks of his heartbeat calmed.

'That's...' she began. 'I don't know what...'

'Don't say anything yet.' He pressed his lips to hers as the noise of the crowd, shouting down the final seconds of the old year, rose to a crescendo outside on the terrace. 'We've got all night for you to make a decision,' he finished.

Taking her hands from around his neck, he turned her back to face the scene outside, folded his arms over her midriff and pulled her slim body back against his. 'Now watch the fireworks.' He bit softly into her ear lobe, heard her breath catch. 'Before I drag you out of here to have my way with you.'

As the crowd roared and cheered Big Ben chimed the hour and a blast of light and colour exploded across the Thames. Cassie tilted her head back against his shoulder, looked up into his face. 'Happy New Year, Jace.'

'Yeah,' he growled, seeing the answer in her eyes. She was going to come with him.

Slanting his lips across hers, he captured her mouth in a harsh, possessive kiss, his heart thumping against his ribs and his arms tightening around her instinctively.

It was going to be a Happy New Year all right. At least for him.

He didn't have to let her go. Not just yet.

CHAPTER SIXTEEN

'So, Cassidy, it's make your mind up time.' Jace tugged her into his lap. Securing his arms round her waist to hold her in place, he asked, 'You want me to book you a ticket to the Big Apple today?'

Cassie's heart leapt into her throat, the sexy smile and the warm weight of his arms making the high she'd been riding since his offer the night before shoot straight into the stratosphere. She swallowed heavily to control the lump of emotion in her throat, ready at last to bare the feelings she had for him.

He wanted to continue their affair; she could see he cared a great deal for her—the way he'd made love to her last night when they'd arrived home from the New Year's celebrations, fast and frantic the first time, then slow and tender the next, was yet more proof of his growing feelings. But she couldn't accept his offer under false pretences. He'd been deliberately casual about how long she would be in New York and about why he wanted her there, she suspected as a defence. He was a man who had never been in love before—not even with the woman he had married—and, from the little she knew of his past and his character, had tried very hard to protect himself from any emotion likely to make him vulnerable.

But if she accepted his offer, she had to let him know that her feelings were not casual. She needed to be honest now, and go with her instinct, that his feelings weren't as casual as he tried to pretend.

Looping her arms round his neck, she gave him a soft smile, her gaze drifting over his harsh, handsome features. The dimple in his cheek, the confidence in his eyes, the locks of unruly hair still glistening from their morning tryst in the shower. She wanted to memorise every aspect of his expression when she told him she was falling in love.

'I want to come. More than anything I've ever—'

'Excellent,' he said, interrupting her. 'I'll give my PA the news. We'll need your passport number.'

He tried to shift her off his lap. She had to cling on. 'I'm not finished, Jace.'

'We need to get the ball rolling,' he said, the flash of impatience in his eye making her hesitate. 'Tickets have to be booked, bags packed and—'

'Jace, stop it. I've got something I want to tell you.'

His shoulders stiffened slightly under her hands. 'Okay, but make it quick.'

'I... If I come to New York... You need to know that I...' She stumbled, her confidence ebbing away. Why did he look so tense all of a sudden? 'This means a lot to me. Because...' She had to force the words out past lips that had dried like parchment. 'I'm falling in love with you.'

His eyebrows rose a fraction, and for a split second she thought she saw something in his face. But it was masked instantly, leaving the precious words hanging in the air between them, sounding foolish and a little corny instead of heartfelt and genuine.

'I'm flattered,' he said, the tone of his voice so condescending she cringed. 'But we've really got to get a move on if we're not going to miss our flight.' Taking her weight, he lifted her off his lap.

She folded her arms round her waist, her insides churning

as the hope and excitement of moments ago turned to bewilderment.

Placing a quick kiss on her nose, he patted her behind. 'Now go and get dressed. I'll drive you round to your place so you can pack after I've called my PA to confirm about the ticket.'

'Jace, wait.' She grasped his arm as he tried to walk past. 'Don't you have anything else to say?'

She'd expected surprise, maybe even shock, had been prepared for him to try to deny her feelings to protect the wall he had kept around his own for so long. What she hadn't expected, or even considered, was his indifference.

He shrugged. 'No,' he said.

She frowned, the tears swelling in her throat making her feel even more foolish. Was she overreacting, being stupidly sentimental? 'I just told you I'm falling in love with you,' she said carefully. She bit down on her quivering lip, knowing that tears would only make this situation a billion times more humiliating. 'Are you sure you don't have anything else to say about it?'

'I told you, I'm flattered,' he said, stressing each syllable. 'I'm glad you like me so much.' But he didn't sound glad, he sounded irritated. She could read him fairly well now, despite the way he always fought to keep his emotions hidden. She could see the slight tension in his jaw, the muscle in his cheek that flexed as he spoke. 'It'll make things more fun when we hit New York,' he finished.

Fun!

The single word sparked something deep inside her. Something that she didn't properly recognise, because she had never let it loose before. Not when her father had left her sitting on the sofa for hours with her best dress on and her hair carefully braided waiting for nothing; not when David had told her in a polite monotone he thought things weren't working out between them; not even when Lance had leapt up from the sofa, his trousers round his ankles, and demanded to know what she thought she was doing walking into her own flat without knocking.

Jace took her arm, steering her towards the bedroom. 'We can talk about this later.'

The curt words had the unfamiliar emotion burning up her torso, searing her throat and exploding through the top of her head.

'Now go and—' he continued, but the ringing in her ears got so loud it cut off the rest of the sentence.

'No, we can't talk about it later.' She wrenched her arm free, glared at him through the mist of tears she refused to shed. 'Because I'm not going.'

'What?' He stared at her as if she'd grown an extra head. 'Why not?'

How ironic, she thought as her hope shattered. That she should finally shock him out of his complacency, not with a declaration of love, but by the simple act of finally standing up for herself.

'Because I don't want to,' she said, her voice rising as she let the surge of temper take over to drown the pain. 'Because I told you I was falling in love with you and you don't even care enough about me to pretend it matters to you.' Her throat ached, her head hurt and her heart felt as if it were breaking into a thousand tiny pieces, but she made herself say what she should have said days ago. 'I didn't expect you to say it back. I'm not an idiot. We've only known each other ten days. But they've been the most wonderful ten days of my life... And I thought they meant something to you too.'

'This is ridiculous, Cassie,' Jace declared, mortified when his voice shook. 'You're overreacting.'

Unfortunately she wasn't the only one, he realised as panic clawed up his throat at the hopelessness on her face.

'Maybe from where you're standing,' she murmured, the brief magnificent show of temper dying as quickly as it had come. A tear dripped off her lashes, and sliced right through the charade of indifference he used to keep a tight rein on his temper. 'But from where I'm standing, I can see now I should have been honest with you much sooner.'

He grasped her arm again as she turned to leave. 'Damn it, Cassie. Can't you see how ridiculous you're being? What do you want me to say?' he said, sickened by the desperation in his voice. 'That I'm falling for you too? If you want me to say it I will.'

She faced him, the sadness in her gaze so much more painful than the anger. 'But you'd be lying, wouldn't you.' It wasn't a question. And how could he deny it when she was right? They were only words to him. A means to an end.

Maybe for a split second, when she'd said she was falling in love in that bright, excited tone, her body soft and pliant in his arms and her gaze glowing, he'd felt that strange sense of rightness, of completeness, but then the truth had registered. And he'd recoiled.

All he'd seen was his mother's face, her lip bleeding, her eyes blackened, her face bruised. And all the guilt and un-happiness, and the crushing feeling of hopelessness had risen up to strangle that ludicrous belief in the impossible.

Cassie grasped his wrist, pulled away from him. 'I can't come to New York.'

'Fine.' He fisted his fingers and buried them in his robe pockets, determined not to give in to the urge to touch her, to cling onto her, to force her to stay. He'd survive without her. Just as he'd survived before. 'I guess this is goodbye, then.'

He watched her lip tremble, but no more tears fell. Instead, she straightened, winning the fight for composure.

She disappeared into the bedroom, and he listened to the muted sounds as she got dressed and packed her bag while he clung onto the frigid control. So he could remain still and silent when she came out and said a quiet, 'Goodbye, Jace.'

But as the front door of the suite closed behind her he marched to the breakfast table, swept up the teacup she had been using and hurled it against the wall. Shattered china bounced on the thick carpet and tea dripped down the silk wallpaper as the old anger and resentment—and a sharp new pain—ripped through his chest.

CHAPTER SEVENTEEN

'HERE'S fine, Dave,' Jace said tightly as the car slid into a space outside the imposing new glass-and-steel structure that housed Heathrow's Terminal Five.

'Are you sure you don't want me to park and help you with your bag, Mr Ryan?' the chauffeur asked through the partition.

'I've got it.' Stepping out of the car, he grasped his holdall. 'Thanks, Dave, you've done a great job.' Pulling five twenty-pound notes out of his wallet, he handed the tip through the window.

The driver smiled and handed Jace a business card. 'It's been a pleasure, Mr Ryan. Just give me a call next time you're in London.'

'Sure.' He gave the man a small salute as he drove off, then flicked the card into a nearby bin before walking into the terminal building.

He was never coming back to this godforsaken city again. Not if he could avoid it.

He'd taken a conference call with the buyers he'd chosen an hour ago and set the wheels in motion. Artisan would belong to someone else as soon as the markets opened tomorrow. He'd informed his PA to have his lawyer contact Helen's solicitors to organise the transfer of funds for her shares. And he'd still have a cool twenty-five mill to invest in his next venture.

He strode through the large, state-of-the-art terminal building, slinging the leather holdall carrying his essential stuff over his shoulder. He'd finally left all those lingering associations from his past behind once and for all. He had no ties to London, no ties to his ex-wife, and no ties to the young, driven and wildly ambitious man who had been so desperate to escape his childhood he'd done things that he'd later been ashamed of.

He was free at last. The last traces of his old life, his old self, were gone. He could start afresh.

The picture of Cassie, her small frame rigid as she walked away from him, flashed into his brain and made his steps falter.

He stopped, shut his eyes, banishing the image for about the five-hundredth time in the last three hours, and ignored the stuttering beat of his heart, and the piercing pain in his chest.

Pull yourself together, Ryan.

She'd done him a favour. He should never have invited her to New York in the first place. As soon as he got home, he'd be grateful that she wasn't going to be with him. And he'd done her a favour too. If he'd taken her to stay in his place in the East Village, knowing how she felt—or rather thought she felt—about him, it would have been even tougher to let her down gently when the time came for her to leave.

But even as he scanned the departure hall, spotted the first-class check-in for his flight to JFK and negotiated the snaking queues of suitcase-laden travellers to get to it, the stupid pain refused to go away. He could feel it like a jagged blade, stabbing at his composure again, slicing through his control just as it had done when the door had shut behind her.

Stop it. Stop thinking about her. She was never more than a good lay.

But even as he said the words in his head the pain and panic rose up his throat like bile and called him a liar.

Standing at the desk, he chucked his bag on the conveyor. 'Hi, my name's Jacob Ryan, I'm on flight three five three,' he said to the young check-in girl as he yanked his passport out of the inside pocket of his leather jacket, slapped it down on the desk. 'My PA, Jeannie Martin, was dealing with the ticket details.'

Just get on the damn plane. Once you're at fifty thousand feet the pain will be gone.

'Yes, Mr Ryan,' the check-in girl said perkily as she tapped his passport number into her computer, scanned it with easy efficiency.

But as hard as he tried to concentrate, on forgetting the memories, ignoring the pain, the sudden crippling sense of sadness, of loss and loneliness that he hadn't felt since he'd last seen his mother, forced its way past the boulder lodged in his throat, releasing a stream of images that flooded his subconscious in quick succession.

Cassie's wild hair and indignant pout as she'd hurled herself into his car; the determined frown as she tried to decide on the perfect gift for her best friend; the expectation on her face when she'd handed him the card she'd made—which was tucked in his jacket pocket because he'd been unable to throw it away while he packed; the soft weight of her lush little body curved against his side as they'd left the funfair; the sheen of tears, and the tenderness and understanding in her gaze when he'd told her about his stepfather; and the lilting hope in her voice when she'd announced she was falling in love.

If she'd only ever been a good lay, why wasn't it the thought of all the really amazing sex he was going to be missing that hurt the most now?

'I'm sorry, Mr Ryan. But we don't have your travelling companion's passport details. And the US Department of Homeland Security requires that—'

'What travelling companion?' he croaked, interrupting the stream of information.

'Ms Cassidy Fitzgerald,' she said, reading off the screen.

'But I...' Just the mention of her name out loud seemed to sharpen the pain unbearably. He swept his hand through his hair, feeling as if bits of him were being hacked off inside. 'How did you know?' he said dumbly. Was this some sort of weird alternative reality? Was he cracking up?

'How did I know what, Mr Ryan?'

'That she's meant to be travelling with me?'

The woman sent him a curious smile, then directed her gaze back to the screen. 'Ms Martin bought her ticket. Online at 1:30 a.m. last night London time. But we did email her to inform her that we would need...'

The woman's words trailed off as Jace recalled keying in the brief text message to Jeannie the night before, telling her to check availability on today's flight. And then the memory of the pleasure that had flooded his chest, that feeling of hope, of excitement, of rightness as he slung his mobile on the bedside table and watched Cassie step out of the bathroom. Her face soft and beautiful in the night light, her curves outlined through the wispy silk nightgown as she stood silhouetted in the doorway.

He'd taken her in the lobby as soon as they'd got back from the New Year's celebration. The passion so hot and raw it had consumed them both. But then she'd rushed off to the bathroom, and he'd waited for her, stretched out on the bed, anticipating how much he was going to enjoy taking her so slowly she begged, now the edge of their hunger had been satisfied.

He'd been so arrogant, so sure, that she was going to say yes to his offer, he'd passed the time by texting Jeannie to let her know he was planning to bring Cassie to New York. And with her usual efficiency his PA had done the rest.

But more than that, he hadn't for a moment worried about the implications of buying a ticket, because all he'd cared about in that instance was that Cassie would be with him, by his side, when he left.

He swore softly. The panic, the regret, the agony and desperation channelling into one simple conviction. He couldn't leave. Not without her. Not if he didn't want to go mad.

Gripping the handle of his holdall, his fingers no longer shaking, he picked the leather bag off the conveyer.

'Your boarding card, Mr Ryan.' The attendant handed the oblong strip of card over the counter.

'Keep it,' he said, his voice firm for the first time since Cassie had walked out. 'I don't need it now.'

CHAPTER EIGHTEEN

A TEARDROP splattered onto the drawing board, smudging the ink line, and Cassie stared at it in dismay. Grabbing a tissue from the box beside her easel, she swiped at her eyes, screwed the tissue up and launched it at the rubbish bin.

'Don't you dare cry,' she whispered to herself.

Placing shaking fingers to her lips, she took several deep breaths, trying to shrink the enormous boulder lodged in her throat. The little hiccup of emotion didn't bode well. She sniffed loudly.

What was wrong with her? It shouldn't hurt this much.

She was being unforgivably self-indulgent. Jace and she were never meant to be. All she'd done was fall into the same stupid, sentimental trap she'd fallen into before. Of believing a guy had stronger feelings for her than he actually had.

He'd made it perfectly clear that she'd blown their fling out of proportion and he didn't return her feelings.

She frowned, swallowing round the huge boulder. So why didn't she feel good about her decision? Why couldn't she stop wishing for the impossible?

Jace Ryan had said he didn't get involved. He'd told her that he didn't even do long-term relationships. She'd misinterpreted his invitation to New York. Put him on the spot and declared her feelings when she'd promised herself she wouldn't do that. But despite the fact that her timing sucked, it had still been the right thing to do to walk away. She didn't want to get her heart shattered just because she'd been foolish enough to believe he was falling for her too.

Cassie's bottom lip quivered. She bit into it, struggling to stem the maelstrom of emotion that had been pummelling her all day.

The only big glaring problem in her carefully worked out logic was that she wasn't falling in love with Jace. She'd fallen. Hard and fast and far too easily. And she was very much afraid that her foolish heart was already shattered.

She stared out of the bedroom's small window, the streetlight outside casting a yellow halo of light in the drizzle of freezing rain. Christmas was over. Jace would be on the plane now, flying back to his home in New York and out of her life.

She'd always regret what they had lost. Because however foolish she'd been, she hadn't been wrong to know she could have given him so much, that they could have given so much to each other.

But she'd offered him her heart and he hadn't wanted it. In the end she had to accept that and get over it. And however much it hurt now, she was much better moving on than struggling all on her own to make it work.

Today was the first day of a whole new year. She took in a deep breath, let it out slowly, glad to note it was only a little shaky. A whole new year and a whole new Cassie.

One day she'd find a guy who loved her the way she loved him. Who needed her and, more importantly, could give her what she needed. Lance had taken away her optimism and her self-respect and her belief in the power of love. And she had never even really loved him. Jace, for all his faults, and despite his resolute refusal to open himself to the possibility of love, had given her those gifts back. And for that she should be grateful.

Their wild Christmas fling hadn't been a mistake. It just hadn't been meant to last.

The loud thumping on the door made her jerk upright, and shattered the quiet moment of reflection.

Giving a little sigh, she climbed down from the stool and crossed to the front door. If that was Nessa, she'd allow herself a good solid cry on her shoulder, but she wouldn't let her best friend bad-mouth Jace. She didn't feel bitter, or used or angry, she just felt sad. But it was a sadness she knew she'd get over in time.

Sliding the deadbolt free, she wiped her eyes one last time and stiffened her stance. Time to give the new improved Cassie a workout. The Cassie who learned from her mistakes, but didn't let them change who she was as a person. But as she swung open the door she saw the handsome face that would likely haunt her dreams and the new improved Cassie turned tail and ran.

'Cass...'

She slammed the door in a flash of blind panic.

'Ow!' he yelled as the heavy oak hit the foot he'd wedged into the gap.

'Go away. You're supposed to be on a plane,' she shouted through the narrow opening.

She couldn't face him now, not after her pep talk. She had to begin the hard process of getting over him. This would only make it harder.

He wrapped his fingers round the door, shoved it back. 'Damn it. I think you've broken my foot.'

She stumbled back, bumped up against the sofa.

'That serves you right,' she said, stifling the prickle of guilt as he limped into the room. 'You shouldn't be here. I didn't invite you.'

'I don't care,' he said, looming over her, his eyes stormy

and his jaw rigid. 'I've come to get you. You're going to New York with me.'

'No, I'm not.' The anger that had been so unfamiliar that morning surged through her veins again, but this time she embraced it.

He had no right. No right to make her go through this all over again.

'Why not?' he said, exasperated, as he grasped her hips, dragged her towards him. 'You know you want to.'

She braced her hands against his chest. 'It's not that I don't want to. It's that I can't.'

'Why can't you? Because you told me you were falling for me?' He snapped the words, his own temper as volatile as hers. 'So what? We'll forget you ever said it. And everything can go back to the way it was before.'

She gasped, astonished not just by his gall, but by his ignorance. How could she be in love with a man who was so clueless about other people's feelings?

'I can't take it back.' She struggled out of his arms. 'That's the way I feel,' she said, her voice rising. 'And I can't stop feeling that way just because you don't.'

'Okay, fine.' He raked his hands through his hair, and she saw something that looked remarkably like panic. 'Feel that way if you want, but why should that stop us from continuing our affair? If you love me, why don't you want to be with me?' The puzzled anguish in his voice had her own temper cooling. How could he not know the answer to this? How could he understand so little about love?

'Because I'd want things you can't give me, Jace,' she said softly, willing him to understand. 'And that would destroy me in the end. Can't you see that?'

'How do you know I can't give you what you need?' he said, grasping her elbow, drawing her back into his arms.

'Maybe I could, if you gave me the chance. Why won't you let me try?'

As he pulled her close, wrapped his arms around her waist, she took a deep trembling breath of his scent and felt her resolve weakening.

'Please, Jace,' she whispered. 'Don't do this.'

She pressed her lips together to stop them trembling, pushed her forearms against his chest. She couldn't give in; she couldn't. Not when she'd come so far. If she went with him, knowing that he didn't love her, she'd only end up trying to convince herself again. She couldn't risk doing that. Not with him. Because with Jace it would be so much more devastating when she was finally forced to face the truth.

Then he touched his forehead to hers, placed a tender kiss on the tip of her nose and whispered, 'Please, Cassie, come with me. I can't go without you.'

The gulping sob racked her body, but she struggled against his grip and forced herself to step back. The tears flooded down her cheeks, the tears she'd held back all day, the tears she'd never shed over her father's neglect, or David's lack of interest or even Lance's betrayal. After thirteen short days, Jace had come to mean more to her than any of them. But as much as she wanted to reach out to him, she knew she couldn't.

'Don't cry, Cassie,' he said, reaching up to cradle her cheek. 'I didn't mean to make you cry. I don't want to hurt you.'

'I know you don't.' She shook her head, brushed the tears away as she crossed her arms under her breasts, lifted her chin to face him. 'But that isn't enough.'

'Then tell me what is?' he said.

She cocked her head to one side, finally acknowledging the desperation in his eyes, the unhappiness, the thin edge of control that was on the brink of shattering. And suddenly she understood how far he'd come. He did care about her, more than she suspected he had ever cared about any woman. He'd opened up to her in a way he probably never had before. The seed of hope that had refused to die pushed through her despair and confusion. Maybe this wasn't actually about her. Had she been unbelievably selfish and naive? Trying to force him to admit feelings that he didn't even understand?

'I need you to be honest about your feelings,' she said softly. 'Why can't you do that?'

He cursed under his breath. Then backed away, sat down heavily on the sofa. Sinking his head into his hands, he spoke, his voice muffled, but shaking with emotion. 'Because I don't want to love you. I don't want to love anyone.'

She sat beside him, placed her hand on his knee, the hope surging back to life now. At last she'd got behind the charm, the confidence and the cast-iron control, to the man beneath. 'Why not, Jace?'

'Because love is a mean, miserable, dirty little trick.' His voice cracked on the word. 'You think you can control it but you can't. And then it ends up controlling you.'

He sounded so angry, but behind the anger she could hear the fear.

'Why would you think that?' she asked gently, but she thought she already knew the answer. And her heart ached for him.

'Because that's exactly what happened to my mother.' He drew a sharp breath in, clasped his hands between his knees and stared blankly into the middle distance. 'She used to be so amazing. So sweet and kind and funny. When it was just the two of us.' His shoulder jerked in a tense shrug, but he didn't sound angry any more, just desperately sad. 'You know, before she met him.' He sucked in a shaky breath, blew it out slowly. 'When I was little and he hit me too, she'd say I should be more careful. That I knew he had a temper and I should try harder not to upset him.' The resigned sigh broke Cassie's heart. 'Then when I got older, and I was big enough to defend her, she hid the injuries. She'd say she walked into a door. Or she tripped and fell. She'd tell any stupid lie to protect him.' He ploughed his fingers through his hair. 'I tried to get her to report the abuse. And she wouldn't. Finally, I couldn't take any more. So I went to the police. She denied it all and kicked me out. That was the night before I got expelled.' He turned to face her. 'She never spoke to me again. All because she loved him.'

He looked shattered, exhausted, the dark memories swirling in his eyes. And her heart broke all over again for that traumatised child and the pitiable woman, destroyed by abuse, who had been unable to protect him.

Cassie covered his hand, threaded her fingers through his and held on, but refused to shed the tears that burned the backs of her eyes and blocked her throat. 'Jace, that wasn't love. Real love isn't a burden. It isn't a punishment. It doesn't hurt. Not intentionally. It heals.'

He stared at her, the muscles in his jaw tensing. 'How can you be sure?' he asked. And she knew in that moment she wasn't talking to the strong, confident, charismatic man, but to the angry and frightened child who had been taught to associate love with something twisted and ugly, a perverted mockery of the real thing.

'Because I love you, Jace. And I know that I would do everything in my power to stop you from being hurt.'

He closed his eyes, let his head drop back. As if absorbing the words. Then he huffed out a strained laugh and slanted her a sideways look. 'Apart from breaking my foot, you mean.'

Her lips tilted, joy surging through her. 'That was an accident. You shouldn't have stuck your foot in the doorway.'

She stroked her hands down his cheeks, then placed her

lips on his, putting all the love and longing she felt into the slow, tender kiss.

His hands grasped her head and he thrust his tongue inside her mouth, deepening the kiss. She opened for him, her tongue tangling with his, tasting his need and desperation as the hot rush of desire eddied up from her core. And the love bloomed inside her, like a garden leaving winter behind and welcoming spring.

This was right. He was right. She hadn't imagined his feelings. They had been as strong as her own. He just hadn't been able to articulate them, because of a childhood marred by violence that had left him terrified to admit them. To even identify them.

He lifted his head, his cheeks flushed, his eyes dark with much more than desire. 'I couldn't get on that plane and leave you behind, even though I tried to make myself.' His eyes roamed over her face. 'When I'm with you, you make me feel that I'm a better person than I'll ever be without you.' His eyes met hers at last and she could see the depth of emotion reflected in them. 'I don't want to tell you I love you, because in the end they're just words to me. Words that I've never trusted. But I can tell you I want to be with you. I want to try and make this work. Whatever *this* is,' he said, sounding unsure of himself, and desperately vulnerable. 'Is that enough for you?'

Tears welling in her eyes, she gave a delighted chuckle. 'That's more than enough.'

As he hugged her close, buried his head in her hair and murmured, 'Thank God for that,' she wondered if he had any idea that he'd just told her he loved her in every way that mattered.

EPILOGUE

'THIS is the absolute last stop,' Jace murmured into his wife's hair, breathing in the cinnamon scent as they stood on the pavement, admiring Selfridges' Christmas window display. 'You've got exactly ten minutes to enjoy the view and then I'm hauling you back to the hotel,' he said firmly, determined not to get sidetracked again. 'No arguments, Mrs Ryan.' He spanned his hands across the firm mound of her belly and drew her back against his chest, his heart jolting into his throat—as it always did when he thought of the child growing inside her. 'I don't care how many presents you've still got to buy.'

They'd been Christmas shopping for three solid hours by his count, and he wanted her back at The Chesterton with her feet up for the rest of the day, before they headed to Nessa and Terrence's place tomorrow for the annual Christmas Day get-together. After the six-hour flight from New York the day before, he was still struggling with jet lag so she must be too. And she was seven months pregnant for heaven's sake. She had to be exhausted.

Cassie laughed and leaned into him. Her palms covered the backs of his hands. 'Don't be such a spoilsport. I'm absolutely fine. And so is Junior.' She tilted her head. 'Now, what do you think of that little red fire engine?' she asked, pointing at the display of traditional children's toys expertly arranged around a silver Christmas tree.

'Oh, no, you don't!' Pulling her round to face him, he slipped his hands beneath her heavy wool coat and held her against him, the round swell of her belly butting his stomach. 'We're not going back in there. The baby's not due 'til February. It can do without a Christmas present.' He kissed her forehead, trying to keep a grip on his frustration. The woman was addicted to Christmas shopping and he wasn't going to feed her damn addiction a moment longer. 'And anyway, the doctor wasn't one hundred per cent sure that was a penis on the scan. It might be a girl.'

'Who says girls can't like fire engines?' she announced. 'You never know, if we have a daughter she might want to be a firefighter.' Flattening her hands against the emerald cashmere she'd bought him three Christmases ago, she grinned up at him. His heart did the little flip-flop it always did when he looked into her expressive face and saw the love she never disguised. 'But that'll have to be next time,' she purred, her eyes twinkling with mischief. 'Because believe me, that was definitely a penis.'

He huffed out a strained laugh, his throat thickening at the memory of that grainy three-dimensional image. But the mention of a 'next time' had the twin tides of terror and excitement surging past his larynx and threatening to cut off his air supply.

Just as they'd been doing consistently for the last seven months. Ever since she'd sat in his lap in their loft apartment in the East Village one morning, wrapped her arms round his shoulders with a calm and decidedly smug smile on her face and announced they were having a baby.

It shouldn't have been that much of a shock. They'd been discussing parenthood for months and—after Cassie had managed to talk him off the ledge of abject panic her original suggestion had caused and finally convinced him that there wasn't a damn thing stopping him from being a decent father—they had agreed to stop using contraception two weeks before. But even so, no way was he contemplating doing this again until Junior was safely out and about—and quite possibly choosing college courses.

'There's not going to be next time,' he said. 'Not until my blood pressure is back to normal. And certainly not until you learn to behave appropriately when you're seven months pregnant.'

A tiny frown creased her brow. 'But I just have to—'

'No, you don't,' he interrupted.

'Only one more...' She shifted, trying to make a break for it, but he held on, keeping her firmly plastered against him.

'We can come back after Christmas for the sales,' he said, although he'd be reserving judgement on that if she didn't get enough sleep in the next few days. 'But there'll be no more shopping today. I can see how exhausted you are.'

Her lips formed into a mutinous pout, so he dipped his head, touched his forehead to hers and brought out the big guns. 'I love you to bits, Mrs Cassidy Ryan. And I love this baby—with or without a penis. And there's no way I'm risking the only two things I care about in this world because you are a shopaholic.'

She melted against him, as he knew she would, and let out a heavy sigh. 'That's not playing fair.' Her hands lifted to caress the side of his head, her fingers threading into his hair as his hands settled on her waist. 'You know I can't resist when you say things like that.'

He chuckled. 'Tough.'

To think he'd once found it so hard to say the words to her. He was so far removed from that man now—he could barely remember him. The man who'd hidden his resentment and his loneliness and his inadequacy behind a veneer of arrogance and lazy charm, and had been so terrified of commitment he'd refused to nurture the simplest of relationships. Cassie had come into his life and changed everything. In the space of three years all the fear and anger and guilt of his childhood had faded to be replaced by a happiness, a contentment, a companionship he had never even believed existed. She was his soul mate, his kindred spirit and every wet dream he'd ever had—all rolled into one.

Because he knew how lucky he was to have found her. He told Cassie he loved her whenever he felt like it now. Which was so damn often, he was in danger of becoming a Hallmark card. But he didn't care. Because it was the truth. And if telling her made her putty in his hands—well, that was just a nice fringe benefit, which he was more than prepared to use whenever the need arose.

Slinging an arm over her shoulder, he directed her away from Selfridges' imposing art deco facade and hailed a cab, secure in the knowledge that he'd won. For now.

'Come on.' He hugged her, kissed the top of her hair. 'This store has been here close to a century. It'll still be here on Boxing Day. I promise.'

Cassie snuggled under Jace's arm as he shouted out their destination to the taxi driver and let his warmth wrap around her. She flexed her feet in her boots, her arches screaming in agony, rubbed her hand over her belly where the baby had finally stopped punching her and felt exhaustion wash over her.

'You're having a nap when we get back to the suite,' Jace declared in that dictatorial tone that he'd been using rather too often recently, as he settled back into the seat and drew her into his arms.

She glanced up to encounter his stern no-nonsense look—and took a deep breath. The clean scent of his soap invaded her senses as his heartbeat hammered under her palm. The familiar flutter of desire pulsed deep in her sex, as love made her heart fly off into the cosmos. She cocked an eyebrow at him, then let her palm drift down the worn, whisper-soft cashmere and felt his abdominal muscles tense beneath.

Gotcha.

'I'm only having a nap if you have one with me,' she murmured. He might have sucker punched her with that declaration of love—something he'd become remarkably adept at doing, she'd noticed—but she wasn't a complete pushover. And she knew just how to sucker punch him right back.

He gave a soft half-laugh. 'No way. You're sleeping this afternoon.' He brushed his thumb across her cheekbone. 'No hanky-panky until those shadows under your eyes have gone.'

'Jace,' she said, letting her fingers delve under the cashmere to encounter the lightly furred skin of his flat belly. 'You really don't want to deny a pregnant lady when she's tired and horny—or she may get cranky.'

Swearing softly, he grasped her hand, halting its descent under his belt, but she'd already seen the flash of desire in his eyes, and the muscle tense in his jaw, which signalled his arousal. And she knew she had him.

She grinned. 'And mind-blowing orgasms always help me sleep more soundly, so it's your duty to supply one.'

'You little...' he muttered, gripping her fingers and bringing them to his mouth. He kissed the knuckles, his gaze alight with laughter and dark with lust. 'All right, damn it. Have it your way. We'll take the nap together.'

'With full hanky-panky privileges,' she clarified. The swell of love and contentment squeezed her heart as arousal stampeded through her system.

She adored this man so much. His honesty, his integrity, his sense of humour, his surly, sexy magnetism and that protective instinct that made her feel so safe and so secure. But most of all she adored the fact that she could love him without having to hold any piece of herself back, because she knew she could trust him to do the same.

She could still remember the first time he'd actually told her he loved her. And she'd made a huge fuss, because she could see how big a deal it had been for him—being able to trust his feelings enough to say the words. But the truth was, she had never needed to hear him say them—even though they had the power to melt her into an emotional puddle every time he'd said them since—because it was the love those three simple words represented that mattered. And he'd already shown her, in so many ways, that she already had that.

'You can have full hanky-panky privileges,' he agreed as his hand settled on her thigh, making the silk of her dress slide over sensitised skin. 'Within reason.' He slanted his lips across hers, gave her a deep, seeking kiss that promised at least one mind-blowing orgasm before naptime.

He smiled down at her as he pulled away. 'Consider it an early Christmas present, Mrs Ryan. But be warned, I plan to seduce you into a coma—and once I'm done with you, you're going to want to sleep for a week.'

She giggled at the seductive boast. 'And miss Christmas tomorrow? I don't think so. But you have my permission to give it your best shot.'

'Don't worry, I intend to.'

As the cab pulled up at the entrance to The Chesterton, the sparkle of Christmas lights in the winter greenery reminded her of the first time she'd arrived at the luxury hotel, in a wet coat and muddy boots, with Nessa's saucy suggestion that she find herself a candy man turning her head.

Paying the driver and stepping out of the cab, the man who had become so much more to her than that hauled out her many bags of shopping and passed them to the waiting doorman with instructions to have them sent to their suite.

As Jace ducked back into the cab to offer her his hand her

heart fluttered at the devastating smile on his face. 'Come on, lover, your candy coma awaits,' he joked, as if he had read her thoughts.

She laughed as she placed her fingers on his rough palm and let him lead her out of the cab. But as she walked up the steps, his arm secure around her waist, emotion welled up in her throat. The thrill of the night ahead, the thought of the Christmas celebrations to come tomorrow, the wonder of the new life growing inside her and the exciting promise of what her future held with Jace by her side soon had the emotion overwhelming her, and making the fairy lights blur.

'Hey, now.' He stopped on the top step, pushed her chin up to examine her face. 'What's with the waterworks?' he asked, concern shadowing his eyes. 'No crying allowed. It's Christmas tomorrow. That's your favourite day of the year.'

'They're happy tears, you twit.' She nudged him with her elbow. 'And FYI, Christmas isn't my favourite day any more,' she said, sniffing back the silly tears that had become a constant companion ever since she'd become pregnant. 'Now I have you, every day is.'

His slow, sexy smile made her heart race into her throat, and the moisture spill over her lids. 'Well, that's good news,' he murmured, reaching into his pocket for a tissue. 'Because when I win the candy war tonight, and seduce you into that coma,' he said, gently dabbing at her cheeks to stem the flow, 'you're going to miss Christmas tomorrow.'

She didn't miss Christmas. Not quite. But it was an extremely close call.

* * * * *

SECRETS OF THE RICH & FAMOUS

CHARLOTTE PHILLIPS

Charlotte Phillips has been reading romantic fiction since her teens and she adores upbeat stories with happy endings. Writing them for Mills & Boon is her dream job. She combines writing with looking after her fabulous husband, two teenagers, a four-year-old and a dachshund. When something has to give, it's usually housework. She lives in Wiltshire.

For my family, with love and thanks

CHAPTER ONE

How To Marry A Millionaire In Ten Easy Steps
by Jennifer Brown
If you can't earn it, marry it!

Champagne receptions, exotic locations, sumptuous food and designer everything. This is the world of the rich and famous, but is it a world of hype? A rich façade which can be infiltrated by following a few rules, wearing the right clothes? Or is there more to snaring one of the UK's most eligible bachelors than a makeover and a pair of fake designer heels?

No rich man will look twice at a woman he believes to be after his money, so to fit into the world of the rich you must look as if you belong there. You must seem like his equal, as if you have money and a beautiful life of your own.

Join me on my undercover mission to find out if an ordinary Miss High Street like me, with a day job and a mortgage, can reinvent herself on a budget to join the world of the beautiful people and win the ultimate prize: the heart of a millionaire!

Rule #1: Move to the right postcode, even if you have to live in a shack

JEN BROWN stood rigid behind the bedroom door in the dark, arm raised, the vase in her hand poised to be broken over the intruder's head the second he entered the room. As the door swung open one last thought dashed through her mind before cold panic set in and impulse took over. She wished, not for the first time this week, that she was back in her mother's cottage in the country, where you could leave your door on the latch all night and still not be murdered in your bed.

A state-of-the-art security system and a massive front door was apparently not enough to guarantee that here in Chelsea.

As the door opened and the light snapped on she leapt with a yell from her hiding place and swung the vase with every ounce of her strength. If this were a movie she would have knocked him out with one crash and then waited smugly for the police to arrive and pat her on the back. But this was reality. And she wasn't movie heroine material.

And so it was that before she could connect vase with scalp, before she had the chance so much as to kick the man in the shins, she was soaring backwards through the air to land with a thump on her own bed. Her wrists were immediately held in an iron grip on either side of her head, and as the intruder loomed above her she drew in a lung-ful of air and screamed as long and as loudly as she could.

She surprised herself with how loudly, in fact. He recoiled a little at the sound, his face catching the light, and she realised with a flash of disbelief just who she was staring at. Last seen yesterday morning on the front of her newspaper, in the flesh he looked even more gorgeous but a lot angrier.

She'd just tried to crack the skull of the most influential figure in British film-making.

* * *

'Calm down, I'm not going to hurt you!' he shouted over her, exasperation lacing the deep voice.

Famous or not, he had her pinned to the bed, so she ignored him and began to suck in another enormous breath.

He took advantage of the break. 'Drop the damn vase and I'll let you go!'

His dark green eyes were just a couple of inches above her own. The sharp woody scent of his expensive aftershave invaded her senses. Hard muscle was contoured against her body as he used his legs to pin her down effortlessly. She struggled, trying everything to move her legs and kick the stuffing out of him, but she couldn't move an inch. The eyes looking into her own were determined, and his breath was warm against her lips.

Drop the vase? She gave it a split-second's consideration. If her hands were free and he tried anything she could grab something else and bash him with that. The place was full of heavy minimalist ornaments—she'd be spoilt for choice.

'Let me go first,' she countered. Her heart thundered as if she'd just done the hundred-metre dash. She held his gaze obstinately.

He made no move to release her but his voice dropped to a *let's-be-reasonable* tone.

'You've just tried to brain me with it. Let the vase go and then perhaps you'd like to tell me what the hell you think you're doing in my house.'

Fear slipped another notch as her mind processed that last sentence.

She should have known the only person who could get past the Fort-Knox-style security system in this place would be the person who'd put it there. And if it had been daylight instead of the dark small hours she might have listened to her common sense instead of turning the situation into a movie plot. No wonder the house-sitting agency kept their property owners' details confidential. She could imagine women queuing up round the block to get this gig. It would be a stalker's dream.

She'd built up a mental picture over the last two days of the person who owned this beautiful apartment: *rich, clearly*. You couldn't rent so much as a shed in Chelsea unless you were *über*-rich and/or famous. Preferably both. *Male, definitely*. Everything in the place was pared-down and masculine. Exposed brickwork, black leather sofas, expensive spotlights, vast flatscreen TVs. No task was left ungadgeted. *And single*. In her opinion there was a serious over-use of art featuring the naked female form. Jen couldn't walk past the huge painting in the hallway without being reminded that her breasts were on the small side and she had no curves to speak of. No, the only women who passed through this apartment were overnight guests with no say in the décor. She was sure of it.

She congratulated herself on her powers of deduction. She was in the wrong profession. Perhaps she should swap journalism for the police force.

Alexander Hammond. Film producer. Award-winner. Millionaire playboy.

She let the vase drop from her fingers. He followed it with his eyes as it rolled away, the look on his face thunderous, and the next moment she was free as he released her hands and stood up.

He straightened the jacket of his impeccably cut dark suit. A pristine white shirt was underneath, open at the collar and devoid of a tie. His thick dark hair was cut short. Faint stubble against a light tan highlighted a strong jaw. He looked as if he'd just stepped off the set of an aftershave commercial. One of those ones filmed in black and white, showing the hero on his way home at sunrise, a glass of champagne in one hand and the perfect woman in the other.

She suddenly realised how she must look, staring at him with her mouth gaping open from her position on the bed. Warmth rose in her cheeks and she snapped her gaze away from him, concentrating on scrambling to her feet with some measure of dignity. Unfortunately on the way up she caught sight of her appearance in the gilt mirror on the wall. One side of her hair was plastered against her face and neck and the other side resembled a bird's nest. Terrific. Add in the greying old shorts and vest she'd been wearing in bed and she wasn't sure she could feel any more insignificant in the face of his gorgeousness.

She made up for it by drawing herself up to her full height and fixing him with a defiant stare. After all, he was the one at fault here. There was a two-day-old signed contract on the massive kitchen table, detailing her right to be here.

'You're paying for me to be here,' she told him.

She suddenly caught herself running her fingers through the tangled side of her hair and folded her arms grimly. What was the point? It would take a damn sight more than a hairbrush to turn small-town Jen Brown into the kind of woman who would impress Alex Hammond.

'I'm what?' he snapped.

'Executivehousesitters.com? I'm here to provide that extra level of security against intruders.'

She searched his face and saw his sudden understanding in the exasperated roll of his eyes.

'By crowning me with my own vase? That was your best effort at security?'

So an apology was too much to expect, then. Typical

arty type. Everything had to be about him. Never mind that he'd scared her half to death.

'What did you expect, creeping around the place when you're meant to be out of the country indefinitely?' She could hear the beginning of temper in her own voice. 'I'm not meant to be some kind of vigilante security guard, you know. I'm just meant to make the place look occupied, that's all.'

Apparently he could hear her temper, too, because he held up a placating hand.

'About grabbing you like that,' he said. 'You were just on me before I had a second to think. I could tell as soon as I got through the door there was someone here, I just assumed I'd had a break-in.' He leaned over the bed and picked up the vase, turned to replace it on the dresser. 'Thank God you're just a house-sitter. My PA booked it up. She must have forgotten to cancel.'

'Cancel?' Her heart plummeted.

He glanced at her. 'There's obviously been some mix-up,' he said. 'Something's come up and I need to use this place at the last minute.'

No kidding, something had come up. Jen had seen the news coverage. She knew instantly where this was heading for her—right out through the door and back to her day job at the *Littleford Gazette*—and she wasn't about to take it.

The *Gazette*, from which she was currently on unpaid leave, was great as far as rural local newspapers went, but she didn't want to be reporting on welly-throwing contests and duck pond vandalism for the rest of her career. She had big plans. Everything was riding on them. And they started right here, in the Chelsea apartment she was passing off as her own.

Having somehow managed to land an internship at *Gossip!*, a huge-selling women's magazine, she'd spent the last three months there, working herself into the ground, soaking up every piece of information she could lay her hands on, living on a pittance in a Hackney bedsit and loving every second of it. As the three months had come to an end she'd pitched an article idea to the Features Editor and got the go-ahead.

An investigation into the millionaire lifestyle from the angle of an ordinary girl. With a twist. This article was her ticket to a permanent job—a job that could change her life—if she could just come up with the goods.

For years she'd had a nagging curiosity about the lifestyle of the rich and beautiful. Who wouldn't, with a father who fulfilled both of those things in spades? Unfortunately he was severely lacking in other qualities, namely those needed to be any kind of parent—although perhaps he reserved that ability for his legitimate children. Pitching an article whose main requirement would be to infiltrate that elusive opulent world had been a natural choice. She'd been wondering what her parallel life might be like since she was a kid. Now she had the chance to find out, and take a huge step forward in her career at the same time.

A career with a top-selling UK women's glossy, living in London, living the dream, or back to covering dog shows at the *Littleford Gazette*, circulation five thousand.

No contest.

She intended—*needed*—to do whatever it took to nail this opportunity, and no man was going to stop her. Even if he was Alex Hammond. And even if it meant fighting a little dirty. The only advantage of having a waste-of-space millionaire for a father was that she wasn't the least bit intimidated by rich men. Although rich, *gorgeous* men were slightly more nerve-racking…

'It's too late to sort it all out now,' he was saying. 'You can stay the rest of the night, then get your things together in the morning and be on your way. I'll get my PA to smooth things over with the agency. No need to worry. I'm sure they'll find you something else quickly.'

He spoke with the air of someone conferring a great favour. To add to the effect he gave her a lopsided winning smile that creased the corners of his eyes and made her traitorous belly perform a backflip. She wrapped her arms defensively across her body. Just because it worked on the rest of the female population—didn't mean she'd let it work on her.

He made a move towards the door, his back already turned. No need to wait for her response, of course, because what he said always went. How kind of him to let her stay the rest of the night. A whole extra four hours. The bitter taste of contempt flooded her mouth, quickly followed by sheer panic. How could she complete her article if she got kicked out? She *had* to stay in this flat.

'I don't think you understand,' she called after him, working hard to stop desperation creeping into her voice. 'I have a contract. You have to give me a month's notice to move out.'

He paused at the door. She waited. He turned back to face her, a frown touching his eyebrows. There was only one thing for it—she was simply going to have to brazen the situation out.

'This house-sitting thing—it's not completely one-sided, you know,' she said. 'I'm still paying rent. I'm here until New Years. I've even put up the Christmas tree. You can't just barge in and throw me out because the mood takes you. I don't care who you are.'

She saw coldness slip into the green eyes, and a slight inclination of his head acknowledged that she'd recognised him. Good. Then he'd know she wasn't about to be starstruck into doing what he wanted. This was her big break, and not even his dazzling looks and reputation could stand in the way of her dreams.

'I see,' he said. 'Of course I'll compensate you for any inconvenience, if that's what you're worried about.'

He thought she was after his cash? She shook her head at him in disgust. 'I don't want your money.'

Why was she even surprised? She knew the type of man he was. She'd known that type her whole life. And not one cell in her body would submit to his insulting assumption that he could simply swan through life buying whatever and whoever he chose, throwing money at anything that stood in his way. As if a man like him could ever understand her desperate need to prove herself on her own terms.

She sat down obstinately on the bed.

He looked down at her for a moment.

'We'll talk about this in the kitchen,' he said.

Alex Hammond glanced through the house-sitting contract which he'd found in full view on the kitchen table. It seemed she had a point. Two minutes later she walked in, barefooted, tying a dressing gown around her. It was short, and he couldn't help but notice the long, long legs and the dishevelled bed-hair that made her look as if she'd been doing something other than sleeping. He felt a spark of heat deep in his abdomen. A couple of weeks earlier and the surprise discovery of a scantily dressed woman in his apartment would probably have led to him trying to talk her back into the bedroom and giving her the one-night stand of her life. That wasn't an option now. As of this week, he needed to be a changed man.

That resolution would be a whole lot easier to stick to without those legs under the same roof as him.

She didn't sit down. Instead she lingered in the doorway watching him, leaning against the jamb.

'I don't want your money,' she reiterated. 'Not everyone can be bought, you know.'

He shrugged.

'In my experience they can,' he said. 'It's just a matter of finding the right price. Tell me yours and we can skip all this tedium, sort the whole thing out, and you can get on your way. Everyone can do with a bit of extra cash at this time of year.'

She shook her head stubbornly.

'I'm staying put. You're welcome to serve me notice, if you like. In fact, let's assume that's what you've just done, shall we? So I've got a month before I need to move out and at the end of that time I'll go. No arguments.'

He had to admire her persistence.

'I've had a look at the contract...' he glanced down at her name on the top sheet of paper '...er...Jennifer, and I can't see what the problem is. I'll make sure the agency finds you somewhere else to stay that's just as good as this, and I'm prepared to offer you generous compensation for the misunderstanding. What's not to like?'

'Somewhere else isn't good enough,' she said. 'It has to be here.'

A lightbulb flickered on in his mind at the desperation clearly audible in her voice. Was that it? She was some kind of obsessive fan? Oh, great. Just what he needed.

He tried to speak kindly. 'Listen, Jennifer, I know there's a strong fan base for my work, and I'm grateful for that, but you have to understand I like to keep my work life and my private life separate.'

More like *have* to, from now on.

He saw her eyes widen, and her lip curled a little. It occurred to him that for a fan she didn't seem particularly keen on him.

'This isn't about you!' she snapped. 'It's about the address.'

She wasn't making any sense. He felt suddenly very tired. Not surprising after the few days he'd had and the night flight in from the States.

'What's so significant about this address if it isn't the fact that I live here?'

She dropped her eyes from his, fiddled with the belt on her dressing gown.

'It's an important part of my cover story,' she said. 'I can't change it now. There's too much riding on it. And I only have limited time and means.'

Her cryptic explanations were beginning to irritate him.

'What the hell are you talking about? Cover story?'

'I'm a journalist.'

The words fell like rocks into his tired mind. He'd just flown thousands of miles to get out of the scrutiny of the press pack only to find that one of them had moved in with him. He fought to keep a neutral expression on his face, to hear her out, when what he really wanted to do was frogmarch her out of the apartment and lock the deadbolt behind her.

'What kind of journalist?'

'I'm working on an article that involves me inventing a different identity,' she said. 'The house-sitting is a cheap way of getting myself an address in the right...' she pursed her lips '...social bracket. I'm working to a tight budget.'

He tried again.

'What paper do you work for?'

The blue eyes cut away from his.

'I'm freelance,' she said.

So she worked anywhere and everywhere she could. Terrific. It was time to wrap this up—immediately.

'Get your stuff right now and leave,' he said. 'I don't

give a damn about any contract. My lawyers will take it from here.'

She tilted her chin up and looked down at him, as if another bargaining tool had suddenly occurred to her. 'Mr Hammond, you must know that with a couple of phone calls to the right people I could have paparazzi outside this flat before the sun comes up,' she said.

He saw steely determination in the blue eyes and braced himself against the surge of rage. These press people—thinking they could manipulate any situation.

'Are you threatening me, Miss Brown?'

She shook her head quickly.

'No, I'm not,' she said. 'You can believe me when I tell you I have absolutely no interest in what's going on in your life.'

She must be the only journalist in the country who didn't.

'I'm working on a very specific project. I don't want any trouble, and neither do you.'

'But you don't seriously expect me to move out of my own house?' he said. This was the best place for him to lie low, decide his next step. He certainly didn't intend to do it with anyone else under the same roof.

'I don't,' she said.

She crossed the room and stood on tiptoe to take a glass from one of the cupboards. The movement made her robe ride up, and he fought to take his eyes off the length of creamy slender thigh it revealed. There was something undeniably alluring about her in a scruffy kind of a way. She went to the water dispenser on the side of the fridge and filled the glass. Not a hint of awkwardness, acting as though she lived here and he was the guest.

'I'll be no trouble. Just imagine you've got a very easy to live with house guest until New Year. God knows the place is big enough for two of us without getting in each other's way.'

For some reason his mind snapped to the bedroom, to that lithe body pinned underneath his, the blue eyes gazing back at his own...

'And what if I refuse?'

She shrugged. 'I've got a lot invested in this. A girl has to make a living, and if you pull the plug on this article I'll have to find something else lucrative to write about.'

The pointed look she gave him said it all. Cross her and her next project would be him.

He'd heard enough.

'Pack your stuff,' he said. 'In fact, no—don't pack your stuff. Get whatever you need for the night and get yourself out of here. I'll have someone send your bags on. You can collect them from the house-sitting agency.'

She didn't move an inch. In fact, she got closer.

'You people are all the same, thinking you can do whatever you like just because you've got a huge bank balance. I have a legal right to be here.' Alex wasn't so tired that he didn't hear the desperate edge to her argument, but right now he *was* too tired to care.

'I don't get this,' he said, levelling his voice with conscious effort. 'I'm prepared to pay all your costs, cover any lost income. You could restart your project without losing anything. An address change can't make that much difference.'

She took a sip of her water and Alex noticed her hands shake slightly. *Good,* she must be feeling nervous.

But she still shook her head. 'No, thanks.'

'Why the hell not?'

'Because I've already set myself up with this address and I'm not screwing around with that. Plus I don't dance to anyone's tune just because they happen to offer me hard cash. I can get where I want to by myself, thanks very much. This way you get to keep a low profile...that *is* what you're doing here, isn't it?...and I get to finish my article. Everyone's a winner.'

She folded her arms. She looked as fresh as a daisy, clearly prepared to argue all night if necessary, and suddenly he was done with it.

'Stay the damn night, then,' he snapped. 'You'll be out in the morning before you've had your first cup of coffee.'

The words were barely out of his mouth before she made a move towards the door, immediately taking him up on it. She disappeared, her bare feet padding softly down the passage back to the bedroom.

He stared at the empty doorway. Let her have her victory. It would be short-lived. In a few hours' time his legal team would have it sorted and he could bolt the door behind her.

Alex switched the phone to his other ear and looked out of the bedroom window onto the square below. It was early and traffic was still light. A couple of hours' sleep hadn't soothed his mood and he was more on edge than ever. Mark Dunn had been his lawyer and close friend for a decade, providing confidential advice he trusted on a personal and business level.

'You're actually telling me I can't evict her from my own apartment? What is the law there for? There has to be some kind of loophole.' He gripped the phone between ear and shoulder so he could flick again through the house-sitting contract.

'Without looking at it I can't be certain, but these things are essentially rental contracts.' Mark's voice was matter-of-fact. 'Fax it over and I'll check it out. Of course you could insist she leaves regardless of what the contract says, but in the circumstances that might not be wise. What's she like?'

Young, slim, minxy blue eyes. Legs that shouldn't be allowed.

'Knows her own mind and is refusing to back down,' he said. 'Hinted that she could make trouble.'

'She most certainly could if she wanted to. Alex, think how this could look if she put the right twist on it. All this stuff in the press about you and Viveca Holt. It's just a few weeks until the awards season kicks off and, trust me, the words "casting couch" are not ones you want bandied about in the run-up to that.'

'You think I don't know that?'

The familiar bite of fury at the backlash resurfaced. How dared people dictate what he did? Who he chose to see? Part of him wanted to issue a statement: *Yeah, so I had a fling with Viveca. A great time was had on both sides, if I say so myself, and I doubt it did her career prospects any harm. But really it's none of your damn business.*

'You need to kill that story stone-dead,' Mark carried on. 'Listen to your PR team for once. You're paying them enough. Go to ground for a few days and then gradually start to be seen again on your own in the right places. Maybe a few carefully chosen public events. Be seen to be having a quiet Christmas away from the limelight. Regain some respectability. Don't give them anything to write about and it will all be forgotten by New Year. What you *don't* need is some loose cannon of a journalist getting a scoop on you assaulting your own tenant and then throwing her out on the street. And that's just one story she could come up with. There could be worse. These people aren't big on truth. Any new story will be used as an excuse to rehash this current scandal. It could run and run if you don't handle it right.'

Alex felt fury begin to mingle with extreme frustration. The last few days had been hell. The constant paparazzi attention had made work impossible, and then there'd been the backlash from the film studios backing the movie. He had no choice but to get things back on track if he wanted to limit the damage to his professional reputation. Since his business empire had been his one priority these last five years, he had no choice but to play the game.

'OK, so if throwing her out isn't an option, what do you suggest?'

'If I were you, while we come up with a solution, I'd let her be and do my best to keep her sweet.' He paused. 'Not *too* sweet, though, Alex. That's the kind of thing that got you into this mess.'

CHAPTER TWO

Rule #2: Get your eye on the prize. Before you can trap the heart of a millionaire you have to be able to identify him. To observe the visible signs that set a wealthy and eligible man apart from the rest of the dross you must observe him in his own environment.

THE kitchen was a vast cold expanse of gleaming cupboards and spotlights and stainless steel. Not so much as a pepper mill cluttered its surfaces. Its clinical sterility reminded her of a hospital, and Jen hated it more than ever this morning. No matter how hard she told herself that she was the exception to the female rule, absolutely *not* attracted to Alex Hammond, her subconscious wasn't getting the message.

The recurring thought of lying on the bed beneath him, his muscular body hard against hers, had invaded her mind and banished sleep for what had been left of the night. The residual adrenaline from facing down a furious Alex hadn't helped, either. As a result she was now edgy and tired, her relief at being able to stay in the flat short-lived. For the first time in weeks she longed for her cosy kitchen back home, with its threadbare sofa in the corner, perfect to curl up on if you shifted the cat to one side before you sat down.

There was no sign of Alex Hammond this morning. He

was obviously sleeping in after the late night. She listened hard for a moment to make sure…

Nothing. The perfect opportunity.

Kneeling down next to the stainless steel dustbin, she pressed the button on the lid to open it and scrabbled around, grimacing as she shoved aside teabags and egg-shells and goodness knew what. At last she found what she was looking for: yesterday's newspaper. She tugged it out, scattering coffee grounds across the glossy grey-tiled floor and smoothed it out with her fist. Folding herself up on the floor, she settled down to read the article she'd only skimmed yesterday.

Now she was sharing a flat with him she wanted every gory detail.

Unfortunately Alex's face in the photo was obscured by a blob of cold scrambled egg from last night's supper. And as she began to read the irony of that fact wasn't wasted on her. Since a costly divorce five years ago he'd been living the life of a rich bachelor to the full. And if you in-sisted on dating a different woman every week, all of them beautiful and most of them famous, it stood to reason that sooner or later one of those affairs would come back and bite you very publicly on the behind. It was a simple mat-ter of probability.

The latest film from Alex Hammond's extremely suc-cessful production company, *The Audacity of Death*, was already tipped to clean up at next year's awards season. Its star, the young and stunningly gorgeous Viveca Holt, had been plucked from obscurity to take the female lead role over a number of well-established actresses. None of this had mattered one bit until pictures had surfaced of Alex Hammond stepping out with Viveca during the film's pro-duction and the rumour mill had begun with a vengeance.

The glamour surrounding the film-maker and the film

star being together was far too good to pass up. Whether or not sour grapes were to blame wasn't clear, but the implication from the press pack was that Viveca had moved from obscurity into the role of a lifetime via Alex's bed, with him pulling strings along the way. Definitely *not* the kind of publicity a serious piece of arty film-making needed, with award nominations being announced next month.

Jen nearly hit the ceiling when Alex Hammond walked unexpectedly into the room. She frantically screwed the newspaper into a ball. He looked down at her as he rounded the corner, at the bin open next to her spilling its contents across the floor, and raised his eyebrows. She coloured.

'What are you doing?' He moved smoothly across to the counter and switched on the coffeepot.

She squashed the paper back into the bin and slammed the lid down on it.

'Recycling,' she lied, getting to her feet. She soaped her hands under the single curved tap in the enormous double sink. Conscious of his far too observant eyes still on her, she added, 'Everyone can play a part in saving the planet.'

Oh, yes, that sounded just *great*.

He was looking at her as though she were a moron, then he shook his head lightly, as if to clear it.

'Coffee?' he asked, coldly polite.

She smoothed her hair back from her face with one hand, drew in a composing breath.

'Yes, please,' she said. 'Black, no sugar.'

He opened one of the many cupboards and took out two mugs. She waited, wondering if he was going to pick up where she'd left off last night on the eviction thing, but he didn't mention it. He simply filled the mugs with coffee and handed one of them to her. Then he leaned back against the counter, mug in hand, watching her.

Even on a couple of hours' sleep he looked fantastic, it

was so unfair. His hair was still damp from the shower, and he was dressed casually—just jeans and a dark grey polo shirt that on its own probably cost more than her entire wardrobe. She folded her arms defensively across her own cheap white shirt and jeans and took a sip of her coffee.

'You checked my contract out with your lawyer, then?' she asked.

He grinned wolfishly. 'Of course I have.'

Of course. Men like him left nothing to chance. She wasn't the least bit surprised. She waited, ready to argue her point. He probably had the best lawyers in the world, more than capable of pulling apart a standard rental agreement, but she knew she'd touched a nerve when she mentioned the press even if it had been just a bluff. She was just a reporter on a small country paper, not a tabloid entertainment correspondent. Her last story before she'd started interning had been about a cat who'd hopped on the bus and travelled from Littleford to the next village all by himself. That was the level of celebrity she was used to dealing with.

He didn't say anything else, just carried on looking at her with that appraising expression in the green eyes which made her self-conscious no matter how hard she tried not to be.

'And?' she prompted, when he didn't say anything.

He sipped his coffee.

'While I *could* break the contract—and I'm sure the house-sitting agency would be prepared to be *reasonable* about it...' His tone made it obvious who he considered the troublemaker to be in this scenario. 'You've told me how important it is to you that you keep this address. And, as I'm all in favour of enterprise, I'm prepared to be the bigger person here and honour the agreement. I wouldn't want to make things difficult for you.'

She bridled a little at his taking the moral high ground but kept her irritation under wraps. She didn't believe a word of it. He needed to keep his nose clean. That much was clear from the newspaper article and his turnaround since last night. Any sniff of scandal and he'd be back on the front pages. She had no intention of going to the press—she just wanted to concentrate on her article, on not letting her big chance, her *only* chance, slip through her fingers—but she didn't need to tell him that.

Let him think she had the editor of every London tabloid on speed dial.

'That's really good of you. Thank you,' she said through gritted teeth.

He raised his mug in acknowledgement.

She waited until he began scrolling through his mobile phone.

'Will Viveca be joining you for Christmas?' she asked pointedly.

His expression as he looked up from the phone was dark and inscrutable. She saw a flash of the arctic coldness from the previous night.

'No, she will not!' he said curtly. 'It's a working relationship, nothing more.'

'That's not what the papers say,' she said.

'And of course they are always right about absolutely everything.' He slammed his mug down, slopping coffee across the granite counter. 'It was a few dates and it was months ago. Can't I go on a couple of nights out without the world reading God knows what into it?'

Clearly not. She would give him her standard live-in-the-public-eye-at-your-peril lecture.

'That's the thing, though. You're happy to court publicity when it suits you. When it's *good* publicity. When

there's a film to promote. You can't then say it's unaccept-
able when people want to know more about you.'

'Well, you would say that, wouldn't you?' he said.
'Seeing as you belong to the *vulture* camp. Hoping to get
the scoop, are you? Well, there's nothing to scoop. I'm
single. I only date when I have to, and I don't see that it's
anyone else's business. There's a line between public and
private. Who I date and why I date them is private.'

She gave her suddenly pricked-up ears a mental slap.
The fact that he was single was definitely of no interest to
her. She didn't care that he was utterly, heart-stoppingly
gorgeous. Firstly, she'd be wasting her time. Even in a
ketchup-smeared photo Viveca was nothing short of exquisite. He'd never look twice at someone like Jen. And
secondly, the only circumstances in which she would look
at a man who paved his way through life with his wealth
would be false ones—as demonstrated perfectly by her undercover article. She wasn't about to repeat the mistakes
her mother had made. No way.

She shrugged. 'You're just too newsworthy. That's the
problem. You need to keep your head down a bit more.
Perhaps if you dated someone a bit more run-of-the-mill
for a change?'

He raised his eyebrows and gave her a suggestive grin
that sent a curl of unwelcome heat through her body.
'Someone like you, you mean?'

The kitchen felt too warm. The look in his eyes took
her right back to the previous night again.

'I don't consider myself to be run-of-the-mill, actually,' she said.

She felt his eyes follow her as she crossed the kitchen.
She could tell just by the heat in her cheeks that her face
was currently approaching tomato-red. No way was she
letting him see that he affected her. She opened a stainless

steel door and stuck her head into the cupboard where she'd stashed her food. She took a few calming breaths and when the flustered feeling was gone took out a loaf of bread.

She'd done a big supermarket food shop during a fleeting visit home a couple of days ago, left half the food in the house for her mum and brought the rest back to London with her. She had enough on her plate here trying to track down millionaires without also having to track down budget food.

She put a couple of slices of bread into the gleaming toaster. His attention was back on his phone again as he leaned against the counter.

She hauled her mind back on task. Sparring with Alex Hammond was all very well, but she needed to concentrate on work.

Thankfully, her accommodation remained sorted. She mentally ticked it off. Now for the next step. Somehow she needed to work out how the hell a girl whose most expensive item of clothing was a fifty-pound pair of shoes could identify whether a men's jacket cost a hundred pounds or a few thousand pounds? She needed to build up a sketch of the kind of man to target, and she had to admit there was a certain satisfaction in the idea of fooling a man of her father's ilk. Someone driven by money and reputation and success, who held all the cards in life and had no qualms about playing them.

Her first proper undercover expedition was tomorrow night. OK, maybe she was running before she could walk—she hadn't even got her wardrobe together yet—but a ticket to the first night of an art exhibition had fallen into her lap via the middle-aged arts correspondent of the *Littleford Gazette*. It turned out boring Gordon was a real culture vulture in his spare time, hanging around galleries and getting himself on exclusive mailing lists. When he'd heard about her planned article he'd thrown a spare ticket her way. She suspected he had a bit of a soft spot for her and feared he might expect a bit more than a cream cake as a thank-you if she had to go back to work at the *Gazette*. There was a lot riding on this project in more ways than one.

The opportunity to attend a champagne reception which would undoubtedly be *stuffed* with rich singletons was too good to pass up. If nothing else she'd be able to observe, and if she was really, really lucky she might be able to highlight a couple of suitable men to target. She hadn't had time to source any designer clothes yet. Instead she was intending to wear her trusty little black dress and blend into the background—use the evening to get an idea of the image she needed to build for herself.

But the thought of going straight from comfort zone to such a glossy affair was terrifying. She somehow needed to ease herself into it. A bit of people-watching would be just the thing to get her in the right mind-set. But knowing where to start was the problem. Where *did* the beautiful people hang out in London on an average week-day?

A sudden movement from Alex made her glance around to catch him checking the huge gold watch on his wrist—probably worth more than her car. Somewhere in her mind a penny dropped.

Standing in front of her was a walking, talking information source on every aspect of the lifestyle of a wealthy single man. Unfortunately with a messy and very expensive divorce in his past he was unlikely to see the funny side of an article on landing a rich bachelor, no matter how tongue-in-cheek it was meant to be. She'd have to find an underhand way to tap the information out of him.

He looked back up at her, a questioning frown knitting his brows in response to her sudden beaming smile.

'Would you like a slice of toast?' she asked him.

Ten minutes later they were seated on stools next to the granite counter. Alex watched Jen finishing her second slice of toast. A few crumbs clung to her full lower lip and he found himself staring at them until the movement of her hand as she brushed them away snapped him out of it. He gave himself a brisk mental shake. He was meant to be keeping on her good side, not ogling her. Mindful of Mark's warning to keep her sweet, he'd only agreed to the toast to appear friendly after snapping at her about Viveca. He surreptitiously pushed the remains of it to one side of his plate and took a large slug of coffee.

He looked up at her to see that she'd finished eating and was now staring at his wrist. She leaned forward on her stool to get a better look.

'That's a lovely watch,' she said.

He smiled distantly. What was she up to now?

'Thanks.'

'Would you mind if I took a closer look?'

Before he could answer she'd jumped down from the stool and taken a step closer. She took his wrist in her slender hands and turned the watch this way and that, examining it.

'Cartier…' she murmured.

He realised that she was the perfect height for him right now, standing next to him as he sat on the stool. This close he could see the big blue eyes, the frown touching her brows lightly. The curve of her top lip above the full pink lower lip was adorable. There were fine tendrils at the nape of her neck where she'd pulled her light brown hair up from her shoulders into a messy ponytail. He was reminded suddenly of the last time he'd been at eye level with her—last night, with her slender wrists in his hands, lush body pinned beneath him on the bed, close enough to kiss her with one short movement of his head. Heat sparked on his skin at her touch and seemed to pool deep in his abdomen.

This was not a good sign. Less than four days since he'd sworn off women and he was mentally wondering what she might taste like. He debated for a moment if he should have ignored Mark's advice and evicted her, anyway.

He tugged his wrist away sharply.

She looked up in surprise, her hands left empty in mid-air.

'I've got a conference call in twenty minutes that I really ought to be preparing for,' he lied.

She took a step back, still eyeing the watch.

'OK, not a problem. I'm planning on going out, anyway, so you can have the place to yourself.'

Honestly, she had more front than Blackpool. Acting as if she was the one doing *him* the favour when it was his own damned apartment.

She tossed his cold toast in the bin and stacked their plates together in the sink.

'Can you recommend somewhere good for lunch?' she asked, her back to him. 'I need to get a bit of background on the area. The kind of people who hang out here, what they wear—that kind of thing.'

He shrugged. 'Depends what you're after. Coffee and a sandwich? Or something a bit more substantial? What do you want to spend? Some places are pretty exclusive and expensive.'

She turned back from the sink in time for him to see the sudden shadows in her blue eyes.

'Not that I'm implying you'd be out of place there,' he

said, wondering why he was worried about hurting her feelings.

'Why don't you just tell me where *you* would go?' she said. 'If you were hypothetically going out for lunch in South-West London.'

He thought for a moment, trying to come up with somewhere she might enjoy.

'La Brasserie,' he said. 'French-style place. It's very popular—decent food.'

'Great, thanks!'

'Don't thank me until you've tried it. We might not like the same kind of food.'

She left the room. Just as he was insisting to himself that she was having zero effect on him he realised he was watching the graceful way her legs moved in the slim-cut jeans. He'd have to find a way of getting her out of here.

The globe lights, the ceiling fans twirling above her, the framed French posters on the walls and the marble-topped bar made stepping into La Brasserie feel like stepping into a little corner of Paris in the middle of London. Strings of white fairy lights and Christmas greenery added a warm festive touch. At a corner table, Jen thought it really was the perfect place to while away an hour or two peoplewatching.

She glanced at the menu and drew in a quick breath at the prices—even after her internship they never failed to amaze her. The coffee shop back home in Littleford did a knockout shepherd's pie for a fraction of the price of the main lunch menu here. Then again, the residents of Littleford wouldn't know what to do with a place that served frogs legs in white wine and parsley, Coquilles St Jacques—whatever *that* was—lobster and steak tartare.

When a waiter in a pristine white shirt and black waist-

coat arrived to take her order she chose only coffee and a
pain au chocolat, with a pang of regret that she couldn't
afford to sample the full deliciousness of the menu. She
needed to eke out her money big-time if she wanted to
frequent places like this and actually look as if she belonged. The group of young women having a girly lunch
at the table opposite made her feel totally invisible. She
was kidding herself, thinking she could pass herself off
as one of them in her High Street wardrobe. She needed
designer *everything*. And on the money she'd scraped together that was going to be no mean feat.

The women were glossy without being in your face.
Hair loose and natural, with gentle highlights, perfect
smiles, less-is-more make-up and not a hint of orange fake
tan. Clothes impeccably cut. Fur seemed to be *the* accessory this winter. No outfit appeared to be complete without
a bit of dead animal attached to it somewhere.

So this was the world her father inhabited, while she and
her mother were an inconvenience he'd written off twenty-
four years ago just by opening his wallet. She didn't think
she'd ever had a stronger feeling of being on the outside
looking in. Jen felt plain, boring, and like an impostor
with her mousy brown hair and her cheap handbag. And
the worst of it was that none of that should matter—not
to her. But still it did.

Wasn't the whole point of her article to look at this
world of luxury from the perspective of an ordinary High
Street girl? Her fresh eyes would enable her to pick up
on all the little things that stood out. Like the way people
air-kissed both cheeks as a greeting. Jen had never done
that in her life.

She was furious with herself. She was an investiga-
tive journalist—a professional gathering background for
an article. She should be finding this interesting, not in-

timidating. But try as she might she couldn't quite squash the needling little voice in her head reminding her that if things had been different, with a shift in circumstances, this could have been *her* world, too.

Darkness was already filtering in as she left the restaurant, and the cold air burned her cheeks, but she forced herself to do a bit of window-shopping on Brompton Road instead of skulking back to the apartment. In the brightly lit Chanel store, with the interlinked Cs logo huge behind an exquisite suit in the window, she could feel the eyes of the perfectly groomed assistants following her in her cheap jeans as she picked up a black tweed jacket—heavy in her hands, impeccably cut. Beautiful. She checked the label and felt the moisture disappear from her mouth. Maybe if she sold her car. And then some.

She put the jacket back slowly, so as not to look as if she couldn't afford it, more as if she'd decided it really just wasn't *her*. And she checked out a couple of handbags and a scarf on her way to the exit in an attempt to leave with some dignity. None of the staff approached her, clearly knowing perfectly well that she wasn't worth attending to. She wasn't the real deal. And all the while she was thinking that what she really wanted was to be back in sleepy Littleford.

She snapped herself out of it. She was just a bit homesick. It wouldn't last. These last three months in London had gone by in a whirl and she'd loved every pacy second of it. Christmas in Chelsea exuded class. It was all twinkly white lights and mistletoe, co-ordinated colours and not a tasteless bauble in sight. It couldn't be further from Littleford, which by now would have its threadbare Christmas tree put up on the village green by local volunteers. The same balding tree had been resurrected every year for as long as Jen could remember.

She wanted to stay in London and this was her chance to do that. Her chance to show she could claw her way up in life by herself. She didn't need a rich father smoothing her path for her.

An hour or so later and things were looking up. It was amazing what people sold online. She scrolled through the auction listings on her laptop, propped up comfortably against the pillows on her bed, mug of hot chocolate next to her. It was gobsmacking how much of a discount you could get for pre-owned clothes. No time to wait for the auction to unfold over a week. She concentrated on the 'Buy Now' options.

Within half an hour she'd been possessed by a kind of madness. It was all too easy to click 'Pay Now'. A pair of jeans, a wear-anywhere shirt, a stunning velvet cocktail dress and a heavily knocked-down pair of nude shoes that she hoped would go with everything—all by designers she'd only ever read about in upmarket women's magazines. She snapped her eyes away from the screen and calmed her racing pulse with the fact that she could sell the whole lot on when the project was over with.

Before she could stop herself she'd clicked 'Pay Now' on a gorgeous leather tote bag. In for a penny, in for…a lot of pounds. Hmm, it was just too easy to get carried away online when the clothes were this delicious. She'd better do a quick recce of the cost. Her wallet was under serious strain. She'd ploughed her meagre savings into her project—after all, you had to speculate to accumulate—but still she needed to watch her spending.

The cost of renting the apartment, although seriously discounted from what it would *really* be to rent a place like this, was still taking up the lion's share of her budget. Add in the anticipated cost of tickets, entry fees, food and drink—all the essentials she needed to actually get herself in the same room as her prey—and she had hardly anything left for her own makeover. And, judging by the young women she'd seen today, she was in serious need of one of *those* if she was to pass herself off as one of *them*.

She tapped the figures into her pocket calculator and stared in disbelief at the total. Clothes alone would never be enough, she needed to look the part inside and out. That meant hair, make-up, fake tan, nails. How the hell was she going to manage all of that on the ten pounds twenty pence she had left in her budget?

'Sorry, could you just say that again? I thought you said you were sharing a flat with Alex Hammond, but that can't be right, can it?'

'You didn't hear me wrong.'

Jen held the phone away from her ear with a grimace, but still the piercing squeal of excitement was audible. When it came to overreaction, Elsie was a professional. Then again, to someone who'd spent a lifetime living in Littleford, and for whom the working week consisted of giving perms and blue rinses to the village's pensioner contingent, the news that your friend was living with a celebrity was probably the highlight of the year. When the squeal subsided she tentatively put the receiver back to her ear.

'Are you sure?' Elsie asked breathlessly. '*The* Alex Hammond? The one on the front of today's newspaper with no shirt on? I've never seen abs like it.'

Jen made a mental note to check out today's paper, then mentally crossed it out. She didn't have time to think about Alex Hammond's abs. She felt mildly offended by Elsie's disbelief. Was it really *that* far-fetched that she could move in these social circles?

'Yes, definitely *that* Alex Hammond,' she said.

Elsie sighed.

'So any chance of you coming home before Christmas Day is even more non-existent, then? I'm dying of boredom here without you. What's he like?'

'Nowhere near as hot in the flesh,' she lied.

She hadn't counted on Elsie being quite so starstruck. It was a good few minutes before she could get her off the subject of Alex's physique and onto the subject of the favour she needed to beg. For Pete's sake, her future career was at stake here.

'I need your help,' she said when she could get a word in. 'The success of my article depends on it.'

She'd bored Elsie rigid with her writing career plans since they'd both been at school.

'What kind of help?'

'I need to look like a goddess—on a budget and in minimum time,' she said. It sounded an extremely tall order spoken out loud.

'How long?' Elsie asked.

'One day would be nice. For a start, is there some over-the-counter product I can use to make my hair look sun-kissed?'

Elsie made a dismissive chuffing sound.

'Pah! You don't need to bother with any of that over-the-counter rubbish. Not when you've got a professional on your team. I'll see you right. Don't you worry.'

'But you're in Littleford. And I can't afford to pay for you to come here even if I was able to let you stay.' She didn't bother to enlighten Elsie about the fight she'd had to keep herself under this roof.

There was a disappointed sigh at the end of the phone.

'I suppose it was too much to hope for a meeting with Alex,' she grumbled. 'And it's been ages since I've seen you. The place has been dead quiet since you took that magazine job.'

Jen squashed the sudden pang of homesickness. No matter how much she had missed her, Elsie would eat Alex alive if she got within touching distance of him.

'Sorry,' she said apologetically. 'He's rarely home, anyway. We barely see each other. And even if you *were* here, what I'm after is that modern, subtle, glossy-but-undone look the It-girls have. I need to look like myself, but better. I'm not sure there's much of a call for that kind of look in Littleford.'

She was trying hard to be tactful but clearly failed, because Elsie gave a derisory sniff.

'A couple of months in London and you think we're all hillbillies,' she complained. 'Just because I spend my days doing shampoo and sets for grannies doesn't mean I don't have all the skills for modern stuff, you know. A tint is a tint, whether it's blue, pink or just-back-from-Cannes-gold. I'll pop some colorant in the post tonight, shall I?'

Jen brightened immediately.

'Is it something I can do myself, then? Can you write me a list of instructions?'

'I can do better than that, honey. I'll instruct you *personally* via Skype.' She spoke in bossy and professional tones, as though she were a stylist to the stars, then ruined it by adding with a touch of stalker, 'Now, give me Alex Hammond's address.'

After a day of catch-up phone calls and e-mails, in which the subject of his swift departure from the States was skated over, Alex wandered into the kitchen on a fact-finding mission. Mark's follow-up phone call had come that afternoon.

'There is no Jennifer Brown that my press contacts

have ever heard of, but it's hardly an unusual name, and the world is stuffed with freelancers trying to get a foot in the door. If anything that makes her more dangerous. She's getting exclusive first-hand experience of your day-to-day life, and at some point—if it hasn't already—it will occur to her that she's sitting on a fantastic scoop.'

The morning papers had brought another spate of articles about him and Viveca, and Alex's never hugely impressive patience was close to breaking point. There were three films in varying stages of production that he should be immersed in, and instead he was stuck here, keeping out of sight, all because the studios backing them financially were unsettled by the sudden tabloid interest in his sex life. At this time of year more than ever he wanted to be busy. *Needed* to be busy. Working hard and partying harder. Anything but sitting here twiddling his thumbs in the flat with time to think about what might have been. He just wanted this whole ridiculous thing wrapped up so he could get back to doing what he did best.

'Then get something on *her*!' he snapped at Mark. 'Get some leverage that we can use if she tries anything.'

'I can't do that when I don't know who she is,' Mark protested. 'I need more background. Though it fills me with dread to say it...' he took a breath '...you're going to have to go and chat her up.'

CHAPTER THREE

FINDING the kitchen deserted, Alex followed the sounds of the TV and found Jen in the small den off the kitchen. It was a small, informal sitting room, cosier than the vast main lounge, with a small sofa, a couple of chairs and a very inferior forty-inch TV set. Where television was concerned, in Alex's opinion, size definitely mattered.

Jen was curled up in the corner of the sofa under a well-worn patchwork quilt that he didn't recognise. In fact, glancing around, he saw quite a few items that couldn't possibly have been put there by the interior designer he'd employed. There were framed snapshots and Christmas cards on the sideboard, tinsel on the mantelpiece and a small potted Christmas tree near the window. A fire crackled in the grate.

From nowhere came an unexpected flash of envy. She'd settled in. Surrounded herself with things that meant something to her, reminded her of her home, her family. When had he last done that anywhere? When had he last bothered with Christmas decorations? These days it didn't seem worth the effort just for him, although Jen clearly didn't see it that way. Home for him was whichever house he happened to be in, and family didn't fit in his life any more. Susan had seen to that.

Jen was wearing glasses and eating cheese on toast from

a plate that was balanced precariously on the arm of the sofa. She looked tiny and somehow fragile.

She glanced up at him.

'Hi,' she said.

He nodded towards one of the empty chairs. 'You mind?'

She shrugged noncommittally, but turned the sound down on the TV and took her glasses off, so he figured she couldn't be dead against him joining her.

'I thought the whole appeal of the executive house-sitting thing was that people get to experience luxury they can't afford themselves,' he said, settling back in the chair. 'You know—get a fabulous pad at a fraction of the rent.'

She was watching him, blue eyes wide. He liked the way she didn't fuss with her appearance. Her hair was piled up in a messy bun and he could see a tiny spray of freckles over her nose. No evidence of hours spent in front of the mirror with a make-up brush. He was used to ultra-groomed women, for whom venturing out was all about the way they looked. She was a breath of fresh air.

'What's your point?'

'So how come you're eating cheese on toast off your lap in the den? The sitting room doesn't look lived-in, and you didn't even bag the master bedroom. This is the only room apart from the kitchen that looks like you've set foot in it. You *are* free to use the whole apartment, you know.'

'Where would you suggest I eat, then?' she asked. 'That enormous glass table in your dining room? The one that seats twelve?' She shrugged. Smiled faintly. 'I'm not that kind of girl.' She glanced around. 'I feel more at home in here. It's cosy. You can keep your huge lounge with that monster TV.'

He felt another uncomfortable twist of nostalgia as for no reason his childhood home slipped into his mind. Not a glass table in sight back then, and they'd been lucky to have one temperamental old television. But Jen had sparked his interest with her indifference to the luxury trappings of the apartment. If anything it seemed more of an aversion. Yet hadn't she said her article was something to do with the opulent side of living in South-West London? Time to charm it out of her.

'Do you want a coffee?' he asked.

When he came back with two mugs she'd finished her toast. The empty plate was on the table.

'How was today, then?' he asked, sitting down. 'What did you think of La Brasserie?'

She held her cup in both hands, like a child, and smiled up at him.

'It was amazing,' she said.

'Did you get the background you were talking about?'

She shrugged. 'I got some,' she said. 'You should have seen the food! There were things on that menu I've never even heard of, let alone tried. And the people were something else. I wanted to get an idea of image, you know? What the young women in the Chelsea set are wearing, how they act.'

Her face became animated as she talked about her project. He felt absurdly touched by her excitement over a restaurant he'd visited more times than he could remember. Over things he no longer noticed.

'And what did you think?'

'I think I've only seen the tip of the iceberg. I mean, there were quite a few touristy types there, too, but it was still an eye-opener. They're all so glamorous. Fantastic clothes! One girl had a dog living in her handbag!'

He burst out laughing and she tentatively smiled back. As the blue eyes lit up he realised she was quite stunning.

Good thing he had Mark to keep him on task. She could be a serious threat to his newly sworn singledom if he let her.

'Where do you live usually, then?' he asked. 'When you're not staking out the Chelsea set? I thought it must be somewhere in London—you know, at the journalistic hub?'

Jen paused for a moment to collect her thoughts. It was one thing to share an apartment with the guy, another to start telling him personal stuff. Then again, she could do with some leverage here. This morning's recce had given her some good ideas about working on her own image—and now she'd got Elsie on board to help with hair and make-up, and hit the online secondhand shops so hard that the thought of it still gave her palpitations.

What she was lacking was information on the type of man she was aiming this image towards. She had no personal experience in that area. Her mother had always avoided talking about her father at all costs, never referring to him without using a variety of colourful expletives. La Brasserie hadn't really been much help there, either. Wealthy businessmen were apparently too busy making themselves richer to be chilling out in the daytime mid-week—no matter how posh the restaurant, and no matter how delicious the food.

Speculate to accumulate. Maybe if she made small talk with Alex she could get some tips out of him and distract herself from the still lingering sense of isolation her afternoon's research had left her with.

'I've been in London for the last few months, but really I'm from Littleford,' she said. 'It's a small village in the West Country. You won't have heard of it.'

No one ever had.

'Not far from Bath?'

'You've been there?' she said, wondering when the hell

he'd have had the need to drop in to a village where the star social attraction of the year was the Farm Festival in July, when everyone got together to admire cows and stuff themselves with local produce.

He shook his head. 'No, but I know the general area quite well.'

When she looked at him expectantly he added, 'I grew up in Bristol.'

'You're from *Bristol*?'

'You make it sound like the moon.' The green eyes looked mocking. 'I haven't always lived like this, you know. My parents are working class. My dad was a lorry driver and my mum was a dinner lady at my school. I could always count on her for extra custard.'

'Really?'

'Your surprise could be construed as insulting, you know,' he said.

'I guess I just assumed you'd had a…well, a privileged upbringing.'

'Why? Because someone from my background couldn't possibly make something of themselves?' His tone was light, but the eyes had a razor-sharp edge to them.

She backtracked. *Hard.*

'I didn't mean that. It's just…well, it's such a glamorous career, what you do. Hollywood, London, Cannes.'

He shook his head.

'I didn't have any of that in mind when I started out.'

He took a sip of his coffee. She waited for him to elaborate, but it seemed his own glam world wasn't as interesting to him as it was to her.

'What's Littleford like, then?' he asked.

'Quiet. One pub, couple of village shops, church, duck pond,' she said, trying to fob him off quickly so she could get the subject back on him. 'So, how did you start out?'

Her plan to pump him for background information on what suits he wore was trampled underfoot by her stampeding curiosity about his childhood. She'd assumed he'd been born to wealthy parents and had had an upbringing involving public school, nannies and a network of contacts that had given him a leg-up until he'd reached the top. Just how wrong had she been?

'I started out small,' he said. He looked down at his coffee mug, a smile touching his lips, creasing the corner of his eyes lightly. 'I guess I just always had big ideas.'

She smiled at that but he shook his head.

'It wasn't particularly a good thing. Where I lived you got through school, then you got out and started earning. Big ideas were seen as a waste of time. I had to fight to get my parents onside about going to college. I worked part-time to fund the course, but there was a real sense that I was wasting that money. I was lucky. I had an inspirational tutor and I was determined to succeed. I made a short film. Just a twenty-minute thing I wrote, produced and directed on a minuscule budget. I knew it was good. I believed in it totally.' He laughed a little. 'Feature films came much later. Ideas above my station never really went away.'

'Nothing wrong with that,' she said. She could definitely relate to it. 'You don't get anywhere by sitting around.'

She realised suddenly that she was feeling hugely impressed by him, and quickly reminded herself that he might have made his own wealth but he didn't seem to be in touch with his roots now. Typical. Get there and never look back. He obviously wasn't above using his money to ride roughshod over other people now he'd got it.

'So you live alone?'

He asked the question casually, without meeting her eyes. The kind of question that might be asked on a date. A spark tingled its way up her spine at the thought and she felt mildly ridiculous. The idea that Alex Hammond might be interested in someone like her when he could call up a model at the drop of a hat was ludicrous.

'With my mum,' she said.

A sudden stab of longing for home made her forget momentarily she was meant to be on a fishing expedition. Try as she might she couldn't really feel at home in this apartment. She was looking forward to going home for Christmas, but she couldn't think past her article right now.

'It's just the two of us. She lost her job recently, and I've been interning, so things have been a bit tight money-wise. I'm hoping this article comes off because it has a great job riding on the back of it. If I can up my earnings, she can slow down a bit.'

An alternative, if their backs were squashed any harder against the wall, *had* been floated. She could contact her father and tap him for a handout—as suggested often by Elsie, for whom pride had no value in the face of hard cash. For Jen it was out of the question. She'd prefer to be poor with her pride intact, thank you very much.

'So you're in the market for lucrative stories, then?' Alex asked.

She didn't miss the suspicious look on his face. Understanding flooded in. A friendly conversation? She knew immediately what this was all about.

'You're wanting to know if I'm planning an exposé on you, aren't you? Is that what this being friendly is all about?'

'I'm just making conversation.' His voice was totally calm.

She put her mug down on the coffee table and pulled herself up from the sofa. She shoved aside an almighty twinge of disappointment. What an idiot she was for thinking he might actually be interested in her and her country background. He was a stereotypical bachelor with enough cash to get his own way on anything he chose. He must be super-nettled by the idea of her living here to go to the trouble of trying to sweet-talk her. Well, good. As long as she didn't have to move out, let him be nettled.

'I told you last night—I've got no interest in you as long as I'm working on this project. As long as you're not planning on throwing me out you have nothing to worry about. Your secrets are safe with me.'

'You don't know any of my secrets.'

She walked around his chair and leaned in behind him, laid a hand on his shoulder and bent down to speak in his ear in what she hoped was a confident *I-won't-be-messed-with* tone. She'd seen it done in the movies, when Mafia bigwigs wanted to be intimidating. Unfortunately she wasn't prepared for the sudden happy flip-flops in her stomach that the scent of his warm skin and expensive aftershave would cause, and she had to talk through gritted teeth to keep up the charade and stop her voice slipping towards soft and melty. That would definitely have ruined the effect.

'I could always make up what I don't know,' she snapped, dropped the TV remote control in his lap and stalked out of the room.

As she made her way to her bedroom she forced herself to focus hard on her article. She wasn't going to get anywhere with the research questions now. She'd just have to wing it at the exhibition tomorrow with no head start at all.

Rule #3: Don't forget…etiquette! If you're going to join the world of the rich, you must act as if you belong there. Blending in isn't just about what you wear—it covers how you speak, what you say, your manners. Do not swear, get drunk, do drugs

*or laugh loudly. Avoid flashy behaviour. You are
aiming for girlfriend to be swiftly followed by wife.
Not mistress. Stand out for the wrong reasons and
your cover will be blown.*

It felt like getting ready for the scariest night of your life.
A cross between a first date and a job interview pretty
much covered it. Jen told herself the nerves were down to
the fact there was so much riding on this project—nothing
to do with the feeling that she was a fraud, that she didn't
belong in this world. She had a perfectly good reason to
be there: research. And this was her first real opportunity
to mingle with the kind of men who thought nothing of
blowing the odd million pounds on a painting.

In fact, there wasn't an enormous amount of stressing
over what she was wearing. She only had one remotely
suitable dress with her. None of her online purchases had
turned up yet. She was still in serious need of a makeover. No millionaire worth his salt was going to look twice
at mousy-haired Jen Brown in her High Street LBD and
shoes, but at least she could stand on the sidelines and
learn to identify the kind of man she should be targeting.

There would be no point changing her own image if
she couldn't tell the difference between real money and
an ordinary culture vulture like Gordon from the *Gazette*.
She needed to nail the difference between bespoke tailoring and mass production. She felt a bit more positive. This
wasn't going to be a wasted evening. It was going to be a
dry run. A learning experience.

And, talking of learning, she had nearly an hour yet before her taxi was due. What would be a more productive
use of that time than a bit of investigation? Alex Hammond
might not be up for twenty questions, but this apartment
was full of the trappings of his rich life, just there to be

examined. She padded down the passageway from her bedroom in her stockinged feet. Alex had been out for most of the day and had shut himself in the study the moment he got back. There was no sign of him emerging any time soon.

She stopped outside the door of his dressing room and hesitated. Dressing room? Honestly! What kind of a man needed one of those?

The kind who had so much hard cash he didn't know what to spend it on, she answered herself, pushing the door open. A little look wouldn't hurt. She was sure he wouldn't mind.

There were dark wood sliding cupboards on either side, a tiled area with his-and-hers smoked glass sinks, and a gleaming mirror took up almost the whole wall at the end of the room. The lighting was unforgiving, and she grimaced as she caught sight of her pale complexion in the mirror. She really would have to get some fake tan sorted out if she wanted to look as if she regularly holidayed in the South of France.

Sliding open cupboards, she was faced with rows of perfectly cut jackets, pristine shirts in every colour, and racks of gleaming shoes stored with wooden moulds inside them. She picked up a pair and studied them. Italian leather. She could see they were beautifully made, but she could hardly spend the evening staring at men's feet. She decided to concentrate on the clothes instead.

She reached into the wardrobe and took out what looked like an evening suit in a very dark slate-grey. She unzipped the transparent dust cover and took the jacket off its hanger. She examined it, trying to burn the look and feel of it into her mind. The fabric was rich and heavy, the cut so sharp that it even looked perfect hanging from her hand.

On impulse she shrugged herself into it, just to see

what it might look like on a person. It smelled faintly of the warm citrus aftershave Alex wore, snapping her straight back to the first time she'd breathed in that scent. The jacket, huge on her, reminded her of the breadth and strength of his toned shoulders as he'd held her down, his green eyes locked on hers. Her breathing speeded up just at the thought of it, and she could see in her reflection the pink hue that rose in her cheeks. She wished her body would get the message that she didn't have time for men like him. Not when she'd spent her whole life grappling with the reason why a man like him had no time for her.

She was turning this way and that, examining the fall of the jacket in the mirror, when the door opened behind her and Alex Hammond stepped into the room.

She felt as though her heart had fallen through the pit of her stomach.

His hair was damp from the shower and he was wearing a sea-green bath towel around his hips, to which her eyes traitorously dipped before she got herself under control and dragged them back up to face level. The toned pecs and biceps were lightly tanned. He looked as if he'd just stepped in from the beach.

For a long moment Alex couldn't quite believe what he was seeing. Hot on the heels of yesterday's thinly veiled threat to make him her next story, now he found her standing next to the open door of his wardrobe, apparently trying on his clothes.

'I can explain,' she said.

At least she had the good grace to look embarrassed. The blush high on her porcelain cheeks made her look very young, and prettier than ever.

This would be interesting.

'Cross-dressing?' he supplied helpfully.

Without looking at him she took the jacket off, hung it back on the hanger, zipped the cover over it and replaced it in the wardrobe. While her back was turned he crossed the room to stand behind her. This close, he was enveloped by her perfume, something light and sweet that knocked his senses. The skin of her shoulders, visible above the boat neckline of the dress, was the colour of double cream against the plain black fabric. Her neck curved delectably. He crushed the impulse to kiss it.

'First you go through my bin and now I find you looking through my clothes,' he said in a low voice.

She spun round, and he heard the small gasp as she realised how close he was to her. He saw in the surprised widening of her eyes that she thought she'd got away with the bin story.

'What the hell is going on here? What are you? Some kind of stalker?'

She stood her ground defiantly, looking boldly into his face. The confident don't-care exterior didn't fool him. He could tell by the way her breath had quickened, the way her eyes met his, that she was attracted to him. She thought she could blag her way out of this, as she did everything else.

'I came in to use the mirror,' she said. 'There isn't a full-length one in my room. And then I wondered if there might be a jacket I could borrow. I only have a pashmina and it's freezing outside.'

'Make a habit of wearing men's clothes, do you?'

'Masculine tailoring is the new black, actually,' she said airily. 'I was just having a try-on. It's a girl thing. You should never trust the way it looks on a hanger.'

She sidestepped him deftly. He let her go, watched her as she pretended to look in the mirror, dabbing her lips with her little finger as if trying on menswear was the most normal thing in the world for a girl to do.

'Naturally I would have asked your permission before I took it.'

'Naturally,' he said sarcastically.

She glanced at him.

It was clear now that she had to be gathering background for some article or other about him. He was shocked to realise how disappointed he felt by that. He'd begun to like her, with her off-the-wall behaviour and her amazing legs. He was used to mixing with women who played the game his way. A couple of dates, a good time, and when he broke it off—which he always did—they left on good terms. No fuss or backlash. Because his good opinion counted in the competitive world of film.

A woman with her own agenda was a refreshing change. And that was not necessarily a good thing.

He considered walking her to the door right now and throwing her out, but he needed to speak to Mark first. Make sure he'd found out something to ensure her confidentiality. That, he insisted, was the only reason he didn't tell her to go and pack now. It had absolutely nothing to do with the way she was affecting him from the waist down.

Obviously tasting victory when he didn't say anything further, she made for the door while the going was good.

'Going anywhere special?' he called after her.

'It's a work thing,' she called back. 'Don't wait up.'

The gallery would have been stunning even without pictures festooning the walls, Jen decided. The building itself was cutting-edge modern, and inside there was major use of glass, highly polished wood floors and superb clear spotlighting to show the art off to its best advantage. At least it would have done if any of the pictures had been Jen's cup of tea. Enormous arrangements of Christmas greenery studded with tiny white pin lights stood near the entrance. Wine waiters mingled effortlessly among the guests, dispensing crystal flutes of champagne and canapés. The artist was up-and-coming and, according to the loud-voiced man dominating the group next to Jen, extremely collectible. The guests were glamorous, their enthusiasm for the exhibits bubbling like the champagne.

Feeling drab and invisible in her plain black shift dress, and unsteady in her borrowed nude heels, she took a third glass of the complimentary champagne from a passing waiter. OK, so she rarely drank, but in this intimidating fish-out-of-water environment at least it gave her something to occupy her hands. She found herself sipping from the glass in an effort to appear busy and avoid speaking. Not that anyone had attempted to start a conversation with *her*.

There were plenty of extremely attractive men in attendance, but they seemed to have at least two or three women keeping them company at all times, all of them beautiful and expensively dressed. A few weeks to go until Christmas and sequins and gold were everywhere. The only way she'd be able to compete might be by tipping her champagne down the designer-clad back of the competition, and that would only get her ejected from the premises before she could so much as speak. Deciding the only way to salvage the evening was to treat it as a serious scouting mission, she chose the least offensive of the eye-wateringly bright oil paintings and picked her way through the crowd to stand on the edge of the group in front of it.

'Fabulous brushwork. So *insistent*,' one woman was saying to no one in particular. Her gold silk sheath dress screamed expensive. Not a hint of tasteless sparkle, more a subtle hint of *luxe*. It made Jen, in her boring man-made-fibre black, want to slink under the nearest rock.

She took a sip of champagne and gazed up at the picture. These people—honestly! Could they not see what was plain as day? To Jen it looked as if a toddler had run amok with a paintbrush.

Confidence shored up by the champagne, she leaned in towards the man standing next to her.

'Not sure about it myself,' she said.

Hah! She'd made a comment. Not so hard, after all! She took another slug of the delicious champagne and glanced sideways at him to see if he was listening. Hmm. Sleek blond hair, haughty but attractive face. Her eyes dipped expertly to his suit. Definitely expensive tailoring.

He smiled and nodded at her. He took a sip from his own glass and his sleeve fell back to reveal his watch.

Cartier!

It was like a message from the gods. She gave him her full attention.

Her confidence was soaring on the back of three glasses of champagne, and she realised with a flash of inspiration that this was the answer to all her problems. Dutch courage! She grabbed a passing waiter by the arm before she missed out, and swapped her empty glass for another full one.

The rest of the group drifted away, but the blond man carried on looking appraisingly at the framed paint explosion in front of them.

'Personally...' Jen leaned in conspiratorially and, extending a finger from the hand encircling her champagne flute, jabbed it towards the picture '...I like what I like. It needs to speak to me on a sentimental level.' She clasped her other hand to her chest to emphasise how heartfelt an opinion that was.

Oh, the champagne was marvellous. And she was just *so* witty and interesting.

'Tell me, what do *you* think of it?' She pasted an expression of interest on her face. Her high heels seemed strangely unsteady and she concentrated hard on not swaying.

The man began an extremely dull monologue on the inspirational brushwork, and she tried valiantly to listen and nod encouragingly when her will to live wanted to dash to the exit and throw itself under the nearest lorry. She glanced around for the wine waiter.

'…name?'

She suddenly realised he'd stopped talking and was looking at her expectantly. The chatter in the rest of the room seemed to have degenerated into a humming background noise.

Name. Right—she'd prepared for this. Something that sounded as if she'd been born into money, because she'd read somewhere that was more respectable than *nouveau riche*.

'Genevieve,' she said. Her tongue felt strangely hard to control.

'Genevieve?' the man asked.

One of her heels suddenly dipped to the side, and she plummeted four inches before managing to right herself by grabbing his sleeve. Champagne slopped from her flute onto his lapel. As she managed to steady herself he pointedly disengaged himself from her grip and took a step backwards, wiping at his suit. People around them began to look over at the disturbance, and she smiled around at them reassuringly—just a little accident, nothing to worry about.

'Genevieve?'

She glanced round at the voice behind her in confusion.

Next thing she knew she was being taken firmly by the elbow and Alex Hammond had control of the situation.

'Genevieve! I wondered where you'd disappeared to!'

His voice was loud and commanding. 'Excuse us…' he added in an aside to the blond man.

She suddenly found her hand encased firmly in his and his arm slid strongly around her waist, propelling her at a stumblingly fast pace towards the exit. Many more heads turned. Interested faces passed Jen by in a blur. As they descended the stone steps onto the frosty street the icy cold air hit her and made her head spin. She was vaguely aware of a crowd moving towards them, saw cameras and mobile phones raised as people clocked just who it was she was in a clinch with.

She struggled free and put a pace between them, intending to swing round on her heel and give Alex a piece of her mind. She didn't care what media grief that might cause him. She'd had it with his interference. Even though her knees went buckly and he caught her again around the waist, before she could hit the frozen pavement, she refused to let him get away with this.

'What the hell do you think you're doing?' She snapped crossly. 'I was well *in* there!'

CHAPTER FOUR

ALEX managed to hold his tongue until they were out of earshot of the press. Having rushed her into the safety of the back of his car, he had his driver head back to the apartment.

'Well in there?' he said through gritted teeth, wondering why he was so angry. 'That was not a school dance and you are not fourteen. Do you realise you just threw champagne over Viscount Dulverwell?'

To his utter amazement, instead of looking ashamed or embarrassed, she actually looked even more pleased with herself.

'Hah! A viscount, eh? I knew it! The watch gave it away.' She hiccupped suddenly and clapped her hand over her mouth.

His lips quirked. The sooner he got some black coffee into her the better.

'Anyway, why are you so annoyed?' She jabbed a finger at his chest. 'What were you doing there? Are you checking up on me?'

'No, I am not!' he snapped in exasperation. 'I'm being seen in the right places. Looking respectable. Looking *single*. And escorting a drunk young woman off the premises was definitely *not* part of my plan.' He glanced sideways at her, taking in her delectably dishevelled state. 'You'd better hope no one got a picture.'

He imagined for a moment the fallout if the chaos of the last fifteen minutes made it into tomorrow's papers. His PR team would have him becoming a hermit next. But suddenly Alex realised none of this made him the slightest bit regretful. If anything, absconding from the dull exhibition, rescuing a delightfully out-of-her-depth Jen, felt like a small victory in the face of the ridiculous media manipulation supposedly taking place on his behalf.

'Why do it, then?' she asked him.

'Do what?'

She gave an exaggerated shrug. 'Why escort me anywhere?'

She leaned in towards him, putting a slim hand on his arm and enveloping him in the vanilla scent of her perfume. His pulse kicked in response, hard.

'Why not just ignore me, let me get on with my evening while you do whatever it is you people do at these places? Buy one of those ghastly pictures, maybe? I didn't ask you to drag me out of there. I was managing perfectly well by myself.'

Thrown by his body's instant reaction to her touch, he plucked her hand from his arm and moved it back into her own personal space.

'I was saving you from making a total fool of yourself,' he said. Not strictly true. The sensible thing would have been to leave her to her own devices, keep as much space between them as he could.

He refused to acknowledge how he'd felt on spotting her across the gallery. At first he'd assumed she was there watching him, convinced as he was that she was now planning to write some story about him. But a few minutes' observation had made it obvious she hadn't a clue that he was there. Intrigued as to what on earth she was doing there on her own, he'd been unable to concentrate on the pictures or the conversation. His eyes had kept dragging themselves back to where she stood, nervously fiddling with her handbag, not speaking to anyone.

He'd seen how her confidence had grown in proportion to her champagne consumption. Watched her grow louder and more animated. And finally he'd watched her throw herself at Viscount Dulverwell, gazing raptly into his face as he talked, only breaking her focus on him to grab yet more champagne. For some reason watching her start out nervous and unspoilt, as if she were at her first grown-up night out, and slowly morph into a vivacious flirt had bothered the hell out of him. Whatever her reasons were, whatever she was doing there, he hadn't been prepared to wait until the end of the evening for an explanation.

Back at the apartment he took her firmly by the shoulders, marched her through the kitchen into the den and deposited her on the sofa while he made industrial-strength black coffee. The silky feel of her shoulders under his hands had him wondering if she felt that satiny all over. He crushed the thought from his mind. Maybe the fact she'd drunk too much was a good thing. If he were to pursue that impulse he would want all her wits and senses at his disposal.

Not that it was even a possibility.

While he waited for the kettle to boil he skimmed an e-mail Mark had sent while he was out. When he came back she'd kicked off the skyscraper heels and pulled the pins out of her hair. It fell in soft waves to her shoulders. She looked suddenly very vulnerable and he curbed the temptation to snap at her.

He sat down opposite her and leaned forward.

'I want to know exactly what is going on. What you're

really doing in London. Why you're in my flat, snooping in my cupboards, and why you were at that reception to-night by yourself. You tell me everything or I put you in a taxi right now.'

'You can't do that,' she said defiantly. She sipped her coffee and grimaced at the strength of it but didn't complain. 'You don't know what I might say to my press contacts.'

He held that defiant blue gaze unwaveringly with his own.

'Which contacts do you mean?' he asked. 'The one who runs the agricultural desk? Or maybe Births, Marriages and Deaths? They're standard fare in a village newspaper, aren't they?'

Mark's e-mail had given full details of her current employment. No tabloid newspaper contacts in sight.

Silence for a long moment, with the blue eyes fixed on his. Then she looked down at her coffee cup.

'You checked up on me,' she said accusingly.

'You turn up out of the blue, living in my apartment and refusing to leave, no matter how much money I put on the table. Not to mention all the weird stalker stuff. Did you honestly think for one second I wouldn't check up on you?'

He didn't add that he checked up on everyone these days, no matter how insignificant they seemed. Trust seemed to have been phased out of his life since Susan had left. After five years it was all but gone.

Jen took another sip of her coffee, pushed her hair back from her face. Her expression was steadier when she looked back at him. Sobriety seemed to be slipping back.

'I'm sorry about the weird stalker stuff,' she said. 'I'm not, in fact, a weird stalker.'

She paused and he waited for her to elaborate, waited to

see if she'd feed him another line or actually come clean this time.

She took a deep breath. 'I'm working on an article I pitched to *Gossip!* magazine.' She searched his face.

He raised mystified eyebrows.

'It's the biggest-selling women's magazine in this country,' she explained. 'I managed to land an internship there for the last three months, and at the end I pitched my own idea for an article.'

The look on her face was disbelief mingled with delight.

'I still can't believe it,' she said. 'I've been trying for the past three years to break into mainstream women's journalism but it's so damn competitive. There's a permanent job vacancy there and the editor said if I can pull this off I've got a great chance of landing it. A proper career. Not just an internship. This is my big break—my foot in the door. Christmas is my deadline, I have to file my copy by then.'

'And how does trying on my clothes and flirting with Viscount Dulverwell fit in to all this?'

She took a breath.

'My article investigates whether it's possible for an ordinary Miss Nobody...' she glanced up at him '...someone like me...to reinvent herself and win the heart of a millionaire.'

He stared at her, wondering if he'd actually heard correctly.

'Obviously a rich man with half a brain wouldn't look twice at me normally, because he'd assume someone like me must be a gold-digger, right?'

A sick feeling rose in the pit of his stomach as Susan flashed into his mind again.

'So I need to give the impression that I have money and success of my own. An address in the right postcode, the right clothes, the right things to say.' She took a sip of her coffee. 'And the right places to go. That's why I was at the exhibition. And that's why I've been taking a bit of an interest in your clothes and your lifestyle. I would have asked you outright but I didn't think you'd take kindly to the idea, given…well, given…'

Incredulity mingled with outrage. *Given the fact that the one person I trusted, wanted to spend my life with, turned out to have pound signs in her eyes and not a lot else…*

'Given my past, right?' he said.

Not for the first time he felt a surge of fury that his private life was public property.

'You mean to tell me you're posing as some socialite so you can bag a rich man? I've never heard anything so ludicrous!'

'It's not *real*. I don't really want to "bag a rich man", as you put it. Personally I'd rather eat my own head than get involved with someone like that.'

Even in his amazement he didn't miss the venom in that comment, and wondered where it had come from.

'It's a way of writing about that whole rich, sumptuous world without it just being a run-of-the-mill description. The editor of *Gossip!* wouldn't have wasted a second on me if I was just writing a straightforward article because that's been done a million times. The way I'm doing it is more fun. It gives an original spin. It's intended to be tongue-in-cheek, not serious.'

'Well, it's never going to work. I can tell you that now. You think a few new clothes and hanging out in the right places is enough?'

'*You* were there, weren't you?'

'What?'

'I said, you were there. Tonight. According to a recent poll you are the thirty-sixth most eligible bachelor in England right now. I checked.'

She'd been checking up on him? His mind zeroed in on that piece of information. He would revisit it later.

'What's your point?'

'That in order to meet a wealthy, eligible man you have to go to the right places. And I did. I just…drank a bit more champagne than I should have.' She rubbed a hand tiredly across her forehead. 'I'm not really used to it.'

'I think the whole article idea is laughable,' he said shortly.

She leaned forward and spoke slowly and clearly. 'It's a tongue-in-cheek social experiment. It isn't serious.'

'Judging by this evening, the experiment isn't panning out all that well.' He felt an unexpected jolt of regret as he saw the look in her eyes. Clearly she wasn't happy with the way it was going. Question was, why the hell did he care?

'I'm not giving up,' she said, 'if that's what you're hoping. That I'll just throw in the towel, pack my bags and be out of your hair. I'm going to make this work, no matter what it takes.'

'Nice though it would be to get my life back, I wouldn't expect you to go quietly.'

And that was the whole point, really, wasn't it? He was used to maintaining absolute control over every aspect of his life, used to excluding anyone or anything that could take advantage of him. If he wanted something he went after it. If he didn't want something he found a way of avoiding it. His wealth and position made that entirely possible. And now his lack of control over this situation, over her, was driving him nuts. Well, not for much longer.

'I've got a proposition for you,' he said.

Interest sparked in her face. She sat forward, the blue eyes shrewd. The only sign of the champagne now was in the dark circles beneath them.

'A confidentiality agreement,' he said. 'You sign that

and I allow you to stay here for the month. Long enough for you to finish your insane undercover article.'

The leave-nothing-to-chance reliability of a signed agreement appealed to him. He'd long since learned from the mistakes of his past.

'A gag order?' Her tone was tinged with contempt. 'You want to control my freedom of speech?'

Had he really expected her to sign on the dotted line without a word of protest?

'It's nothing out of the ordinary. It's a standard contract. All my staff sign one as a condition of their employment.'

'I'm not staff. And *you* might consider giving someone else control over your life to be nothing out of the ordinary, but I don't.'

'We'll both benefit from it. I'm not asking you to cut your tongue out—you can write about any other damn thing you like except for me.'

He felt a stab of exasperation. Did she have any clue at all what it was like to be on the receiving end of the press pack? To go through the worst of times and have to elbow your way through photographers just to leave the house? And, when they couldn't get what they wanted from you, to have them hound your family? To read about private details of your marriage break-up in the papers, your heartbreak there in black and white for anyone to see?

He watched her staring into her coffee for a moment, deep in thought. Eventually she looked up at him, a frown touching her eyebrows.

'I could do with a new approach, I'll admit,' she said slowly. 'So how about we strike a deal?'

Mark would have insisted he halt the conversation right there, withdraw the offer and tell her to go and pack. But there was something about her defiant attitude that he couldn't help responding to. In spite of himself, it stirred

him. In more ways than one. To put his business interests first he had to curb his socialising. Yet solitude did
not come easily to him, and having her here would offer
some diversion. The question was whether that was a good
thing or not.

He put his coffee cup down and met her gaze.

'What kind of deal?'

She shrugged.

'I admit you might have a point about my press contacts.
I don't know anyone in the national press. But I could still
make trouble. It wouldn't take much for me to ring up the
entertainment correspondent of one of the daily tabloids
and give the inside story of my few days in your company
following your scandal.'

A counter-threat. He wouldn't have expected anything
less.

'So you understand where I'm coming from?' he said.

She nodded. 'And I'm prepared to sign your agreement
if you change the conditions. Your offer is to let me stay
here, but I'm going to ask for a bit more than that.'

He wasn't sure he'd ever met anyone who pushed their
luck so hard.

'Go on,' he said slowly.

'What I need right now is an adviser. To help me get my
article back on track. Someone who knows the world I'm
writing about and can give me a few pointers.'

He stared at her.

'You want me to help you trick some unsuspecting millionaire into thinking you're a rich socialite?'

'In a nutshell, yes. But not in a direct way. I just want
to be able to ask your opinion on a few things, that's all.
Clothes, locations, that kind of thing.'

He needed time out to think.

'I think it's a fair offer,' she added.

As she put her empty coffee cup down on the table he got to his feet and reached for it.

'I'll make some more coffee,' he said.

She grabbed his hand as he picked up her mug. Sparks of heat tingled through his wrist and zipped down his spine. There was something so alluring about her—and it messed with his body, not just with his mind. Her upturned face was imploring, the blue eyes clear.

'I'm no threat to you. I honestly have no interest in making trouble for you. And we're not that different. You told me you started out with ideas above your station and that's what I've got. I just need this chance.'

He looked into the pleading blue eyes. He must be mad.

She took her hand back and he straightened up, made his way back to the kitchen, knowing that he should be ejecting her from the apartment right now.

She was right about selling her story. She could still make life difficult for him if she wanted to.

He had a choice. He could make her move out now, take a chance that any fuel she added to the scandal fire would be short-lived. Or he could go along with her crazy scheme, get the gag order in place and keep her here with him for the month. The inherent danger in that thought made his pulse-rate climb. He ignored it.

It burned that he was expected to toe the line of the studios, the management, to restrain his private life. After clawing his way up from nothing to get where he was, and having been knocked halfway down again by Susan, being held back in any way now was abhorrent to him. His one failed attempt at family life had been dissected and trampled on by the media. Living the high life was payback for that. He enjoyed spending time in the company of beautiful women, but he never let it get serious enough to have emotional consequences. Let them print that he was screwing this model, or that actress. He didn't care whether it was true or not.

Jen wanted him to spend a bit of time giving his opinion on clothes and the like? How hard could that be? With his social life reined in he'd have plenty of time on his hands. Let her stay here and work on her mad project. It would give him a few laughs if nothing else. And he'd far rather look at her long legs and big blue eyes than stare at these four walls.

He could tell Mark he'd secured her silence. No need to mention that he'd given in a little on the terms of the agreement. Or that he found the prospect of spending a month living side-by-side with Jen dangerously attractive.

He refilled their coffee cups and made his way back into the den. He stopped in the doorway. She was curled up in the corner of the sofa, brown hair spilling over the cushion, sleeping. His heart turned over gently. For a split second he toyed with picking her up and carrying her to her bed. And then the memory of the other night drifted back—the thought of her beneath him, his for the taking. He mouth felt too dry all of a sudden.

There was kicking back and there was recklessness.

He put the coffee down on the table and grabbed the hideous patchwork throw she was so attached to. He tucked it around her and left the room.

Every movement around the kitchen jarred Jen's aching head. She cooked dry toast, took headache pills, then sat on one of the stools and swigged orange juice. All the usual tricks for dealing with a hangover. If she was going to feel this grim at the very least she should have had the luxury of memory loss—the kind where you missed hour-long sections from the previous night as if you'd been abducted by aliens rather than drunk too much champagne.

The humiliation of being escorted from the exhibition by Alex played on a loop in her head. She'd tossed a drink over a member of the aristocracy. For a professional journalist she knew her behaviour had been pitiful. And the *coup de grâce* that really made her cringe? Collapsing in Alex Hammond's arms on the gallery steps. Her face burned just at the thought of it. That they hadn't been swamped by the gawping paparazzi was down to pure luck and Alex's super-fast driver. Clearly the press had been as surprised as she was to see him at the gallery, and the car had pulled away with seconds to spare.

As soon as her head calmed down she would go and pack. All hope was gone of his letting her stay here. The champagne might have given her the courage to propose they strike a deal, but that had been her big mistake. Alex Hammond would never stoop to negotiate with someone like her. He'd see it as a challenge to his authority. Men like him did what worked for them. He'd wanted rid of her from the moment he arrived and now he'd got his way.

Deep down it wasn't the leaving that was the problem. Yes, it would be a setback. She had a ton of designer clobber winging its way to this address. A pain, but fixable. No, the thing that really rankled was that he'd got what he wanted despite her best efforts. Another rich man letting nothing get in his way—especially a nobody like her. She knew she could sell a story about him, but she was in this for the long haul. She didn't want fifteen minutes of fame for a flash-in-the-pan exposé and a one-off payment. She wanted to make a serious career out of writing, and that meant maintaining journalistic integrity. What if she wanted to interview a celebrity at some time in the future? She would never be trustworthy if she sold Alex out now.

He had no idea what it had cost her to agree to the gag order. The only way she'd been able to stomach it was to throw in some terms of her own, to try and hang on to some control. Well, much good it had done. Was this what it had felt like for her mum when she'd been pushed into signing the piece of paper that had let her father buy his way out of her future? As if she was painted in a corner with no other option left?

She glanced up and her heart began to thud as Alex walked into the kitchen.

'Morning, Genevieve,' he said.

She flushed. He'd got what he wanted. She'd be moving out. She didn't need to put up with him teasing her too. She jumped down from the stool, grimacing as the sharp movement jerked her head, and made for the door.

'When do we start, then?' he called after her.

'When you said you'd need a few pointers, I didn't expect to have to read women's magazines,' Alex muttered, flipping through the pile of glossies she'd handed him with a dubious expression on his face.

They were sitting opposite each other in the main sitting room on the leather sofas, a roaring fire burning in the enormous fireplace. A low coffee table separated them, upon which was a jumble of her handwritten notes, magazines, photos and a coffee mug each.

She wasn't about to let him off the hook now. Initially amazed that he'd agreed to her request, she'd quickly forged ahead with her plans before he could change his mind, booking proper slots in his diary so he couldn't make excuses. This was the first—deliberately late that afternoon, so her hangover headache had had the chance to dissipate completely. She felt totally alert and focused again.

'I think it's important you understand the kind of article I'm pitching. It isn't some serious literary thing, it's meant to be light-hearted and fun.' She took a slug from her coffee. 'And, anyway, you should be thanking me instead of complaining. These magazines are an insight into the mind of the modern woman.'

'"*Christmas party make-up for every skin-type...*"' he read aloud. 'Very insightful.'

She ignored the teasing.

'I'm talking about the stuff on relationships, not the make-up column. Articles on what women really think about foreplay. How to decipher what he really thinks of you by studying his behaviour.' She jabbed her pen towards him. 'There's a whole underground conspiracy between those pages that men just aren't aware of. A sisterhood. A sharing of information that arms us against the wiles of the opposite sex. Did you know that the majority of women at some point fake orgasm?'

'The minority who sleep with me don't,' he said.

Sparks tingled up and down her spine as he deliberately and firmly held her gaze, the heat clear in his expression. She picked up another of the magazines and began to flick through it, not seeing the content, just using it to deflect the moment. It didn't help that she knew exactly what it felt like to have his body held hard against hers. Without conscious effort her mind wasn't above taking that scenario further step by step. What it might feel like to be kissed by him, touched by him. She wasn't about to let him play with her the way he undoubtedly played with all the women in his life. She knew his type. What possible interest could he have in someone like her, besides amusement?

'Men have magazines, too, you know,' he said, apparently giving up on getting a reaction from her. 'Women don't have the monopoly on this stuff.'

She flapped a dismissive hand at him, glad to be back on task.

'You can't possibly compare lads' mags with the serious issues covered in women's magazines. They're just an excuse to show pictures of scantily clad women with the odd article about cars and football thrown in.'

'Nothing wrong with that,' he said, grinning.

He wasn't going to take this seriously, was he? She should have just launched straight into the stuff about image. Gathering up the magazines, she stacked them in a pile under the table and picked up her notebook.

'There's two areas where I need your input,' she said, keeping her tone efficient. 'Firstly, background on the kind of men I'm writing about. It should be easy. Just tell me about yourself. Where you go to socialise, what you wear, what subjects interest you, what sports you like—that kind of thing.'

He leaned back on the sofa, arms behind his head.

'You want to know about what makes me tick?'

The question was loaded. She could feel it. It made her stomach feel soft and squiggly.

'In as much as it relates to my article, yes,' she said, trying to keep her focus.

'And the other area?'

'My own image,' she said. 'I've ordered a stack of second-hand designer clothes. I just need you to give me a thumbs-up or down as to whether or not they would do it for you.'

'*Do it* for me?'

She felt heat rise in her cheeks. This would be so much easier if he was middle-aged, short and dumpy. It was hard to keep things businesslike with him looking like an Adonis. She didn't relish the thought of asking his opinion on her looks, but she was determined to give her absolute all to this article. She was more than capable of crushing any stupid embarrassment in the interest of the bigger goal.

'Make me look like I'd fit into your social circle without standing out,' she rephrased. 'Like I have plenty of money of my own.'

'Got you,' he said. 'I assume that's what the name-change was about, then, Genevieve.'

He seemed determined to keep a blush on her face.

'You have to agree that Jennifer Brown doesn't sound rich.'

'You could double-barrel your surname,' he suggested. 'What about adding your mother's maiden name?'

'Brown is my mother's maiden name.'

'OK. Add in your father's name, then.'

'I've got to twenty-five without using anything of his. I'm not about to start now,' she said, more forcefully than she'd intended. The fact that her father's name could open doors had only made her even more determined not to use it. She was determined to prove that money and string-pulling weren't the only way to get where you wanted in life—something Alex Hammond could do with remembering.

He raised his eyebrows but made no comment.

'Street name?' he said. 'Add your street name to your surname.'

'That would be Farmer-Brown.'

He burst out laughing and she couldn't help grinning back. He looked absolutely heartstopping when he laughed. Maybe if she got to know him she could talk him into giving her an interview somewhere down the line.

She marvelled at herself. Here she was, country mouse Jen, career-building and networking without even thinking about it.

'Maybe it's a sign. I think I'll just forget the name thing for now and concentrate on the way I look and speak. Having a name like a princess isn't going to convince anyone if I look and sound like trailer trash.' She frowned. 'Not that I do.'

'Sounds like a good idea,' he said. 'And next time you might want to lay off the champagne.'

CHAPTER FIVE

Rule #4: Get the right look. Don't be yourself. Be better. Walk better. Dress better. Groom yourself better. Ditch High Street for designer but avoid labels that show. Think simple, understated, classy. Get a decent haircut and colour and keep make-up subtle but pretty. On a budget? Trawl internet auction sites, or try charity shops in rich locations, for second-hand clothes and put together an expensive look that's versatile enough for different occasions...

'ARE you sure this will have worked?' Jen asked dubiously.

'Relax. It'll be a piece of cake. You followed my instructions, didn't you? You can't go wrong.'

Elsie's face, her hair in a new upswept bouffant style with a pink fabric flower pinned at one side, filled the screen of Jen's laptop. Alex was out for the afternoon and she'd taken over his dressing room. Mainly because there was a sink available and the floor was tiled, so any splashes of hair colorant would be easy to clean instead of carpet-ruining.

She'd stashed her laptop to one side of the sink unit and had mixed the colour under Elsie's virtual supervision before painting it onto her head. That had been a while ago and now it was time to rinse.

Alarm bells began ringing as soon as she began pouring jugfuls of hot water over her head.

'Er…Elsie?'

'Mmm?'

'Is the water meant to be this colour?'

Water the shade of what could only be described as fluorescent carrot swirled down the plughole, and she felt a pang of dread as she pulled the towel tighter around her shoulders and steeled herself to take a glance in the mirror.

Dark shock descended and she felt suddenly as if there was a brick in the pit of her stomach.

The aimed-for delicate shade of kissed-by-the-sun-blonde had turned out a rancid head-in-a-bucket-of-sick neon orange. Worse, the usually soft, silky texture of her hair seemed to have ended up somewhere between straw and candy floss.

Her reflection in the mirror gaped at her, lips pulled back from her teeth in a grimace of horror.

'Elsie, what have you done to me?' she howled.

Elsie put down her nail file and peered from the laptop screen.

'Oh, dear. That's a bit intense, isn't it? You can't have followed my instructions properly.'

'Don't you dare blame me for this! I've done everything you told me to do.'

'Perhaps it's the colorant,' Elsie said, pursing her lips thoughtfully. 'I know it had been lying around for a while but that shouldn't have made a difference. There isn't much call for sunkissed blonde in Littleford. Maybe it'll tone down a bit when it's dried. Mind you,' she added, 'it does look quite festive.'

So, under the guidance of her so-called friend, she'd just plastered her hair in out-of-date chemicals.

'Festive?' she yelled. 'The brief was myself, but better. Not *Sesame Street*!'

'What the hell is all the noise about?' Alex snapped irritably, banging the door open.

She saw the expression of annoyance on his face change to one of shock as he caught sight of her hair. She scrabbled frantically to hide it by throwing the towel over her head. Oh, please, not him—not now. Humiliation burned in her cheeks, turning them a shade of beetroot that clashed horribly with her new hair.

'Is that him?' Elsie squawked excitedly over Skype. Her face was suddenly enormous on the screen as she peered closer to the camera. 'Is that Alex? Oh, my God, I'm such a fan. You can't possibly imagine! Jen, could you budge to the left a bit so I can see him properly?'

Jen reached out in exasperation and slammed the lid of the laptop shut.

Alex stared at her, aghast.

'Who was that?' he asked. 'And what in the name of hell has happened to your hair?'

She burst into tears.

He took a step backwards.

'There's no need to cry!'

Livid with herself for making such a fuss, Jen unwound a large corner of the towel from her head and wiped it furiously over her face, swallowing hard to get herself under control.

'I've ruined everything,' she said, between snuffles. 'I might as well throw in the towel on the whole project right now. What's the point in wearing designer clobber when you've got radioactive hair? Looking like this, the only way I could trap a millionaire would be by drugging him. And it's all my own fault for thinking that someone who spends their days putting curlers in pensioners' hair could turn me into Viveca Holt!'

'Viveca?'

Why the hell had *that* particular name sprung to mind? There was absolutely no reason why she would want to look like Viveca. Alex would think this was some sad attempt to make herself attractive to him. She quickly flapped a dismissive hand at him.

'Figure of speech.' She clenched her hands in exasperated fury. 'Oh, if I'd just been a bit more restrained online this would never have happened.'

Clearly confused, he held up a hand.

'You're not making any sense. Calm down and tell me what's going on.'

She took a deep breath.

'I'm on a minuscule budget for my whole project,' she said. 'I've ploughed all my savings into it, but it isn't like I'm made of money. Every penny counts. I went a bit mad buying designer clothes online and realised I had hardly any money left for a makeover. Elsie agreed to show me how to do the whole lot for free,' she said, nodding at the laptop. 'Hair, make-up, nails, fake tan. Only I might as well have entrusted the job to Laurel and bloody Hardy!'

Her temper was on the rise again as her tears dried.

Alex pulled out his mobile phone and began scrolling through it. The bitter reality of what this meant hit home. The final straw.

'Oh, yes, go on—ring the lawyer again!' she said. 'I can't even blame you. Who needs this kind of chaos in their life? I think you'll find there's nothing in that agreement that says you can evict me because of comedy hair!' She raised her voice to a shout. 'I read the small print!'

Frowning, he held up a hand in a shushing gesture. She sank into a chair by the sink and put her head in her hands.

'Marlon?' he said into the phone. 'It's Alex. Great, thanks, and you? Good, good. Listen, can I arrange an appointment? Hair, make-up, styling, the lot. Soon as you can? We'll come to you. Sorry it's out of the blue but it's a bit of an emergency.'

Jen peered out at him from between her fingers, ears pricked up, heart suddenly racing.

'First thing tomorrow? Perfect!'

He hung up.

'Marlon?' she asked.

'Marlon Cobelli. He's the stylist I use when I'm shooting in London. He does a lot of work on my film projects. Bit of a drama queen but he knows his stuff. He'll soon sort you out.'

She saw his eyes dart upwards to the towel on her head. Hope rose as she realised what he was saying, only to be dashed again as the implications clicked into her mind.

'I can't afford London prices!' she wailed miserably.

He rolled his eyes in exasperation.

'I wasn't expecting you to,' he said. 'I'll throw it in with the accommodation. Call it a Christmas bonus—whatever you like.'

Her long-held principles held steady even against the current vile situation. Alex Hammond, cruising through life on a bed of cash. Well, she didn't *do* charity—she did it alone. She slowly shook her head even as her heart plummeted.

'Thanks, but I can't possibly accept that. I'll have to think of something else.'

Maybe she could sell something. She had some jewellery with her—not that it would fetch much.

'Why on earth not?'

'It's nothing personal. I just don't like to rely on other people, that's all.'

'You relied on Scary Laptop Girl.' He nodded at the computer. 'Why such a problem with me?'

'That's different.'

'How?'

'Because she's an old friend who owes me a favour. And you're throwing money at someone you don't even know.'

'But you've just said you'll have to throw the towel in. You'd rather do that, give up on your dream, than accept a bit of help?' His tone was incredulous, making her feel like a stupid amateur.

'This article's all about proving myself, showing that I can make my own success,' she said. She didn't want that principle diluted. She shrugged. 'I don't expect you to understand.'

He was watching her intently.

'Do you think the fact that I roped my friends into helping with my first film for free makes me any less of a success now?' he asked her. 'Or that I borrowed five hundred pounds from my college tutor to buy props?'

'That's different.'

'No, it isn't. It's fine to accept help sometimes. Everyone needs a friend.'

The expression on his face was unexpectedly sympathetic. It made her stomach feel soft and she felt tears approach again.

The fact obviously didn't escape him, because he gave an exasperated sigh. 'Oh, for Pete's sake. I'm under contract to help you with your image, aren't I? Terms negotiated by you in return for which you signed away your beloved freedom of speech. Just look at this as me delegating my responsibilities. Trust me, you'll do a lot better with Marlon on the case than you would with me. I mean, do I *look* like an expert on women's clothing?'

She looked down at her hands, thinking it through. It was this or hightail it back to Littleford. Back to covering country fêtes and dog shows. The thought filled her with despair. And what he'd said made her feel somehow less as if it would be accepting something for nothing. It wasn't a failure to take him up on it. Failure would be to go back. She slowly allowed blissful relief to bubble through her. Before she knew it excitement was back, and without thinking what she was doing she stood up and threw her arms around him.

'Thank you!' she said into his shoulder.

She was suddenly aware of his hand sliding around her waist in response. It sent simmering heat flying up her spine. And the delicious smell of his aftershave made a lovely replacement for the horrendous pungent odour of hair chemicals.

'No need to thank me. I'm doing it for me, really, not you,' he said over her head. 'I'm not sure I could face living with a Muppet for the next four weeks.'

The local hair salon in Littleford where Elsie trimmed Jen's ends every couple of months had a row of hood hairdryers along one side, a waiting room full of gossiping pensioners, a tin of traditional biscuits and a stack of years-out-of-date magazines on the side table. Jen couldn't help comparing it to the glossy mirror-lined walls and spotlighting of Marlon Cobelli's cutting-edge studio. A spiky black Christmas tree stood in one corner. The salon was clearly at the cutting edge of Christmas as well as everything else. It was a world away from anything she knew.

Jen's stereotype of a stylist to the stars involved someone impossibly trendy, bossy to the point of offensive and brutally honest in pointing out things like saddlebags and bingo wings. In pre-emptive self-defence she pasted a don't-care expression on her face and clung to the hope that he would also be the polar opposite of Elsie when it came to styling skills, and this hideous embarrassment would all be worth it.

Marlon turned out to be all of these things. He was also camp as Christmas, and greeted Alex with a smacking kiss on both cheeks. She noticed Alex returned the embrace without an ounce of self-consciousness.

She couldn't help feeling a touch of admiration. Now, *there* was a man who was comfortable with his sexuality. Her ex-boyfriend Joe, who worked as a farm hand and who'd put up with her for six months—a personal relationship best—would have deepened his voice and launched into a football anecdote before running a mile.

'This is Jen,' Alex said, pushing her forward and holding her there, as if he could sense she wanted to bolt back into the background.

The firm slide of his hand around her waist as he stood just behind her made her stomach flutter with more than just nerves. He was close enough for her to pick up the scent of aftershave on warm skin. She swallowed hard and tried to focus her attention on the stylist.

Marlon wore a slim-cut shirt with a flower print over skinny black jeans, and his shoes had the sharpest toe-points she'd ever seen. His eyes widened in surprise as she removed the baseball cap Alex had lent her and shook her horrific neon hair free.

'Oh, my darling!' he exclaimed sympathetically. Then, to Alex, 'We definitely start with the hair.' He bustled over and looped his arm through hers.

She threw a backward glance at Alex as Marlon propelled her from the room. He was settling into the lounge area with its leather sofas and complimentary wi-fi. As she watched he gave her a supportive grin and a wink. Her heart gave a warm and fuzzy little leap in return. He was impossibly gorgeous, and now he'd turned out to be less self-centred than she'd given him credit for. As he opened his laptop she looked away and caught a glimpse of herself in one of the mirrors. She grimaced. That had to have been a sympathy wink. The man dated the likes of Viveca Holt. He wasn't about to be making eyes at Ronald McDonald.

Marlon patted her hand comfortingly.

'Don't worry, sweetie,' he said. 'I like a challenge.'

If that was intended to make her feel better it failed miserably.

Ushered into a swivel chair in the hair salon and swathed in a protective gown, she was assigned a hairstylist who was intimidatingly young and trendy but who turned out also to be very sweet.

'I did a season on that reality talent show,' she confided reassuringly. 'Transforming contestants for the live performances. It takes more than a dodgy dye-job to faze me.'

A couple of hours and a make-up lesson later and Jen couldn't believe the girl in the mirror was her. Her new hair colour was gorgeous, with multi-layered tones of toffee and gold, and long layers made it swingy and glossy. The make-up was subtle—a bit of mascara, bronzer and pink-toned lippy. She could blend in easily with the girls at La Brasserie. Excitement bubbled in her stomach. After everything that had gone wrong, she finally felt as if she might be able to pull the article off, after all.

Marlon reappeared as she stood up and took off the gown.

'You look *fabulous*, darling!' he exclaimed delightedly, but then, as she glanced up to smile at him, he caught sight of the High Street jeans and old T-shirt combo she was wearing underneath and pulled a face. 'Shame about the ghastly clothes. Let's go and look through this stuff you've bought.' He led the way through another door. 'Don't you just love the internet?'

Her heart sank as she followed him into a dressing room with glossy black floor tiles and a three-hundred-and-sixty-degree range of brightly lit mirrors. She'd be able to view her bony hips and flat chest from every angle. Terrific.

He ushered her behind a screen.

Alex flipped idly through his e-mails and ordered another coffee from the starstruck junior. Jen had been gone a good couple of hours now. Enough time for him to finish making notes on a new and exciting script idea which made him itch more than ever to get back to work. Jen was fast becoming the only thing taking his mind off it, and he wondered if there were any other ways he could help her—other contacts he could enlist to help her succeed with her project. Living with her was anything but dull. He never knew what she might throw at him next. He realised with a flash of uneasiness that he was beginning to get off on that unpredictability.

He glanced through an e-mail from his PR company which recommended that he attend a charity ball this week, despite the fact he thought it would be media suicide. The charity funded grants for underprivileged youngsters wanting to build a career in film and Alex was a patron. Surely with the words 'casting couch' hanging over his head it wouldn't take much for a savvy journalist to come up with some sordid story about his association with them.

The PR company didn't see it that way. Reverse psychology, apparently. To be seen at the ball would show he had nothing to hide, that the stories about him and Viveca were groundless tabloid pap when they actually weren't.

It struck him with sudden amusement that his desire to party seemed to be disappearing. Since his life after Susan had been rebuilt as one long social event that was pretty damn unheard of for him. After failing so miserably at family life he'd gone for the opposite end of the spectrum, enjoying his situation to the full with no responsibilities to hold him back.

Worryingly, staying in was beginning to be more attractive than going out.

Once you realised his bonkers exterior was actually total perfectionism, Marlon turned out to be hilarious. And he was clearly harbouring a huge crush on Alex. He was devoted to him.

'He's never done this before.'

Standing in the middle of the circle of mirrors in flesh-coloured underwear, Jen was being treated to a view of her bony straight-up-and-down body that she could most definitely have done without.

'Done what?' she asked.

Marlon glanced up from the rail of clothes. She could see her own purchases in there among other stuff. He must have unpacked them while her hair was being fixed.

'Brought in a waif and stray.' He handed her the catsuit she'd bought with nightclubbing in mind. 'Put this on.'

She began to step into it, hackles rising.

'In fact, he's never brought in anyone on a one-to-one basis like this. We go to *him*, usually. Film sets. Awards ceremonies. He doesn't come to us.'

'I am not a waif or a stray,' she said, trying to look dignified with one leg in and one leg out of the catsuit. 'We have a working arrangement.'

He raised sceptical eyebrows at her over the rim of his statement glasses.

'He's helping me with an article,' she said. 'I'm a writer.' Oh, it filled her with joy to be able to say that to someone. 'He's using his contacts, one professional to another.'

'Sweetie, this is the first time he's ever had me style someone who isn't on his payroll. So you tell me what that means. And you're staying with him?' His voice rose with a hint of awe. 'People would *kill*! You've got closer than the rest of the population in the last five years. Not for the want of trying.'

He winked at her and she shook her head at him.

'You don't understand. We're not *together* at all.'

'Not yet, maybe.'

She didn't tell him she had Alex over a barrel with the threat of a front page tell-all. It was just so delicious to be thought alluring enough for it even to be *plausible* that Alex might be interested in someone like her. She opened her mouth to remind Marlon that Alex had seen her at her worst with her neon hair, but he cut her off with his own horrified squawk.

'Oh, my life! What blind, tasteless person chose *that*?'

Her intended pirouette in front of the scary mirrors in the brightly printed catsuit turned at the last moment into a damp squib of a wiggle. It *was* a designer label, wasn't it? Hadn't it cost practically a week's wages?

'It cost me two hundred pounds,' she said pointedly. 'Second-hand.'

'Sweetie, you were screwed,' he said to her reflection. 'Lesson one: bling does not equal class, girlfriend. Just because you spent a fortune on it, does not mean it will look good.'

He spent the next twenty minutes ordering her in and out of clothes, mixing and matching, adding accessories.

'I can't believe I'm the first person he's introduced to you who isn't working for him,' she said, dragging the subject back to Alex the first chance she got. 'I mean, come on.' She gave him a wink. 'I've seen the papers. He's always dating.'

'Exactly,' Marlon mumbled, then removed the pin he was holding in his mouth to speak clearly. 'He *dates*. That's the important word. It never lasts. He's never really interested and it's usually a mutual benefit.'

'How do you mean?'

'Those women he sees—all the same type, usually up and coming. Maybe with a movie in the pipeline or a DVD release to publicise. Nothing like being seen on Alex's arm to get a bit of exposure, and he gets a no-strings date out of it. Genius.'

'So it's more of a publicity stunt than anything?'

Her heart felt suddenly floaty. Maybe his playboy image was just that—hype, the papers twisting things. Perhaps there *could* be more to his helping her out than the damn agreement between them. He didn't have to do any of this, after all. She would have been happy with a few nuggets of advice from him. Her stomach felt suddenly melty at the thought of his interest in her being more than just... well, a *contractual requirement*.

'Well, of course he beds them,' Marlon said with brutal matter-of-factness, making her floaty heart plummet as if he'd stuck it with a pin. 'I mean Viveca Holt. Exquisite. Of course he beds them—who wouldn't?'

'Of course!' she said, with a chummy laugh that wasn't quite convincing enough to hide the fact he'd stamped on her feelings. Stupid feelings that she shouldn't be having.

'That's all it is, though, darling,' he comforted her. 'Don't you fret. He hasn't shown any real interest in anyone since the nightmare with his ex-wife.'

'I am *not* fretting!' she snapped.

Marlon made a cynical face. *Whatever you say,* it said.

'Did you know Susan?' she asked.

He pressed his lips together in a hard line.

'The wife?' He pulled a face. 'I knew them both. I worked on his first film. I wasn't long qualified myself, then. She was very normal. Not famous. Miss Ordinary. They were at college together.'

So Susan was like her, then. Nothing like the film star conquests Alex was linked to now.

'He's always been very close to his family. Probably thought he had it all. Happy families, career booming. No wonder it hit him so hard when it all went pearshaped.'

He flicked through the rack of clothes and produced a silk shift dress, cornflower-blue.

'You need to cinch in that waist to give you an illusion of curves while making the most of those legs,' he said.

'Did it come as a surprise to you when they broke up? she asked, hungry for more information.

'I think it came as a surprise to everyone—including Alex. Imagine that. You build yourself up from nothing, just get to the point where you don't have to worry about money, and then your wife calls the whole thing off and takes half of everything. Can't have been easy.' He fiddled with the waistline of the dress, not looking at her. 'And of course he didn't have a pre-nup. He wasn't anyone at all when they married, so she really did take him to the cleaners.'

She let Marlon finish the outfit. So the press stories were true. Susan had really hit him where it hurt—in the wallet. No wonder Alex wasn't keen on promoting any of his conquests from overnight guest to a more permanent position.

Had he thought he could trust Susan because she knew

the real Alex? The one before he became a celebrity gold-mine? She could see now why he surrounded himself with superficial relationships.

She was too preoccupied to be shy about Marlon's no-feelings-spared advice. By the time he'd put together out-fits for casual wear, dinner, cocktails and lunches, she was desensitised to standing in her underwear and wasn't even cringing any more.

'I'll just get changed back and then I'll be on my way,' she said, when he announced that he'd finished.

'You will *not*!'

He grabbed her saggy-kneed old jeans out of her hand, balled them up and threw them in the nearest bin.

'There's no going back now,' he said. 'Wear the clothes. Think class, not chav. Get yourself in character and stay there.'

He took her proudly by the arm.

'Now, let's show Alex what he's missing.'

Alex glanced up as the door opened, heaving a sigh of re-lief. He hadn't banked on it taking this long. Clearly what-ever horrific process Marlon had had to put Jen through to restore normality was more complicated he'd expected.

It was a moment before he saw her because she was shuffling nervously about behind Marlon.

'Well, what do you think?' Marlon beamed smugly, stepping aside. 'Isn't she just stunning?' He waited, clearly ready to bask in anticipated praise.

It took a moment for Alex to reply because his tongue had momentarily stuck to the roof of his mouth. When he'd driven her here this morning, half-eaten toast in her hand, his own borrowed baseball hat jammed over her eyes, she'd been girl-next-door Jen, still hanging her head over the monstrous hair mistake, and in spite of himself he'd been beginning to like having around far too much. Somewhere in the last few hours, under Marlon's supervision, the double cream skin had become lightly sunkissed and the ghastly orange hair had morphed into soft golden tresses.

'Wow,' he said eventually, because he'd only just regained control of the hinge of his jaw. A one-syllable word was about the limit of his capability right now. The golden tan made her blue eyes stand out more than ever, and the blonde highlights and freckled nose with her skinny figure made her look like an off-duty model just back from a shoot in the Bahamas.

He suddenly wondered at what point he had thought it would be a good idea to let Marlon loose on Jen. After all, she was never going to look *less* attractive, was she? Focusing on getting her out of her latest scrape with the horror hair and, he had to admit, enjoying the madness of it all along the way, it hadn't occurred to him that he might be making the situation a whole lot worse. If he was getting off on just being around her when her hair looked like a fright wig, it stood to reason that a makeover was only going to make things a shedload more complicated. He could kick himself.

A blush rose in her cheeks, making her look prettier than ever, and she ran a hand self-consciously through her hair.

'Does it look OK?' she asked him. 'Come on—give me your opinion.'

There was an awkward smile on her face that told him she wasn't completely comfortable with this. His heart gave a soft flip. The dark slim jeans made her legs look longer than ever. The shirt looked classy and expensive. She bore little resemblance to the shorts-clad indignant young woman with the bed-hair he'd found in his apartment a few nights ago. His stomach knotted with tension.

OK didn't even start to cover it. The collar of his shirt felt strangely tight, and it suddenly seemed degrees hotter in there. The freezing air outside was suddenly attractive. He'd been cooped up way too long.

'Terrific,' he blurted out. 'Excellent job, Marlon, as ever. We must get together soon and catch up.' He stacked his papers on top of his laptop and got to his feet. 'I need to get back and make some calls.'

What he really needed was to get out of this situation *right now.* He ignored her puzzled expression and made for the front door of the studio, bandying about promises to meet Marlon for lunch soon. Unfortunately not looking at her didn't go any way at all to numbing his sharp awareness of her as she followed him out, her high heels sounding every step she took on the tiled floor.

CHAPTER SIX

It was fantastic to wake up and look in the mirror and actually quite like what she saw for a change. Makeovers were seriously underrated, Jen decided. A few blonde highlights and make-up tips and she felt as if she could conquer the world single-handedly.

As long as the world didn't include Alex.

She squashed the churning disappointment she still felt at his lack of enthusiasm yesterday. He'd made barely any comment about her transformation and had disappeared to his study the moment they'd got back from Marlon's studio. She was furious with herself for minding so much. What was she expecting? That Alex Hammond, who had the pick of the world's most beautiful women, would swoon at the sight of her in a pair of designer jeans?

Yesterday had been a turning point. She'd been building their friendship up in her mind when to him it was clearly no more than a distraction from his own problem situation. He'd been sticking to his side of the gag order, nothing more, and she had been a fool to read anything else into it. Well, she was truly back on task now. Being here was all about work, nothing more. She intended to live the rich life properly, really get into character, do her article justice and make the sale.

Wearing the new jeans and a casual fitted shirt, she made her way to the kitchen for toast.

He was there, looking at his laptop screen with a face like thunder. He glanced up as she breezed into the room and went to the fridge. She removed a pint of milk and went to switch the kettle on.

'Morning,' she said, without looking round. Flatmates, that was all they were. 'Coffee?'

Alex realised he was staring at her with his mouth open and snapped his gaze away.

'Please,' he said automatically, not caring one way or the other about coffee. Watching the lithe way she moved around the kitchen was making him wonder what it might feel like to have those long, long legs wrapped around him.

For the hundredth time since yesterday he wondered just who would end up getting the benefit of her transformation. Who would she be targeting on her next madcap trip out? The thought caused a burning sensation deep in his chest. She might look like a super-confident socialite, but underneath all that gloss she was a kid with big aspirations. He felt an irrational angry aversion to this whole project that was so damned important to her.

'Can't you just write your article based on research?' he said suddenly. 'You know—do a few interviews, surf the net a bit?'

She turned from the coffee to stare at him, a bemused expression on her face.

'Well, I could, if I wanted to be like every other writer out there,' she said. She ran a hand distractedly through the perfectly undone hair. 'The whole point is that I live the experiment. Doesn't matter whether or not the plan works. It's the process that provides the background for the article. It's meant to be light-hearted, remember?'

'You mean it doesn't make any difference whether or not you actually manage to score a date with a guy?'

'Not to my article, no. I could write about where I went wrong and why it didn't work. But it would be great if it did work, because it would give me more material to play with. Why are you suddenly so interested?'

That was a good question. Why the hell was the idea of her throwing herself at some rich Lothario bothering him so hideously? Staring at these four walls was obviously making him lose the plot. He needed to get outside, get some perspective.

He didn't answer. Instead he looked back down at his laptop and forced himself actually to digest the e-mail from his PR manager, which he'd read now three times without actually taking in.

'...stay home as much as possible. Do not allow yourself to be photographed, except at events expressly cleared by us first. Any outings that may bring you into contact with members of the press should be approved by a member of the team...'

He stared at the words, anger finally tipping over the edge. Enough was enough. Right now he didn't care how many people had a stake in this film's success. He just wanted to live his own life again.

He logged out and shut the laptop, glancing up at Jen as she handed him a mug of coffee.

'What are you doing today?' he asked on impulse.

She took a sip of her drink, shrugged.

'Getting out and about,' she said. 'Testing out my new look.'

With a supreme effort he managed to stop himself looking down at her legs again.

'I'm going stir crazy here,' he said. 'Want some company?'

She stared at him, mouth open in surprise.

'Aren't you meant to be under house arrest?'

He stood up.

'A couple of hours won't hurt. I need to get out of here.'

'What if you get recognised?'

He crossed the kitchen and put the coffee down on the counter next to her. She was looking up at him dubiously, as if they were at school and he'd suggested they play some prank on a teacher. There was something irresistibly unspoiled about her. Before he could stop himself he'd slipped an arm around her shoulders and given her a squeeze.

'Don't worry,' he said. 'I've got a few places up my sleeve. And, anyway, what are they going to do? Give me detention?'

'Kensington Gardens?' she said.

He'd brought her to the smaller entrance to the gardens on the Bayswater Road—a low-key gate in black wrought-iron that was less attractive to tourists. So he wasn't completely throwing caution to the wind, then, no matter how stir-crazy he claimed to be feeling. She'd returned his baseball cap and he was wearing it himself today. With that partially obscuring his face, and a jacket with turned-up collar, he didn't seem to be drawing any second glances from passers-by.

He glanced sideways at her.

'You sound surprised.'

'That's because I am. You don't strike me as the kind of person who likes the great outdoors.'

They began walking down one of the elegant tree-lined avenues. The air was crisp but there was a hazy glow of winter sunshine tempering it. The trees were completely bare, dusted icy white. Their breath puffed out in soft clouds.

'Well, that just goes to show how little you know me,' he said. 'Sometimes a bit of open space is just the thing.'

'This is lovely. I've never been before.'

'You should do the sights. You've missed out.'

They began walking again down the avenue of trees. Frost clung to the grass. It felt as if they were walking through a Christmas card.

'Except for the Science Museum,' she added.

'The Science Museum?'

'School trip.'

He grinned down at her.

'London can be a fantastic place for kids,' he said.

'I'll expect you to relocate back here, then, shall I? In a few years, maybe, when you meet the right film star?'

'Very funny.'

'I'm being serious.' She kept her face straight. 'I'll probably be a senior editor by then, maybe on one of those glossy celebrity mags.' She looked up at the sky dreamily. 'I could do a fantastic photo spread. *Alex Hammond and family at their London home.*'

He didn't smile.

'That's never going to happen.'

'I'm a gifted journalist, you know! And I'm aiming high. The cheek!'

He still only cracked a faint ghost of a smile.

'I don't mean your ambitions. I wouldn't put it past you to end up editing *Vogue*. I mean me.' He paused. 'I'm not family material.'

She'd obviously touched a nerve. Her curiosity flared.

'Everyone is family material. Some people just don't know it yet. You're not exactly over the hill.'

'Not me.'

'I thought you had a happy family background? You told me you were close to your parents.'

She deliberately didn't mention his wife.

'I did. I had a good childhood. Hardly any money, but a happy home. Parents who loved me, not to mention each other. Brother who was also a good friend. I'm a psychologist's nightmare—there's nothing they could pin on my upbringing.'

'Don't you want to replicate that, then?' She was genuinely puzzled. 'With your financial position, you could do an even better job than your parents.'

'Yeah, well, I used to think that, too. But look at my life—the public scrutiny, the constant demands. Hell, my own ambition. How does all of that fit with having a family? We were always there for each other. That's how I was brought up. That's why they weren't crazy about my big career ideas. We were encouraged to be happy with what we had. My parents put us and each other first.' He shook his head. 'I can't be a father *and* make films at the level I want to. Not if I don't want to do one or both of those things substandard.'

The sound of children playing grew louder as they neared a playground. She dug her hands in her pockets to warm her fingers.

'Coffee?' he asked as they approached a café. The play area was bathed in hazy sunshine, with tepees and a huge pirate boat climbing frame with kids hanging off it.

'Hot chocolate,' she countered. 'I'll buy.'

He watched her queue for drinks. The place was full of families enjoying the winter sunshine. A long-discarded desire of his own had resurfaced and he crushed it down again. Family life or work success? That same old dilemma. To have both just wasn't an option. He knew that.

His choice was long since made—Susan's betrayal had certainly hammered the last nail in the coffin of any desire for a wife and kids—and he never discussed it. So why the hell was he revisiting it now?

She returned with the drinks and they carried on walking. Her cheeks and the tip of her nose were pink from the cold, frost sparkled on her eyelashes, and he fixed his gaze straight ahead to avoid watching her slowly sip the hot chocolate. As if he needed any more attention drawn to that soft pink mouth.

'There are lots of ways to crack a nut, you know,' she said, wrapping both her hands around her cup. 'My father wasn't there at all and I never felt neglected. It doesn't have to be all or nothing.'

She only vaguely registered two women approaching on the opposite side of the path—until one of them did a sharp double-take as they passed.

'Excuse me?' the dark-haired woman called out.

Jen stopped and turned, was aware of Alex doing the same. The woman was staring at Alex intently.

'Alex Hammond? It *is* you, isn't it?' She elbowed her companion. 'I told you I was right!'

Jen sensed rather than felt Alex tense next to her and squashed her own irritation at the interruption. She had felt for the first time that she was seeing beyond the exterior he showed everyone else. His being recognised now was the last thing he needed. She acted on impulse.

'Hah! He wishes!' she said, loudly enough to talk over any admission Alex might be thinking about making. 'I wish, too, come to that. Wouldn't mind Alex Hammond's money.'

Both women looked uncertainly towards her. Jen crossed her arms and looked appraisingly at Alex. He stared back at her, eyebrows raised.

'Can't say you're the first to say it, though,' she added.

'Really?' The woman eyed Alex with a frown. 'It's a remarkable resemblance.'

'You think so?' Jen said. 'That Alex bloke is far better looking, in my opinion. Roland's eyes are too close together.' She gave Alex a friendly punch on the arm. He was looking at her as if she were completely insane. 'No offence, honey.'

The woman took a couple of steps back, clearly disappointed.

'I was going to get my photo taken with him, post it online. I'm a mad fan. I've got loads of press cuttings about him.'

She saw a look of horror cross Alex's face, could see the unspoken word in his eyes. *Stalker!*

'You can have your picture taken with Roland if you like,' Jen offered. 'Better be quick, though, we're pitching for the management contract on the toilet servicing for the park. On our way to do a quick survey.'

That seemed to do the trick. The women drifted away.

Alex looked down at her, a grin lifting the corner of his mouth.

'Roland?' He said. 'That's the name that springs to mind when you look at me?'

'I was trying to put you as far away from reality as possible,' she protested.

'And my eyes are too close together?'

He fixed them on her and her belly gave an excited little flip in response.

'Nobody's perfect,' she said.

As they began walking again Jen tucked her arm through his. He was sharply aware of it, of the closeness of her. She probably walked arm-in-arm like that with all her friends, but it didn't stop his body reading more into it. Heat zipped up his spine and simmered on his skin just at the touch of her.

'Maybe we should make a move before she realises that actually your eyes *aren't* too close together,' Jen said, glancing over her shoulder. The women seemed to be lingering, still in sight.

He felt an unexpected pang of regret at the thought of ending the outing. He hadn't realised how much he enjoyed her ability to make him laugh, to put a light-hearted spin on every situation. The deep heat in his abdomen warned him that friendship was not the limit of his wanting and he crushed it. He wasn't about to lose control of his feelings just because she happened to make him smile.

'Let's find somewhere and grab something to eat. I know just the place,' he said.

On their way back, just a few turnings away from the apartment, was a small restaurant, smart but relaxed, with dark wood tables and a select menu. Coloured fairy lights were strung around the walls. The sky had darkened as they left the park and a thin veil of icy rain now coated the windows. Jen didn't mind. It felt intimate and cosy. They sat at a corner table and ordered steaks with caramelised onions, thin-cut crispy fries and hot coffee.

'You're not worried about being mobbed? I'd have thought you'd want to go home, not go to another public place,' she said as soon as the waiter had brought their food.

He sliced into his steak.

'I've yet to be mobbed in here,' he said. 'It's off the beaten track so it doesn't get touristy. Plus it's nearly two o'clock. The lunchtime rush is over.'

There were only two other tables occupied besides

theirs. No one gave them a second glance. She forked up some fries.

'So your father left when you were small?' he asked.

Jen felt the age-old defiance kick in. *Do not feel sorry for me.* 'Before I was born,' she corrected, and flashed back an I'm-not-bothered smile.

'That can't have been easy.'

She shrugged.

'You're assuming that he would have been someone worth knowing.'

'You don't know who he is?'

'Oh, I know,' she said, attacking her steak and slicing it into minuscule pieces. 'I just don't care.'

He looked questioningly at her and she put her knife and fork down, sat back for a moment, knowing she should just kill the conversation right there and then. She didn't have to tell him anything about her background. She found she wanted to. Maybe just a little.

'I was the result of a relationship my mother had with him,' she said. 'Well, I say relationship. It was a few nights, nothing more. He was her boss. He was married.'

She looked down at her meal, pushed the steak around a little with her fork, remembering.

'When she found she was expecting me, you can imagine it went down like a rat sandwich.' She grinned up at him ruefully but he only looked at her. 'As far as he was concerned he already had a family and a career. He didn't want to complicate any of that. My mother refused to have a termination so he dealt with it his way. Withdrew from her completely, never acknowledged me, went back to his comfortable life as if I never existed.'

'Your mum didn't spill the beans at all, then? To his family?'

She shook her head. 'She wanted to bring me up herself, without worrying about his intervention, so she never stirred things up.'

She felt a pang of love as she thought of her mother. How dignified she was. She'd accepted a one-off payment and that was an end to it as far as she was concerned. But Jen didn't want to go into that with Alex.

'And he's never tried to get in touch?'

She took a sip of her coffee and thought about the question for a moment, ran her mind back down the years when she'd struggled with that lack of interest from her father.

'No,' she said, and considered how she felt about that. 'It probably bothered me most when I was school age. Only because you don't want anything then that makes you stand out from the crowd. And I wondered if I might hear from him when I hit eighteen.'

'Bit of a milestone?'

She smiled bitterly.

'Also the age when you stop needing maintenance payments. I thought he might show his face. But nothing. So when I hit twenty-one I didn't expect anything, and it turned out I was right.'

'And if he turned up out of the blue now?'

'I couldn't be less interested.'

She forked up some steak and onions and carried on eating her meal, not looking at him.

He watched her. All bravado. No wonder she was so set on proving herself, so desperate for personal success, to show herself as worthwhile. Despite the impression of indifference she gave, it must hurt terribly that her father had never even been intrigued enough about her to get in touch. Not even once.

'Back to the grindstone after this, then?' he said, groping for matter-of-fact conversation, wanting to lighten things up for her. And to distract himself from the compelling need to ask more, dig deeper behind the façade to find the true Jen Brown.

She sighed. 'Yes. Shame, really. I could have spent all day in the park.'

'What's next up on your mad agenda, then? Now you're done with sorting out the clothes and hair?'

'Next I put it all into practice. Get myself into the same room as the target. I'm still on a budget, so I've thought up some ways of throwing myself into the path of eligible men without having to bankrupt myself on gallery tickets.'

Her voice became animated as she talked about her project. Alarm bells began ringing. What the hell was she cooking up now?

'What ways are you talking about?'

'There's a nightclub I thought I might try tonight. Christmas cocktails—that kind of thing. The younger royals hang out there sometimes. It's at the cutting edge of nightlife for the rich.'

He felt as if a bucket of sleet had been sloshed over him. The thought of her putting herself out there in some cattle market nightclub by herself, looking the way she did, filled him with cold horror. No man in his right mind would pass up the chance to spend time with her.

'You are *not* going out on your own to some nightclub,' he said before he could stop himself. 'I don't care if the Queen herself is a patron. You'll end up dead in a ditch somewhere.'

'There aren't any ditches that I'm aware of in Chelsea,' she said. Her excitement seemed to have slipped into obstinacy. 'And what's it to you where I go, anyway? I'd have thought you'd be pleased your part of the deal is finished. I've had the makeover, you've given me free rein to look through your wardrobe, and you've given me some pointers. I'm really grateful for all your input but I can manage on my own now. I've honed my skills and I'm confident I won't be throwing myself at any man worth less than a million.'

Alex was absolutely furious, and not inclined to explore too carefully where that level of feeling was coming from. He struggled to stay calm. He knew her well enough by now to be certain that if he forbade her to do something she'd press ahead with it all the harder. What he needed was something to divert her.

'Actually, I've got a better idea,' he said, thinking on his feet. 'And it would give you a lot more material for your article than you'd get hanging out at some nightclub.'

She looked at him suspiciously.

'What's that?'

'It's a Christmas ball tonight—for the Youth in Film charitable trust,' he said. 'I'm a patron. It's at a five-star hotel in Mayfair. There'll be a champagne reception, dinner, dancing. And an open charity auction. There'll be a big presence there from the film and media world. How about I get you a ticket there instead? You won't be able to move without falling over an eligible bachelor.'

And that way he could keep an eye on her from a distance. Make sure she was safe and not getting herself into any trouble. Surely that was the only reason he wanted her there?

Her eyes widened. 'Those events are way above my budget. They don't let just anyone in. In fact, it's probably not in keeping with the tone of my article—Miss Ordinary would never be able to afford to go.'

He rolled his eyes. Not this again.

'We've been through all this when I booked you in with Marlon. You need to start seeing past your principles if you're going to get the most top-quality material you can and write this thing. Who cares if you don't stick to the letter of the idea as long as you come up with an entertaining article that will blow their socks off? You keep telling me it's tongue-in-cheek. No Miss High Street from the back of beyond is really going to come to London armed with your article and intending to land a rich bloke. It's just meant to be entertainment.'

'I suppose so,' she said. Then she frowned suddenly.

'How come you didn't mention it before?' she said. 'I thought you were meant to be keeping out of the spotlight for a while? I know you've made a break for it today, but Kensington Gardens is hardly a paparazzi hangout.'

'I was in two minds about going, because it's a bit of a sensitive subject in light of the recent press stories about me. *Patron of charity that helps youngsters into film in casting couch scandal*—I can see the headlines now. But this way I'm showing I've got nothing to hide. Plus the charity relies on my profile, and it's a great cause. It would have made a massive difference to me when I was starting out if I'd had access to resources like that.'

She was practically jumping up and down with excitement now.

'Are you sure you can get me in? I can't believe this! I'll be able to get loads of background material.'

She tugged at his arm and leaned forward suddenly, gave him an impulsive quick peck on the cheek. Her skin was against his for a split second, but it was enough to send dizzying sparks sizzling from his skin to his abdomen via his spine. His heart began to race in his chest.

'Thank you,' she said. 'I'll give you a credit in the article.'

He leaned back deliberately in his chair, as if physically distancing himself would have the same effect on his mind.

'That won't be necessary.' He tried to keep himself on task. 'And there will be ground rules. I won't be able to spend the evening with you—you understand that, don't you? This isn't a date.'

She chuffed out laughter and he felt a little piqued. Was it really so outrageous a thought to her?

'Don't be daft,' she said. 'Last thing I need is *you* hanging around me, cramping my style.'

They finished their meal and began walking back to the apartment. Jen upped her pace considerably.

'Come on!' she called over her shoulder.

'What's the rush?' The crisp air caught in his throat after the warmth of the restaurant as he stared after her.

'Are you kidding me? It's going to be the poshest night of my life. I need to get back home and start getting ready.'

He checked his watch.

'But it's only mid-afternoon.'

'And your point?'

'The ball doesn't start until seven thirty. How much time do you need, for Pete's sake?'

She walked back to him impatiently, grabbed his hand and began walking backwards, pulling him along.

'You know what your problem is? You're just such a *man*. I have to look perfect.' Her voice rose excitedly. 'Ooooh, I get to wear my cocktail dress—yippee!'

He tried to stop himself zeroing in on the touch of her hand on his, on her bubbling enthusiasm. As he gave in and let her increase their pace he raised his other hand and snapped his fingers in front of her face.

'Pay attention. We'll have to arrive separately, leave separately, and no acknowledgment of each other beyond basic politeness. I can't afford to be linked with anyone else in the press—not now. The whole Viveca thing will be rehashed if I give them half a chance. So above all—

and this is really important—there cannot be a repeat of the art exhibition debacle. Whatever you do, you must *not* get drunk!'

CHAPTER SEVEN

Rule #5: Get thee to the right locations. Save as much of your budget as you can for some choice tickets to the right occasions. Charity dinners are the perfect choice—they are stuffed with the über-rich, desperate to part with their money for a good cause. All you need to do is watch and make your move...

EVENING wear. *Christmas party* evening wear. Glittery, goldy, silk, satin, velvet. A dream night out.

Make-up applied and hair finished, she held up the dress she'd chosen from an amateurish online photo which had passed Marlon's approval. A sumptuous full-length velvet gown in midnight-blue with spaghetti straps and a low draped décolletage. She put it on, zipped it up and walked down to the dressing room to stand in front of the mirror. It hung on her straight-up-and-down figure like a dishrag and the draped neckline looked like a huge wodge of spare flappy fabric. She took it off.

Thank goodness for shapewear. A girl's best friend.

She shrugged her way into a nude push-up bra and stuffed in the large-sized gel pads. Fortunately she wasn't planning on getting naked with anyone any time soon. They'd be in for a shock if she did. She stepped back into the dress and adjusted the neckline. Unbelievable. She could hardly recognise herself. She felt suddenly absurdly shy. Even though there was hardly an inch of her body that wasn't now fake in some way or other, in this dress she felt like a million dollars.

She glanced at the door, suddenly wanting Alex to see her looking her best for once, instead of her worst. Just to show him she wasn't only country bumpkin Jen. If she could impress him, with his string of supermodel girl-friends, she could impress anyone at the ball.

Before she could chicken out, she stepped into nude heels and made her way out of the room. Heart thumping in her ears, she checked the kitchen, then looked into the sitting room. The whole place was silent.

He'd already left.

Alex had spent what felt like hours mingling, being seen with the right people and saying the right things. Following PR advice, he deliberately hadn't avoided the press stalking the red carpet. He'd given a statement about the stellar work done by the foundation, and waited for the inevitable question about Viveca Holt. When it came he'd dashed off a carefully prepared reply.

'I'm grateful to Viveca for the outstanding work she's done on *The Audacity of Death*,' he'd said. 'Ours is a pro-fessional relationship. Anything more than that is pure speculation and, frankly, I think we should be focusing our attention this evening on the work of this charity in-stead of on idle gossip.'

He'd avoided follow-up questions, instead moving quickly through the glass revolving doors into the cool glossy cream of the hotel lobby, relieved that once inside the building the press were no longer a concern. Ushered to the silver and white elegant luxury of the ballroom, he'd taken a flute of champagne from an instantly present waiter and concentrated on socialising.

Half an hour in and not a foot wrong so far. He should be relaxing into the evening, but he couldn't shake the feeling of edginess that gnawed at his gut.

She was late. He should have insisted she use his driver instead of getting a cab.

He mentally kicked himself into touch. What the hell did it matter when she arrived? Or even *if* she did? This was him doing a favour for a friend, that was all. It meant no more than that.

'Looking for someone?'

Mark Dunn approached, hand outstretched, his wife trailing in his wake. Alex hadn't realised he was scanning the room so obviously. He pulled himself up mentally, forced himself to focus on his friend.

'Just seeing who's shown up,' he said, shaking his hand.

'Nice job with the press,' Mark said. 'You're getting to be something of an expert. Talking of which, how's the resident journalist?'

Late.

He shrugged. 'Since we got the gag order sorted, no problem at all,' he said. 'We barely see each other. She'll be moving out at the end of the month.'

He had no desire to discuss Jen with Mark or anyone else. She was already occupying far too much of his head. It suddenly occurred to him that she might have changed her mind at the last minute and gone to the nightclub, after all, what with her warped principles about not accepting help. The thought made him suddenly feel cold, and he turned to Mark to excuse himself, go outside and ring her on his mobile phone.

The words never made it past his lips. Instead the room seemed to freeze.

He found himself staring, mouth hanging open, over Mark's shoulder at the doorway, past the vibrant buzzing crowd. Because suddenly there she was.

He felt as if his eyes must be on stalks. When had Jen got curves like that? He was sure he would have noticed that cleavage if it had been there before. He could see growing confidence in her assured smile, in the way she walked tall, head held high. She was absolutely stunning.

He felt a thin sheen of sweat break out on his fore-head and ran a finger around his suddenly tight collar. Moisture leeched from his mouth and he cut his eyes away in a hurry.

Oh, he was in so much trouble here.

He should have acted on that initial attraction the first night he'd met her. Seduced her into a quick fling, a few nights of fun—done and dusted. That was the root cause of all this. She'd have been out of his system by now, gone the way of all the others, Viveca Holt included. Instead he'd followed the stupid PR advice and kept his distance. He'd let himself get to know her, and in the process it seemed she'd somehow got under his skin, inside his mind. And he had no idea how to stop her.

Jen was one of a table of ten, and found herself included from the outset in buzzing, friendly conversation. The room was lit by huge chandeliers suspended from an ornate domed ceiling. Christmas flowers and swags of greenery studded with tiny pearly lights made everything festive. Circular tables were dressed in pristine white and silver, with sparkling crystal glasses and perfect silver cutlery. The waiting staff were smoothly efficient. A month ago this situation would have made her quake so badly with nerves that holding a knife and fork would have been a challenge. Now she tucked into the starter of roasted scallops with a celeriac purée without so much as a tremble.

She realised with a pang of something akin to guilt that there was a part of her that could really come to like this opulent lifestyle. Not just the beautiful food and elegant surroundings here tonight, but the luxury of living in a Chelsea apartment, too, and beautiful clothes. She'd spent so long belittling this world in her mind, determined to believe it a façade filled with shallow people, that to admit she was enjoying herself made her feel like a hypocrite. She tried to focus on the fact that this was a means to an end, about work not play. Enjoyment shouldn't come into it.

As the meal finished the auction began, hosted by a well-known comedian who held the room effortlessly in the palm of his hand. The man on her left knew exactly what he wanted. She watched as he treated the just-for-fun ambience with absolute seriousness.

'Not bidding?' he said as he won a weekend of hunting and fishing on an exclusive estate somewhere in the North for an unspeakable amount.

'I don't fish,' she said.

He grinned, raised his glass. 'Richard Moran,' he said.

Mid-thirties, with the most inscrutable dark eyes she'd ever seen made even more striking by their contrast with his fair hair. He was good-looking, she decided, in a menacing kind of a way.

He held out his hand.

She smiled and shook it.

'Genevieve Hendon,' she said. It actually helped, having a false name. It was calming somehow. Jen Brown didn't look like this—didn't come alone to places like these.

'On your own?' he asked.

'I am,' she said. 'I was meant to be here with a friend,

but something came up at the last minute. I couldn't bear to miss it so I came alone. How about you?'

She wanted to get as much background on him as she could in the shortest possible time. No point wasting her energy getting to know him if he wasn't eligible, after all.

He inclined his head.

'I came alone, yes, but I know a lot of people here. This is my field.'

She smiled, pouring as much interest into her tone as she could.

'Would I know any of your work?'

He gave her his full attention. 'Possibly,' he said. 'Have you heard of the *Faith* trilogy?'

Her heart began to pick up speed. The only way someone could avoid hearing of the *Faith* trilogy would be if they lived in a cave. Not award-winning arty stuff, by any means, but a total crowd-pleaser of a swashbuckling adventure franchise. It had broken box office records. She ran through her mental checklist.

Good-looking? Yes, despite the slightly unnerving eyes.

Rich? Definitely, definitely, definitely.

Eligible? Still to be discovered.

'What do you do?' he asked her. 'Are you in the industry?'

She laughed lightly.

'Nothing that exciting, I'm afraid. I'm building up to launching my own bespoke jewellery business.'

Marlon had helped her come up with that occupation. Something creative that might fit in with a wealthy background and didn't have her sitting on her backside living off her trust fund.

The bidding restarted. This time on VIP tickets to a sell-out Christmas race meeting. There was a buzz of excitement in the room.

'Excuse me one second,' he said, standing up. 'Someone I must speak to.'

She took the opportunity to scan the room. The women's outfits were nothing short of stunning, in every jewel colour she could think of and in the richest of fabrics—velvet, silk, lace. The men looked pristine in black tie. Way towards the front of the room at another table she was able to pick out Alex Hammond. She thought him the most handsome man in the room. Her heart turned over softly, making her catch her breath. No doubt along with every other woman in the room.

To her surprise his eyes seemed to be fixed on hers. She'd been expecting him to avoid her like the plague after the pre-ball pep talk he'd given her on the importance of keeping her distance. And now, bizarrely, he appeared to wave at her.

Surreptitiously she took a glance behind her—in case Viveca Holt was at the next table or something. Because surely he wouldn't be blowing his cover, not to mention hers, by openly greeting her like that. Nope, he was definitely waving at *her*. For Pete's sake. She gave him a smile that was more of a grimace and inclined her head as slightly as she could, hoping that would be enough of an acknowledgement to stop him.

Apparently it wasn't, because he raised a hand again. She looked away, heat rising in her face. Maybe he'd decided keeping his distance wasn't so important to him, after all. Her heart rate picked up at the thought. The idea that he might actually be interested in her filled her belly with butterflies and she took a deep calming breath. Tonight was about gathering material, not about swooning like some stupid teenager over Alex.

She would acknowledge him now and then stick to the original plan.

Raising a hand, she waved back to him in what she hoped was a coolly discreet fashion.

'Table sixteen. Thank you very much, miss. The total now stands at one thousand pounds exactly.'

The butterflies in her belly turned into concrete. A blinding spotlight pooled over her, making her blink like an owl. The eyes of the nine other guests at her table swivelled towards her, and she was favoured with approving smiles and claps as she realised what had happened.

She'd just bid a thousand pounds she didn't have on a trip to the races.

The room felt suddenly boiling. He hadn't been waving at her at all. He'd been bidding on the damn auction.

'Any advances on one thousand pounds?' the compère said.

She searched desperately for Alex across the room, but the spotlight made it impossible for her to pick him out. *Please let him bid. Please, please, please.*

Silence apart from background conversation.

She felt perspiration break out on her forehead. Much more of this and her make-up would begin to slide off.

'One thousand, one hundred with the gentleman at the bar…'

The spotlight slipped away as quickly as it had arrived and she felt suddenly as if she could breathe again. She took a calming swig from her wine glass, despite the fact she was determinedly pacing herself. The bidding carried on and she made a conscious effort not to move another muscle while the auction was going on. Crisis averted— no thanks to Alex. Wait until she got her hands on him.

Returning to the table in time for coffee, Richard Moran talked about himself animatedly. Within minutes she'd established he was single. That was all the boxes ticked. The perfect target. Plus he was openly flirting with her.

The problem was she felt anything but enthusiastic about spending the evening with him. As she tried to work out why there was a nagging feeling of disappointment deep inside her, she found her eyes straying far too often to the table across the room where Alex was talking seriously to the stunningly beautiful woman seated on his right.

As soon as the auction had closed the band began a classy jazz set, and Alex watched as Richard Moran led Jen by the hand to the dance floor. He took her in his arms, his hand pressed against the small of her back.

There was no point even bothering to deny it any more. The seething heat deep in his gut was too strong. He was horribly, angrily jealous. Of all the men she could have ended up with it had to be *him*. A business rival he truly disliked. He insisted to himself that this was about Richard Moran, not about Jen, and refused to acknowledge the needling thought that he'd be feeling like this about any man in the room she spoke to.

Good intentions or not, he'd had enough. He had to intervene before she went too far. She wasn't the worldly-wise socialite she was pretending to be. And that meant she was out of her depth without even knowing it. As Moran led Jen to the edge of the dance floor he crossed the room towards them and waited to pick his moment.

'Another drink?' he heard Moran ask.

'Just mineral water, please,' Jen said.

At least she was pacing herself with the alcohol. With any luck she'd keep her wits about her and take on board what he was about to say.

As soon as she was left standing alone by one of the huge marble pillars Alex approached, took her hand and led her firmly back onto the dance floor. The band played a slow number, and the dance floor slowly filled up. He steeled himself against the heat that climbed through his body as he pulled her against him, slid a hand around her tiny waist. The soft velvet of the dress clung to every contour of her body, giving an intoxicating hint of how it might feel to hold her naked against him. The sweet scent of her hair made his mind spin. She looked up at him in surprise, the soft pink mouth close enough for him to kiss her with just a short movement of his head.

With a stupendous effort he focused on the task at hand and hissed at her in an urgent whisper. 'What the hell are you doing?'

Her brows knitted. 'I might ask you the same thing. Thanks to you I nearly bought a trip to a race meeting when I've got zero cash and I loathe horses. I thought you were waving at me. And I thought we were meant to be avoiding each other at all costs.'

'We are,' he said. 'I just can't stand by and watch you spend the evening with Richard Moran without warning you about him.'

She pulled away a little to look up into his face, a puzzled expression in her eyes.

'Why would you want to warn me about him? It's going brilliantly. He's the perfect target. Did you see how high he went with the bidding for that vile hunting holiday? He's obviously completely minted, he's here on his own and he isn't a total nightmare to look at. In my book that ticks pretty much all the boxes.'

'It doesn't matter if he gives millions to charity. He can't be trusted. He'll do anything to get what he wants.'

She came to a standstill, forcing him to do the same. They stood motionless, surrounded by dancing couples. Her expression was fierce.

'He's in film production, isn't he? Just like you.' She held up a hand and cut her eyes away from his. 'Look, I'm really grateful for all the help you've given me, but that doesn't give you some kind of creative veto over my work. I can take it from here by myself, thank you very much. He's perfect, and I'm not backing off just because he happens to be some work rival of yours.'

If only the reason was that simple.

'That has nothing to do with it. I'm looking out for you. He's not a nice guy.'

She rolled her eyes. 'What do you mean?'

'Let's just say he's involved in some pretty shady stuff. If he gets a sniff that you're chatting him up under false pretences it won't be pretty. Don't kid yourself that he'd see the funny side of your damn article. He could ruin your whole career with one phone call if he wanted to. You're not used to mixing with these people. You haven't a clue what you might be dealing with.'

He could see immediately that he'd said the wrong thing. Her eyes widened in anger.

'Don't you *dare* patronise me! Just because I'm not swimming in cash doesn't mean I'm not up to dealing with people who are. You make it sound like I'm some social moron. I thought you were different, but I was wrong. You're just like the rest of them here—certain that you're better than everyone else.'

'I didn't mean it like that,' he said. Where on earth did this paranoia of hers about not fitting in come from?

'I can handle Richard Moran,' she snapped. 'He's never going to know who I really am. It's one evening. That's all. I'm hardly likely to get much further than small talk, but I am going to end up with *tons* of information for my article. So if you could make yourself scarce that would be great.'

She raised her eyebrows and kept them there until he took a step back, and then she turned to walk back across the room to where Richard Moran waited for her like a predator, with a drink in each hand. His blood felt as if it might hit boiling point at any moment. He pushed his way through twirling couples to the other side of the room and was quickly surrounded by people wanting to discuss the evening, the charity, any forthcoming award nominations. He tried to focus outwardly on his own purpose for the evening—being seen to be on the straight and narrow, championing a good cause.

It felt to him as if Jen was lit up by a huge spotlight that kept everyone else in the room in shadow. What was happening to him? He barely remembered his girlfriends' names usually, and now he seemed to be aware of every tiny detail about *her*. The gorgeous curve of her neck softened by the tumbling golden curls, the stunning slender figure hugged in all the right places by the rich velvet of the dress. He wanted to slide his arms around her again and feel her body against his, responding to his every movement.

He forced himself to get a grip. He was meant to be keeping his nose clean, living a quiet life, focusing as he always did on work. She had brought nothing but trouble since the day they'd met. He'd long since given everything to his career, and he damn well wasn't going to let that be compromised again by a woman.

As Jen took to the dance floor again, back in the arms of Moran, Alex forced himself to look anywhere but at them.

Inside he fought the impulse to cross the room and tear Richard Moran's head from his shoulders.

CHAPTER EIGHT

Rule #6: Rich men can always be found near boats, horses and ski slopes. Get yourself to any of these locations and make sure you know what you're talking about.

ALEX unlocked the door to the apartment and tried to engage his tired brain, which currently felt as if it was packed in cotton wool. A reversion to type had seemed like a great idea earlier, as he'd watched Richard Moran twirling Jen expertly around the dance floor. The ideal way to get back some perspective—which he'd clearly lost if he'd begun to obsess like this about a woman.

It was the stress of his recent press exposure. Had to be. Pressure from all sides to get some positive publicity had taken its toll. His enforced abstention from the opposite sex had made him become preoccupied by the nearest woman. One who couldn't be more unsuitable if she tried. She might look delectable, but that didn't compensate for the fact she was a walking disaster area, always causing chaos, always in some kind of scrape.

At first the decision to let her get on with it had seemed a liberating one. Let her spend the evening with that idiot Moran. It didn't mean he had to watch her do it. He'd made his excuses at the ball and gone on to a club. Maybe exactly what he needed was to get back to normal, and have a full-on meaningless fling, and damn the consequences.

The problem was none of the women at the ball or the club had held the remotest speck of interest for him. Try as he might, there was only one woman he wanted to spend time with. He could deny it all he wanted. Apparently it wasn't going to go away.

He headed to the kitchen to make some coffee. He would go to the study, work for a couple of hours. Sleep was beyond him now. The anger that had seethed all evening as he watched Jen flirt with Richard Moran was still simmering just below the surface. And adding to it was hatred of these insane feelings for her that were apparently beyond his control.

'Richard Moran was nothing short of the perfect gentleman,' Jen said airily the moment Alex stepped into the kitchen. For some reason the satisfaction she'd expected to get from saying that to him didn't live up to the anticipation.

'You waited up for me just so you could say *I told you so*?'

Hmm. She supposed it did really boil down to that. Not that she was going to tell him.

He threw his keys on the counter, filled a glass with water from the fridge and immediately downed half of it. *Hah!* Obviously dehydrated. She'd been looking forward to being the sober one with the moral high ground for a change. Surely sloping in at one-thirty a.m. automatically meant a few drinks too many?

Unfortunately not. The green eyes were absolutely sharp and lucid. Worse, the intense way he was looking at her over the rim of the glass was making her stomach feel melty and her pulse pick up speed.

'I am *not* waiting up for you,' she snapped. 'I've got a ton of notes to write up on the evening. Best to do it while it's still fresh.' She waved a hand at the laptop and the notes covering the counter in front of her. 'I just didn't realise it was so late.'

She narrowed her eyes at him suddenly.

'Anyway, how do you know I didn't just get in myself? For all you know I could have been whisked off to dance the night away.'

'Er…you're wearing pyjamas.' He raised an eyebrow and nodded down at her open dressing gown and shorts and vest combo.

Damn. She'd forgotten about that. Understandable, considering how annoyed she was with him. His implication that she was out of her social depth with men like Richard Moran had really rankled. She knew she was overreacting, but she couldn't seem to help herself. It had needled her more and more as the evening had progressed.

When Richard's driver had dropped her home at half past eleven her first thought had been to sweep inside and run through the huge success of the evening with Alex. Prove him wrong. OK, so Richard had a bit of a propensity to ogle her fake cleavage, but she could put up with that because he also loved the sound of his own voice and had given her loads of material to write about. She'd seen no sign of the scary villain Alex had made him out to be.

Having to wait two hours to prove him wrong had somehow made her irritation spread into a massive annoyance with herself for wondering where he was, what he was doing and, worst of all, who he was doing it with. Because she really shouldn't give a damn about any of those things.

No way was she letting on that she'd been sitting here that long. Not when he was obviously more than happy to have got some distance between them. He'd taken her at her word and disengaged himself totally from her and her project. She hadn't even seen him again after he'd warned her off Richard.

So much for his concern for her safety and wellbeing. He was so concerned that the moment their conversation was over he'd disappeared for the rest of the night. No doubt living it up—probably with the exquisite blonde from his table at the ball.

He pulled a stool up next to hers and looked at the mess of papers and the open laptop in front of them. She was acutely aware of how close he was. Well within touching distance. She could breathe in the scent of his aftershave and she felt a dangerous flutter deep in her stomach.

'Aren't you going to ask me how I got on?' she asked.

He took another sip of water.

'Nope.'

'Well, I'll tell you,' she said, ignoring the *here-we-go* roll of his eyes. 'Richard told me all about his home in Hollywood, and his ranch in Montana. Not to mention his mansion in the Cotswolds. He has a yacht, he dabbles in horse racing and he's fed up with airhead women who aren't up to the challenge of stimulating conversation.'

Alex rubbed his eyes with a thumb and forefinger.

'Let me guess—that's where you come in, is it?'

'Absolutely,' she said triumphantly. 'Once you've found out a man's background and interests, you're well on the way to snaring him. It stands to reason. He barely left me alone for five minutes. He was gobsmacked by how much we have in common. Well, how much he *thinks* we have in common.'

He gave a bitter laugh.

'I just bet he was.'

She threw her hands up in exasperation.

'I don't understand this. Why can't you be pleased for

me? I thought we were friends. You've helped me do all this groundwork for my article—getting Marlon involved, helping me prepare. And now, when I start to have some success, when I actually manage to engage a man's interest, you tell me I'm not up to the challenge of dealing with him. Your implication that I'm some hopeless case who can't hold her own in rich company was *so* offensive.'

Elbows on the counter, he ran both hands through his hair.

'That is *not* what I was saying!'

She could tell by the strangled tone of his voice that he was struggling to maintain control.

'I was trying to do you a favour, look out for you, and for some reason—God only knows what—you've chosen to see it as criticism of *you*. You've got this huge chip on your shoulder about fitting into what, let me tell you, is nothing but a false world full of shallow people. Why the hell do you want so much to be a part of *that*? You saw it tonight. It's all about getting along with the right people, keeping them sweet, greasing palms. You think I actually *like* half those people I was with tonight?'

She felt oddly naked, as if he could suddenly see inside her, pick out her insecurities. She dropped her eyes from his as if they were giving her away, fiddled with the papers on the counter.

'It's not that I want to be a part of it,' she said, and in her tired and overemotional state she added before she could check herself, 'It's that I could have been. If my life had panned out differently.'

He frowned. 'You're not making any sense.'

She almost told him then. Who her father was. The way he'd paid off her mother instead of accepting Jen as his child before melting back into his opulent life with his wife and privileged legitimate children. There was so much bitterness there that she didn't know how to start—wasn't sure she wanted to. She bolted back to her comfort zone, where the whole situation was about work and nothing else.

'Forget it,' she said. 'It doesn't matter. What matters is my work. Getting this article finished and sold. And, like it or not, Richard Moran has given me better material than I could have hoped for.'

He clenched his hands, glanced up at the ceiling.

'OK, I apologise! Is that what you want to hear? I'm sorry if I belittled your achievement. That wasn't my intention.'

'What *was* your intention, then?' she snapped.

She sought the answer in his green eyes, waited for him to speak. And in the depths of that moment he was suddenly on his feet, reaching for her, one hand sliding into her hair, cupping the side of her face, tilting her mouth to meet his, the other claiming her waist.

The attraction she'd tried so hard to crush since she'd lain beneath him that first night flooded back. Sparks tingled on her skin at his touch, zinged down her spine, and heat seemed to pool at the top of her legs. If it hadn't been for the stool she might well have folded like jelly onto the floor.

The space between them was hers for the taking, and before she had time to think take it she did. She was on her feet, too, palms sliding up the taut muscle of his chest to meet around his neck, fingers sinking into his hair. His hand curled around her waist in an urgent caress as he moved backwards again to the stool, hooked one foot around her and pulled her greedily into the gap between his legs. He moulded her body hard against his and she moved her hips against him in response. She could feel the effect she was having on him. He uttered a low guttural moan. She felt his hand slip beneath her pyjama vest, sliding across her skin and making her jump and writhe with desire. The other hand tangled in her hair, tilting her head to the perfect angle as he parted her lips hungrily with his tongue.

Only now she'd responded to him did he take full control. And that was what finally made common sense kick back into her spinning mind.

Better late than never.

Equal responsibility. That was how he wanted it. No comeback. That was how he played it with women, wasn't it?

He was obviously missing his social life. He'd gone out partying after the charity dinner, had stuck to his stupid single-in-public rule. Was that because he knew he had his own manufactured socialite back at home, gag order in place, ready to go? She'd turned herself into his kind of arm candy, signed away her right to tell anyone what happened between them and suddenly—what a coincidence—she was fair game.

She disengaged herself from him, took a good couple of paces backwards. He didn't protest, didn't try to move towards her. He simply stayed where he was on the stool, watching her. He rubbed his lips with his fingers as if savouring the taste of her.

She tried to take control of her racing heart.

'Got your gag order in place so now it's all systems go?' she said, trying not to pant.

His eyes held hers, widening slightly in surprise.

'The gag order has nothing to do with this,' he said.

'Really? Your models and actresses are off the menu, aren't they? I've been living under your roof these past couple of weeks and the only time you noticed the way I looked was when my hair turned into a fright wig. But add a load of gloss and fake extras…the nails…the breasts…

and get yourself a gag order—suddenly I'm up for grabs. Now that I look like a clone of one of your conquests.'

He smiled at her, the lopsided grin melting her very bones.

'I can see where you might get that idea from, but you're wrong,' he said. 'The agreement has nothing to do with this. I wanted to kiss you. You gave as good as you got. Don't try and hide that by criticising my motives. Why kiss me back if you didn't want to?'

She ignored him—along with the frantic pounding of her blood and the vague sense that she might be overreacting.

'I know the kind of man you are. Your life is an open newspaper. The women you step out with are the kind who spend a fortune on their appearance and always look perfect. It's obvious that's what does it for you these days.'

'So you think you only look good to me now you've spent hours getting your hair and nails and goodness-knows-what-else done?'

He got down from the stool, closed the gap between them so that she needed to look up to watch his face. She was hotly aware of his muscled body inches from hers, of every cell in her body wanting to take that one pace back into his arms.

She stood her ground and looked at him boldly. 'In a word, yes.'

He gazed right into her eyes as he spoke.

'You. Are. Gorgeous,' he said. 'In that dress tonight. In jeans and a T-shirt. And most of all in these hideous short pyjamas with your hair looking like you've spent the night screwing instead of sleeping. I really wish you weren't. The idea was for me to avoid women, play the single professional for a bit, and having to share my roof with you, and those legs, was *not* part of the plan.'

Her oversensitised body fought for control over her mind. She was furious with herself for responding to him and livid with the unfairness of it all. The strongest physical reaction she'd ever had to any guy and it had to be someone like him—someone who held all the cards.

'And you see this as more than a one-night stand, do you?' she asked. 'More than your usual casual fling? You want to step out with me in public? Or maybe introduce me to your parents? Are you looking beyond tomorrow morning for a change? Possibly the end of the week? Maybe New Year?'

He simply looked at her. And in his silence she realised how stupidly disappointed she was.

She was most definitely *not* going to have a fling with him. No matter how gorgeous he was. No matter how much her body wanted her to. She was in total control here. Let him realise he wasn't irresistible. Kick that arrogance into touch. So his kiss turned her legs to jelly? That didn't mean she had to betray the effects, give him the satisfaction.

His lips were inches from hers.

'It isn't going to happen,' she said softly, looking into his eyes. His warm breath mingled with hers. 'I don't do rich men, I don't do flings and I definitely don't do flings with rich men. Especially ones who manipulate their way through life with gag orders, contracts and cash. So why don't we stick to our own plans? I'll get my article finished and be out of your hair by Christmas. And you can get on with sorting out your reputation. If you've still got one.'

With enormous effort she took a step back from him, then put another pace between them, and another. His gaze didn't waver, meeting hers without a hitch until she cut her eyes away and left the room, slamming the door behind her. She knew just from the way her nerves were on edge that she'd be lucky to get any sleep tonight, but she didn't care. She was in control, not Alex, and that was the only thing that mattered.

Alex stared for a long moment at the closed kitchen door. She'd had to kick the doorstop away because she was so determined to have something to slam. If his head wasn't so mixed up he might have found that amusing.

Desire burned deep in his abdomen. He rubbed his fingers slowly over his mouth again. He could still taste her, still smell her. His senses were vibrantly alive. He couldn't remember the last time he'd felt so tuned in to a woman, and he was so damn sexually frustrated he felt like gnawing the granite worktop.

Kissing her hadn't been the plan. Of course it hadn't. He'd been fighting those mad feelings like crazy all evening. And suddenly those soft lips had been against his. He was shocked by the overpowering hunger that suffused every part of his body. Rational thought was driven away. The pent-up anger and jealousy he'd suppressed all evening as he watched her in someone else's arms boiled to the surface. His one desire at that moment was to kiss and kiss and kiss her again, and ride that delicious wave as far as he could.

He stood up and made coffee. The familiar motions of filling the mug, adding milk, calmed him, brought a more solid reality back.

It gnawed at him that she'd painted him as some kind of predator, out to take advantage of her. And it annoyed him even more that he cared so much what she thought. He'd had a lucky escape. He was tired, wasn't thinking straight. She might look like Miss Chelsea now, but underneath she was country village girl through and through.

Miss Ordinary. Like Susan. Do-not-touch-with-bargepole. Rationality clicked coldly back in.

He drained his coffee and threw the dregs down the sink. As he made his way to his bedroom he felt the momentary lapse in control disappear. She'd done him a favour, backing off like that. The next time he saw her he'd make sure he kept a safe distance. Physically and mentally. And surely now her work would be done she'd be moving out. That was a good thing.

Yet sleep was still a very long time coming.

On edge through lack of sleep, Jen was dressed by seven, making coffee and breaking eggs into a frying pan. She added milk and began to scramble them. Her head felt fuzzy and out of focus.

Alex came into the kitchen and her heart skipped a beat. Despite her mental determination to put distance between them her body was apparently refusing to stand down. Even when obviously tired he still looked gorgeous. He poured his own coffee. The tension in the room was palpable.

'Hi,' she said uncertainly.

He barely glanced around.

'Morning.'

'I'm going to be working on a draft of my article today—the material I've got so far. I thought I'd set myself up in the den, if that's OK with you?'

There was a pause, as if he was considering whether to mention the elephant in the room.

'About last night...' he said.

She'd prepared for this. Somewhere in the long restless hours between leaving him in the kitchen and finally giving up on the prospect of sleep.

'There was no last night.'

He looked vaguely amused. 'You can deny it as much as you like. I was there, too, remember?'

'I meant what I said. Let's just be professional. Concentrate on our own lives.'

'I couldn't agree more. But first, for the record, I did *not* take advantage of you, despite your determination to paint things that way. You kissed me back.'

'You made me.'

He laughed in disbelief. 'I'm sorry?'

'I said, you made me.' She had to admit, as arguments went, it wasn't her strongest.

'I've only known you a matter of days but I think I can say with confidence that I can't imagine anyone *making* you do something you didn't want to. Ever.'

Deep down there was the frustrating reality that he was right. She *had* kissed him back. But only after *he'd* instigated the intimacy. She rounded on him, determined to put an end to this once and for all.

'However you want to paint things, we both played a part,' she said. 'I don't see why this has to turn into a huge *atmosphere*. I just want to make it clear that last night was a blip. I'd never be interested in a one-night stand.' She tipped the eggs onto a plate. 'It's nothing personal.'

He gave a bitter laugh. 'One-night stand? Is that what you think it would be?'

'What do you expect me to think? You don't do relationships. You do work. You made it clear how you live your life. You want short-term flings with no comeback. That's fine by me, but I'm not about to be a one-hit wonder. Not for any man.'

Alex thought of Susan. The sweetness of their early relationship, the distance that had grown gradually between them as his work became more and more demanding in line with his success. And the end, when he'd realised he no longer knew her at all. If he ever had. The side of the story the press hadn't covered.

'Of course you're at such an advantage because you think you know all about me,' he said. 'Everything there is to know about my past. Because everything printed about me is, of course, always true.' His voice rose to an exasperated snap.

She didn't rise, kept her voice calm. 'Tell me what you're really like, then. What am I missing? Why shouldn't I believe everything I read about you?'

How the hell was he supposed to answer that? And, more to the point, why did he even want to? She had the weight of years of tabloid stories on her side, painting him as a playboy. He'd been linked to so many women. Some were just speculation, but plenty had been correct. Oh, yes, the papers had made much of the financial cost of his divorce. But there had been other costs, too—ones which didn't make such great column inches. He was so much more newsworthy as a bachelor playboy rather than a workaholic who dated superficially because he had no time to be a family man.

He gripped the edge of the granite counter, took a breath, and wondered where to start. Wondered whether to start at all.

The sound of the exterior intercom buzzing cut like a knife through the tension in the kitchen. For a moment both of them stuck to their rigid defensive posture. Jen looked at him expectantly for what she was no doubt certain would be a rubbish explanation. Then she threw her hands up and left the room for the front door.

He heard her speaking, heard the door open and shut, and then she re-entered the room. The only visible part of her was the long legs. The rest was obscured by a gigantic arrangement of red roses, holly berries and Christmas greenery. An explosion of red and green, vulgar in its hugeness. He felt his jaw drop.

She heaved the arrangement onto the kitchen table. He couldn't help noticing that her cheeks were flushed pink with excitement as she emerged from behind the flowers. She pulled out the card and flipped it open.

A sharp intake of breath gave away her delight. 'They're from Richard Moran!' she said.

Of course they were. Hadn't he known that the moment he saw them? The man had no style. The massive bouquet dominated the room. Moran had never been one to stick to the mantra of less is more.

Lack of subtlety didn't seem to make a poor impression on Jen. She looked at him, card held aloft, delighted excitement in her eyes.

'He's invited me to the racing!' she gasped. 'That VIP Christmas meeting I accidentally bid for. He must have thought I wanted to win it and couldn't afford to go higher!'

Alex felt a nauseating stab of jealous irritation that told him that, however hard he denied it, last night's kiss definitely meant more than he wanted it to. What a creep! He couldn't believe she was falling for this.

'You can't seriously be thinking about going? You just finished telling me how much fantastic material you've got. How much more do you need, for Pete's sake?'

She looked at him with an incredulous expression.

'Of course I'm going! Are you insane? I need to ride this out as far as it goes now. That's the whole point of the article. This is better than I could ever have hoped.'

'The longer you go on with this, the more likely it is he'll clock who you are. It might have been OK last night, with all those people, the dancing and the auction in the background, but if you spend the day at the races, just the two of you, he's bound to ask you some awkward questions.'

'Your confidence in me is really heartening,' she said, giving him a sarcastic grin.

'Your insistence on pushing ahead with the project is very telling,' he snapped back angrily. 'Are you sure it's *really* still about the article? Are you sure you're not getting carried away with the moment?'

The flush on her cheeks intensified and she cut her eyes away from his.

'Don't be ridiculous! Nothing is more important to me than nailing this article. Everything is riding on it. All my savings are sunk into it, and my future career depends on it. I don't care what it takes.'

'Don't you think you might be protesting a bit too much? You don't care if you're taking a risk because you're so busy swooning over your new fake life, being wined and dined by a millionaire. So much for social experiments.'

He knew he'd touched a nerve. Fury took over her face.

'You have absolutely no idea what you're talking about. I am here to work. Last night was about research for my article—not cosying up to some rich guy, getting what I could out of it. This whole thing is about making my own success without the need for any of that.'

'You expect me to believe that?'

'I don't care if you believe it.'

'I've seen all this before, you know. Starting out grounded, determined the lifestyle won't change you. Then you have a taste of the high life, start to enjoy the trappings. It's one slippery slope to letting the luxury take over. You lose your grip on reality, on what was really important to you at the outset.'

He saw from the knit of her eyebrows, the sudden

shrewd gaze, that he had her full attention now. But her next question still floored him.

'Are you talking about yourself?' she said.

He wanted to kick himself for giving away so much, and cursed her insight.

'Not just about me,' he said shortly.

'You mean your marriage?'

He was done with this conversation. 'Yes, I mean my marriage. I won't bother to elaborate. I'm sure you already know all the details as you're so up to speed with the press coverage of me. And if you don't you can always research me on the internet.'

He left the room. Left her to the flowers. He didn't see her blush because she'd actually done that way back, on the first day she met him.

CHAPTER NINE

'LET me get this right. Alex Hammond snogged you and you've told him you're not interested?' Elsie's incredulity was immense. 'Have you lost your mind?'

'No, I haven't! And that's exactly the point. I'm in total control of the situation. Men like Alex Hammond do not go for women like me. Not for any good reason, anyway. He only took an interest because he's had to swear off women after all that stuff about Viveca Holt in the news. He can't get his hands on one of his usual conquests so he thought he'd have a punt at me. He'd probably cosy up to a gorilla right now if it had a makeover and signed a gag order.'

'Who cares what his reasons are? You passed up the chance of a fling with Alex Hammond!' Elsie spoke as if Jen had won the lottery and handed the ticket back.

'Yes! Exactly! All it would ever be is a *fling*. Because that's all he ever has.' Jen smoothed her hair back from her face, took a dignified breath, drew herself up to her full height. 'I'm better than that.'

Perhaps if she said that often enough, in lots of different ways, she might actually begin to feel as triumphant about her decision as she wanted to feel. Instead of this miserable dragging in her stomach as if the butterflies he'd evoked there last night had been doused in icy water. The idea that she might be different, more than a week-long fling, was something she refused to entertain. She'd bet all his girlfriends thought they'd be the ones to change him, and if Viveca Holt hadn't managed it Jen from the country wasn't likely to, was she?

She made a huge effort to squash everything out of her mind apart from her article. It was about time she got her mind back on task.

'Only problem is, now I need some background information on horse racing and I can't ask him. I'm having to rely on the internet and I feel like I'm floundering. I don't suppose you know anything?'

'Nope. Sorry.'

Impossible to distract, Elsie returned to the subject that mystified her. 'Was he a good kisser?'

Just the flashback that question prompted made Jen feel like melting into a puddle on the floor.

'I'm not going to answer that,' she said. 'I'm going now.'

She moved to press the disconnect button, but not before she managed to catch Elsie's parting comment.

'That means yes.'

Rule #7: Never fall at a millionaire's feet. Remember he has hundreds of women doing that. Remain cool, classy and in control at all times.

It turned out that the careful couple of glasses of champagne at the ball—just enough to make her feel confident and bubbly, not enough to turn her into loudmouthed ladette—combined with the twinkly subdued lighting, had given her a bit of a rose-tinted goggles effect when it came to Richard Moran.

Perching uncomfortably on one side of the leather back seat as his car purred smoothly towards the racetrack, it briefly occurred to Jen that Alex's warning her off him might also have pushed Richard up a few notches on the attractive scale. She'd been told many times, mainly by her mother, that there was a definite streak in her that didn't appreciate being told what to do.

In the cold light of day Richard was ogling her cleavage rather too much for comfort. Then again, the moss-green dress with its pretty floral print and empire line didn't need stuffing with chicken fillets to make it look half decent. Perhaps he was simply wondering where her curves had gone.

His incessant talking about himself and name-dropping was also beginning to grate on her, and his hands were getting a bit wandery, making her grateful to whoever had invented the maxi-dress that it banned access from ankle to neckline. She sat up stoically in the seat. She wanted so much to write a mind-blowingly brilliant article. One the editor of *Gossip!* magazine simply couldn't refuse. The consummate professional, that was her. She was prepared to do anything to pull that off.

She wriggled away as Richard's hand brushed her thigh.

Not quite anything.

Alex drained his fifth coffee and tried to apply his caffeine-buzzing mind to his work. Just his work. Everything else excluded. Doing that was meant to be second nature by now. Relationships, *people*, didn't distract him like this. He didn't allow them to.

The attitude he'd taken—let Jen go her own obstinate way and see how far it got her—had become somehow harder to stick to the moment the front door slammed behind her.

He was concerned about her.

Whatever else that kiss had meant, he didn't know. Wasn't sure he wanted to know. Concern was the first step on a slippery slope towards caring, and he no longer did that. But somewhere along the way they'd become friends, and he couldn't now just let this go. It hadn't been so bad at the ball. He'd been around to keep tabs on the situation. This was completely different. She was on her own.

Richard Moran was not just a ruthless businessman, he also had a very nasty accusation of sexual harassment lurking in his not-too-distant past. An accusation hastily dropped, yet rumoured to be true. And that was just one of many indicators of the unsavoury side of his personality.

Alex threw his cup into the sink and grabbed his keys. However things were between them, he should never have let Jen go today. He might as well have let her go swimming with a very hungry shark. She wouldn't thank him, he knew that, but anything would be better than sitting here driving himself nuts. He'd blag his way into the VIP enclosure when he got there.

The Christmas race meet was a jovial affair. The VIP enclosure was festooned with decorations in subtle shades of blue and aqua, perfectly co-ordinated. Spicy mulled cider and canapés were served in the warmth of the glass-fronted bar as horses thundered past outside, their breath clouding the frosty air.

After talking about himself for the entire car journey, Richard Moran seemed alarmingly determined to turn the tables on her as soon as they arrived. It was much harder to work the perfect date when you were constantly being kept on your toes about your fictional background.

The first person he introduced her to turned out to be a successful jewellery designer with her own exclusive studio and website. Jen felt a line of perspiration break out along her spine as Richard mentioned her own invented jewellery business, and then watched beadily as she tried

not to squirm while fielding questions about what was and
wasn't hot in jewellery right now.

As the afternoon progressed being with him felt more
and more like walking on eggshells.

She'd no sooner pasted on a breezy smile as he introduced her to Annabel and Cosmo—'Old, old friends, darling. Cosmo and I studied together at Cambridge.'—than
she was fighting back a wave of nausea as he pointed
out that Annabel had attended the fictional private school
she'd chosen.

'Prior Park College, wasn't it? You must have been there
around the same time,' he said.

Annabel flicked back her glossy chestnut bob and surveyed her with perfectly made-up eyes.

'I don't remember you,' she said.

'Ah, well, it's a big school, isn't it? Perhaps we were
there at different times.' Jen groped desperately for a way
to change the subject.

'What house were you in?'

'Aha! Those canapés look delicious!' she gabbled.

She made a beeline for a waiter a few paces away and
returned munching a port and stilton tartlet. She couldn't
think of any other way of causing a diversion, and etiquette
rules forbade her from speaking with her mouth full. She
glanced at Richard and realised with a cold flash that she
wasn't doing half as well as she'd thought she was. He gave
her a penetrating look which made her nerves fray. She
tried to stop the rising heat in her cheeks by force of the
mind, certain that he would pick up on the slightest blush.

He was suspicious of her.

The friendly, upbeat façade had switched like lightning
to coldness, and she felt a dark twinge of unease as she
remembered Alex's warnings about him. She suddenly
wished she'd heeded his advice and quit while she was

ahead with the success of the ball to write about. But, no, she'd been so stupidly flattered by the in-your-face flowers and attention, and the idea of proving a point to Alex, that she'd failed to keep a clear head.

Her only option was to stick to her story and try to avoid being alone with him.

Richard drew Cosmo aside for a private discussion, and Annabel propelled Jen towards a group of glossy women who eyed her up and down as if she was some new and interesting life form. She took a deep breath. *Intimidated* didn't really cover it, but at least Richard was distracted.

'You can always count on Richard to bring along someone new.' Annabel gave a tinkly laugh.

Jen bit back a sarcastic reply. Yes, she knew he was a playboy—but surely it must be bad form to point that out?

She soon found that belittling the girlfriend of a rich bachelor was practically a sport in itself among these women.

'I had that dress, too—what a coincidence! It's darling, isn't it?'

Jen glanced at the skinny blonde woman, introduced to her as Sukie.

The three other women leaned backwards in unison and looked at her dress. As a spectator she might even have found it funny. She concentrated hard on keeping her posture relaxed.

'Thank you,' she said.

'Designer. Last season.'

Jen didn't miss the challenge. Pointing out that the dress wasn't brand-new was an underhand move. She didn't rise.

'Unfortunately I had a bit of an accident in mine,' Sukie said. 'Someone spilled red wine down it at a wedding back in January. Landed mainly on the hemline. I remember it flapping around my ankles all wet. I could never quite get the…' her voice trailed off '…stain out.'

If this had been a movie the camera would have moved in on Jen for an immediate close-up. She tried desperately to keep a dignified look on her face when what it wanted to do was fold in on herself. Four pairs of beady rich eyes swivelled downwards to the hem of her dress. Jen didn't need to glance down herself. She could tell just from their expressions what she would see if she did. The sweet floral print on the deep green fabric was busy enough for the stain to blend in on cursory checking. If you didn't know it was there you would miss it. Turned out, she had.

'I donated it to Oxfam,' Sukie added, to no one in particular. 'In Knightsbridge.'

So Sukie had no compunction about donating imperfect clothing to charity without pointing out the flaw. Jen really couldn't give a damn what someone like that thought about her. Her temper flared.

'I'm all for wearing second-hand clothing,' she said. 'Too much emphasis is placed on the price tag in my opinion. No one cares if it costs more than a car as long as it's by an in-vogue designer. It's incredibly shallow. And by the way…' she frowned at Sukie, who took a step backwards '…you were supposed to point out to the store that there's a stain on the dress.'

She realised that the elegant, quiet tone she'd consciously been trying to maintain had disappeared and her loud voice was making heads turn.

Richard Moran swiftly rejoined the group, tumbler of whisky in hand.

'What's going on?'

'Genevieve appears to be wearing one of Sukie's cast-offs,' Annabel said smoothly, with that tinkly laugh again. 'I think she's finding the situation a little awkward, Richard.'

Jen's heart plummeted. Not one face in the group was friendly. They saw her as an impostor, and she supposed that was exactly what she was.

Richard Moran grabbed her by the elbow and pulled her aside.

'Do you want to tell me what's going on here?' he barked in a stage whisper. 'Your big talk about a jewellery business just doesn't stack up, you fobbed Annabel off when she asked about school and now it turns out your dress is from a charity shop. What are you? Some kind of stalker?'

Jen felt a hot flash of contempt at the way he was treating her. And he thought she was pursuing him because she was infatuated? How arrogant could you be?

'Don't be ridiculous.' She yanked her elbow free and snapped impulsively, 'I'm not a stalker. I'm a journalist!'

The words were barely out of her mouth before he'd grabbed her a second time, one arm clamped around her waist, the other digging sharply into her arm. The black eyes had a sinister tinge in them. He pulled her hard towards the roped-off exit.

She struggled. 'What are you doing? Let go of me.'

He clamped her against him and spoke with absolute clarity in her ear as he propelled her along. She was vaguely aware that he was simultaneously smiling and nodding at people as they passed. Keeping up appearances.

'You are going to walk out of here with me without making any fuss,' he hissed. 'We are going to go somewhere quiet and you are going to tell me exactly what you are up to and who you are working for.'

His grip bit bruisingly hard into her arm and she felt the first dark tendrils of real fright twisting their way through

her. Her instincts told her Alex had been right. This was
not a man to be trifled with. She forced her whirling mind
to *think*. She needed to get herself away from Richard before he could find out any more about her. Thank goodness she'd used a false name. If she made a run for it there
was no way he could trace her.

Gathering all her strength, she kicked him as hard as
she could in the shins—but instead of releasing her he
unclamped his hand from her arm and grabbed a handful of her hair. She struggled madly and drew in a huge
breath to scream.

The sound died on her lips as Richard Moran lurched
suddenly sideways. Letting go of her, he fell into a nearby
dark blue spiral Christmas tree. She stumbled to keep her
own balance. As he got to his feet, covered in blue glitter
and dabbing the corner of his mouth with the back of his
hand, she found herself dragged away at speed.

It was Alex.

He'd come, after all.

They barely spoke at first as the car sped back to London.
Her emotions were in turmoil. Hideous disappointment at
the failure of Mission Racing churned deep in her stomach along with the humiliation of being manhandled to the
exit, VIP heads turning her way. The dreadful feeling of
being frighteningly out of her depth was something she
loathed. But underneath it all there was a tentative glim-
mering of deep-down happiness at what Alex's dramatic
intervention might mean.

He'd bailed her out again. This time at huge cost to
himself. Would he really do that for a potential one-night
stand he never needed to cross paths with again?

Eventually she could stand it no longer.

'Thank you,' she said. 'For not saying it.'

'Saying what?'

She gave him a rueful smile.

'I told you so. The temptation must be huge.'

She saw the tension in his shoulders soften a little.

'It is,' he said.

Silence fell again.

'VIP tickets weren't as scarce as they made out, then,' she said. 'Seems a bit of a scam.'

'What?' He glanced at her.

'The auction,' she said. 'The other night. I almost got stung for a grand on supposedly gold-dust tickets, but you just strolled in like you owned the place.'

Strolled in was actually way off the mark. Vaulted into the fray was more like it.

He stared straight ahead.

'No big deal.'

'No big deal? You *hit* him! There were enough diamond-encrusted mobile phones in that VIP enclosure to guarantee you a place on tomorrow's front pages. You're probably already an internet sensation.'

'I don't care,' he said.

Her stomach gave a dizzying flip. Being rescued shouldn't really sit well with her lifelong determination to go it alone. And yet the deliciousness of it took her breath away.

They were almost at the apartment now.

'What about the movie? All your PR rules? You've probably broken every single one in the space of two minutes.' The grief this was likely to cause him suddenly hit home, and she felt a sickening stab of guilt at what she'd dragged him into.

'Yeah, well, I've spent my entire career worrying about how my every move affects my work, chasing success at the expense of everything else. Maybe I just decided to do what I want for a change, without reference to any of that.'

'So all this is about you making a point? Nothing more?'

'What do you mean?'

'All this…' She waved her hands in an all-encompassing gesture. 'Everything you've done. Gatecrashing the racing.'

He pulled the car to a standstill in his apartment's parking space, turned the engine off, got out. She followed him into the lobby, waiting for an answer.

'Come on,' she said. 'Am I just a distraction because you've been forced to stay in and miss the party for a few lousy weeks? What's this all about?'

He stopped, laughed into the darkness.

'A distraction?' he said. 'You're right. I've never been so distracted by anything or anyone. And it has nothing to do with my PR team or the award prospects for my damn movie.'

In two quick strides he was right back beside her. Her stomach melted into softness.

'I should never have let you go with him today.'

'Then why did you?'

'Because you were so determined to prove a point, and you would have argued me down until you were blue in the face.'

He looked up at the ceiling briefly.

'And because I didn't want to admit how much I want you.'

Heat tingled through her as he slid one hand firmly around her waist, traced the other along her collarbone. Sparks jolted deliciously down her spine.

'Since when?'

He smiled down at her.

'To be honest I think I was halfway there the first

night—just finding you in the apartment like that, with your long legs and all that attitude. But I think what really sealed it was the orange hair.'

All sense and rationality left her, pushed out by the intensity of the desire that rushed through her under his touch. She let her arms circle his neck, let his thick hair slide through her fingers. The green depths of his gaze met her own. She felt as if her knees had melted and might quit holding her up very soon.

'I could always dye it back,' she said into his mouth, and she felt the grin on his lips as he kissed her, his hands sliding lower to press her hard against him.

She felt him tighten his hold enough to lift her and then he was walking down the hall, her toes skimming the floor in the semi-darkness. She heard him mash the key blindly into the lock as he kissed her hungrily. Then, as he carried her inside and kicked the door shut behind him, all reservation was gone. She locked her legs behind his waist and let him carry her through to his bedroom.

Sunlight slanted into the room through a chink in the heavy curtains and fell on the pillow next to Jen, pulling her back to consciousness. Alex's side of the bed was empty. She slid her hand beneath the cover.

Still warm.

She glanced around, collecting her thoughts. The room was pure Alex, like the rest of the apartment. Nothing personal or sentimental. No indication that he'd put down roots here. It felt like sleeping in a hotel room. A very expensive one. A full flashback of what had happened between them zoomed into her mind and she threw the sheets back quickly.

The deep feeling of hot euphoria that had enveloped her very bones at the feel of him the previous night was fast regressing into cold tension. She stood up, glanced round the room for her clothes. Her panties had somehow ended up under the chest of drawers, and she hooked them out and stepped into them.

What had she done?

Carried away by her very own Sir Galahad, stepping in yet again to save her. Was that what had removed her sanity? The novelty of having someone actually *be* there for her for a change, for her to rely on? She'd told herself she was happy with her life, yet there had always been that sniff of what might have been lingering just out of her reach. Hell, that was what had driven the whole article idea. Had she let him under her radar because he represented that parallel universe for her—the one where she really was a rich socialite instead of just playing a part?

Rationality was sinking in deeper with every moment, driving away the delicious feeling of happiness she'd encountered in his arms, with his hands her skin.

She could hear his muffled voice somewhere outside the room and paused near the door, listening hard. He was obviously on the telephone. That meant he could be back in here at any moment. She looked hurriedly around for the rest of her clothes and suddenly registered a swatch of dialogue.

'...tomorrow. Send me the flight details through...'

Cold regret seeped into her heart as she followed what he was saying. Along with anger at herself for letting things go so far.

Where exactly had she *thought* it would go from here? She knew what his priorities were. He hadn't made a secret of it. Work came first. Would always come first with him.

Flight details.

So he wasn't even staying in the country for Christmas, then? What would he give her? A couple of days before he jetted off back to his life? What had she been thinking? She'd fallen into his arms like some simpering idiot, all because he'd rescued her from a scary situation. She'd slept with him and now he was going.

The only thing stopping her from becoming her mother right now was the fact he'd used a condom.

She dashed around the room, picking up her dress and cardigan. Now reality had bitten she knew only that she had to put a stop to any further repeat of history. There was only one way forward if she were to retain the control her mother had given up.

She'd have to dump him before he got in first.

CHAPTER TEN

ALEX returned to the bedroom via the kitchen fridge, thinking they would have a slow and languorous champagne-breakfast-fuelled second round. Just the thought of the warm softness of her body curled up in his bed made hot desire rush through him again.

The bed was empty, sheets strewn haphazardly across it. As he glanced at the half-open *en suite* bathroom door, of the darkness beyond it, she popped up suddenly from behind the far side of the bed. She was naked except for lace panties and clutching the rest of her clothes to her chest, hiding her modesty as if he *hadn't* just spent half the night exploring every silken inch of her body. He stared at her.

'What are you doing?'

She avoided his eyes, bent down and retrieved a shoe from under the bed.

'I need to get going.'

He shoved the tray down on the chest of drawers as she moved towards him. On her way out.

'To do what, exactly?'

'I need to get to work. This article won't write itself.'

'Come back to bed. Have some breakfast. Another hour isn't going to make a difference.'

'Well, if that's your attitude I'm amazed you've made

such a success of your career,' she said. 'Lying in bed until all hours.'

'It's only seven-thirty,' he pointed out.

She was next to him now, next to the open door, shoes balanced on top of her clothes. She apparently really was going.

'So you're choosing work over a lie-in with me?' Surely she couldn't be serious. 'Let's just have something to eat and then you can get started, spend the day on it. You can use the office, if you like.'

'I don't need to use the office. I need to get packed and then I'll be out of your hair.'

His mind whirled. What the hell *was* this?

'Out of my hair?'

She shrugged.

'It's been fun, but we both knew it was never going anywhere…right?'

He didn't answer. He was too busy trying to fathom how things had gone from the intimate sizzling passion of the night to this detached coldness.

Not bothering to wait for an answer, she finally pushed past him and walked barefoot down the hall towards her own room, still clutching her clothes against her. He followed her, the smooth contours of her naked back tantalising him. Messy waves of hair were tumbling every which way over her shoulders.

She talked loudly without looking round. 'Won't take me long to get my stuff sorted.'

'You're moving out?'

'Yes, our agreement's reached an end. I told you I needed to stay until I got enough material. I've done that.' She paused. 'It's over.'

She walked into her room, made as if to close the door. He grabbed it and stood in the way.

'But you haven't written it yet.'

'Oh, I can write the thing anywhere,' she said. 'I've got all my notes. Once it's done I'll just e-mail it in and hope it's good enough. I'm going to see my mum.'

'You're going home to the country?'

'For Christmas,' she said. She turned. Faced him. 'Let's face it, Alex, I was always going to be going home to the country for Christmas. This can't come as a big surprise.'

'But last night…'

'Was great. But you're not exactly the marrying kind, are you?'

She smiled at him, as if she was perfectly fine with that, but it was a perfunctory effort and didn't really touch the blue eyes. He'd seen what a proper smile looked like on her face and this was a poor imitation. Whatever was going on here, he wasn't buying it.

'I've got ambitions,' she said. 'There's a lot riding on this project for me. I don't have time to take a few more days out for sex with you just because you're stuck here and you happen to have an empty diary.'

That was all it was to her? Sex? He couldn't believe what he was hearing.

'Let's just cut our losses and get back to normal. You must be going back to work any day now, anyway, aren't you?'

There was a loaded tone to that question, a hint of contempt. Or maybe he'd imagined it.

He dropped his eyes for a moment, but there was no point trying to hide it.

'I do have to fly out to the States,' he admitted. 'My spat with Richard Moran is going to be plastered all over the papers for the next day or so, but my PR team will smooth it over. We're well known as business rivals, and it isn't the first time we've crossed swords, so they'll pass it off as a long-running feud and your name shouldn't come into it.' He gave her a small smile. 'And even if it does it won't be your real name.'

'Good,' she said. She didn't smile back. 'So I've become Viveca Holt. You sleep with me, there's a scandal in the press and you make yourself scarce. History repeats itself.'

'What happened with Viveca has nothing to do with this. Don't you think I'd stay here if I could? Ride out the storm with you? There's been a hitch with the funding for one of my films—the kind of thing I don't want to leave to anyone else to sort out. That's the reason I have to go. I need to get back in control. I've been gone long enough.'

That urge to be back in charge was as strong as ever. He had a hands-on involvement in every film. Delegation didn't come naturally. He found it hard to believe anyone else had the commitment and standards that he did. And yet now he found it tempered by the want, the *need* to be with her.

'When?' she asked, matter-of-fact.

'Tomorrow,' he said.

'Well, there you go, then!'

He clenched his hands at her sudden dismissive attitude.

'It's the States, Jen. It's not the moon. I'm not disappearing off the face of the earth. There are phones. There's Skype. And I'll be back.'

'Of course you will. Next time your work demands it. I'm sure I'll read about it in the papers.'

Her tone was don't-care.

She turned her back on him, dropped the ball of clothes on the bed and stood momentarily naked except for her panties, shrugging her way as fast as she could into a T-shirt. He could be across the room with her in three quick strides, sliding his hands around her to cup her breasts, kissing the back of her neck. It took huge will-power not to do exactly that, to use sex in that way he was used to—to divert a woman from anything with more depth and importance. But he didn't go. He didn't know where he wanted this…this *thing* between them to go, but he suddenly realised he wanted more from her than just sex. And to pitch them at that level now would, he instinctively knew, be a huge mistake.

Now wearing T-shirt and panties, she hauled a suitcase out from under her bed and crossed the room to the bureau, pulling open drawers, gathering up clothes and belongings. He crossed the room and shut the lid of her suitcase, stood between it and her.

'Will you quit packing for a minute?'

She took a deep breath and stood still, a T-shirt in each hand. Her expression was one of sad resignation and his heart lurched.

'I don't want this to be it between us. Don't you understand?' he said. He made an effort to curb his tone. In his determination to make her understand his temper was fraying. 'I know the situation isn't perfect. We've both got huge demands on us, on our time. But I want to carry on seeing you.'

'For what? A couple of dates? Or are you after an easy date whenever you happen to be in town? Call me up and I'll drop everything and be there? Is that it?'

'Jen, I know why you're acting like this. You're cutting me out because you think you know me. You're judging me, judging *us*, by a million stories you've read about me in the press. And that's not fair. I'm serious about this. Don't you think you at least owe me the chance to show you that?'

She looked at him, eyebrows raised.

'How do you plan to do that?'

He thought her tone had warmed up slightly, almost imperceptibly. Maybe at last he was getting through to her.

He took a deep breath. He couldn't quite believe what he was about to suggest.

'I fly out tomorrow to LA. Spend today with me. And at the end of it, if you still want out, I won't argue with you. Your damn article can wait one day.'

'You think spending one day in bed with you is enough to convince me you're serious about me?'

'Not you, no,' he said. 'But then you're not run-of-the-mill, are you? Get showered and dressed. We're going out.'

'The M4?'

She glanced at the motorway sign. The main route to her home village.

'I thought you were talking me out of going home. Trust me, my mother won't thank me for turning up out of the blue with a guest in tow. She'll be up to her elbows in pastry, making the famous Brown mince pies. Or, worse, she could be stuffing the turkey.'

'The M4 doesn't just serve Littleford, you know,' he said, not taking his eyes off the road.

Light snow was falling against the windscreen, but it was deliciously snug in the Maserati with its seat-warming gadgetry and perfect climate control.

She caught on.

'We're going to Bristol?'

'We're visiting my parents,' he said. 'The Hammond Christmas drinks and nibbles. You'd better brace yourself.'

Jen sat in silence as he took the Bristol slip road, mulling over what this could mean. She'd challenged him with this, hadn't she? With taking her to meet his family? Was Alex proving a point? Nervous butterflies pinged around her stomach.

It seemed the bonkers British weather hadn't put off the traditional last-minute rush of Christmas shoppers. The roads to the town centre were stuffed with traffic, which finally began to ease as they headed for the Downs and Clifton.

'I should warn you they're likely to be a bit narky,' he said as he pulled the car into a wide avenue lined with snow-dusted trees. They came to a standstill outside a beautiful three-storey townhouse. 'On account of the fact I haven't visited for a while.'

She crunched across the frozen gravel driveway behind him. He rang the bell.

'How long is "a while"?' she asked as the front door opened and a man stepped into view.

Alex shrugged. 'Eighteen months-ish.'

'More like two years,' the man said.

He had to be Alex's father. The resemblance was strong. Sixty-ish, he had the same thick hair, though it was steel-grey, and glasses. Alex had his green eyes.

And then they were surrounded. Alex's mother appeared from nowhere, petite with a short light brown haircut to match her elfin features. Alex made an apologetic face at Jen over her head as she dragged him into an enormous hug. There was a brother, there was a small niece and nephew who hung off Alex's legs, there was a grandma sitting in a high-backed chair by the fireplace, and there were uncles, aunts and cousins. A total of four generations of the Hammond family.

Cheesy Christmas music was belting out from somewhere within.

The rich exterior of the house didn't match the inside. It was stuffed to breaking point with mismatched furniture and no surface was left uncluttered. There were ornaments and knick-knacks everywhere she looked.

'I bought them the house seven years ago,' Alex said as they were ushered through the hall. 'Not long after I got my first big break. Took me ages to persuade them to move out of their old house, and when they eventually did they told my interior designer to get stuffed and basically moved the interior of their old place as it was.'

In the corner of the sitting room there was an enormous fake Christmas tree, festooned with a combination of hideous baubles and homemade ornaments that spelled the word *family* in a way that nothing else at Christmas quite did. A threadbare fairy perched on the top, well past her best but clearly there for years to come based on sentimentality instead of appearance.

Alex was subjected to an inquisition from the entire family that he clearly deserved and took calmly in his stride.

'Good of you to finally show your face,' his father said when they'd been each been given a glass of cranberry-red Christmas punch.

Yep, there was definitely an air of narkiness.

'I've invited you and Mum to visit me in LA loads of times,' Alex protested. 'Tried to persuade you to come and have a holiday. You never take me up on it.'

'You know your mother is afraid of flying. And I don't hold with that foreign food. It doesn't agree with me.'

Everywhere Jen looked there were framed pictures of Alex with his younger brother, growing up. There was an enormous table groaning with quiche, sausage rolls and sandwiches. Good hearty food, not the one-bite-and-it's-gone canapés she'd been served these last few weeks.

The argument went on.

'Would it kill you to phone your mother once a week? Or even once a month? I know your every move, Alexander Hammond, I read the red-top newspapers. I know when

you're in this country, skulking in London, not bothering to nip down the M4 for an hour or so to see your family. And then just this morning there's a picture of you
smacking someone at some racetrack. Off the rails! Are
you on drugs?'

Alex held both hands up to ward him off.

'No, I am not on drugs! And I was staying out of the
way because I wanted to protect you lot from all that.'
He turned to Jen. 'The press hounded them when I broke
up with Susan,' he explained. 'They'd follow my mother
when she walked down the street, barking out questions.'
He looked at his parents. 'I didn't want that for you again.'

'We've taken more grief than that in our time,' his
mother snapped. 'When our Michael got caught shoplifting
I couldn't hold my head up in the supermarket for weeks.
A few gutter press weren't going to bother me after that.'

'What's shoplifting, Daddy?' Alex's six-year-old niece
piped up.

Michael threw his hands up. 'Oh, cheers, Mum. Trying
to be a role model here and you bring that up.'

As the day progressed and the punchbowl emptied
things slowly began to thaw. As darkness fell Jen stood
in a corner of the warm kitchen watching Alex deep in
conversation with his father and brother.

'You're the first girlfriend he's brought home in a long
time,' his mother said, joining her. She topped up Jen's
glass, then her own.

'I'm sure it's just because work keeps him away so
much.'

A pause and an unconvinced smile.

'Come and let me show you something.'

Jen followed her out of the kitchen.

There was an enormous ball of mistletoe suspended
from the doorway into the sitting room, and Alex's eccen-

tric uncle Norman seemed to be hanging around it rather more than necessary. He flashed her a toothy smile as she sidled past him into the room.

'I'm amazed to see him,' Alex's mother said as they sat down on the sofa. 'He has no need for us any more. We're lucky to get a phone call now and then. He's got all he needs—all those rich friends. There's nothing here that he wants to come back for.'

Jen shook her head. 'You're wrong. He misses you. He misses *this*.'

She was fascinated. It had always been just her and her mum. Her grandparents were long gone. She envied him the warmth, the buzz of it. You'd never be on your own with a family like this.

Unless you took yourself out of it. Which was what he had done.

'I've kept all the cuttings from his career.'

She produced a groaning photo album. Jen forced her face to keep a smile on it as she flipped through a few pages. It was full of tabloid pictures of Alex with various models and starlets. Here was Alex on the red carpet with a gorgeous redhead. And here he was cavorting in the surf somewhere tropical, with Viveca Holt of all people.

Photos of ex-girlfriends. Exactly what you needed to boost your ailing confidence when you met the parents for the first time. *Not.*

'Fabulous!' she exclaimed, smiling so hard her cheeks ached. 'And have you seen all his films?'

'Oh, yes,' she said. 'We've got all the DVDs.'

Alex's mother leaned in conspiratorially and added in a stage whisper, 'Some of them are a bit dull, to be perfectly honest, a bit too arty for us. Still, I'd never tell him that. It's brilliant that he's won all those awards. Graham and I prefer more of an action film, like that *Faith* trilogy. We love those—have you seen them?'

As they said their goodbyes Alex bandied about promises of regular visits and phone calls. In the silent warmth of the car on the drive back to London Jen wondered if he'd meant them. Or whether the whole day had really been about proving a point.

CHAPTER ELEVEN

Rule #8: When you've snared your millionaire, gradually introduce him to the real you one step at a time.

'WHY did you take me to meet them?'

Alex stared into the fireplace for a moment. She was curled warmly against him on the sofa in the den, back in his apartment. The room was lit only by the soft glow of the fire and the coloured lights on her little Christmas tree. She followed his gaze, watched sparks flying from the logs into the velvety darkness. Two glasses of wine and the remains of scrambled eggs on toast lay on the coffee table to the side of them.

'I wanted to show you my roots,' he said. 'You were so determined to accept the newspaper view of me as a playboy, and I don't blame you. I've never tried to correct it either publicly or privately. To be honest I haven't cared either way what was written about me.' He glanced at her. 'Not until now.'

'Why now?' Her heart beat faster as she waited for his reply.

'I want you to know what I'm really like. Not the press image. The real me. If you're going to do a bunk I want it to be because you're not happy with *me*, not some illusion.'

'Why haven't you seen them for so long?' she asked. 'They were so delighted to see you I thought you were going to be lynched, and you obviously love them all to bits.'

He took a sip of his wine.

'Part of it was the demands of work keeping me away. I wasn't lying to them about that. But it isn't the only reason.'

He sighed.

'After Susan left it was just such a reminder of what I was missing, seeing them all. My brother became a dad, something I could never see happening for me after she went, and it became easier somehow to just stay away. They've never been excited by what I do. Not when I was a kid starting out and not even when I became a success at it. Michael's given them grandchildren. He sees them all the time. Those are things they can relate to. His life is real to them.'

He ran a hand distractedly through his hair.

'I think they see me in the newspapers and wonder who the hell I am. When I see them they act like I think I'm better than them. I sometimes think they'd have been happier if I drove a taxi for a living or worked down at the docks.'

She could see his agitation in the tensing of his shoulders and was touched. If today had been about proving to her he was serious, it hadn't been an easy gesture for him to make.

'But what conclusion did you *want* them to make? You've encouraged them to think that way by staying away so much. They think you're ashamed of them because you don't see them.'

He flinched, and she knew she'd touched a nerve, but she wasn't about to back down.

'I can see where you're coming from,' she said. 'They're happy in their own little bubble. Flying halfway round the world fills them with dread. But it isn't that they aren't proud of you. It's just that they're so in awe of the world you live in.'

He was shaking his head. She put a hand on his arm.

'Your parents own all your films, you know,' she said. 'They've got them all, every single one, on DVD. I saw. And your mum subjected me to a scrapbook of newspaper clippings. You in the arms of half of Hollywood. I was expecting baby photos and I got you frolicking in the surf with Viveca Holt. They're your biggest fans, you idiot. Just because they don't really understand what you do it doesn't mean they aren't proud of your achievements.'

A pause. He watched the fire.

'Maybe,' he said.

'You should see more of them.'

'I know.'

'That Christmas tree is a shrine to your childhood,' she said.

He grimaced.

'I know. It's hideous. Sorry.'

She shook her head. 'No, I like it. That's the kind of Christmas tree I want to have one day. You can keep those ludicrous black trees with minimalist lights and those deconstructed turkey dinners. It's like wearing designer clothes and not caring if you look like a moose as long as they cost a fortune. Christmas at your parents' has been fine-tuned over years and years. It actually has something concrete behind it instead of vacuous self-importance.'

'So your Christmas tree will be festooned with tat?'

'Decorations made by toddlers do not fall into the *tat* category.'

He laughed, gave her a squeeze.

'I thought you were aiming for editor-in-chief of Vogue.'

His tone was neutral, almost deliberately so. 'How are you going to fit family in with that?'

'This isn't the Dark Ages. I know you think it's impossible to mix business with family life but I don't agree. I definitely want kids one day. You just need to be good at juggling and working as a team. Women are fabulous at that kind of thing.' She pointed an emphatic finger at him. 'Your big problem is you think it has to be all or nothing. Anything less than white-picket-fence-two-kids-and-a-dog-perfection doesn't cut it for you. But, like I told you before, there's more than one way to crack a nut. As long as both parents are never away for work at the same time, maybe downsize their hours a bit, delegate more, cut down on travelling. There's loads of ways you could make it work.' She leaned forward, picked up her wine glass and took a sip. 'I intend to have it all. Nothing's going to stop me.'

'I guess I thought the way things were with your father and your insane sense of ambition, that you weren't big on family.'

'I'm not right now. But give me a few years working my way up and family is next up.' She paused. 'My father is irrelevant.'

He glanced her way. 'Is he?'

She leaned against him for a moment, savouring the warmth of him, the feeling of security his closeness gave.

'Almost doing a bunk this morning was about me, too,' she said. 'Not just about you.'

He moved sideways a little so he could see her face.

'It's not you, it's me?' he said, eyebrows raised. 'You don't have to spare my feelings. I just want you to be honest with me.'

'Remember when we talked about false names for my article and you suggested I use my father's surname?'

He frowned.

'Yes.'

'Well, the fact he's a waste of space wasn't the only reason I didn't use it. I didn't want to draw attention.'

'How do you mean?'

She took a deep breath.

'My father is Dominic Armstrong.'

She waited. The fire spat softly in the background.

'You don't mean *the* Dominic Armstrong? The—'

'The media giant,' she finished for him. 'Yes.'

He looked sharply down at her, his interest clearly buzzing. Of course it was. She met his gaze, ready for the questions.

'But he owns two or three newspapers, doesn't he? Not to mention magazines and that TV news channel?'

'He does.'

'Then I don't get it. All it would take is a bit of name-dropping and you could land yourself a job on the magazine of your choice. But instead you've slogged your way up with an internship after working for a newspaper from the back of beyond.'

'It's how I wanted it. I've never wanted to be indebted to him for anything. Twenty-five years and not a card. Not a phone call. The only part he's ever played in my life was on his way out of it. He had my mother sign a contract—gave her a lump sum in return for relinquishing all parental responsibility.'

'He paid her off?' He sounded appalled.

'Exactly. And that's why I was trying to make a quick exit this morning. Because when you get down to basics he saw me and my mother as a hitch in his life. So he fixed the problem and then disappeared.' She paused. 'Like you did with Viveca Holt.'

'You're comparing *me* to your father?'

She could hear the edge in his voice, grabbed his hand, held it.

'Not now. But I was this morning.'

He'd pulled away from her, a frown touching his brows. She spoke quickly, needing to make him understand.

'Think about how it looked to me. You had an affair with Viveca, it began to cause you problems in the media, so you got your PR people onto it and got the hell out of the country. And then we spent the night together, you're plastered across the press for belting Richard Moran in the chops—a situation caused by me—and suddenly your PR people are on the case and you're jetting off to LA. What was I supposed to think? I wanted to jump before I was pushed. I don't want to make the same mistakes my mother did.'

He took her face softly in his hands, looked steadily into her eyes. The woody scent of the fire mingled with the fresh citrus of his aftershave.

'This is not a mistake. I am not getting on a plane to fly out of your life. Don't judge me by the way your father behaved.'

'I couldn't help it. After twenty-five years it gets to be a bit of a mind-set.'

'Give me time and I'll change that.'

He pulled her against him in the firelight, held her, kissed her so deeply it made her light-headed, and then he was easing her onto his lap, his hands sliding deliciously beneath her clothes, and she let hot desire for him crush away doubt.

Afterwards she lay in his arms, watched the fire flicker. He grabbed the patchwork throw from the armchair and tugged it around them.

'You really think this can work?'

She wondered where they could go from here. Would he suggest that she move her work ambitions across the pond? Or even drop them altogether? Take on a new job as Alex Hammond's Other Half? With his views on putting each other first, surely that was how he would see things progressing. Susan had supposedly left him because he wasn't in the same room as her often enough, so chances were he'd view working on different continents as a bit of a hitch.

She looked up at him to gauge his response and he kissed her forehead gently.

'Yes, I really think this can work.'

'With you on the other side of the Atlantic?'

She waited.

'You could come with me, you know,' he said.

There it was.

She wriggled away enough to raise herself on an elbow. The glow from the fire lit the strong contours of his face. His green eyes held her gaze and her heart turned over softly. There was a part of her that wanted to leap in immediately, agree to anything he asked just to keep him. But the self-sufficient part of her, honed over twenty-five years, easily held its own.

'I can't do that,' she said, and waited for it all to begin unravelling.

'I didn't think so,' he said, 'which is why I'll be relying on air travel.'

'Air travel?' Her heart did a happy little skip.

'When you get this new job—'

'*If,*' she interrupted.

'OK, *if* you get this new job, you're going to be even more career-obsessed than you are now, right?'

'Obsessed is going a bit far,' she said, and then saw his raised eyebrows. She sighed. 'Maybe you have a point.'

'And I'm not going to lie to you, my work schedule can be fierce. I've built it up to be exactly that. It's been everything for me these last few years. I can't downsize my hours overnight.'

'I wouldn't expect you to.'

'But I could start to rebuild things from now—work my schedule so it fits with yours. We both work hard when we're apart, and we make the most of every moment we're together. Starting now.'

He slid his hands beneath the throw and turned with her so she was on her back, the softness of the velvet sofa against her naked skin as he loomed above her. He leaned down to kiss the line of her collarbone, sending sparks fizzing right down to her toes, and then moved back up to look into her eyes, his forehead pressed lightly against hers, his warm breath on her mouth.

'I'm serious about this,' he said. 'I'm serious about you. And even though I'm as scared of letting people close as you are, a few thousand miles aren't about to stop me.'

Perfect man, perfect Christmas. And now New Year, new job.

She straightened her new short jacket. Now she had a proper regular income and an image to keep up. She had money for clothes. Not the designer level stuff she'd bought to play Genevieve, but a wardrobe that was a cut above her old jeans-and-T-shirt uniform. Marlon's makeover had been all about playing a part for her article, but somewhere along the way she'd begun to like feeling a bit more polished.

Plus she wanted to look her best for Alex. He'd managed two visits since Christmas—one a four-day break and the other a forty-eight-hour turnaround spent almost entirely in bed that made her toes curl and her stomach melt whenever she thought about it. He called every day, and used Skype whenever he could, but she was still competing for his attention with film stars and models, and a new suit seemed *essential* under the circumstances.

She stacked her papers together and put them away in her briefcase, shook her editor's hand. The delicious feeling of having made it hadn't gone away yet. Four weeks in and she was still in pinch-yourself mode.

She'd done it. Actually done it. Sold her article to *Gossip!* magazine and been offered a permanent role in the Features Department. She was on her way. She'd just finished a meeting at which she'd pitched new article ideas and the reception had been great.

Her editor accompanied her down the hallway, a sheaf of papers in one arm.

'Really pleased to have you on board,' she said. 'Always on the lookout for a fresh approach.'

'I'm just so happy to have the opportunity.'

'No need to thank me.' She shifted the papers to the other arm. 'You came highly recommended, after all.'

Jen frowned. What the hell did *that* mean?

'Recommended? By who?'

No one at the *Littleford Gazette* had an ounce of clout in this universe. Maybe if she'd gone for a job with *Pig-Farming Monthly...*

'Our Entertainment Editor.' She smiled at Jen. 'Apparently Alex Hammond mentioned you to her a few weeks ago. The film producer. I had no idea you knew him. He gave her an exclusive interview on account of the fact you now work here. Fantastic scoop for her. She was delighted. That's exactly the kind of networking we should be doing.'

They'd reached Reception, the lifts. The editor gave Jen

a parting smile and she returned it automatically, oblivious to her surroundings, her mind working overtime.

Disbelief came first.

He wouldn't have done that. He knew how she felt about that article, how hard she'd worked, how she'd spent everything on it—not just in money terms. He wouldn't have undermined all that by pulling strings and namedropping.

Would he?

She didn't notice the other people in the lift as she descended to the ground floor. Didn't register anyone she passed.

It was in his nature to manipulate situations to get the outcome he wanted. She knew that much. Life had moulded him that way. He had all his staff sign confidentiality agreements. When they'd first met he'd tried to buy her off to get her out of his apartment. He paid a PR company to manipulate his image in the press. And he'd slept with Viveca Holt who, not so coincidentally, had then managed to get the showbiz break of her life. The list was endless. He wasn't above throwing money or influence at any situation to get the desired result. Why would this be any different?

Maybe he was too used to it after Susan's betrayal to act in any other way. Why leave anything to chance when you could manipulate the outcome?

Her mobile phone rang. She checked the screen. As if he had some sixth sense, it was Alex. She pressed 'call reject.'

Rule #9: If it doesn't work out, don't be downhearted. Have a Plan B. Go it alone and get rich and successful yourself.

Six missed calls and now she knew why. She'd forgotten the date.

She watched the annual award nominations as they were read out on the news channel. It was a good year for British film.

The Audacity of Death had eight nominations. One of them was Best Actress for Viveca Holt.

Hot anger boiled through her.

His success. His glory. No one else's. He could bask in his achievements, knowing his full worth, knowing they were down to him. His management, his drive.

He'd stolen that feeling from her. What meaning did her job have now?

The phone rang again and she answered it on autopilot, still looking at the TV screen.

'Hey,' he said.

His voice. The voice she loved. She lay awake at night waiting to hear it, just so she could go to sleep with it resonating in her mind.

'Hi.'

'Have you seen the news?' he asked.

'Eight nominations. Congratulations.'

He hadn't managed to screw things up, after all. Whatever publicity his exploits before Christmas had generated, it hadn't done the movie any harm.

'Will you come to the ceremony with me?' he asked.

Before she'd gone to work this morning that question would have filled her with excitement and delight. Not just at the prospect of attending what had to be one of the most glitzy evenings on any social calendar anywhere but because he wanted to share that event, that huge achievement, with *her*. It would have given her that happy little tummy-flip you got when the fabulous new boyfriend with whom you were totally smitten suggested you booked a holiday for later in the year. That insecurity-crushing fact you could repeat in your head at confidence crisis moments:

He intends to still be with me for the awards ceremony. He's serious about me. She would have been able to say that to herself in those moments when she missed him.

Instead she felt numb, as if all her senses had been wrapped in cotton wool.

'I can't, I'm afraid. I'll be working.'

There was a long pause. He was probably wondering if he'd heard correctly.

'This is a bad line. What did you say?'

'I said I'll be too busy,' she repeated. Speaking to him seemed to have opened the door on her pent-up anger. Just ajar at the moment, but it wouldn't take much for it to swing wide and bury her. 'Work's really taken off, and you know how I've given everything to get where I am. In fact, I'm not sure a relationship is the right thing for me just at the moment.'

'Jen, what the hell is this about?' His voice was strong in her ear, confusion and anger tingeing the edges.

Good. Let him be confused and angry. Just like her.

Her heart felt as if it was disintegrating. He wanted a woman he could control. He'd made her think he wanted to get close, maybe he'd even believed that himself, but in reality he'd been busy cobbling safety nets, making sure their life would be perfect, heading off anything that might cause a problem or challenge their happiness.

She didn't want that. She wanted to stand and fall on her own merits. To share her successes with him and lean on him through her failures. Would life with him just be one long cushioned ride? She wanted to *feel* life, the ups as well as the downs, taking whatever it threw at her head on. And she couldn't do that with him.

'You pulled strings at *Gossip!* magazine to swing me that job,' she said.

His silence on the end of the phone told her all she needed to know.

'Jen, listen to me,' he said at last. She could hear the urgency in his voice. 'It wasn't like that. You're reading too much into it.'

'You're saying you *didn't* promise an exclusive interview to *Gossip!* while I was staying with you at the apartment? While I was busting a gut, busting everything I had, to nail that job *on my own merit*?'

A long pause. She waited.

'I did promise them an interview, yes,' he said quietly. 'But it was not some calculated move to get them to accept your article. I know how much that job means to you, I know how hard you worked. Do you really think I would openly do something to jeopardise that?'

'I don't think you can help yourself,' she said. 'You have all this money, all this power, and you look at life and think about how you want this or that situation to turn out. And then you sort it. You went to *Gossip!* bandying my name about and offering an exclusive, and you expect me to believe you didn't ask for anything in return? You said it yourself at that Christmas ball—in this world it's all about knowing the right people, about greasing palms. Well, I can't live like that. I can't be with you like that. Catching me when I fall is one thing, but you'd have me living in a damn great safety harness.'

'You're not listening to me.'

'I don't need to listen to any more of this. What could you possibly say that can undo this? It's over, Alex.'

She hung up before she could break down. Waited for the phone to ring, for him to text, steeling herself to ignore him, not expecting for a moment that he would let things lie. Not Alex, who was used to getting his own way in everything.

The phone stayed silent.

Grief began to seep in alongside her anger. He was going to accept what she'd told him this time, without trying to manipulate what he wanted from the situation.

Maybe he was finally getting to understand her, after all. Now that it was too late.

CHAPTER TWELVE

SIXTEEN-HOUR days had kept Alex sane when his marriage had ended, and throwing himself into work now had its advantages. Funding was secured on three new films, and publicity for *The Audacity of Death* was frenzied. He tried to convince himself that his relationship with Jen had been a stupid mistake. A reminder that life for him worked best when he lived it alone. He turned back to the solace of work, the one focus that had always driven him, always given him a purpose, even in the face of Susan's betrayal.

And now it wasn't enough.

Somehow he'd managed to fall for her in a way he'd never fallen for anyone. Even Susan felt like a distant wisp of a memory now. The way she'd fleeced him had tortured him for the last five years and yet now it failed to raise so much as a stab of resentment. Work had slipped from being inspiring and satisfying to being nothing more than a way of occupying his mind, of shutting out the constant ache for her. What had she done to him? He could barely feel anything any more.

Dozens of times he went for the phone. He needed to hear her voice, to try and convince her how sorry he was. But he couldn't call her because she had been right.

He'd agreed to the interview with *Gossip!* while he'd waited for her during her makeover at Marlon's salon, thinking it might raise her profile a little at the magazine, smooth the way a bit for her. He hadn't done anything to actively pull strings. But there was no point denying he'd probably had some influence. Mentioning that Jen was connected to him was never going to do her any harm, was it? Just as it hadn't done Viveca any harm at the casting for *The Audacity of Death*. But while Viveca had been more than happy to take any opportunity that came her way, for Jen opportunity had to be made by *her*, not dropped in her lap.

He knew that now because he knew her better. They'd talked about her father, her past. He understood her single-minded ambition, her need to prove herself. But that had been later, when they were together. And by then the damage was done.

And now, more than a month on, work and the bachelor lifestyle were still not enough to block out the ache for her. He wasn't sure they ever would be again.

'Settling in OK?'

Jen turned from the counter. The coffee house was just around the corner from *Gossip!* HQ and she was addicted. No more Littleford Tea Rooms for her.

Angela West. Entertainment Editor. Whippet-thin. Super-intimidating designer suit. Jen had learned more about designer clobber in a couple of weeks living with Alex than she had in a lifetime in Littleford.

Oh, but it hurt to think about Alex. There was a raw ache deep inside her at the thought of never seeing him again, never being held by him again. In any other break-up situation throwing herself into work might have helped take her mind off it, but every move she made in the office was a bitter reminder of his betrayal. The constant wondering about whether she deserved this job at all crushed any joy she had in her work.

He'd not only broken her heart, he'd taken away the one thing that might have helped her get over it.

'Great, thanks,' she said. She took her full-fat latte and sprinkled it liberally with chocolate shavings. Added a white chocolate muffin to her tray. At least now she didn't have to worry about her weight or her skin breaking out, since she intended never to get naked with another man. *Ever.*

'And how's the fabulous Alex Hammond?' Angela asked, peering through the display cabinet glass, probably in search of something with zero calories. A plain rice cake, perhaps.

Jen felt as if she had been doused with cold water. Of course. Entertainment Editor. The penny dropped. The string Alex had pulled had apparently been attached to *her.*

'I haven't spoken to him recently,' she said vaguely.

'You two know each other, don't you? Surely you must know how he is?'

Part of her, the part that hurt the most, wanted to ask this intimidating woman how he was. If he was OK. If he was getting on with his life as if she'd never existed. She refused to let that want take hold.

Angela West ordered a skinny cappuccino and duly decided against eating anything. Was this what it was like when you spent your working life interviewing celebrities? Did you become weight-obsessed in the face of all that glossy gorgeousness?

'Unfortunately I can't really say we know each other,' she said. 'Shame, I'd love to have him on my Christmas card list. I only spoke to him the once. He was doing the publicity rounds for that film he'd just made, with the awards season looming. He mentioned he knew some-

one who worked for *Gossip!*—that was it.' She winked.
'Lucky you!'

A spike of uneasiness slipped unexpectedly into Jen's
mind.

'Did he mention my article at all? My internship?' she
asked, finding it hard to form the words because her mouth
seemed suddenly dry.

'Which article was that, honey? Is it something on him?
I could use a bit of extra background.'

Jen ignored the slight in that sentence, the implication
that something *she* produced wouldn't be of any more
value than 'background', because of the mounting feeling of cold awfulness in her stomach. She needed to clarify this. Right now.

'The article I wrote at the end of my internship. As
part of my permanent job application. *How To Marry A
Millionaire in Ten Easy Steps.*'

Angela laughed out loud. 'Good grief—is that the
kind of thing they're commissioning now in the Features
Department?'

The laugh wasn't light-hearted or friendly. Jen liked
her less and less.

'No, honey, he never mentioned you really at all, except for saying he knew you and you worked here. Sorry.'

The catty flash in Angela's dark eyes gave away what
she was thinking. *Starstruck kid, thinking Alex was into
her.*

'Don't worry about the extra background if you don't
know him that well. I'll call him up myself, cover some
more ground.'

Jen barely noticed her sashaying away, tray in hand.
She put her own tray down untouched on one of the empty
tables on her way out.

She felt physically sick. She'd been so convinced he'd

swung the job for her and now it turned out he hadn't even mentioned her article. Dropping her name into conversation wasn't the same thing as pulling strings, was it? Would he have passed it off as nothing more than—what had her editor called it?—*networking*, if she'd given him the chance to explain? Which she hadn't. She was so prejudiced by her useless father that she hadn't wanted to listen.

What had she done?

Rule #10: If you do manage to land your millionaire, always, always agree to a pre-nup. This is your payment, your insurance that all your hard work will pay off. You weren't in it for love, anyway, right?

'I can't understand why you didn't let me come to stay with *you*,' Elsie grumbled for the hundredth time. 'We could have gone clubbing in London—maybe one of those clubs where the footballers go. We could have *really* washed that man right out of your hair. But instead you think pie and chips at the village pub is going to cut the mustard.'

She looked questioningly into Jen's face.

'I just fancied a quiet weekend away,' she said, because she had to say something. How could she tell Elsie that the job she'd aspired to for years now made her feel miserable and bitter. And that living in London, which had filled her with excitement while she did her internship, now felt lonely. The friends she'd made at *Gossip!* just reminded her of the mess she was in, cruising along rudderless because she now had no clue what she wanted from life.

Elsie waited, apparently for something more, then gave an exasperated snort and stood up.

'I'll get another round in. Might as well get plastered. There's nothing else to do.'

'I'll have a pint.'

Broken though it might be, Jen's heart was apparently still capable of beating crazily at the sound of Alex's voice, the sight of him.

Elsie's eyes were practically on stalks.

Hollywood Alex had come to Littleford. What a scoop that would be for the *Gazette*.

'Jen? Do you want to talk to him? Or shall I…?' Elsie paused, clearly fighting the urge to fall at Alex's feet. 'Get him out of here?'

Jen looked up at him. He looked tired, drawn.

Because of me, her mind whispered hopefully. She crushed the thought. He'd flown in from the States. He was jetlagged. It didn't mean anything.

'Elsie, could you give us a minute?' she said.

His green eyes held hers steadily and she suddenly re-alised Elsie hadn't moved an inch, apart from possibly dropping her jaw even wider.

'Elsie?' she hissed through gritted teeth.

'Hmm? Right. No problem. Leave you to it.'

Elsie backed reluctantly away towards the bar. Alex slid onto the bench opposite her.

'How did you find me?' she asked.

'I went to your house and your mum told me you were at the pub. There's only one in the village. It wasn't hard.'

She took a deep breath.

'Why are you here?'

'I want to make things right between us,' he said.

'Have you got a time machine?'

He didn't answer.

'I know you didn't pull strings,' she said. 'Not intention-ally, anyway. I want to tell you I'm sorry for not believing you, for thinking you'd undermine me like that, but when you didn't get in touch again I thought you'd just put us behind you and moved on.'

'I tried,' he said. 'But it didn't work.'

Her heart gave a half-skip but she ignored it. Nothing mattered now apart from making him understand.

'I've never criticised my mum for taking that payoff when I was a baby. She had her reasons. It meant she could buy the cottage in Littleford and at least not have to worry about having a roof over our heads. But it made me wary of anyone like my father, who has money and power, and it made me determined to make something of myself—an achievement that I could call my own, without help from anyone like that.'

'You wanted to prove that you never needed him, anyway?'

She gave a wry smile, thinking that somehow he'd managed to get closer to the hub of it all than she had.

'Yes, I suppose I did. And that's why I overreacted so badly. I thought you'd taken that chance away from me.'

'Jen—'

She held up a hand. 'Please. Let me finish. Let me explain.'

He leaned back against the bench.

'I found it hard at first to take any help from you, but then, as I got to know you, I began to realise there's a difference between offering help and trying to control someone. I should have trusted you and I'm so sorry that I didn't.'

'It's OK,' he said.

'Is it?'

He put a hand over hers and she felt sweet relief. Even if they couldn't go back to how things were, maybe at least she hadn't lost him altogether.

'It isn't your fault,' he said. 'I should have thought what it meant when I offered that interview. Just being connected with me opens doors—and I'm not saying that to be arrogant. It's just a fact. You're the first person I've come across that wanted those doors left shut.'

She gave a small smile. 'That makes me an idiot, doesn't it?'

'No, it makes you different. You've never wanted anything from me. It's never been about what publicity you could get, never a mutual benefit thing. When we're together it's about us, nothing else. All the help I gave you I had to bargain with you to take, and I loved that attitude. I would never have consciously screwed around with it and I'm truly sorry.'

The green eyes were full of remorse and her heart turned over softly.

'It's OK.'

'It isn't OK. After my divorce I fell into the habit of keeping control over every aspect of my life—to protect myself, I suppose. And because of that I messed with yours. None of this is down to you. It's the fallout from my damn marriage, and I should have let it go years ago.'

He squeezed her fingers.

'You saw what my family is like,' he said. 'There's never a dull moment, always someone to talk to. When I was a kid there was always someone to play with. I wanted that in my future, and that's what my marriage to Susan was about. I was building my work reputation up from scratch, giving it everything I had. It was all for us—for Susan and me and the family we'd have one day.'

He frowned.

'Things were easy at first, when we were both students. But when my career took off and I got serious studio backing that's when it started going wrong. I was away a lot and she didn't like it. Then when we were together things began to be strained. There was press interest even then. I was pictured out with people I worked with. There was never anything in it, but she just didn't have that level of trust in me that enabled her to let it go. By the time we broke up I'd made good money. I'd bought my parents that house, bought a place for us in London. I'd reached a point where I could start to pick and choose projects to work on. And then she took me to the absolute cleaners.'

'Maybe she thought she deserved a decent settlement,' Jen ventured. 'It can't have been easy with you away so much.'

'I offered her a decent settlement,' he snapped. 'It included the London house. But she got some good advice. She refused my offer and went to court to take as much as she could. I'd worked for that money from nothing. I'd poured my heart and soul into it to get where I was. And in one court judgement fifty percent of it was gone. Just like that.'

'It must have hurt.'

'I was furious. Absolutely livid for a very long time. I made the decision then that I wouldn't get involved again. That was it for me with relationships. If I couldn't trust someone who'd known me when I had nothing, how could I trust anyone?'

'But what about the family you wanted?'

He dropped his eyes briefly.

'That's what hurt the most. The papers went on about the financial cost of my divorce, but it cost me a lot more than that. If I couldn't give enough time and commitment to Susan because of my work, how the hell could I hope to make it work once children were thrown into the mix? My whole future crumbled when she left me the way she did.'

He looked back up at her, his gaze clear and unapologetic.

'So I made a new one. I was rich, I was successful, I had plenty of pretty girls crossing my path, so I decided to enjoy the bachelor party lifestyle without letting anyone get close. And for a while I thought I'd made the right decision. I had a scream of a time.' He paused. 'It's just recently that it's begun to feel like not enough.'

'Recently?'

'I began to wonder just who the hell I was slogging away like this *for*. And when I met you I began to understand.'

'Understand?'

'I'm still a family man underneath it all. Depriving myself of my family couldn't change that. For the first time in so long I started to think my life could be about more than just work. You make me want that, and if you give me a chance I promise we will always be an equal partnership. I will never do anything to undermine you again. I love you too much to want to restrict you.'

Jen was distracted from delicious shock at the fact he'd used the L-word by Elsie's gobsmacked gasp from across the bar as he put a tiny blue velvet box on the table in front of her.

'Is that…?'

'A proposal? Yes, it is. But before you say anything there's something I want to mention.'

She stared at the box on the table between them. In that box was the moment her life diverged. Two paths. One way with him. One way alone. And suddenly she knew what was coming.

The caveat.

She didn't blame him. She understood his reasons perfectly. And yet there was disappointment. That he thought she would be interested in half a fortune she'd had no part in earning and that her life was to be overshadowed by yet another contract. She'd thought he knew her better than that.

'You want to talk about a pre-nup,' she said.

He looked at her for a long moment.

'Why? Do you want one?' he asked.

She stared at him, unsmiling, and he dropped the light-hearted tone.

'You probably think a pre-nup is a given with me, right? Based on my past.'

She nodded slowly.

'Based on everything. You don't leave anything to chance, and that's something I'd have to try and work on if we were to go with this. Make you fly by the seat of your pants a bit more.' She offered him a smile. 'I don't blame you for being that way after what happened with your marriage.'

She glanced down again at the box in front of her. Give up Alex because of a principle? Could she do that? Her heart twisted at the thought of being without him again.

She could let all the prejudices her father had given her slide and just be with him. What did she care if there was a pre-nup, anyway? If they ever broke up she knew perfectly well she wouldn't want anything from him that she didn't deserve.

She could forgive him for giving *Gossip!* the interview, because despite all the angst and bitterness he hadn't swung the job for her. Not really. Just being connected to him opened doors, and if she wanted to be with him that was something she'd have to swallow however hard it stuck in her throat.

The choice was simple. She could be lonely and feel victorious or get rid of her stupid pride and be happy.

For him she would compromise. For *him*.

'*If* we were to go with this?' he said. 'How big is that "if" exactly?'

She took a deep breath.

'I love you,' she said. She saw his eyes light up at that

and it strengthened her resolve still further. 'I'm willing to sign a pre-nup, if that's what you want.' She paused. 'If that's what you need.'

He visibly tensed, and a light frown touched his face. Her hands were suddenly in his, surrounded by them.

'Thank you,' he said.

She smiled a little.

'But that won't be necessary.'

Her heartbeat jolted into action. She looked at him through narrowed eyes.

'What do you mean?'

'I'm guessing the thought of a monetary get-out-clause isn't something you want in your future, being as you have the one from hell in your past,' he said. 'So the answer is no, I won't be wanting a pre-nup. I don't intend to need one. I love you. I've never been more certain of anything.'

He lifted one hand to her cheek, stroked it gently. Heat sparkled along her cheekbone as if it might burst into flames. Her stomach did a slow and delicious cartwheel. She felt such love for him that it made her throat dry, and she knew tears might follow pretty soon if she didn't swallow hard.

'Jen, will you quit with all the questions and marry me?'

She waited a moment, just to let the full deliciousness of that question sink in and envelop her.

He got her.

It filled her with happiness. He lived his life with a safety net and he was letting that go. For her. Because he understood how important it was for her.

As he opened the box she looked down in awe at the square-cut diamond, yet nothing could have meant more than the trust he was putting in her.

'Yes,' she said, finally letting excitement bubble over. She wanted to jump up and down, leap around the bar.

He slid the ring on her finger, then held her hand tightly in his. He leaned forward to give her a hot kiss that made the locals gawp, and then something occurred to her. She put a hand on his shoulder, broke the kiss gently.

'Hang on,' she said. 'Didn't you say there were a few points you wanted to bring up before I gave you my answer?'

'I meant wedding details, you idiot. You can choose whatever you want—location, theme, guest lists. Anything. Just one condition.'

'What's that?'

'You have to include my family in there. I've got some bridges to build. Otherwise you get *carte blanche*. Marlon can do the styling, if you like. He really took to you.'

They both turned at the sound of exaggerated throat-clearing.

Elsie drew herself up to her full height.

'If there's any styling to be done,' she said, an indignant tilt to her chin, 'look no further.'

* * * * *

TRUTH-OR-DATE.COM

NINA HARRINGTON

Nina Harrington grew up in rural Northumberland, and decided at the age of eleven that she was going to be a librarian—because then she could read *all* of the books in the public library whenever she wanted! Since then she has been a shop assistant, community pharmacist, technical writer, university lecturer, volcano walker and industrial scientist, before taking a career break to realise her dream of being a fiction writer. When she is not creating stories which make her readers smile, her hobbies are cooking, eating, enjoying good wine—and talking, for which she has had specialist training.

CHAPTER ONE

From: Andromeda@ConstellationOfficeServices
To: saffie@saffronthechef
Subject: Our least favourite school friend and online dating
Hey Saffie.

I know, I know. I should have listened when you tried to warn me against working part-time for Elise van der Kamp in the first place.

Do you remember when Elise signed up with that expensive Internet dating agency for young executives? Well, now she has decided she is too busy to write her own emails and that I should do it for her. Write a few emails, she said. Then a few more. Just to get the ball rolling. After all, what else are personal assistants for?

Right.

I almost told her what to do with her job, but then she offered me a special bonus, which should be enough to pay for that professional illustrator's course I've been yearning to go on. It would be perfect. And just what I need to be taken seriously as an artist.

Not much has changed from school, has it? Elise knew I couldn't turn it down.

So guess who has been wooing potential Christmas party arm candy for our least favourite school friend every evening for the past week? Oh, yes.

Well, things have just sunk to a new low.

Ten minutes ago she texted me to say that she has to

dash off to Brazil on some urgent business and—wait for it—she has changed her mind about the whole online dating thing. Apparently it is far too sordid and risky and she doesn't want her reputation sullied by that kind of thing.

Sullied! Can you believe it? I don't think she even read one of the emails I sent or the lovely replies I got back from the boys who had rearranged their schedules to meet her for coffee this week.

The real problem is that the first coffee date is tonight. As in half an hour from now, and it is far too late to cancel. This one's username is #sportybloke and he sounds really nice over the Internet. I can't stand the idea of the poor man sitting there all alone waiting for #citygirl Elise to show. I know what it's like to be stood up and I wouldn't wish that on anyone. And I do feel sort of responsible.

Do you think I should go and meet him? And explain? Ahhrrggg.

Hope that slave-driver of a master chef isn't working you too hard in Paris.

Wish me luck. Andy

From: saffie@saffronthechef
To: Andromeda@ConstellationOfficeServices
Andy Davies, you are making my head spin. I cannot believe that you would agree to go onto an Internet dating site posing as Elise van der Kamp. I mean…Elise? Social skills of a piranha and twice as mean? Sheesh.

I am not in the least surprised that she chose a friendly person to write her emails for her.

As for the coffee date? I think you would feel better if you took a minute to go there and apologise in person. But be careful. Executive type? Being stood up and lied to? He could get cross. Use your charm. And take extra sharp pencils. Just in case.

Love ya. Saffie the kitchen slave

ANDROMEDA Davies stepped down from the red London bus and darted under the shelter of the nearest shop doorway.

The November rain pounded on the fabric awning above her head and bounced off the pavement of the narrow street in this smart part of the city.

Her gaze skipped between the pedestrians scurrying for cover until it settled on the giant mocha-cup bistro sign directly across the street.

Light from within the coffee shop streamed out in vertical bands like strobe lights between the pedestrians onto the wet pavement. She had already been here twice that week on a mission to find the perfect location for a first Internet date for Elise. It was ideal. Central, well lit, spacious and very public. They served hot food and the coffee was pretty good too.

Taking a deep breath, Andy tugged her shoulder bag across her chest, and hit the button on the handle of her umbrella with her thumb. It was so typical that the only umbrella she possessed was purple with pink cartoon flowers on the top and had been a gift from when she'd worked as a temp at a company that made novelty items for children's parties.

In her current financial state she was hardly one to complain and if it kept her dry that would be a bonus— but Elise would have taken one look at it and thrown it in the bin.

Her cover story was that it was a unique design from an up-and-coming fashion designer who specialised in one-off graphics. Nobody else would have an umbrella just like it and…

Lies, lies, lies, lies. All lies. Some little fluffy cloud white lies and some great big stonking massive thundercloud of lies. But lies just the same.

Andy closed her eyes and wallowed in ten seconds of self-pity and shame before shaking herself out of it.

This had been her decision. Nobody had forced her to

agree to impersonate Elise van der Kamp on the dating site. She could have refused and insisted that Elise write her own correspondence with these busy city boys. But Elise knew that she wouldn't turn it down. Not when she was waving a sweet cash bonus as bait to lure her in.

Andy dropped her shoulders, and shoved her free hand into the pocket of her trendy dark navy raincoat with white piping, which she had snatched up from a charity shop in an exclusive part of town.

The things she did for her art!

She really didn't have to worry about her umbrella or how she looked as long as she kept to her plan. All she had to do was dash in, wait for #sportybloke to arrive, apologise politely on behalf of Elise and then leave. The whole thing would be over in ten minutes.

Of course the girl he was expecting was the efficient and sophisticated executive director of one of the largest corporate promotion companies in Britain. Or, as Elise had insisted that she add to her online dating profile, aspiring marketing guru to the world.

Gag.

Ten minutes. And then she could get back on the bus and switch to being plain old Andy Davies, part-time personal assistant to Elise during the day, mostly unpaid illustrator in the evenings and weekend art historian, aspiring to pay the bills.

She would not be here at all if Elise had not suggested that she could 'take care' of the first round of emails—'so that she was not wasting her time on the no-hopers'.

Charming. And some of the men sounded lovely. *On their profiles.*

'I know I can rely on you completely to manage my social diary,' Elise had said with her full-beam smile. 'There is simply no one else I could trust with my personal information. But we have been friends for so long, Andromeda. I just know that you will be totally discreet. Wonderful!'

Um. *Right.* It had probably never even crossed Elise's mind that Andy had to juggle her hours at the last minute to fit all of the work in. But she had done it—just. Maybe now that Elise had pulled the plug on the Internet dating, they could both go back to what passed for a normal life in her crazy world. Like planning the Christmas and New Year party circuit.

Providing, of course, she survived explaining to #sporty-bloke that #citygirl had no intention of turning up to meet him.

Now that did give her the shivers. That and the rivulet of rain water spilling out from the awning.

Exhaling slowly, Andy glanced from side to side to find a gap in the stream of people who had their heads down, their umbrellas braced forward against the driving rain and oblivious to anyone who might walk in their way.

Seizing on a momentary lull, Andy lifted her umbrella high and dashed out onto the road in the stationary rush hour traffic. She had almost made it, when she had to dive sideways to dodge a bicycle courier and planted her right foot into a deep puddle. Dirty cold water splashed up into her smart high-heeled ankle boots and trickled down inside, making her gasp with shock.

Hissing under her breath, Andy stepped up onto the kerb, closed her umbrella, which had totally failed to keep her dry, and opened the door to the coffee shop and stepped inside.

Water dripping from every part of her, Andy shook the rain from her hair and inhaled the glorious deep, rich aroma of the freshly ground coffee beans. She was looking forward to the day when she could afford real coffee at home to replace the cheapest supermarket-brand instant coffee. The aroma combined with the background noise of the coffee shop—a low steady hum of voices, coffee grinders and espresso machines—created a wonderful soundtrack that she had every intention of enjoying, seeing as Elise was picking up the bill.

Andy gazed around the terracotta and cream walls to the groups of people sitting on the pale oak chairs behind red-and-white gingham check tablecloths.

No sign of the Hawaiian shirt #sportybloke had said that he was going to wear—and she was not likely to miss that type of clothing on a cold wet evening in early November in the centre of London.

Andy moved to the counter, bought her Americano coffee and took a seat at the small square table in the corner with her back to the wall. She propped her pink-and-purple umbrella against the wall, slipped off her raincoat over the back of the chair and ran her hands down the skirt of her favourite grey business suit.

A flutter of nervous apprehension winged across her stomach.

This was so ridiculous.

She wasn't here on a real date. There was no need to be nervous.

She was here to apologise for Elise. That was all.

So what if she had tried to imagine what #sportybloke would look like in person? You could only tell so much from an online thumbnail photograph, and they could certainly be deceptive.

It was only natural to be curious, wasn't it? Especially when #sportybloke told stories about the social life of a surfer in exotic places like Hawaii and California that had made her laugh out loud. He had a sense of humour…and he would certainly need one if he was dating Elise.

Andy bit down on her lower lip. Maybe coming here was not such a good idea. What if he was a total disappointment? And Saffie had a point. He had every right to be annoyed with her—and Elise—for tricking him. But she had to put it right with #sportybloke, tell him the truth face to face and apologise in person. She owed it to him—and herself.

Andy looked around the coffee shop at all of the happy couples, laughing and chatting merrily away over their lattes and pastries, and her heart twanged a little. But she sniffed and shook it off.

She wasn't looking for a date. Far from it—this was her time to do her own thing without having to worry about rushing back to the office where she had worked with her so-called ex-boyfriend, Nigel, to sort out his project for him. She had learnt her lesson. No more lies. No more half-truths and self-delusion. In fact, no more boyfriends at all, if her last one was anything to go by. She was quite happy on her own. *Thank you!*

Andy checked her wristwatch. Ten minutes. Then she would finally be able to steal back the few spare hours she had in the day to work on the type of paperwork she loved most.

Hiding a quick smirk, Andy dived into her large shoulder bag and pulled out her sketch pad and pencil. The museum she worked at part-time had agreed to see her five favourite hand-crafted Christmas card designs with the view to possibly selling them in their shop and she was so close to being finished! This was her chance to persuade the museum to showcase her calligraphy and artwork.

Andy was so engrossed in a sketch of a decorative scroll of strawberries and clover leaves that it took a blast of cold damp air from the open door to snap her back into the present moment. She shivered in her thin suit and looked up in surprise.

A towering dark-haired man filled the space where the entrance had been, before he closed the door behind him.

His tanned face was glowing from the rain and wind and he ran the fingers of his right hand back through his long damp hair from forehead to neck in a single natural motion.

The water droplets stood proud on the shoulders of a hip-length waterproof sailing jacket, which he was slowly unzipping as if he were a male stripper in a cabaret act. Umm. And she would be right there in the front row telling him not to rush.

Wow. He certainly had the body to pull it off should he decide on a change in direction, and as he rolled back his shoulders with a casual shrug Andy sucked in a breath in anticipation, and then exhaled very slowly.

Yup. *Hawaiian shirt.*

His square jaw was so taut it might have been sculpted. But it was his mouth that knocked the air out of her lungs, and had her clinging onto the edge of the table for support.

Plump lips smiled wide above his lightly stubbled chin, so that the bow was sharp between the smile lines. It was a mouth made for smiling, with slight dimples either side.

The short-haired #sportybloke who had posed for the corporate shot on the online profile had been wearing a suit and tie and looked like a clone of all the other business execs. But the man in the flesh was something else. For once the photo had not done him justice. At all.

His button-fly denims sat low on his slim hips but there was no mistaking that he was pure muscle beneath those tight pants. Because as he stood there for a second, his hands thrust deep into his trouser pockets, looking from table to table, scanning the horizon that was the confines of the coffee shop, every movement he made seemed magnified and as glaringly in your face as the scarlet-and-blue tropical flowers on his shirt.

The entire room seemed to shrink around him.

How did he do that? How did he just waltz in and master the room as though he were in command of the space and everyone in it?

This man was outdoors taken to the next level. No wonder he worked for a company making sports clothing. She could certainly imagine him standing at the helm of some racing yacht, head high, legs braced. The master of all he surveyed.

The hair on the back of her neck prickled with recognition. Her father had been like that once, when he worked in the city. So confident in his right to be the self-proclaimed master of the universe that when the financial crash came his world, his sanity and his identity tumbled down with it.

It was a pity that she was on a boyfriend ban. Because #sportybloke was truly the best-looking man she had seen in a very long time.

And then he saw her, but instead of giving her the up-and-down, toes-to-hair 'beauty pageant' special once-over, his gaze locked onto her face and stayed there, unmoving for a few seconds, before the corner of his mouth slid into a lazy smile.

The corners of those amazing eyes crinkled slightly and the warmth of that smile seemed to heat the air between them. And at that moment, this smile was for her. And her heart leapt. More than a little. But just enough to recognise that the blush of heat racing through her neck and face were not only due to the piping-hot coffee she had barely sipped.

In that instant Andy knew what it felt like to be the most important and most beautiful person in the room, but instead of squirming and wanting to slide under the table she lifted her chin. Heart thumping. Brain spinning. An odd and unfamiliar tension hummed down her veins. Every cell of her suddenly alive and tuned into the vibrations emanating from his body.

Suddenly she wanted to preen and flick her hair and roll her shoulders back so that she could stick her chest out.

It was as if she had been dusted with instant lust powder. *Wow*.

#sportybloke had truly arrived.

Sitting up a little straighter on her chair, Andy quickly swept away her sketch pad and focused her gaze on the arrangement of the menus on the table, trying to find something to do with her hands, only too aware that he was still watching her.

She could practically feel the heat of that laser-beam gaze burning a hole through her forehead and was surprised that there was no smell of smoke or a scorch mark on the wall behind her.

Even though she had chosen the most spacious coffee shop she could find, this man weaving his way towards her seemed to block the light. According to his profile he was six feet two inches but he certainly filled every inch. He was tall and tanned and broad-shouldered and muscular and every ounce of his attention was totally focused on her.

His feet slowed as he reached her table and she looked up into a pair of eyes the colour of dark bitter chocolate below heavy dark eyebrows and wavy brown hair. He had eyes a girl could drown in and not want to come up for air. And they locked onto hers as though they could see into her soul, wander around for a while, looking for trouble, then move on leaving her lonely and bereft.

'I'm a sort of a sportybloke. You may be expecting me, city girl.'

His transatlantic voice was rich, deep and came from

low down in his diaphragm, giving it a certain roughness
that resonated inside her head.

It was the kind of voice that should be on the radio
promoting late-night ballads, but it had no place at all in
a small London coffee shop where she was in touching
distance of its owner.

He just stood there, patiently waiting for her reply, with
a smile on his lips and a body aimed at her. A male cover
model made flesh.

Just hearing his voice made her glad that she was sitting
down and, judging by the glances from the other women
on the nearby tables, allure this powerful had a range of
at least ten feet.

*What was he doing here? On an Internet date of all
things? This man could win a gold medal in charming
women without even trying hard!*

'Absolutely,' she lied, horrified at how pathetic and
squeaky her voice sounded, and she tugged at the lilac silk
scarf Elise had chosen as her marker. 'Scarf and all.'

'I am sorry I'm late.' He smiled, shrugging off his
waterproof and throwing it casually onto the wooden floor
behind her chair, showering the planks and smothering her
umbrella in the process. 'Had to take someone to the airport
and the traffic was pretty bad. Thanks for waiting.'

'No problem,' she replied, and held out her hand. 'It's
nice to finally meet you in person.'

He stepped forward and grasped hold of her hand and his
long fingers wrapped around hers with a strong, masterful
grip, which was probably perfect for grappling ropes on
sailboats and back-slapping athletes, but left her fingers
feeling as though she had been sitting on them for several
minutes. But who needed blood anyway?

Inappropriate and totally crazy thoughts about the effect
those same fingers could have on other parts of her body

flitted through Andy's mind and it was a relief when he broke contact first and slid down into the smallish wooden chair opposite, which seemed far too flimsy for his body.

'You too. Corporate promotions. Tricky stuff.'

Andy felt her heart rate increase several notches as he moved even closer.

Keep to the script. Keep to the script. Give him five minutes to get a coffee, and then break it to him gently. Talk business. That usually works.

She took a long drink of coffee to give her brain a chance to catch up and form something close to a sensible reply. 'It can be. But I suspect that every successful entrepreneur has to take risks. Even in sportswear.'

His brown eyes focused on her face, but there was just enough of a crunch between the dark brows to capture her attention. 'Damn right.'

Then one side of his mouth lifted into a half-smile. 'You could almost say that was the best part. Pushing yourself against the limits, knowing just what kind of risk you are taking. Yeah. I guess that we are both in the risk business. Can I get you another coffee?'

And without waiting for her reply he lifted his head and, like a genie from a lamp, the barista instantly appeared on their side of the counter. 'Two of what the lady had and I'll take an omelette. Three eggs, ham and mushroom. No onion, heavy on the herbs. And can you throw in some of those Panini and a couple of cookies? Cheers.'

Two fingers to the forehead and their server was gone. Amazing.

Andy looked in astonishment to the counter, where the two girls were feverishly working on the order, and then back to #sportybloke, who was sitting back, legs outstretched to one side. Watching her.

'Do you always do that?' She asked with a quick jab of her head towards the counter.

He blinked and hit her with a grin that displayed his straight white teeth to best effect. 'Do what? Order coffee? Yeah, I might do that now and again. Especially in a coffee shop.'

'I mean, do you always just shout out the order from your chair instead of going up to the counter like everyone else? And how do you know that I needed another coffee? I might have preferred a tea for a change. Or maybe even one of those hot steak sandwiches?'

His reply was to rest his bare arms on the table, hands loose and relaxed, and lean the top half of his long wide frame towards her from the hips so that she had to fight the urge to lean back against the wall and protect her space.

The top two buttons of his shirt stretched open as the fabric stretched over a broad chest, and revealed a hint of deeply tanned skin, and more than a few dark chest hairs.

At this distance she could have reached out and touched the curved flicks of dark wavy hair that had fallen over one side of his temple, but she had the idea that he would like that far too much, so she simply lifted her chin and inhaled a long calming breath through her nose.

Big mistake.

Instead of a background aroma of coffee and baked goods, she was overwhelmed with the scent of gentle rain on fresh-cut grass blended with lime zest, which was tangy against the sweetness of the air.

He smelt wonderful. Fresh, distinctive and on a scale of one to ten on the testosterone level she would give it a twelve. Because there was no mistake. The man below the flamboyant floral shirt that the dreadful Nigel would have completely refused to wear, even for a bet, was certainly adding a lot of himself to the mix. From the sun-bleached hair on his arms and the way the muscles in his neck flexed when he moved, to the 'know it all' confidence in the smile he was giving her at that moment, he was off the scale.

And then he ramped it up a notch by lowering the tone of his voice so that she was the only person who would be able to hear him whisper in words that were as smooth as molten chocolate.

'I took a chance. *City girl.*'

Then he slid his arms into his lap, sat back against the wooden chair and winked at her.

CHAPTER TWO

A CHANCE? He took a chance? Oh! Could he *be* more of a caveman and testosterone driven?

And he knew it! He knew exactly what effect he was having.

And suddenly every alarm bell in her body started sounding all at once.

Why on earth did a man this gorgeous need to meet women on the Internet?

It was obvious from his emails that he was a flirt, but this man looked as though he was getting ready to beat his chest and roar or if that didn't work, sling the nearest stone club over his shoulder and head out into the rain looking for dinosaurs to slay.

His too-long dark chocolate-brown hair was tousled and so unkempt that one heady thick wave fell forward across his high cheekbone, and he flicked it back with his fingertips. It was a move that any professional fashion model would be proud to have mastered so perfectly—while still looking manly and gruff.

Then there was that mouth.

#sportybloke had an expression that was somewhere between suggestive and cheeky and as infectious as chicken pox. Andy had to fight from smiling automatically in return.

Until now she had believed that she was immune to such

charms. After all, she had been exposed to this type of infection many times before and just about survived.

But this man was a carrier for a super powerful version of charm that no amount of medical science and previous experience had a chance of fighting off.

She might have guessed.

#sportybloke was one of *them*.

According to his online profile he ran a sportswear company with his brother and spent a lot of time promoting water sports overseas. Their speciality was surfing gear.

Well, from the looks of #sportybloke he was just another wealthy, arrogant and handsome entrepreneur who had been in the right place at the right time and had made his pile of money and was determined to flash it at every opportunity. A man like him spent his winters at some luxury ski resort and his summers bumming it around the Caribbean on other people's yachts while his was being built to his own specifications.

Little wonder that he probably expected everyone to jump when he clicked his fingers, when, in fact, CEOs of international sports companies had all the time and money in the world.

Sheesh. Well, Andy had news for #sportybloke. The dinosaur was right here in the room and she was looking at him. Okay, so that was no hardship, but it was definitely time to get back to the script and earn that bonus that she knew Elise would pay, even if she had pulled the plug on the whole Internet dating business.

Just tell him and get it over with. He can cope!

Andy took a breath for courage, her back braced. But just as she was about to blurt out who she was and why she was there, the food and fresh coffees arrived and she was temporarily distracted by the delicious aroma from two cheese and ham freshly grilled Panini and crisp chocolate-chunk-and-hazelnut cookies.

One of the bar staff actually whimpered slightly under her breath as she slid the plate of steaming hot, fragrant herby omelette in front of #sportybloke, who thanked her with a smile.

Unbelievable.

'Ladies first,' he breathed and gestured towards the Panini; he had deftly cut each in half diagonally and left them in the centre of the table. They were oozing with molten cheese and tomato in between the crunchy bread and her mouth was already watering at the aroma, but just as she was about to say no her stomach growled in anticipation of the fat and carb treat that was on display.

'Thank you,' she murmured, leaning forward towards him, 'but there is something I need to tell you and it is quite urgent. You see, I'm not who you think I am. When I sent you those emails I...'

Suddenly a chair was knocked over on the next table only inches away from where Andy was sitting. An older man was on his feet, gasping in air through his nose, his hands clutched tight onto the sides of the table. He was panicking, his eyes darting from side to side. Face and neck red.

Without waiting for permission Andy darted out from her seat. 'Someone please help. He's choking.' Oblivious to the sound of people standing and shuffling chairs, she gave the man an almighty thump between his shoulder blades with the heel of her hand. Her hand ached with the effort and she was puffing slightly but her back slap had no effect.

Andy stepped back to inhale and was just about to repeat the process when #sportybloke appeared at her side, stepped into the gap, linked his hands in front of the now very wheezy and panicky diner and pulled sharply upwards with all the force that a muscular man over six feet tall with long arms could produce on a crouched person's stomach. A sizeable piece of unchewed steak sandwich shot out onto the check tablecloth and the diner sucked in breath after breath, his shoulders shaking with relief.

#sportybloke gave him a quick nod in reply to the handshake and man-thumped the stranger on the arm before stepping back to their table. Apparently oblivious to the slight cheer that had gone up from the other patrons and the anxious waitresses.

But instead of sitting down, he clamped his fingers tightly around the back of his chair and exhaled slowly from deep inside his chest, with a definite wince.

'Anything the matter?' she asked, quietly.

His gaze shot onto her face. It was fierce and intense, and for one microsecond she had an insight into the power and strength of this man who could freeze her to ice with just one glance.

But then he blinked and his eyes softened. 'Leg cramp.' He coughed and slapped his upper thigh with the flat of his hand. 'I'm not used to sitting around for long periods. But I'm fine. Thanks.'

And he immediately pushed his chair closer to the wall so that he could sit down with his right leg stretched out in front of him.

Andy slid back in the chair and sat back to wait for her heart to stop thumping before blinking, swallowing hard and pulling her chair to the table.

'Well. If you're okay. That was…different,' she said, looking over #sportybloke's shoulder. 'If I was the suspicious type I might think that you set that up just to impress me. Luckily for you I'm not, but I didn't see emergency first aid on your online dating profile. Is that new?'

'My first regular paid job was as a lifeguard in Cornwall. Compulsory first-aid training. Although I can't say that I have used that move for a while. Glad to have helped—but you did okay for a city girl. One tip? Thump harder next time.'

'Next time? I don't want there to be a next time, thank you.'

She held out her right hand in front of her and watched the fingers tremble. 'How can you stay so cool? I'm a wreck.'

His reply was to smile and seize hold of her hand between the palms of both of his, trapping it inside as he slowly moved his hands up and down, inch by inch, massaging life and heat and stimulation into the nerves.

His skin was warm and surprisingly soft except for the callouses on the fingers and inside his palms, but there was no mistaking the hidden strength in those hands and fingers.

She liked hands, always had. It was usually one of the first things she noticed about a person. And this man had spectacular hands. Long slender fingers with clean short nails. His knuckles were scarred and bruised as though they had been bashed at regular intervals.. Sinewy. Powerful.

They were clever, fast, working hands, and for the first time Andy wondered if she had made a mistake slotting #sportybloke into the arrogant CEO slot. These were not the hands of an office worker like the men she usually met. Far from it.

Um. Maybe he had been telling the truth about his surfing line in those emails?

'Being cool has nothing to do with it. I simply knew what I had to do and did it. Feeling better now? Great. Let's eat.'

He slid his hands away and her rock-steady fingers waggled back. But to her disgust she already missed having his warm strong hand around hers.

Then he cut the omelette into quarters, then eighths before spearing a portion with some of the salad garnish and carefully closing his mouth around the fork. Then slowly, slowly, drew the fork from his mouth.

And suddenly Andy found that her neck had become amazingly hot for some reason and she put down her dinner to loosen her scarf.

He was eating an omelette using cutlery. That was all. And the whole fork thing was not sensuous at all. Oh, no. Not a bit. Well… Maybe a little.

Well, that clinched it.

This man was way too handsome to be single and looking for girls online. And he could speak in joined-up sentences and use cutlery.

There had to be something wrong with him.

She had heard about married or engaged men who went on Internet dating sites to have extramarital affairs with unsuspecting girls. Perhaps he already had a perfectly charming lovely lady back at home? Or he was actually a journalist doing a documentary about desperate sad girls who met men through Internet dating.

She inhaled sharply.

Focus, Andy, focus. Stop letting your imagination run away with you.

She took a breath and her words came tumbling out in one huge rush.

'I need to tell you something. I am not the #citygirl executive you were expecting. My boss is. Only she had to go away on urgent business and it was too late to cancel. So, I came instead to apologise. Sorry.'

And then she sat back, dropped her hands into her lap, focused her gaze on his chin and waited for the fireworks to start.

The man on the other side of the table continued chewing for a moment, then put down his cutlery, crossed his arms, stretched out his neck and seemed to double his size. If he was intending to be imposing and maybe a little intimidating, his plan was working perfectly.

He stared at her through slightly narrowed eyes, his eyebrows low and dark, and she had to fight down the sudden urge to start chewing at her fingernails.

'So let me get this straight. You're not the girl I was supposed to meet here tonight.'

Andy pressed her lips together and risked a small apologetic shrug.

'And you're not a company executive?'

She shook her head very rapidly from side to side.

'I see,' he replied with something close to disappointment in his voice. 'So how do I get to meet the girl who wrote those emails? Or has she got cold feet?'

She blinked twice before answering. 'Oh, that was me. I wrote the emails. My boss paid me to write them for her, you see, and I really enjoyed chatting to you and learning about your life as...'

A low growl stopped her mid tracks. 'Paid you? To write them. Right. So just who are you and what are you really doing here?' he asked, and slid the whole top half of his body across the table towards her.

She tried shuffling backwards as he invaded what little personal space she had left but it was no use. Unless she wanted to leap sideways like a gazelle and make a run for it she was stuck. It was confession time. If he let her get a word in edgeways.

'Is this some sort of game you and your boss play with men you set up on the Internet? For all I know you could be pretending to be your PA because you don't like what you see or maybe you're using your boss's Internet account to meet someone above your pay scale. Am I close? Which one is it?'

Andy stared at him in horror, the blood pounding in her neck.

'A game? Of course it isn't a game. Elise doesn't even know that I'm here. And I would never use her account to meet people. That's a terrible accusation. No, it's nothing like that. Nothing at all.'

'Okay. Then what is this all about? Why are you here?'

'Well, I am beginning to wonder, because, if you must know, my boss cancelled less than an hour ago and I didn't like the thought of you sitting here all alone waiting for a date who has stood you up. There. That's it. Happy now?'

And before he had a chance to answer, Andy picked up the Panini with both hands and took a huge bite. And the second her teeth hit the toasted bread, a large squeeze of tomato shot out and hit her straight on the chest. And her white blouse. Her only, her favourite, her best and most expensive, white blouse.

Gulping down the rest of her overfull mouthful of food, she tried to scrub at the spot with her napkin. Only it was pink and made out of paper so that she now had a pink dye and a hot tomato stain on her blouse.

She put down her shredded napkin, took a quick glance at #sportybloke, who was looking at her in disbelief.

'Fast food. Always a risky business. The steak sandwich is not the only dangerous item on the menu,' she murmured, sighed out loud, picked up the Panini and took another bite. She couldn't do any more damage so she might as well finish her food.

#sportybloke blinked several times, pushed his shoulders hard back against the chair and unfolded his arms so he could stretch them out on the table, his palms flat on the gingham. The white scars on the backs of his hands and knuckles were just large enough for her to notice, but then she had to look at something, because he was doing the laser stare again.

His gaze seemed to be locked onto her face, as though he was looking for something, and she tried desperately not to squirm. And failed.

'Happy would be pushing it, but I completely agree.' He nodded, a strange smirk on his face, then tapped his forefinger against his full pink lower lip, then pointed towards her. 'About the food. Especially the cheese.'

Cheese? What cheese?

Andy patted her napkin against her lip in a dainty and ladylike fashion and all was going well until she dropped it back to her lap to reveal a string of molten yellow plastic-looking cheese, which must have been dangling from the corner of her mouth.

Well. So much for the sophisticated and elegant look.

'That's better,' he said with a fixed smile, sitting back. 'And the name is Miles, by the way. Now where were we? Oh, yes. Being stood up. Does that still happen?'

Miles? She looked at him with raised eyebrows.

She had rain-damp hair, a stained blouse and she had been sitting there in blissful ignorance of the fact that cheese strings were dangling from her lips.

Why did he trust her with his real name? If it was his real name.

Her mouth opened, ready to share her name, but then she closed it again. *Not yet. But she could answer his question.*

She paused and looked up at the ceiling. 'Oh, yes, it has happened to me more than once. I think that's why I hated the idea of doing it to someone else. Yes, I know that we have only talked through emails, but texting is not the same as apologising in person. Or at least it isn't to me. That probably makes me sound very old-fashioned, but that's the way I am.'

He seemed to think about that for a second before replying. 'I happen to agree. And your boss doesn't know that you are here?'

Andy shook her head. 'She's changed her mind about the whole Internet dating business. But there wasn't enough time to call you and cancel. So here I am.'

Then she braved a smile over the top of her sandwich. 'I hope you're not too annoyed or disappointed. Especially since I've eaten most of your food and I'm not actually your proper date.'

He sat back, eyebrows high, and pressed one hand to his chest. 'My pleasure. You have seen through my evil plan to win over a lady with toasted cheese and coffee. I feel the shame.'

'You should.' Andy nodded and inspected the last part of her Panini. 'Even though this was a most superior cheesy snack. So thank you for that.'

'Glad you approve,' he murmured, and raised his coffee beaker. 'Here's to cheesy snacks, although I am curious about something. Does your boss often ask you to pimp for her?'

Only just as the words left his mouth Andy was swallowing some coffee and between spluttering and coughing it took her a while before she could attempt to reply with a raspy voice. 'First time. And the last. We went to school together so I suppose Elise trusted me not to let her down.' She flashed him a glance. 'Did I? Let her down?'

A long, slow, languorous smile crept like dawn across the whole of his face, and then he wrapped his hands around his beaker. 'I might have chatted to a couple of girls. But this is the first Internet date I have ever agreed to.'

He rested his elbows on the table to support his chin. 'The only one. Does that answer your question?'

Andy froze, her coffee beaker suspended in mid-air.

'This is your first Internet date?'

'Absolutely. So far, not quite what I expected, but getting better by the minute.'

Her hand dropped. 'Oh.'

Of course it is—fool. He doesn't need to go on the Internet to meet women. But it did make her wonder. *Why? Why now?*

'I enjoyed reading about all the wonderful countries you have visited for your work.' She twirled one hand towards his shirt. 'I suppose that must be a problem for your, um... romantic relationships.'

Oh, shut up now before you make an even greater fool of yourself, you idiot. Andy winced and picked at some salad, to avoid looking at him.

'My romantic relationships?' He sniffed. 'Actually my romantic relationships, as you call them, are just fine. That isn't the problem. Just the opposite if anything—I spend my days surrounded by sporty girls of all shapes and sizes, and usually they are wearing remarkably little in the way of clothing.'

He lifted his chin and smiled. 'Did I mention that we specialise in water sports? Everything from paddle boarding to kite surfing. Our bikinis are very popular.'

A short chuckle and a nasal snort made her blink. 'No, I have plenty of female company. But I don't get to meet other kinds of women. And now I'm back in London, it might be interesting to meet girls who know more about the city than surfboards and sunblock. Plus I happen to enjoy meeting new people and getting to know them.'

She leant forwards, glancing from side to side as though about to tell him a secret of some sort.

'I have a terrible fault.'

His eyebrows rose towards the ceiling but he did not take the bait.

'Curiosity.' Andy nodded. 'I am well known for it. So you see, I can't help but wonder…why now? What made you decide to come out on a wet night to meet this particular girl when you don't even know her name?'

And without permission or any kind of warning, he clasped his long fingers around the palm of her right hand, raised it to his mouth and kissed her knuckles for two seconds before releasing her hand.

'I wanted to meet the girl who wrote those emails. The girl I am looking at right now.'

His lips had been warm and full and soft and she was so totally taken back by how gentle and tender that ultra-soft whisper of his lips on her skin had been that she just sat there, still, and in silence. While he smiled at her. And this time his eyes were smiling as well as his mouth and all she could hear was the sound of his breathing, slow and deep, which matched hers perfectly, breath for breath.

The coffee shop and the background clatter of people and machine and chairs being dragged on wooden floors faded into some other world which she no longer had any part in.

The air in the space between them seemed to bristle with electricity, tense and thick with unspoken words and silences. The pulse at the side of his neck was mesmerising, strong and steady in tune with his breathing.

Killer. Absolute killer.

Then he leant slightly forwards and said in a low whisper, 'I have a confession too. My brother Jason was the one who set up my profile and filled in the forms. Apparently he got fed up of my constant complaints about not being able to find a date for when I am in London.'

He raised his coffee cup and looked at her over the top of it—but his gaze was locked onto hers and somehow it was impossible for her to look away. 'To online dating virgins everywhere,' he whispered and took a long sip of coffee. 'Perhaps we should exchange notes?'

Ah...so that was it. She should have worked it out. Miles was a sailor with a girl in every port. Online dating virgin indeed!

They looked across at one another in silence, his mouth curled into a smile for so long that the air crackled across the table.

Andy felt as though a small thermonuclear device had just been planted somewhere low in her stomach and was threatening to emerge as a girly giggle.

She did not do giggling, simpering or anything that came close. Not even for hunky hotties like the one sitting opposite her nonchalantly drinking his coffee as his gaze stared into hers, waiting to see how she responded. Maybe this was some sort of test?

'I'll drink to that,' she replied, with a smirk. 'Although it does make me wonder.'

'Wonder?'

'What were you planning to do with the hazelnut cookies?' she replied in a flash, and pressed both of her lips tight together before sitting back in her chair, her head tilted to one side.

He roared with laughter. A real laugh, head back, shoulders shaking, holding onto the flimsy table, making it rock as his whole body joined in the joke, and this time she could not help herself. And for the first time in a very long while, Andy Davies laughed. Really laughed. Laughed until the tears were running down her cheeks and she was starting to wheeze.

She never laughed like this. Ever. And it was wonderful.

Even if people on the other tables had started to give them furtive glances.

Oh, Nigel would have been *so* mortified if she had made this kind of a scene on the few times when he was with her.

Nigel. Andy felt as if a bucket of icy water had been thrown over her head, and she instantly sat up straighter in her chair and tried to clear her head.

Stupid girl. She was not here to flirt and laugh with Miles. No matter how much he had brightened up her cold, wet evening. She was not ready to flirt and laugh with anyone.

She glanced up into his smiling face and a small shiver of disappointment and regret fluttered across her shoulders.

This was a horrible mistake.

It should be Elise sitting here, not her.

But he was worth meeting. If anything he was more open and extrovert than his emails had suggested. She couldn't lie.

Andy's gaze slid over to his long, muscular, tanned arms and she inhaled slowly.

Men like Miles stood at the helm of sailing ships and jumped off mountain peaks with only a pair of skis strapped to their legs. They did not do executive buffet lunches with mini canapés and fizzy pink water, which Elise specialised in.

It was time to call a halt to this embarrassing charade and make a quick getaway.

Stealing a secret smile, Andy was just about to make her excuses and leave when her view was blocked by the long cream designer raincoat of the most notorious gossip in Nigel's office, who was standing right in front of her.

Leering.

Andy reared back in horror, a fixed smile cemented onto her face. She had walked out of Nigel's office in tears six weeks ago and this was the first time that she had met any of the people she used to work with.

Worse. There were two of them. The second most feared, time-wasting gossip in the whole office building was glaring at Miles, her mouth hanging open in shock and lust.

'Hello, Andy,' the gossip whined, her eyes flicking from Andy to Miles and then back to Andy again. 'Fancy seeing you here. I heard that you were working nights somewhere.'

'Oh. Just taking an evening off,' Andy replied, in a casual voice, refusing to get involved in any kind of conversation with these two. 'You?'

'Thought we would catch a movie,' came the casual reply. Then her lips twisted into a knowing smirk. 'Amazing who you meet on the way.'

'Isn't it? Have a good time at the movie. See you around,' Andy replied with a quick wave of her hand, then her fingers clamped around her coffee beaker instead of the girl's neck.

Sniffing at being so obviously dismissed without being introduced to Andy's mysterious date, the two shuffled over to the only spare table, which thankfully meant that they were facing away from Andy, but from the sly sniggering glances they were giving her it was obvious that their lives were now complete.

Who needed a movie when they had just found out that Andy Davies was out with a hunky bloke in a coffee shop? Just think! Who would have thought she had the nerve, after Nigel had made such a fool of her?

It would be around the office in five minutes. In fact, they were probably texting all of their *pals* and her colleagues on their mobile phones at that very minute.

'Friends of yours?' a male voice asked from across the table.

She opened her eyes and blinked. Not only was Miles still there, but he was smiling at her and had started work picking out the whole hazelnuts from his cookie. She had been so absorbed in her own dilemma that she had forgotten about him.

'Girls I used to work with in my last job. And no, they certainly are not my friends. Far from it. I despise them.'

Now why had she said that? It wasn't their fault that she had fallen for all of the lies Nigel had told her so that she would work on his business proposals for nothing, night after night, while all the time he was living with the boss's daughter and taking the credit for her work. And she was the only one who was not in on the joke. The rest of the office had been laughing behind her back for weeks. Just waiting for Nigel to dump her the second he got his promotion. And he had. Oh, yes. And in public. And in style.

That familiar cold dark blanket of humiliation and bitter disappointment wrapped itself around Andy's shoulders, and she shivered inside her thin suit jacket.

'I see. They tell me that girls can be hard to work with. I'm sorry if my being here is going to cause you a problem back in the office.'

'Problem?' She whimpered and slumped down. 'You don't know the half of it.' Then she caught his change in breathing, and saw a flash of concern in his eyes. Tossing her head, she ran her fingers through her hair and smiled. 'Sorry. It's fine. Let's try and ignore them. They have nothing to do with my life now.'

He rested both elbows on the table and leaned forwards until his fingers were almost touching hers, and nobody else could hear what he was saying, his back to the room. 'None of my business but in my mind there are two ways to deal with office gossips. You say so what, and shrug it off. Or…' He picked up Andy's hand and started playing with it.

'What are you doing?' Andy snapped, trying to pull her hand away, but he was holding it in a vicelike grip. 'They're looking this way and taking photos on their cell phones,' she groaned in a strangled voice, as if things could get any worse.

'Excellent,' he replied, in a low calm voice. 'So let's try the other option, and give them something to really talk about.'

There was something in his voice that should have warned her that actually things were going to suddenly get a lot worse, but her gaze was locked on his mouth as he licked his lower lip with the tip of his tongue.

Then without warning his entire body moved in one single continuous motion, so that as he lifted slightly from his chair his right hand reached back and cradled the base of her head.

And then he kissed her.

Not just a peck on the cheek. Oh, no. His warm, full, moist lips moved gently across hers in a kiss so tender and so loving that her eyes instantly filled with tears and she had to blink them away as she closed her eyes and tilted her head so that he could kiss her again.

Only this time it was deeper and she felt just the slightest tingle of his tongue, chocolate and coffee on hers before he slid his mouth away, leaving her staggered, wobbly and unable to speak and attempting to breathe again.

Wow.

Andy opened her eyes and he was breathing as hard as she was. She could not resist staring at his full mouth, which was still wet from her kiss, and in another place and another universe she would have liked to know what it would feel like to lift that shirt over his head and find out what kind of man was able to kiss a perfect stranger like that.

She wasn't sure if she was meant to push him away and hit him for taking advantage, or pull him closer, and jump into his lap.

He did it for her. 'Andy?'

'Yes?'

'Do you think that is enough to keep the gossips happy?' he asked in a hoarse, breathless whisper.

'Oh, yes. That would do it,' Andy answered, and looked over to the girls who seemed to be huddled together over their phones. 'That will definitely do it.'

She pulled back, scraping her chair along the floor, grabbed her bag and stood up. 'Back in a moment. Too much caffeine,' she lied and almost ran to the ladies' room.

'I'll be right here,' he murmured behind her back. She turned back to look at him, as his fingers started flicking across the screen of his smart phone. The way his fingertips pressed the keys told her a lot more about his finesse and gentle touch than any online profile could.

Miles would be amazing in bed. She sighed as she turned away.

And it was only when she got inside the stall and had locked the door firmly behind her that her brain caught up with her hormones.

Miles had just called her Andy. And now he knew her real name!

She sat down, fully clothed, her elbows resting on her knees, chewing at her raggedy small fingernail, trying to come up with a cunning plan as to how to:

#Thank Miles for his understanding about Elise and pray that he had enough cash for the bill. Then thank him for the nice kiss. No—make that a very nice kiss.

#Sneak out of the coffee shop alone past the two gossips. Or maybe she should stride past with her head high? Nigel the suit was nothing compared to the gorgeousness of the man she had just left at the table.

#Come clean to Saffie. It had to be done. Elise's online coffee date had kissed her within an hour of walking through the door. Which either made her extremely lucky or a total strumpet. And she did not do strumpet. Never had. Not even when she was at school. The boys from their rival high school did not call her frosty knickers without good reason.

#Try and ignore the fact that Miles was the most attractive man that she had met in a very long time and that she would be reliving every moment of the last hour for a long time to come.

She keyed in the list on her organiser, looked at it, then shut the gizmo down and stuffed it into her bag, ripped off a long strip of toilet tissue and blew her nose loudly.

One thing was for sure. She was not going to get anything done sitting here feeling sorry for herself. Time to get going.

Andy pushed herself to her wobbly legs, turned the door handle and hobbled over to the washbasins in her high-heeled boots to try and repair the damage before facing Miles again.

She took one look at the medium-height, medium-pretty woman with the medium-brown scraggy hair in the mirror and winced.

Why had she stayed long enough to let Miles kiss her?

Miles was a flirt. A professional, Greek-god-handsome, used-to-women-falling-at-his-feet flirt. He had higher qualifications in manly allure and an honorary degree from the university of flirting and female dazzling.

And she was not in a place where she could handle that. Any of it.

He was everything she'd thought he might be from his emails. And more.

She simply wasn't up to flirting with a man like Miles and the truth was...she didn't know whether she ever would be. Time to go home.

CHAPTER THREE

MILES watched Andy stroll away from him to the other side of the room.

So what if he was a leg man?

Those cute little ankle boots showed off her shapely legs to perfection, and not even that shapeless grey business suit could hide the fact that Andy had a body that would look amazing in a swimsuit.

What was the Andy short for? Andrea? Maybe he would have a chance to find out.

If she let him.

Miles chortled to himself as he finished his coffee. It wasn't often that the old Gibson charm let him down, and he had a sneaking suspicion that there might be a back door to this coffee shop and Andy had made a run for it.

And he could hardly blame her. He had felt like doing exactly the same thing after the little announcement she had made earlier.

The whole idea that he had been set up was the one thing guaranteed to flick his switches. When she told him that she was a replacement for her boss, his first reaction was to walk out and not look back.

Which was only natural after what happened with Lori.

But that was before he realised that Andy was the girl

who had written the emails that had made all of those trips to the physio almost tolerable over the past week.

Well. Jason had warned him that this #citygirl might not be the date he was expecting—and he had got that right.

She was a whole lot more.

It took guts to come here and apologise in person. Guts and a heart that did not want him to sit here on his own waiting for his date to show up. Maybe that was what he had seen in those emails? That Andy cared about people. People other than herself.

One thing was sure.

He had trusted his gut reaction every day of his sporting life, and right now it was telling him that Andy was telling him the truth. This was no trick—she had not even bothered to look the same as the girl whose blurry photo was attached to the online dating profile.

Of course he could be wrong. Lori had proved that. But there was even more to this girl Andy than he had expected. She was curious about him—and he was just as curious about her. Why on earth did she agree to write emails for her boss? This girl had a story to tell and he wouldn't mind hearing it.

At the very least she could provide the kind of distraction he would need to get through the sports event a week on Saturday.

He peered around in the direction of the ladies' room. She had taken off pretty quickly after he had kissed her. Maybe that had been a mistake? She hadn't stopped him but unless he had read the signals wrong she hadn't been expecting it, either.

Maybe she was hiding and afraid to come out in case he was actually a sex fiend who lured nice girls into coffee shops. Then kissed them in front of their least favourite workmates.

Jason was going to be furious.

Miles scanned his emails and opened the latest from Jason with a link to an article from a London magazine giving a list of the Brainiest Millionaire Bachelors in London.

And there he was—Jason Gibson of Cory Sports.

His identical twin brother.

The photographer must have come to their London office because Jason was in full city-boy mode. He was wearing his trademark long-sleeved black shirt with the diamond cufflinks in the shape of a surfboard and black formal trousers. Something must have amused Jason because he had broken into a half-smile as he looked into the camera.

Miles shook his head. Even though they were so totally different in so many ways, there was no denying the fact that there had been a time when their own parents could not tell them apart.

Of course that had been before he filled out and Jason stayed boy slender.

When he thought about all of the times they had swopped places and fooled people over the years. Playing tricks on teachers and girls was their favourite—Jason was naturally more academic and a whizz at exams. He could never understand why Miles only wanted to learn about the things that interested him—like sports science and geology and the weather.

Then there had been that one time when Miles had taken the boat out to show off to some girl and it had run out of diesel in the middle of nowhere. And Jason had taken the initiative to sit the exam in his place, and not one of their tutors realised. What made it especially annoying was that Miles had been given top marks, and Jason had only studied climatology for a few months before dropping it for computer science.

But somehow it had worked. Jason was the brains of the family and Miles was the professional sportsman who was on the way to being world champion.

And that was okay. Hell—it was better than okay. The Gibson twins were the stars of the surfing world and Cory Sports went global.

Miles inhaled slowly and rolled his shoulders back as that cold icy feeling of dread welled up from the pit of his stomach.

Correction. That *had* been okay. Until the accident.

Now he was back in London to pretend to the sporting world that it was business as usual for Cory Sports.

If only that were true.

Oh—he knew what the sports journalists were asking. Jason was at the helm and still one of the brainiest bachelors in London. But what about his brother? What was Miles doing in the business apart from learning to walk again? What future did he have when he stopped being the sporting hero? Good question. Pity that he did not have a smart answer for them. Not yet. But he would. He had to.

Sitting up taller, Miles decided to focus on something he could control and snorted in derision at the fawning press article before sending a suitable reply about how Jason's smart-boy haircut was bound to wow the ladies—if, *big if,* he ever found the time to meet any.

Jason was brilliant and had taken Cory Sports to places neither of them had ever expected.

But when it came to girls? Hopeless. No. Make that worse than hopeless.

His brother seemed to attract girls who either saw him as someone who they could get free sportswear from, or as a geek who they could persuade to run the IT in their companies in his spare time, then dumped him when they found out that he did not have any spare time.

Or then there were the worst kind. The professional gold-diggers who were happy to pursue any man who could even vaguely be described as a millionaire. Or, in their case, multimillionaire, although Jason would be the last person to brag about the money.

And Miles knew all about gold diggers.

Lori had been in his life for three years and not once did it cross his mind that she was using him and his status to get where she wanted to be. He was actually deluded enough to believe that she wanted to be with the real Miles Gibson, when in fact, she had a lot more interest in how he could further her career.

But when he had the accident? Well. He had stopped being useful to her any more and she had moved on to the next world-class sportsman who could give her the A-list profile she wanted. Having her own TV show was just part of the perks of that celebrity world.

And so was being invited to the Sports Personality Award show next week.

Which made it even more important that he walk into that sports event, on his own two feet, with a new woman on his arm and a twinkle in his eye.

The twinkle he could manage on his own.

But the woman? He wanted the right woman. Not another lingerie model like Lori.

No—he needed a stand-in date for one night—and just one night—who could hold her own.

A date with spark and energy and her own life and independence who could guard his back when he showed the world that Miles Gibson was not going to let a car accident stop him doing what he wanted.

Moaning to Jason that he did not want to go solo to the sports personality event had been a mistake. The last thing he had expected Jason to do was set him up on an Internet dating site. And he hated it when Jason got it so right. Andy was interesting. Funny. Oblivious to the fact that her real personality was there in every line of the emails that she had sent.

She had been worth coming out on a wet November evening.

All he had to do was turn on the charm and talk her into coming with him to the event. Done deal.

Suddenly there was a bustle of activity and Andy breezed past him, picked up her coat from the back of her chair, slipped it on without saying a word, and slung her bag over one shoulder.

He was just about to say something when she turned towards him, and the words stuck in his throat. Her skin was as white as paper, and from the quivering mouth it was obvious that she was upset about something.

Over him? Damn. Those girls must have got to her. Kissing her just to make an impression had been a big mistake, even if it had been the highlight of his day.

'It was very nice to have met you, but I need to head back. Urgent business. Thank you very much for the dinner and best of luck with the dating scene.' Then she gave a quick nod and turned away from him towards the door.

'Hey. Wait a moment,' he said, not wanting to draw attention to her, but if she heard him she pretended not to, and in one smooth motion flicked her collar up, flung open the door and strode away into the rain as fast as her legs could carry her. And was gone.

Miles stood up and tried to move after her, but he had been sitting in the one place too long again. His leg instantly cramped up and the pain in his knee switched from being just tolerable to pass-the-painkillers so quickly that he had to sit back down and massage the injured muscle back into life.

Well, this day got better and better.

He had just driven away the only online date he had agreed to meet.

And then he spotted something purple and umbrella shaped propped up next to her chair.

Saffie's house was in complete darkness when Andy walked up the path and turned the key in the front door. The rain had turned into a driving sleet and as the warm air hit her face and ears she could feel her cheeks tingle from the icy blast.

She had already been halfway down the street before she realised that she had left her purple umbrella back in the coffee shop—probably hidden below Miles's jacket. So she had waited for the bus that never came. So then she had gritted her teeth and walked for twenty minutes in her smart boots rather than just stand there and wait.

Waiting was for losers. Miles would never have waited—and neither would she.

Because standing on her own at that freezing bus stop with the rain running down her neck and inside her boots Andromeda Elizabeth Davies had come to a major conclusion. After twenty-eight years on this planet she had done enough waiting for other people in life.

She had waited for her parents to stop working just long enough to pay her some attention.

She had waited for someone to explain why they had to move out of her home and her own room with her own things into the hastily rearranged study of her grandparents' apartment, which she would be sharing with a lifetime of hoarded unwanted clutter.

She had waited for her parents to stop telling her how lucky she was to go to the private boarding school that was soaking up the trust fund her parents had started when they were rich and had money to throw away.

And then she had waited for her school friends to realise that she was just the same girl, only without any money. Saffie and her close pals had been brilliant but the others like Elise had dropped her in a week.

She had been prepared to wait for Nigel to make the first move and start dating her properly. Too busy with the project work, he had said. The presentation to the board for the new promotional plans for the coming year had to be perfect—but then they could relax and spend a weekend away together and tell the other people in the office that they were a couple. Surely she could wait a few more weeks?

She was his guilty little secret.

Sordid. Dirty. Expendable—and something he would simply throw away when he had used her enough. So he could get back to the girl he was living with.

Well, that was then and this was now. And she had waited long enough.

Meeting with #sportybloke Miles that evening had shown her just what she had been missing in her life—and it hurt that she did not feel able to open her heart to relax and enjoy his company as though it were a real date.

Because it had never been a real date, and she had to remember that. No matter how lovely his smile, his touch and the feeling of his lips on hers.

Slipping off her wet coat, she strolled slowly up the staircase, her feet dragging and her wet boots feeling like lead weights on her feet. Each tread of the old wooden staircase creaked as she put her weight on the boards and echoed around the tall empty hallway, but she had become used to each familiar sound in this comfortable family-sized home. Her faithful friends were the chiming of the grandfather clock in the hall and the faint clanking from the central heating as it tried to bring some warmth to so many unoccupied rooms.

When Saffie had asked her if she wanted to come and keep her company, Andy had jumped at the chance to share a house with a girl she was proud to call her friend.

But that was two years ago, when Saffie was working in London and she could jump on a bus and be at the restaurant in twenty minutes. Now she was in Paris and not even a fast train link could make the distance any smaller.

Andy looked up at the stained-glass window at the top of the stairs. In summer the house was filled with coloured light and seemed a magical place, bright and positive and bursting with life.

But at that moment, it was dark, wet and windy and the rain lashed against the stained-glass and the only light was from the street light outside streaming in from the glass panel over the front door.

And as she stood there on the staircase, halfway to the landing, a huge weight suddenly seemed to press down on her shoulders.

Andy slid sideways onto the stair with her back against the wall as though the events of the day were too heavy to carry any longer.

She let her head drop back and just sat there, listening to the sound of her breathing and gentle sobs in the darkness.

It wasn't the dark, or the silence.

No, it was the crushing feeling of loneliness that drove her to feel sorry for herself. She had never got used to being so lonely. There was no one she could talk to about her life and her problems. Nobody understood her or was truly interested in her life.

Saffie was the nearest thing she had to a family. It would be the middle of the dinner service in Paris around now, so she couldn't talk to her best pal until the morning—and

Saffie worked so hard, driven by her passion for food to be the best she could be, and Andy admired her for that.

Goodness knew, Saffie could have trained as a lawyer as her parents wanted her to, but that wasn't what she wanted and she had started at the bottom washing dishes and ended up with a first-class degree in catering and a chance to show what she could do in a serious restaurant in Paris.

And nobody was prouder than Andy.

Saffie had been her best friend at boarding school when her parents were working silly hours in the city and sending the chauffeur to pick her up on a Friday afternoon. But what made her truly special was that Saffie had stuck by her even when the stock market exploded and her father's bank went under. Helping her friend out while finding somewhere else to live had seemed a brilliant solution to two problems. Win, win, as Nigel would have said.

Nigel.

Andy pressed her hand to her mouth, and then wiped away the tears from her cheeks.

Oh, what a fool she had been.

It had been the right decision to resign from her nice clean office job once she understood that he already had a girlfriend. No. Make that a rich girlfriend. The boss's daughter. There was no going back from that. Even if it had meant leaving a full-time job to work part-time for Elise to pay her bills.

It was just—sometimes she felt that she could touch the silence in this house which was more than her home—it was where she had her studio.

A small smile creased her lips and Andy blinked away her tears and sniffed.

Yes. She had her painting and her studying—and that was enough for anyone.

Maybe Miles was having a bad influence on her? Now

there was a true entrepreneur who acted first then asked for permission later. What had he said? He took a chance. A risk.

She had been snatching an hour here and there over the past few months to work on what Saffie called her secret squirrel passion. Illustrating. The one thing in this world she would love to do more than anything else. That was why Nigel's betrayal hurt so much. She had sacrificed the time she could have spent on her true passion for him.

A man like Miles would never have put up with him.

Lesson learnt. Not again. Never again. No more waiting. No more putting it off until later.

Andy wrapped her hand tightly around the bannister and was just about to pull herself to her feet when her mobile phone rang out from her bag.

Saffie! She scurried around in her bag, terrified that she would ring off before she found her phone in the near darkness of the hall, and flicked it open, instantly creating a bright panel of light. Her shoulders slumped down in disappointment. It wasn't her friend. It was an email.

Then she froze. What if it was from Nigel?

Hardly daring to look, she quickly scanned down the list.

It was the online dating agency. #sportybloke had sent her a message.

Drat. Closing Elise's account was on tomorrow's list of things to do.

Exhaling slowly, she paused for a second before clicking on the email. He must think that she was a total idiot, running out on him into the rain like that without even a decent explanation.

Then her eyes widened and she sat back on the stair and looked through the stair rails to the hall before reading the message again.

From: #sportybloke
To: #citygirl
Hi Andy.
Hope that you managed to dodge the rain and are not working too late.

I wanted to apologise for my rash act in the coffee shop this evening. Kissing you in front of the office gossips was neither tactful nor courteous. I do hope that it does not complicate things.

After you left I found a purple flowery umbrella which might be yours.

If you can stand it, I would like to meet you again and return your property in person.

You said in one of your emails that you like modern European food, and I happen to know about a new Spanish restaurant which has just opened in Soho.

How about dinner? Thursday. 7.30pm. Looking forward to it.

Say yes. Miles.

P.S. They have good cheese.

Andy stared at the screen, put down the phone and pressed her hand against her mouth, her mind buzzing with questions and options and excuses.

This was her get-out clause.

All she had to do was to thank him politely for the invitation and tell him that it hadn't worked out. Sorry. Best of luck. And that would be it. Job done.

She put the phone down on the stair and rubbed both of her hands across her face, then back over her hair to her neck. Her fingers massaged her neck for a few minutes, her eyes closed.

Nigel had deceived her. Tricked her. Used her for his own advantage.

And then she had done exactly the same with these online

coffee dates. She had lied in every one of the many emails she had sent for Elise.

This was so wrong it was not funny. So many lies.

Well, that was over now. She was done with being used by other people who lied to her.

These men deserved better. Miles deserved better. A lot better. He had been nothing but nice to her and he was even more of the man she had imagined from his emails.

Andy read the message again on the brightly lit screen that was illuminating her small strip of staircase. And the more times she read it, the more clearly the hidden message screamed out at her.

This was a pity date.

Miles felt sorry for her. Sorry for kissing her. Sorry for the trouble he might have caused. Sorry for being a nuisance—so he offered her a meal out as an apology which would make him feel better. He wasn't interested in her. Not really.

Her fingers moved over the tiny keyboard with the only answer possible.

To: #sportybloke
From: #citygirl
Hello Miles.
Thank you for your message but there is no need to apologise.

Spanish food sounds wonderful, and I am deeply flattered by your kind invitation, but I don't think seeing each other again would be a good idea. Hope that you enjoy your time in London. And best of luck with the online dating.

Please keep the umbrella. I think it would suit you.
Andy.
P.S. I love cheese.

Her finger hovered over the send button before she pressed hard down and watched the message go off into the ether.

Finished. Over. Done.

Andy pulled herself to her feet and inhaled deeply before lifting her leg and moving forwards. One step at a time, girl. One step at a time. Time to feed Saffie's goldfish Madge and relive a kiss from a sporty bloke that for a few brief moments had made her world a much brighter place.

CHAPTER FOUR

From: saffie@saffronthechef
To: Andromeda@ConstellationOfficeServices
Subject: Moment of madness

Hiya Gorgeous—thanks for the update. And for the good news about Miles—your hunky sporty bloke. Now we're talking. And I still cannot believe you turned him down!

Here's an outrageous idea. Track down this Miles and tell him that you have changed your mind and would LOVE to go out for dinner so that he can feed you cheese then dance the flamenco with a rose between his teeth. Tight pants and all. [I shall require photos]

What you need is a large dose of Aunty Saffie's famous remedy for getting over a rubbish relationship. Have a fling! Throw caution to the wind, raid my wardrobe for glad rags and go out and let your hair down and have some fun.

Otherwise I have this sneaky suspicion that you will be sitting hunched over your drawing board for days on end. Don't do it.

Anyhow. Must dash. Or I will be in mucho troublo.

Have fun. Saffie

P.S. I mean it. Put down that pen and ink, right now. And, yes, I know that I am bossy but that is why you love me. J

MILES sat up against the bed head and flicked on the bedside lamp, his lungs fighting for air, squinting against the light until he could see all around him.

Heart thumping, his skin shiny with sweat, he swung his legs over the side of the bed, onto the solid oak floorboards, and felt the slight roughness of the wood under his toes. Reassuring. Real.

It had been the same dream again.

A memory played out so many times it had become like a scene from a favourite movie. A video played over and over until the words and images were embedded in the subconscious. Until the reality was lost, and the dream took its place.

Miles looked around the room.

Where was he? *Focus.*

The Cory Sports building. Upstairs in Jason's penthouse apartment.

London, he was in London.

In a too quiet, too calm and way too white bedroom, which looked just like all of the hospital rooms he had got to know over the past eleven months. Only without the smell.

Air. He needed air! Action. Sound. Movement. Colour. Life!

A cold autumn dawn was trying to creep around the edges of the window blind at the patio doors and he tried to push himself off the bed.

But his knee did not like that idea one little bit, and he winced in pain and lay down flat again, his fingers crushed into fists of anger and frustration.

How long had he slept?

Miles squinted at the electronic gizmo with about twenty dials that Jason called a clock. Five hours. Maybe six. Not enough.

The latest physiotherapist had given him strict instructions to get off his feet as much as possible and give his knee some chance at recovery.

Yeah. Right.

Miles lay back, legs stretched out in front of him, but the pain was too much to ignore and his right hand automatically rubbed his right knee.

When would he be able to block out that movie clip from his memory?

Probably never.

He could still hear the voices in his head.

Have you heard that Miles Gibson has been in a car accident? Now he really has lost everything, hasn't he? Poor guy. He won't ever get up on a board again. Must be hard not having any career left.

Well, they were wrong. And he was going to prove just how wrong they were, then prove it again and again until they got the message straight. Miles Gibson was back on his feet and the same man he had always been.

The Gibson family had built up Cory Sports on the strength of having world champion kite surfer Miles Gibson at the helm. They were a good team. But these were hard economic times and the competition was fierce. His family had sacrificed everything to make his dream of being a professional surfer a reality. They needed him to get up there and tell the world that he was back to stay.

He would not let them down. No matter how much it cost him.

He was a fighter. And that was what he should focus on now.

Fighting. Every hard-won step of the way. Fighting through the pain.

Miles scrubbed harder at his leg, trying to massage the blood back into muscles and joints.

He had spent most of the past week visiting specialists all

over London and they had all come to the same conclusion. There were no magical treatments or remarkable new experts that he could fly in to save the day, no extra medical equipment he could buy or new procedures.

The brilliant surgeons who had pinned his left leg back together had taken one look at his right knee and done the best they could. But it was no good and they knew it. His career had ended inside a vintage sports car that was never intended to comply with modern safety regulations. There was no airbag, no protective roll cage. Just a few layers of metal between him and the road.

His life as a professional kite surfer was dead. Gone. Finished.

Twenty years of hard work and pushing himself to be the very best in his profession. Over in an instant.

And he hated that. He hated it with a passion that very few things in this life could match. One of them required the kind of escort agencies that might give him some distraction in the short-term, but were a terrible idea at any time, and the other needed sea, surf, high waves, quality boards and acrobatic kites.

Problem was—he still actually needed his knee in some sort of working order to be able to walk. Anything to avoid being confined to a wheelchair again.

Miles stopped punching at the innocent headboard, sat up and scrubbed at his hair with his fingertips just as Jason stumbled into the room, wiping his eyes then blinking at Miles over the top of his spectacles.

'I heard yelling. You appear to be alone so it can't be the obvious. The old dream again?'

'Yeah. Sorry if I woke you,' Miles answered as Jason flopped down on the bed and pulled the pillow under his head.

'No problem.' Jason yawned. 'I need to get in early anyway.

That pretty receptionist the agency sent over knows nothing about sports and still managed to crash our complete online ordering system yesterday, so that's my morning wasted on interviews. How about you? Back to the physio?'

'No. Not today. But one thing is for sure—I need to get out of this apartment. I don't know how you do it, Jase. Seriously. I had no idea it would be so hard to stay indoors for more than a few days at a time. I didn't have any choice in the hospitals but this office work is killing me. Don't you ever yearn for fresh air and a beach now and then? No?'

Miles sighed and shook his head. 'Cabin fever.' He scanned the room, then shrugged. 'Great apartment. But you might have added something in the way of colour? All I can see are plain cream walls and if I look out the window I see grey skies, greyer buildings and most of the people in this city could use some sun and a humour transplant.'

Instantly he thought of #citygirl Andy and broke into a smile.

'One more thing to add to that list of things to do, Jase. Email that online dating service and tell them that the coffee date was a hit but the lady has decided that Internet dating was not for her.'

'Oh, no,' Jason groaned. 'Do I have to call lawyers? What did you do this time?'

'Relax, I didn't do anything unusual.'

'That's what I'm afraid of.' Jason inhaled sharply and lifted his chin. 'Hit me with it. Was she ancient, desperate, frigid or a gold-digger?'

Miles thought for a moment and did a rerun of their conversation, especially the part when she confessed that she was a stand-in for her boss. 'None of those things. Andy was different, cute. Although I'm not totally surprised that she didn't want to see me again seeing that…I might have, maybe, possibly…'

'Bro. Out with it. You didn't strip off in the middle of the restaurant to impress her with your tattoos or abs again, did you?'

'Worse. I embarrassed her in front of a couple of girls she used to know. She ran off before I could apologise. And there may be photographs.'

Jason winced. 'And you are supposed to be the ladies' man in the family. Well, our press cuttings agency will pick up anything that hits the gossip columns. What does this Andy look like?'

Miles conjured up an image of a girl with delicate cheekbones, silky fine brown hair curling at her ears and full pink lips, which had made one Panini the highlight of his day, and chuckled.

'Brunette. Green eyes. Dainty. Sassy in a suit. Doesn't freak when she drops food on her top and knows first aid. Nice hands. And she likes cheese.'

'Hands. Sassy. Cheese. Got it,' Jason said, slipping off the bed and polishing his spectacles on his tee shirt.

'You like this Andy, and don't try and deny it. Usually the only thing you are interested in is how she looks in or out of swimwear. I know you way too well. Pity you blew it.'

'What did I say?' Miles raised his arms in protest. 'You were the one who talked me into this online-dating game. All I need is a date for next week. One night. Not a relationship. End of story. And in case you have forgotten I am off the dating circuit and will be until further notice, remember?'

'I don't know why. Lori made her decision to dump you at the worst time possible. Fact. But that was months ago and you are more or less back on your feet. Another fact. You have been whining at me for weeks about having to find a date for the show. Don't blame me for taking the initiative.'

'Initiative? I'll give you initiative,' Miles growled. 'I am staying in this dull grey city long enough to show my face at the Sports Personality Award show, and then I am taking the initiative and getting out of the city to get some colour and spark back into my life. The Cory Sports roadshow hits Australia in less than eight weeks. Sun. Sea and surf. And it couldn't come soon enough.'

Andy grinned as a madcap bike courier jumped his cycle onto the pavement at breakneck speed, only feet in front of her, to overtake a stationary car, and then whipped back onto the road with a quick wave and was gone.

Normally she would have taken a second to steady herself and call after him with a cutting critique of what she thought about his driving skills. *But not today.*

Today she was going to the museum to show her friend the shop manager her Christmas card designs. There were so many fabulous commercial cards on display—but hers were hand painted, personalised and based on her favourite designs in the illuminated manuscripts room.

This was it. This was what she had been working on in every spare moment over the past year or more. Experimenting with new ideas for colours and borders and working late into the night until she was happy with the final result.

And she was happy with her work. *Very happy.*

Plus it was a bright sunny November afternoon and she had only one more party invitation to deliver for Elise—and then she would be free. *Free!*

Which was most excellent.

It was such a lovely day that she had walked through Covent Garden and up towards Holborn through streets she had known all of her life. The trees still had some of their leaves and the deep russets, reds and golds were stunning in the pale late-autumn sunshine. Shop windows were bright and bursting with colour from their displays of Christmas gifts and decorations. She had always loved autumn in the city. Especially when the sun was shining and she had the whole day ahead of her to enjoy.

Andy double-checked the address and map, turned the corner through a high stone archway and stood quietly for a moment, admiring the stunning ornate architecture of the exclusive side street. Cory Sports had their London office in a converted four-storey stone Victorian building, which had been built when the British Empire was at its peak. Now the marble and glass entrance was modern and clean and welcoming rather than intimidating, but somehow it fitted in perfectly on this quiet pedestrianised area with its flower tubs and boutique shops and restaurants.

Elise had already paid her to hand paint the party invitations for her client's annual fundraising party in aid of high school art projects in London. Those A-list celebrities and senior business leaders expected a promotions company to send them a special invitation with a difference. Last year it was engraved crystal glassware—this year, hand-painted cards, each one designed to fit the person being invited.

No pressure, then.

Of course Andy would never tell Elise but she had loved every minute of this work. It was challenging, intricate and detailed. And she'd adored doing these pieces. But now they were done.

Thirty invitations. All personal. All hand drawn with the guest name written in calligraphy.

Cory Sports had been a special delight. It had only taken a quick glance at their online sales brochure to see that Cory was short for the Spanish word for the heart—Corazon.

Spanish. Perhaps she could have picked up a few more Spanish words if she had accepted the dinner invitation from Miles?

Andy gave a little chuckle. *Oh, Saffie. No flings for me. The last thing I need is another boyfriend.*

This was her time to make a new life for herself! And she could hardly wait.

Grinning from ear to ear, she only took a moment to leave the hand-embossed envelope with the friendly receptionist at the main desk, who promised faithfully to make sure that Mr Jason Gibson received the letter the moment he got back.

Tugging down her warm jacket, Andy stood outside in the warm sunshine, head back, her messenger bag across her body, and closed her eyes.

Finally! Now she could relax.

Except that as she dropped her shoulders and inhaled, the most delicious aroma of freshly roasted coffee and baking filled her head and set her stomach growling.

Why not? The sun was shining, and she had just delivered the last VIP invitation. She could spare a few minutes to buy some lunch as a treat.

Strange how just the smell of that coffee took her straight back to the coffee shop and the way Miles had stirred his cup of coffee three times, clockwise, before taking a sip. She had never seen anyone do that before. Not adding sugar or cream, just stirring the grounds in the coffee.

He was such an interesting man. Pity that she would probably never see him again. Because the more she thought about him, and it was bizarre how often his face popped into her head, the more she wondered what he was really doing there that evening.

Of course she was flattered that he had come to meet her, the girl who had written to him, rather than Elise, but she was not stupid enough to think that a man like Miles would ever date her.

He was a chancer. A player. Turning on the charm to

persuade a girl to provide some temporary amusement for him while he was in London.

And he had obviously done it before.

Well, not this girl. Not even if he was arrogant and bossy and funny and intriguing and all wrapped up in a gorgeous hunky package.

Shaking her head, she caved in and took the few steps across the street to the ornate French patisserie and coffee shop. Ah. *Temptation came in so many forms.*

Miles was just as luscious and bad for her health as the wonderful creamy cakes and pastries artfully arranged on glass shelves in the window.

Andy stepped into the shop with a skip in her step and a smile on her lips.

And froze. Her breath turning to ice in her lungs.

Because sitting at a corner table, laughing into the face of a glamorous blonde girl, was Miles.

Not that he was paying any attention at all to the customers waiting at the bakery counter.

Oh, no.

Miles was far too busy running the fingers of one hand up and down the blonde's arm, while the other hand rested on her knee. Her V-neck blouse had been designed to make the best of her substantial assets and he certainly seemed to be appreciating them. At very close range.

The blonde was wearing a very red short skirt that highlighted her perfect slim figure, high-heel red mules and had tanned bare legs that seemed to go on for ever. Her make-up was perfect, her long straight blonde hair salon sleek and overall she was just about as different from Andy as it was possible while still being in the same species.

Little wonder that he had now started to play footsie under the table.

Andy could have marched in playing the trumpet and Miles would not have noticed.

The cheek of the man!

Only a few days ago he had asked her out to dinner, and yet here he was, laughing and chatting up another girl in a coffee shop. And look at him! Short hair. Flash black business suit. Where had the sportsman gone?

She had been right all along. He was just another executive looking for a girl to adore him and tell him how marvellous he was. A chancer, pushing his luck in the hope that he would pick up some temporary female by dazzling them with his full-on charm offensive.

And if that blonde he was pawing was eating a Panini she would scream.

Andy glanced at their table. Of course. How silly of her. No carbs would contaminate that beautiful creature's lips.

Which only served to make her even more of a fool than she had been before.

This was the man she had been dreaming about every night, reliving his kiss and his gentle touch. While he had spent the time since they met on the lookout for his next date.

She had fallen for his little game. Which was so infuriating that she could hardly speak.

If there was any justice in the world, she should leap onto a table and denounce him to the world. But she wouldn't. There were limits to how much humiliation she was prepared to put up with, and she had already wasted enough time on this one.

Then her breath caught in her throat.

Miles pushed back his chair, whispered something to the glamorous blonde, who giggled in reply, then he stood up and started walking towards the counter.

Perhaps he had recognised her and wanted to warn her off?

But instead of scooting back outside, her feet felt as if they were glued to the floor and belonged to someone else, leaving her standing there like an idiot, staring at the shelves of baked goods as he casually strolled up and stood not more than a foot away.

And did not say a word to her. Nothing. Not even a curt hello.

In the second it took him to place his order for two more cappuccinos she gave him the once-over.

Someone who knew hair had given him the perfect tousled cut. The other evening his overlong dark chocolate hair had kept falling forwards but now it was smart city-boy short over his ears. With an edge.

He was wearing a black shirt, suit jacket and black trousers, which made him appear a lot slimmer and narrower in the shoulders. She could tell that it was expensive designer black, but he looked so different. Professional, businesslike and a lot paler than she had remembered. He must keep his rough-and-tumble charm and all-weather gear for outside work. Shame. Although she hated to admit it, she had liked that about him.

And he was still totally ignoring her. Which was more than rude.

'This is new,' she said to him in a low calm voice. 'I thought ordering from the table was more to your liking. Or have you decided to join the common people for a change?'

Miles turned to look at her with a smile, then glanced around as though looking to see who she could be speaking to.

'I'm sorry but I think you have the wrong person.' He shrugged, and then he added with a dismissive smile, 'I just have one of those faces,' and turned back to the counter where the barista was loading his coffees onto a tray.

What? Wrong person? One of those faces?

He turned and smiled at the blonde, and the penny dropped. Of course, Miles would not want his new date to think that he made a regular habit of meeting girls in coffee shops. No wonder that he was pretending that they had never met.

So she stepped forward and stood so close to him that their shoulders were touching, which seemed to startle him a little. 'I am so sorry about leaving so quickly the other night.' She swallowed down her nerves and gave a small cough. 'But thank you again for the dinner invitation.'

Miles looked at her with his mouth slightly open, blinked several times, then licked his lips and nodded slowly.

'I'm sorry. Have we met before? Which evening was this?'

The barista chose precisely that moment to bring the second cappuccino to the bar and must have overheard what Miles said because he instantly covered a snigger with his hand.

Brilliant. First Miles pretends he does not know her, and then even the barista starts sniggering at her.

She gave the barista a freezer glare, which sent him scurrying back to the coffee machine.

Come on, girl. Get it over and done with.

'Does online dating ring a bell? Monday evening?' she snapped, in a small, trembling voice, and lifted her eyebrows.

He stared at her with a tight closed mouth for so long that she wondered if he was okay, then suddenly Miles leant against the counter, his brows tight with concentration.

'Online. Right.' Then he nodded his head, just the once, his eyebrows headed skywards and he flashed her a polite smile. 'Of course. Andy. You have to be Andy. Well, I am delighted to see you, but, tell me, how did you manage to track us down?'

Andy closed her eyes and counted to ten but he was still looking at her when she blinked into his wide-eyed face. 'I am not a stalker. I haven't tracked you down and I didn't know that you would be here. Okay?'

She lifted her chin, straightened her back to try and gain another few inches and planted a hand on each hip. Suddenly furious. Miles didn't respect her—he didn't know how. He was just like all of the other people—just like Nigel—who had used her over the years, and then walked out and pretended that she was not important as a human being. And she was not putting up with that. For one more minute.

'I cannot believe that I actually wanted to apologise to you for the other night. Well, Mr hot surfing sportybloke, you can forget it. Forget that you kissed me, forget that you asked me out on a dinner date. In fact, it would be better if you forget that we ever met. And here is the drink I owe you, since you like water so much.'

And without thinking past the fury of the blood rolling in her veins, Andy picked up one of the water jugs brimming with ice cubes from the counter and poured the whole lot in one single gush all over the very startled head of the handsome idiot.

'Goodbye. We will not be meeting each other again.'

And with that, she clenched her teeth, turned on her heel and walked slap bang straight into a solid mass of man muscle.

'Well, that would be a real pity because that was the most fun I've had around here in a long time.'

It was him.

Right down to the hair and the attitude and the voice and

a presence that made every other man in the room suddenly look smaller.

Andy reared back in shocked silence, opened her mouth to reply, then looked up into the face of the Miles she recognised from the coffee shop, and then back to the version who was still standing next to the bar, and then back to the man she was pressed up against.

Twins. *Identical twins.*

Oh, dear.

Her Miles lifted an eyebrow at her and, blast him, his gaze moved slowly from the tips of her comfy old green walking shoes to the red tartan beret she had chosen as a last-minute hat seconds before leaving the house to go to the museum.

She didn't like being trapped between this tall hunk of man and the solid wooden bakery counter. And she especially didn't like the fact that just looking at him, and inhaling his manly scent, had something pinging low in her belly.

It was just muscles, she thought in annoyance and frustration, and tried to stare him out.

Lunch. That was it. She needed lunch… At…the… museum.

She looked over at his twin, who was now being swabbed at with paper napkins by the glamorous blonde girl. His eyebrows were high and he was clearly waiting for an explanation as to why there were ice cubes in his hair.

She needed to get out of here.

'Wait a minute.' She blinked, trying to be casual. 'Whose date was I on last week? Yours—' she thumped him on the chest with the heel of her hand, which only made her hand sore and he didn't even blink '—or—' her fingers waved towards the man with the coffees '—the other yours?'

The suit coughed and tugged at the surfboard cufflinks

in his tailored slim-fit black shirt before picking the ice cubes off his lap and stretching one arm out. 'Miles, over to you,' he replied.

The only sign that he felt even the tiniest bit guilty was a slight bunching of his jaw.

Andy whirled back to muscle man and her brain made the connections at lightning speed.

Go for it.

She took a breath and her words came tumbling out. 'I was honest with you from the start. I am not, and never have been, a stalker.'

She held her breath, not knowing what Miles would do.

'So just what are you doing here? Andy?' he asked, and took a step closer, so that her back was pressed against the counter. His hands were pushed inside the pockets of his cargo pants and he looked annoyingly casual and in control.

'Well, I certainly didn't come looking for you,' she snapped. 'But if you must know, I have been making a delivery to the office across the street.'

He glanced quickly through the coffee shop window, then back into her face and then inhaled sharply through his nose. 'Do you mean the Cory Sports office? I'll take that look as a yes. So are you a messenger service?'

'No! Well, yes, but no.' She shook her head. 'Elise asked me to help her organise a fundraiser event and I painted the invitations myself.' She pointed to the office. 'I didn't want it to get lost in the mail so I delivered it myself. Okay?'

'So now you're an artist as well as a personal assistant and a messenger girl?' he asked in a voice of molten chocolate spiked with hot chili.

'Oh, that is just for starters. I have so many talents it's hard to keep up,' she answered in a low hoarse voice, her eyes locked onto his. And this time she had no intention of looking away first.

The air was so thick with electricity between them she could have cut it with a knife. Time seemed to stretch and she could see the muscles in the side of his face twitching with supressed energy, but she was not going to give in.

'My, it's awfully hot in here,' the suit said as he stepped in front of his brother, breaking their connection and creating a space just large enough for Andy to step through, fully aware that she was still being glared at.

'Apologies for the misunderstanding.' The suit sighed, brushing the water from his trousers. 'That explains a great deal.' Then he stretched out his wet hand and shook hers as if he were about to hold a business meeting.

'Jason Gibson. Cory Sports. It appears that you have already met my brother, Miles. Delighted to meet you, Miss…'

Andy shook Jason's hand and tilted her head to one side, determined not to take the bait. 'Cory Sports? Ah. Fancy that. Enjoy your coffee.'

And with that she tugged the strap of her bag higher onto her shoulder, darted out of the patisserie, turned and gave the two men with the same faces who were both standing there, watching her, a small one-handed finger wave before the ornate painted glass door closed behind her.

Jason rocked back on his heels for a second before sniffing and glancing at Miles.

'You kissed her? And set up a dinner date?'

'Yes. And yes. I thought Mayte's new place.'

'Good choice,' Jason replied, with a nod towards the door. 'You had better get after her, then. Because, brother, I think you may have just met your match and you still need a date for the sports awards. Maybe there is something in this online dating after all?'

CHAPTER FIVE

MILES winced with pain from his knee as he half jogged across the cobblestoned side street. He had a cane back in the apartment but he would be damned before he used it in public... But the agony was worth it, because Andy was still waiting to cross the busy main road, her gaze focused on the contents of the messenger bag across the chest.

'Andy—wait up,' he called.

Her head shot up like a meerkat and she looked from one side to another before half turning back towards him. Instantly her shoulders slumped and she sighed and shook her head in disbelief.

'What? Have I not embarrassed myself enough for you for one day?'

She lifted both hands in the air and pretended to surrender. 'Okay. I admit it. I faked being Elise when I wrote those emails to the dating agency. There. Done. Can I get back to my life now please? I hope you have better luck with the other lucky ladies.'

She glanced at her watch and winced. 'Lovely to chat but I need to be somewhere. Bye.' She turned on her heel and lifted her chin as she strode out into the sunshine. Opaque black tights. Green laced flat shoes. A navy padded jacket above a preppy red tartan swing skirt with a matching beret.

Her outfit was bright, colourful and in his eyes looked

as sexy as anything. Correction—she looked as sexy as anything. What had he told Jason? That he was looking for some life and colour to make London bearable?

Well, he was looking at the perfect example right now. In the shape of a girl who had made him laugh not once, but twice. And that took some doing.

He hadn't met a girl as open and expressive as Andy for a very long time. If anything she was too open. Too honest.

Miles slowed his pace.

The self-protection mechanisms he had built up after Lori dumped him were still there, at the back of his mind, reminding him that he had made the same mistake with her. He had believed her, trusted her, shared his dreams and goals, given her everything. *Everything.*

And she had turned out to be just one more charming, beautiful gold-digger who was happy to be with him for as long as he was useful to her.

So why was he chasing a girl down a London street when his self-defences were screaming that Andy almost seemed to be too good to be true?

Well, there was only one way to find out. No way was he going to let Andy escape that easily. Not without her last name and a phone number.

He needed a date for one night.

And one night only. Not a relationship. Not a lover. A date. And Andy could be exactly the breath of fresh air that he had been looking for.

She marched ahead, totally engrossed in the busy traffic, and only stopped to glance behind her as they stood on the pavement waiting to cross the street. Andy whirled around to face him, her brows squeezed together, hands planted firmly on each hip. 'Are you following me? There are laws against that, you know. Are you really so bored?'

'I might be, or I could just be walking along, enjoying the

fine weather.' He whistled casually. 'And I am not bored in the least. In fact, my day has suddenly become a lot more interesting. It isn't often that someone gets the better of Jason Gibson.'

'Right.' Then she ran her fingers back through her hair, slipping off her beret. 'Look, Mr Gibson. I have already apologised for the pretence. Elise had to go overseas at the last minute and she really did not want to reschedule the coffee date. But I made a mistake. I...I should have insisted that she write her own emails to the guys she was interested in...I was interested in. Oh, you know what I mean.'

'Ah. So you *were* interested in me?' He nodded. 'Pleased that we got that misunderstanding cleared up. And 1 am glad you were. Otherwise we would never have met face to face. Your emails were...interesting. Intriguing, even. I enjoyed reading them.'

Andy flicked her tongue out and licked her upper lip and suddenly the late-afternoon sunshine got a lot brighter. 'People don't realise just how much of themselves they reveal in these emails. I...was expecting someone different. More executive and less...' she flicked her fingers towards him '...athletic, I suppose.'

'Right back at you, girl. Maybe I was expecting someone different as well. And we both made a mistake. So here is an idea. Why don't we call a truce? And it's Miles, remember?'

'A truce?' she replied, her gaze scanning his face much longer than he had expected. Whatever she was looking for, she must have found it, because slowly, hesitantly, she nodded. 'If I say yes, will you stop stalking me, because I really do have a business meeting to go to? And it's important to me.'

'Say yes, and I promise not to stalk you. Okay?'

She exhaled slowly, then stuck out her hand and they

shook on it. 'Truce it is. Now. Have a lovely day, Miles.
See you around.'

And then she was off—practically skipping ahead.

But he was in luck—the traffic lights turned to green
just as she tried to cross the road. Giving him the chance
to catch up.

But then his luck ran out. Because driving down the
small London street was a vintage English sports car, which
looked so familiar it took his breath away in shock.

He closed his eyes for a second and he was back inside
his beloved little red sports car. His dad had bought it
second-hand from a friend in Cornwall, and the two of
them had worked hard to restore it with loving care in the
family's tiny draughty wooden garage just in time for his
seventeenth birthday. He had done the heavy lifting and his
dad had supplied the technical knowhow.

It had been his first real motor and the envy of every
other boy in the school. Even Jason, who had never shown
any interest in cars and opted for a home computer for his
seventeenth instead.

He had loved that car. Loved just taking off to the beach
for the day, during the school holidays or a family picnic
on a summer Sunday.

It had taken him three days to drive it down to Spain and
take the ferry across to Tenerife—but it had been worth it
to have his own car. Sunshine. Top down. Classic.

And it had never let him down. Not once. And then he'd
had to listen to every sound it made as it was crushed and
wrecked beyond repair by a drunken truck driver. With him
still inside. Together to the end.

He could recall every aspect of that morning in full
colour.

The car radio had been playing classic songs from the
sixties. The sun was shining. The road was clear. In the

dream memory, the unreal Miles knows that something is about to happen, and even though the next few minutes have played themselves over and over again in the past months Miles still cannot avoid the inevitable. He is powerless to do anything to change it. He becomes a passive observer, just watching, as the traffic lights change to green and he engages first gear and moves slowly forward before changing into second.

And then the soundtrack changes. Metal being crushed. Bags and loose papers and sports kit flying around from side to side, the horizon spinning around, over and under the car before it stops rolling and smashes back down to rest on its side.

He remembered leaning, half suspended from his seat belt, his lower body trapped below the hips. And someone was screaming. And was still screaming when the ambulance and police arrived and he realised that he was the one doing the screaming.

Miles forced open his eyes into the real world that was London in November.

He knew what would happen next. He had to control his breathing. Come on, he knew the routine. Deep breaths right down to the abdomen.

Forget the fact he couldn't even drive. And seeing that car killed him all over again.

Time to wake up and live. Wasn't that what all of those doctors had told him to do? Focus on the positive. Focus on the fact that most of him was still functioning and by some fluke and good safety belts he had escaped a head injury?

Miles glanced around and took his bearings. Andy was still standing at the pavement.

She was as good a place to start as any. He had a new goal.

'Not so fast, girl. I'm not used to being turned down, so I have to wonder. What was the real reason you decided to turn up in the place of your boss the other night? Just curious. Not stalking. Curious.'

'Curious?' she replied as they walked across into a wide piazza in front of an impressive stone building, but he could hear a supressed smile in her voice. 'Well. What a coincidence.'

'Isn't it? My biggest failing. Can't help it. Was it just for the money? Or were you wondering what I looked like? In the flesh, as it were.'

She stopped and scowled at him. 'Yes and maybe. But mostly I did not like the idea of you just sitting there on your own waiting for a girl who is never going to show up because she is in Brazil and has changed her mind. And you. Are an incorrigible pest. Do you know that?'

'Hey. Flattery. I am a businessman,' Miles replied, then stopped and gave her a small nod. 'Thanks for taking the time to turn up. It was sweet. But you need not have worried. I don't wait for girls. And I will not be thwarted. That dinner invitation still stands.'

Her reply was to sigh low in her throat and walk towards a huge arched stone portico that formed the entrance to the building. She gestured to a large marble plaque on the entrance with the words 'The Harcourt Collection' engraved onto the surface in gold lettering.

'Far too busy. Busy, busy, busy.'

'I'll wait. Where are we headed?'

'This is one of the finest museums in London, and my favourite place in the whole world. I also happen to work here at weekends. So the staff know me and I would be mightily miffed if someone—' and she lifted her eyebrows high '—was to diss me once we get through these doors. So if you can't agree, maybe we should say our goodbyes here.'

Miles blinked at the plaque a few times. *A museum? She worked in a museum? Well, this got more bizarre and intriguing by the minute.* Maybe she was as multitalented as she claimed.

Andy turned to go but he stepped in front of her.

'Not so fast. I don't get to London very often. I didn't even know this place existed. It would be a shame to miss the chance to see what it looks like on the inside. In fact, seeing as you know the museum so well, how about a guided tour?'

'A tour? No. Sorry. I have to plan my sales pitch before the meeting and calm down on my own. I need this quiet time to myself. But if you ask at the information desk I am sure that you could join the next tour. Tourists are always welcome.'

Miles growled at her through narrowed eyes. 'Nice try. Not going to work. But you mentioned those magical two words, sales and pitch. Why didn't you say so? You act as my guide and I'll write your pitch for you. Deal?'

She glanced from side to side and swallowed before stepping closer to him so that she could reply in a harsh whisper. 'I don't mean to offend you, but I am an illustrator and I want to persuade the museum to sell my hand-crafted greetings cards through their shop.'

She lifted her right hand, palm up, and stared at it. 'Sporting goods.' Then she did the same thing with her left hand. 'Illustrated greetings cards.' She stared at one hand, and then back to the other. 'Note the difference.'

Then she dropped both hands and stared up at the imposing entrance. 'This is me sticking my neck out and taking a chance and I am rather nervous so thank you but no. I need a moment on my own.'

Her long dark eyelashes fluttered close to her smooth pale cheek as she dropped her head, eyes closed, her chest rising and falling below her jacket as she took several calming breaths.

And every cell of his body twanged to attention.

Either this girl was an extraordinary actress or his instincts had been right and she was someone worth getting to know.

Time to switch up a gear and clinch his date for the night.

Miles chuckled and grabbed her hand. 'You haven't heard my pitch yet. Take the risk. You won't regret it.' And in one smooth motion he flung open the heavy embossed door and stepped inside, dragging Andy with him, complaining loudly all the way.

'And you really think that I can ask that much for each card?' Andy asked as they strolled out of the collection of eastern jade and porcelain.

'Absolutely,' Miles replied, his eyes focused on one of the Christmas card samples that Andy had brought with her. 'You haven't taken account of your hourly rate. This is excellent work and beautifully painted. Offer the museum the cut I suggested and you both benefit—but don't undervalue your workmanship. People pay for quality—I know I do. And you have already customised it for this outlet.'

'I hadn't thought of it that way. But the inspiration did come from this museum.'

Andy pointed to the central gold-and-blue design on the card he was holding. 'Each central motif is based on a letter from a medieval illuminated manuscript, which are so wonderful it is hard to put into words.'

She paused, gave a quick nod and pointed to a room just down the corridor and flashed him a grin that made him blink. 'Actually it's easier to show you than try to describe it. The books and documents are in here.'

Miles followed on as fast as he could but he had been on his pinned and dodgy legs for way too long so that Andy was already crouched over a long glass display cabinet when he joined her.

And then she looked up at him.

And the transformation on her face was so miraculous that he was taken aback by it.

Her whole body seemed to have come alive, so that her eyes sparkled with life and energy and when she spoke her voice was completely different.

It was as if something had flicked a switch inside this girl.

This version of Andy was bursting with enthusiasm and excitement and joy.

He knew that look. He had seen it before.

It was the look of someone with the fire in their belly that burned hot with the passion of doing the one thing they loved most in the world.

A passion that nothing else in life could replace or come close to matching.

And he knew exactly what that felt like.

A cold hand clasped around his heart.

Would he ever feel that passion again? That glow that beamed out from Andy's face at that moment when she looked at these books with the coloured pages?

He envied her that. More than he could say.

Bitter bile at the injustice of what had happened to him roiled deep inside, but he pushed it away. Not her fault. It was his job to deal with the fact that his world had shifted.

There was a good chance that he would never stand on a surfboard again or feel the rush of a kite lifting his body high above the waves. Not if he wanted to walk or live his life without wheelchairs or canes.

One thing was certain.

This kind of passion could never be faked or copied.

She was the real deal.

Not an actress or someone out to con him—but someone who was as passionate about these handwritten and decorated books as he had been about his sport.

Was this what he had glimpsed between the lines of those few emails that she had sent him? He had certainly sensed that there was something special about her, but passion like this? No. This was a bonus.

But it was more than that. The Andy he had met in the café was pretty and sassy, but this Andy was transformed by her happiness and joy into a very remarkable woman who was intent on telling him all about the royal families who had commissioned these hand-painted books in a world before the printing press had been invented. Her expertise and knowledge streamed out of her.

Andy was not just pretty. This Andy looked stunningly beautiful.

And right there and then, he made the decision.

I want you to look at me with that passion in your eyes. I want you to warm my cold disappointment at the fire of your passion while I have the chance.

This one. I choose this one.

Heart thumping, he could barely drag his gaze from her face to the pages she was describing.

Andy leant her elbows on the frame around the glass case and sighed in wonder at the pages of the book on display.

'Isn't it astonishing?' she said and her shoulders seemed to drop several inches as she grinned up at him, her eyes sparkling with fire and happiness and delight.

Her joy was so contagious that Miles could not help but grin back and move closer, so that they could look down at the exhibit together.

His hand seemed to move to her waist all on its own and, judging by the instant flash of a grin she gave him, the lady was not complaining. She was having way too much fun.

While Andy's gaze was totally locked onto the beautiful manuscript, Miles took the time to look at her close up. In the natural light her hair was not brown but a blend of every shade of gold and brown with copper and russet blended in. Lori used to spend the cost of a new surfboard on having her hair coloured and it had never even been close to this fabulous.

It hurt him to think that Andy had no clue about how very naturally beautiful and gifted she was.

He moved closer and pointed to the left page where a giant bird in the shape of the letter P had been covered with the most intricate and startling of ancient circles and birds and flowers and animals.

'Tell me about how they made those colours. And is that real gold?'

'The colours?' she replied, blinking up at him and clearly delighted that he was showing any interest at all. 'Oh, yes. This is real gold. This set of gospels was meant to be a royal gift so the monks had the very best of everything. The blue is azurite and lapis lazuli from Afghanistan rather than native indigo and that fresh green colour is most likely malachite. It truly is a masterpiece. And I love it so much. I could look at it all day.'

All day?

His leg was already complaining about walking about for an hour and he had just about reached his limit on his other knee.

He might have to ask the guard if he could borrow his chair.

Luckily he did not have to, because just as he was about

to reply the sound of a herd of baby elephants echoed up from the stone staircase. He took a tighter hold of Andy and they both turned to see what all the noise was about—just in time to see an entire junior school of jostling, jabbering, running, curious and mega-excited children burst into the exhibition space. All desperate to be the first ones to see the books and all competing in decibels to get the attention of their already harried teachers.

Andy stepped back from her precious book with a sigh, looked up at Miles and shrugged.

'I have a suggestion.'

She glanced from side to side around the room. The way into the café area was blocked by the second wave of children, who all wanted drinks at that very minute, and they would have to fight their way back to the main exit. *Time for Plan B.*

'What would you say if I told you that I knew a secret exit onto the dome and we could escape the school party and read the guide book in peace?'

Miles replied by taking what was a surprisingly firm hold around her waist, which made her gasp, before he whispered, 'I would tell you that I will follow you to the ends of the earth. But make it fast. The teacher is heading this way. And she has a clipboard.'

'Okay, now I am intrigued,' Miles whispered as they stood at the railing and looked out through the curved glass at the busy London street below. Above their heads was the curved dome of the ceiling of the museum, which was a masterpiece of metal and stone and arched beams, inset with decorated panels of stars and mythological creatures.

The walkway they were standing on ran the complete circle of the dome of the building and was a hidden gem, offering a complete three-hundred-and-sixty degree view over the entire city of London in all directions through the row of heavy glass wall panels.

The sound of clinking glasses and children's chatter and the noise from the buses and taxi cabs outside filtered into the space and yet they were quite alone. Separate.

'How on earth did you know about that secret staircase leading up from the exhibition?'

Andy looked up at him and her lips curled into a smirk before she replied. 'Oh, I have explored most of these corridors and they haven't changed at all. In fact...' and at this she paused. 'They are exactly the same as I remember them.'

Then Andy took pity on his confusion and she smiled and leant forward before adding, as casually as she could, 'I grew up in a house not very far from here. So you see, I have been coming to this museum all of my life.'

She stopped suddenly, dropped her shoulders back and pointed towards the ceiling. 'When I was little I had a copy of that zodiac in the ceiling of my bedroom so that I could lie in bed at night and watch them and dream about what they all meant. It was magical!'

'Your parents must have loved bringing you here,' he replied.

'My parents? Not exactly,' she answered with a shrug. 'They both worked in the city and they didn't have a lot of free time, even at weekends.'

Andy tilted her head and was grateful that his gaze was fixed on the window glass so that he could not see the glint in her eyes. Talking about those sad times still hurt.

'I had a series of au pairs and nannies who soon found out that they could take off to the café to chat and leave me to explore the exhibits.' Andy waved one hand, then let it fall as she turned back to face him. 'So when they weren't looking I took off to explore on my own. The curators and security guards soon got to know me and I never made a mess or got into trouble. This was my personal playground.'

'Wow,' he replied, with the look of something close to awe in his face. 'Are you serious? Did you really grow up wandering around in a museum?'

'Oh, yes,' she answered with a tiny shrug. 'And don't say it as though that was a bad thing. I loved it here. My folks eventually worked out that I was spending far too much time learning about ancient Persian history so they sent me to boarding school at the age of eleven. Too late, of course. By then the damage was done. I was a history geek and proud and nothing my parents told me about the advantages of a career in hedge funds was going to change my mind.'

His reply was a low snort of disbelief.

'Quite. No, I have wonderful memories of sitting up here all alone, dreaming about the wonderful research I was going to do and all of the ancient manuscripts that were still out there for me to explore.' Her voice faded slowly away as the contrast between her life and the life she had imagined for herself flashed into sharp focus. 'My life was going to be so magical.'

Miles must have picked up on her change of mood because he moved closer so that their coats were touching.

She instantly switched her smile back on. *Not his problem.*

'Now I have started some freelance PA work for my friend Elise and work on the information desk here on Saturdays but we are always mad busy. This is a rare treat.'

'That is because you love this place so much and you miss it,' he replied in a gentle voice, and chuckled at her gasp of surprise. 'Yes. It is fairly obvious. Especially...'

'Especially?' Andy asked in a shaky breath. She was

not used to opening up to a millionaire that she had just met in this way, and it startled her, and yet was strangely reassuring. *Weird.*

'I was going to say, especially considering that there must be so little work for history graduates.' He blew out hard and blinked. 'Research on ancient documents! That's hard for me to get my head around. It must be hard to do office work when you have such expert knowledge of the subject.'

Hard? How did she even begin to explain to a stranger the misery of having to turn down her place at a prestigious university, which she had worked so hard for, because there simply was not the money to pay for her parents' new business disasters at the same time as sending her to university? They wanted her to study for a degree that would guarantee her a secure future as a professional, not some ridiculous foolishness about art history. That was not going to get her anywhere. After all, she was not gifted or talented.

She had begged her grandparents to support her, and applied for grant after grant, but it had all been for nothing and in the end she had had to face the truth.

If she wanted to make the world of illuminated manuscripts her life, then she would have to do it with money that she earned.

Her whole world had shifted under her feet and was still shifting now.

Even after ten years of living in rented accommodation, and now as a house sitter, there were some days where she had to remind herself that she could still do it. She read and studied and practised her techniques, constantly working to become the best she could be. Evening classes. Museum workshops. Anything that would improve her knowledge and skills.

Andy blinked hard. The blur of constant activity that she used to fill each day created a very effective distraction, but even talking about those sad times brought memories percolating up into her consciousness. Memories she had to put back in their place where they belonged.

Then she looked up at the new moon rising in the clear sky above the tall stone buildings across the street and felt the sting of tears in the corners of her eyes as the memory of the lost opportunities flooded back into her mind. She was so overwhelmed that when Miles shifted next to her on the railing, she suddenly came crashing down to earth and the harsh reality that her life was so very different from the one she had imagined for herself as a girl.

'Oh, I am so sorry,' she said through a tight, sore throat. 'Here I am, rambling on about illuminated manuscripts and my boring life history. How embarrassing! I don't usually go on like this but this has been a tough week. But thank you for listening.'

Miles inclined his head towards her. 'I got the feeling that you needed to talk. Apparently I was right. And you were not boring, not in the least.'

Andy instantly whipped her head around to check if he was making fun of her, as Nigel had, as so many of the men she had met had. But instead of supressed ridicule, he was doing the laser stare through the centre of her forehead again. No laughter. Just something close to sincere curiosity.

And it totally disarmed her.

'Thank you,' she replied, then gave a small cough to cover her embarrassment. 'How about you?' Andy asked with a lift in her voice, eyebrows high. 'Where did you live growing up?'

'Ah. Nothing like this,' he replied with a chortle. 'I was born in Cornwall. My dad was a sports teacher so we spent most of our free time on the beach or helping him to run training sessions for local schools and colleges. But in the winter we went to my grandparents' beach house on Tenerife. Sunshine and surfing.'

Miles shrugged deeper into his down coat. 'I soon found out that Cornwall was amazing in the summer but in January? Technical surfing was a lot easier in the Canary Islands.'

'Oh, I so agree,' Andy said with a knowing nod. 'Technical surfing. Absolutely.'

'Even so,' Miles said as he moved closer so that he could stand next to her with his arms stretched out on the metal railing as they both gazed onto the London street, 'I envy you growing up here. There is something special about the city at this time of year.'

The tall London plane trees had been strung with white party lights and Christmas decorations so the front entrance of the hotel opposite looked like a fairy-tale picture of Christmas from a children's book.

Huge white plastic snowflakes, bright red-and-gold baubles and lots of silver-and-gold-dusted ivy dotted with crimson holly berries were suspended from wires to form perfect garlands and wreaths.

The shops along this busy high street had decorated their windows with wonderful displays of toys and gifts and the finest luxury goods to be had in the city in magical winter wonderlands of huge stores and designer shops and specialist food outlets.

And as Andy and Miles looked into the early evening dusk the first Christmas street lights twinkled bright and colourful and cheerful. Pedestrians hurried along, bundled up against the cold, children and adults smiling and enjoying the bustle and energy of the city street.

The whole scene was so familiar to her and yet still so

magical that Andy felt her shoulders relax for the first time
in many days.

This was why she'd never found peace when she had
lived in boarding school or with her grandparents. They
had never come close to this special place in her life.

She leant in contented silence and grasped the balustrade
with both hands, quietly aware of how very close she was
standing next to this man she had only just met. Close
enough that she could hear his breathing and the sound
his boots made as he shifted his weight from one foot to
the next. The sharp tang of his aftershave combined with
the dust and polish from a large building to create a heady
scent.

Should she tell him that he was the first man that she had
ever brought to the roof dome? Perhaps not. He had already
teased her about being an online dating virgin.

But as she fixed her gaze on the thick glass panel, she
knew that it was more than that.

Miles had come here to be with her—because he wanted
to.

He even appeared happy to enjoy the view and remain
in silence and allow her to do all the talking, since she
was relaxed enough in his presence to enjoy the type of
conversation that could only happen between strangers,
unfettered by past history.

Strangers.

Tears pricked the corners of her eyes and she looked
away from Miles out over the city.

Stupid! Why had she just told so much of her life to this
stranger?

Miles wasn't her friend. *Far from it.*

She knew his laugh, his smile, the way he stirred his
coffee, but she had no clue who he was or why he wanted
to spend his afternoon in a museum with her.

This was Miles Gibson of Cory Sports. Multimillionaire sportsman. Driven, intense and determined to succeed in the business he had built up with his brother.

Instinctively she felt the man in the black down coat looking at her, watching her, one elbow on the metal railing.

She turned slightly towards him and noticed for the first time, in the fading natural light and the twinkling stars in the street, that his eyes were not brown but a shade of copper the colour of autumn leaves. And at that moment those eyes were staring very intently at her.

On another day and another time she might even have said that he was more gorgeous than merely handsome. Tall, broad and so athletic it was a joke.

Dazzle factor and allure of this quality did not come cheap.

Some lucky girl was going to have a wonderful online date.

He took a step closer in the fading light and in the harsh shadows his cheekbones were sharp angles and his chin strong and resigned.

The masculine strength and power positively beamed out from every pore and grabbed her. It was in the way that he held his body, the way his head turned to face her and the way he looked at her as though she was the most fascinating woman he had ever met, and, oh, yes, the laser focus of those intelligent copper brown eyes had a lot to do with it as well.

He was so close that she could touch him if she wanted to. She could practically feel the softness of his breath on her skin as he gazed intently into her eyes. The background noise in the museum seemed to fade away until all of her senses were totally focused on this man who had outspokenly captivated her.

She couldn't move.

She did not want to move.

'What are you doing here, Miles Gibson? What do you want from me?'

CHAPTER SIX

HER words blurted out in a much stronger voice than she had intended, and she instantly warmed them with a small shoulder shrug. 'Your brother probably has a stack of work waiting for you back in the office. Shouldn't you be getting back?'

Miles straightened his back and lifted his chin before releasing the railing and turning to face her.

'What am I doing here? Well, I thought that was fairly obvious. Since you don't want to have dinner with me, I had to find some other way of satisfying that terrible curiosity I am cursed with. And, yes, he certainly does have a mountain of admin waiting for me, and, yes, I probably should, because my knee...' Then he pushed his lips out, licked the bottom one with his tongue and said in a clear calm voice as though he were reading from a script. 'Car accident. Still having physio. Hurts when I stand. And we have been doing a lot of that this afternoon.'

'Oh, no,' she gasped and clutched onto the sleeve of his jacket as she looked down to his trousers. 'You should have said something. I am so sorry.'

'Not a problem,' he replied in a voice of finely sharpened steel that cut the air. 'I'm fine.'

She snatched up her head and stared into his eyes, shocked by the change of tone in his voice.

Whatever casual friendly atmosphere they had built up—was gone. Vanished into smoke. And it was as if a blast of ice-cold air had just blown into the dome, making her shiver.

She closed her eyes for a second, and when she opened them, she almost jumped back because Miles was standing so close to her that the front of his soft jacket was almost touching her sleeve.

'It was worth it to share another person's passion first-hand. And that is what you have, Andy. You have passion.' He sniffed. 'Takes one fanatic to recognise another one. So thank you.' He took another step closer, so that when she looked into his eyes she had to lift her chin to do it. 'For being my guide into another world I knew absolutely nothing about.'

And with one tiny nod he stepped back, his hands sliding up and down the sleeves of her coat. 'Come on, girl, it's getting cold up here. You're trembling. I'm taking you for a hot coffee. Tea. Whatever. And on the way I want to hear you practise your sales pitch. Shall we?'

He stuck out his hand and she looked at it for a fraction of a second. Taking his hand would mean saying yes to spending more time with him, the coffee, everything. But before she had a chance to think, he grabbed it firmly and laughed out loud. 'One more thing. I think it's about time you told me your real name. What does the Andy stand for?'

She hesitated for a moment before raising her gaze to the ceiling and blurting out, 'You had better not laugh—it's Andromeda. Andromeda Davies.'

He lifted his head and nodded. 'Andromeda. It totally suits you.'

He raised one fingertip and traced it along her cheekbone.

'And in case you were wondering—I know about dreams. So does Jason. Do you think we were handed Cory Sports on a silver platter? No. We had to wash dishes and work weekends and school holidays to earn the money to buy the kit and teach and learn and teach and learn some more before we were even close to being ready to go professional. But you know the true meaning of the word amateur, don't you?'

He dropped his hand so that it rested lightly on her hip and she could feel the warmth and the weight of his fingers through several layers of fabric.

She shook her head slowly from side to side, speech impossible.

'It comes from the Latin word *amator*—the lover. Now a girl who loves what she does so much that she can keep the fire of her passion for history burning for ten years…that is a girl who I would like to know more about. See more.'

Then he kissed her on the tip of her nose. And the touch of his lips was as gentle as a butterfly landing and she closed her eyes to revel in that tiny moment when her skin was in contact with his.

'What do you say, Andromeda Davies? Are you willing to be seen in public eating Spanish food with me? Oh— and this time? This time it will be a real date. You and me. First-name terms. I would like to hear a lot more about those dreams of yours. Tempted?'

Tempted?

Andy stared into his face for a second in total silence, aware that she was probably ogling and looking as bewildered as she felt.

Of course she was tempted.

Had he no clue what he was asking?

Why could he possibly want to have dinner with her? To hear about her dreams? Listen to her plans and fantasy ambitions?

She had no fabulous stories of international travel and

achievement to amuse a man like Miles. Did he feel sorry for her and the life she led? Or simply need someone to talk to because he was lonely? She didn't need that either.

Andy inhaled deeply, his gaze on her face as he waited for her answer.

But when he moved even closer, she took two steps back, away from the temptation—the danger.

Her heart was thumping so loudly he could probably hear it from where he was standing. He smelt wonderful, his touch sent her brain spinning and he was so handsome that her heart melted just looking at him.

She had felt that wicked pull of attraction in the coffee shop the other evening and run away. And she would have to do the same now, because the high-tension wire that was pulling her closer and closer towards Miles Gibson would only lead one way—to her heartbreak and pain.

She had learnt her lesson with Nigel and dared not place her trust in a man like this again. She just couldn't risk being used then cast aside.

She wasn't ready to date anyone. Nowhere near.

'A dinner date? Thank you, but I don't think that would be a very good idea, Miles. But perhaps Jason could find you another online date in my place?'

'Not a good idea?' Miles frowned. 'I don't know about that. The girl who runs it comes from our part of Tenerife and her whole family are terrific cooks. Mayte will look after us well. And no squishy tomatoes in sight.'

'Then that is a very good reason why I am the last person you should ask out as your date. A friend of your family might get the wrong idea. And I am really not looking for another boyfriend at the moment.'

Miles paused for a moment, pressed his lips together, winced and then slapped the heel of his hand to his forehead as he took several steps back towards the entrance. 'You already have a boyfriend. Of course you do. It was your boss who needed the online dating agency.'

He gave her a short bow. 'Apologies. I jumped to conclusions. Another one of those flaws I was talking about. I only hope your boyfriend doesn't turn up at the office and thump me for asking his girl out. I'm not sure my brother could take any more surprises today.'

There was just enough of a change in his voice to make her look up. Unless he was a very good actor and she was completely misreading the signals, she saw a glimmer of genuine regret and disappointment cross that handsome face before he covered it up.

Interesting.

Decision time. Pretend she was seeing someone and lie through her teeth...or not.

'Jason is safe. What I meant was that I recently broke up with someone and I don't feel comfortable going on any kind of date just yet. But thanks again for the invitation.'

It was astonishing to see how fast Miles could switch on that killer smile.

'Ha. So you are single. That makes two of us.' He looked at her quizzically, eyebrows high. 'But you do know what that means, don't you?'

He stepped closer, ran his hands up both sleeves of her jacket and smiled as his gaze locked onto her eyes.

'I simply won't take no for an answer, Andromeda. Not going to happen.' And he winked at her. Just as he had done in the coffee shop the other evening. So smug and confident in his dazzling power. And with just the same power to make her roll her eyes and sigh out loud as she slithered out of his grasp.

'Which part of not wanting another boyfriend right now do you not understand, Miles? I appreciate the offer but I really am not ready for a new relationship—with anyone. So, thank you, but no.'

Then she patted the front of his coat briskly with her fingertips and gestured with her head towards the stairs, before glancing at her watch. 'And look at the time. I have been keeping you chatting for far too long. Thank you for keeping me company and for the kind advice about the pitch, but I think I had better put those tips to good use while they are still fresh in my mind.'

Andy stretched out her hand. 'Goodbye, Miles Gibson. And thanks for the business tips.'

Miles inhaled the heady atmosphere of the dusty museum and the light floral perfume that Andy wore and tasted the slight tang that came with the possibility that his fine plans were about to be scuppered.

She was serious! She was actually turning him down.

There had to be *some* way to persuade her to change her mind and agree to be his date. What did she want? There had to be something. And just as that thought popped into his brain she shuffled her shoulder bag higher and the corner of one of her greeting-card folders popped out of the top.

And then he had it.

Her artwork.

That was it. He was going to fuel the fire of her passion by offering her the one thing that could make a difference. Fire for fire. A date in exchange for her heart's desire. He knew that her passion would never allow her to turn down an offer like that.

His fingers closed around hers and his mouth curled into a warm smile as her smooth-skinned, cool, clever fingers moved against his. 'Thank you, Andromeda Davies, and it was my pleasure.' But instead of releasing her, he kept hold of her hand as though reluctant to let her go, and although she coughed and glanced down at her fingers he did not move an inch.

'You asked me earlier what I wanted from you, and do you know, I never did answer your question. How very rude of me. Do you still want to know my answer?' He paused, knowing that he had her full attention, then moved half a step closer and pressed a fingertip to her lips just as Andy was about to reply.

'One of the reasons I am in London is to attend the annual Sports Personality Award show. Cory Sports is the main sponsor. And I need a date for the evening. That's why Jason signed me up with the online dating agency.'

And he lifted his eyebrows and grinned. 'If you don't want to eat dinner with me, how about going to the awards show as my date for the evening?'

'Your date at the sports awards? You? Miles Gibson?' Andy asked, her eyes wide with disbelief.

'Hell, yes. And only the best for you, girl. Top table all the way. From what I am paying that celebrity chef we should have a decent meal. Couple of glasses of wine. And if my memory serves me correctly you would be sitting next to that film actor who does his own stunts in the Bond movies. You know the one?' Miles sniffed. 'I shall take that squeak to be a yes. The athletes will want to talk sport but I am sure you can cope for a few hours before we hit the real party. What do you say? Are you willing to take a risk on having a brilliant time?'

'Are you on medication?'

'No…well, actually, yes. But only at night so I can sleep for a few hours.'

'Thought so. Miles, I don't know the first thing about sport. I hate having my photograph taken and I would probably be asleep with my head on the table after a couple of glasses of wine. This is not a good look when you are the sponsor and probably have several members of the royal family presenting awards. Thank you, but I am so *not* the girl you want to have as your date for a prestigious event like this.'

Miles was silent for a few seconds, his gaze flitting across her face. Then he took both of her hands in his, flashed a closed-mouth smile and tilted his head slightly to one side.

'Two royal princes, plus several radio and TV presenters. And as it happens, I would be honoured to have you on my arm for the evening.'

That seemed to knock the wind out of her sails and he seized the opportunity to dive in before she could bluster another refusal.

'Why not come along and have some fun? It's the perfect opportunity for you to meet the great and good of the sporting world. The after-show party can go on all night and there will be plenty of famous names there. I know, I won it a couple of years ago.'

Andy looked at him, wide eyed, as though he had just suggested running down the street wearing nothing but a cheeky grin and a pair of red stilettos.

'*Fun?* Perhaps it sounds like fun to you, but to me it is my worst possible nightmare.'

'Why? These celebrities are just people, the same as you and I.'

'Celebrities? That award ceremony has television crews, reporters and paparazzi six feet deep at the red carpet. If I went to an event like that I would be the wallflower who sneaks off to the kitchens to get some peace and quiet.'

Andy took a breath and shuddered for effect. 'Thank you for the invitation but that is not my kind of scene. *At all*. You can tell me all about it when you get back and I'll watch the highlights on TV. Have a nice time.'

'I intend to. But I didn't explain myself. You wouldn't be in the kitchens, and there is no way that you could ever be mistaken for a wallflower. Oh, no. I would never let you out of my sight for a second.'

Andy flung her arms out wide. 'You are still not listening. You need a glamorous sleek girl like that gorgeous blonde Jason was talking to just now.'

'Ah.' Miles nodded, his brow creased. 'The lovely Tiffany. Great girl, but unfortunately her talents did not extend to filing anything other than her nails and she cried when my dear brother asked her to coordinate the press for the award ceremony on Saturday night. *Actually cried.*'

'Stop it,' she said, trying not to laugh, and waggled her hands at him. 'I'm not sleek. I'm one of the ordinary girls who actually runs the place but from behind the scenes. Just the thought of those cameras pointing at me when I totter down a red carpet gives me palpitations.' And she gave a loud sigh and leant back on the balustrade, eyes closed.

'Andy,' he said in his best melted-chocolate voice, and as she half opened one eye he shuffled forwards, his gaze fixed on her face. And the look he was giving her was so absolutely carnivorous that she forgot to breathe.

'Don't let anyone tell you that you are ordinary. From what I have seen, you are one of the most extraordinary women I have ever met. And as for sleek?' His lips lifted into a smile that sent hot flames to warm the pit of her stomach. 'Sleek is much overrated in my opinion. I'm looking for more than sleek. I'm looking for real.'

Heat shimmered in the air and she could almost hear the clock chiming in the gallery in the cutting silence that separated her from Miles.

'Are we still talking about the date?' she finally murmured, his hot gaze still burning her face.

'What do you think?' he replied, biting his lip to suppress
a smile.

Andy inhaled slowly, trying to make her brain work
while Miles was looking at her like that and failing.

'I could use a girl who has no truck with this ridiculous
game we all play called fame, but is polite enough not to
tell someone that to their face. With a girl like that, I might
be able to survive the night without socking someone or
showing Jason up.'

His gaze slid up from her hands to her face, but his
thumbs continued to stroke the back of her hand as he
locked eyes with hers.

'That girl is you, Andy Davies. I choose you. Say yes
and in return…I promise to do everything I can to help you
with your career.'

She took a sharp intake of breath and her eyes flickered
into life with that same fire he had seen back in the gallery.

'What do you mean? My career? You don't know
anything about my career.'

Miles shrugged. 'Yes, I do. I know passion and talent
when I see it and, from what you've just told me, you have
not had the opportunity to make your dream a reality until
now. Those cards you have in that bag are only the start,
Andy. Cory Sports uses professional designers who are
always looking out for new talent. Talent like yours.'

'So now you are bribing me to be your date in exchange
for helping me to find an outlet for my designs. Is that what
you are saying?' Andy asked, with disbelief in her voice.

'Absolutely,' he replied with a single slow nod.

'You should be ashamed of yourself.'

'Not in the slightest. Because I am quite serious. Come
out with me for one date. One. And I give you my word

that I will do what I can to help your career. It's not often I have the chance to make a girl's dream come true. I rather like it. What do you say?'

She licked her lips and seemed to be working through the options.

It was now or never.

'One date.'

He nodded his head slowly up and down. 'One evening. And of course, as my date you should prepare yourself to be pampered with every luxury known to woman along the way. All part of the deal. No extra charge.'

Andy seemed to be biting on the inside of her lip, but then her shoulders dropped and she gave him a small, but warm half-smile.

'Pampering?' she replied, breaking the thick tense air that filled the few inches of space between them. 'Why didn't you say that in the first place? It has been a while since I had some pampering.'

'Then you will come with me? A week on Saturday. Eight till late?' Miles said as he leant forwards and kissed her forehead with the lightest possible touch of his lips, then her temple. 'Yes? Excellent,' he whispered in her ear before sliding away with a beaming grin. 'It is going to be quite a night.'

Then without warning he wrapped his arms around her slight body in a great bear hug, which seemed to force her air from her lungs, then stood back and rubbed his hands together.

'Right. Down to business,' he smouldered. 'You have taken time out of your life to show me those wonderful art works that make your heart sing. The very least I can do is offer to give you some idea of my passion in return. That way you'll have a fighting chance of keeping up with what we are talking about during the show.'

'I have to go surfing?' she gasped in disbelief.

'Not unless I can kidnap you and whisk you off to Tenerife. I was actually thinking of something a little closer to home. But I'll be in touch.'

And he lifted both of her hands to his lips and gave them one kiss before releasing her.

'We just have enough time to go through that pitch again before your meeting. Ready? Let's go and dazzle them,' he smirked, then grabbed her hand and took off, bad leg and all, dragging her behind him.

'I must be hearing things,' Jason said, peering at Miles over the top of his spectacles. 'For a moment there I thought you just said that you had to bribe the lovely Andy to go on a date after she turned you down. I'm shocked.'

'That would be correct,' Miles replied through bites of sandwich made from four slices of bread, half a pound of cheese, smothered in mayonnaise and several sliced tomatoes, which passed for a light snack. 'On the other hand, remind me again who you are taking to the most important event of our season? Um? Oh, yes, I remember now. Going solo. Again.'

Jason blew out long and low. 'True. But I am not the one who has been pacing the floor for the last hour and cannot sit still for more than ten minutes at a time—and, yes, I know your knee needs work, but please, just tell me that Andy is not just another form of distraction? Because I am the one staying in London who will have to pick up the pieces.'

'Distraction?' Miles sniffed. 'Maybe. Because talking to Andy certainly beats being cooped up in an airless office all day. But I meant what I told her. We have business skills and contacts she can use. And you can stop looking at me like that. One night. And that's it. No expectations on either side. Just how I like it.'

Jason looked at Miles through narrowed eyes. 'You have been whining on for months that you are not prepared to go solo in front of the other sportsmen and I get that. Truly. I do. You are back on your feet and you want the rest of the world to see you in your full glory with a lovely lady on your arm. All hail the great hero. But why am I getting the feeling that it is more than that?'

'Never mind the great hero part. We need to show the people who matter that the business is still in good hands. And I never asked you to set me up with some dates.'

'No, you didn't, because you have a problem asking anyone for help, even if they are your own family.'

Jason sat back in his computer chair and twirled it around to face Miles.

'Why are you going to this much trouble? Remember that fashion shoot we did in Bali last year? Those lovely ladies were all from the same London agency. I can pick up the phone to any one of ten girls who would be happy to be your date for the evening. Why don't you want to take the easy route this time? After all, it's only one night.'

Miles put down his sandwich, his appetite suddenly gone, and turned back from the open patio door. 'You really are clueless sometimes, do you know that? The last thing I need is another bikini model. Great girls, every one of them. But for this event I need someone different, and not in showbiz if I can help it. Andy is great. Quirky. I like her.'

Jason tapped his fingers on the edge of his chair as Miles glowered at him, then leant forwards and rested his elbows on his knees before asking in a low voice, 'Is this about Lori? Because I am happy to cover the meet and greet at the award ceremony if you are worried about seeing her again.'

'Worried?' Miles snorted as he pushed himself to his

feet. 'Why should I be worried? Lori has already moved on to become the official girlfriend of one of the world's finest footballers. I am happy for her.'

'Happy,' Jason repeated. 'Oh, boy. I should have known. Here's an idea. Walk away. Why put yourself through the awkward moment when you see each other again for the first time since the accident? The latest range of surf gear is due to roll out at the trade fair in Honolulu next week. The manager would love for you to be there. Sun. Sea. Fun. And think of the publicity.'

'Not going to happen. I am fine. Professional and fine.'

Miles slapped his hand down hard on Jason's shoulder, making him wince. 'You worry too much. It's okay. Besides, I would much rather supervise the aqua-therapy programme this afternoon than squeeze myself behind a desk for any longer than I have to or into an aircraft seat. My knee won't take a long flight. Not yet.'

His hand suddenly stilled. 'Aqua therapy. I wonder…' And with a laugh he hobbled off to his room. 'I might just be able to persuade the lovely Andy to spend time with me after all. See you later and best of luck with the office systems.'

'Yes, fine. Go,' Jason sighed loudly and slapped his forehead. 'Don't worry about me. Just leave me to sort the mess out. I'll be okay. You go ahead and enjoy yourself.'

'No doubt about that,' Miles replied with a hand gesture. 'No doubt at all.'

'Charming. But aren't you forgetting something?'

Jason dived into his trouser pocket and pulled out a folded scrap of paper. 'I might have noted down the telephone number when Andy called this afternoon… She wanted to tell you that the museum have asked to see her complete range of greetings cards. Oh—didn't I mention that before? Silly me… Miles, what are you doing with that fork? Get off me!'

CHAPTER SEVEN

From: Andromeda@ConstellationOfficeServices
To: saffie@saffronthechef
Subject: What to do about the millionaire

I wish you would stop scolding me so much. Blame Nigel if you like, but the last thing I want or need right now is a dinner date where I won't know what cutlery to use for what course, and I am bound to say the wrong thing. He is just being kind. That's all.

You know that I am clueless when it comes to sport.

And no. I won't organise a double date for you, me and the Gibson twins.

My life is already complicated enough.

Oh, must go—cards to paint.

Love ya, Andy the professional artist or something like that.

ANDY sat down at the worktop she was using as her bedroom desk and stroked the thick paper and lustrous colours of the print she had bought at the museum. This was where she was happiest. Alone with her illustrations. This was where she could most truly express what she was made of and what she did best.

Picking up the calligraphy pen she had been using for the lettering on one of her Christmas card designs, she carefully and slowly wrote his name in a round font, then italics, then gothic script.

Miles Gibson.

It was a strong name with two wonderful leading capitals.

A strong name for a strong man. A powerful man.

A smile crept up on her and she pressed her lips together tight.

Contrary. Unpredictable. Sporty. Domineering. And those were just his finer qualities. The list could go on.

Tempted? Oh, yes, she had been tempted.

Andy was so preoccupied with writing his name that when her mobile rang she picked it up without checking to see who the caller was, flipped it open, lifted it to her ear and said, 'Andy Davies.'

'Hey, girl,' a deep male voice said, and the pen she was holding dug into the paper, made a splodge of red ink and twisted the nib.

'Oh, rats,' she hissed, and tried to soak up the ink.

'I prefer hello,' Miles replied, his voice lifting up at the end in amusement.

'Oh, no, not you.' She frowned. 'I just spilt some ink, but it was only a test piece, nothing to worry about.'

She held the phone away from her mouth, rolled her eyes and grimaced. Was it possible to sound more stupid and pathetic?

She took a breath, smiled and tried to speak as though her brain was connected to the mouth. 'Back now. Shall we start again? Hello. What are you up to? And how did you find my number?'

He breathed out hot and fast. 'It turns out that my brother is a member of the gym at the hotel next door. And they have a hot tub. And Jason made a note of your number when you called today.'

Then his voice dropped several decibels and he half

whispered in a tone that she could pour over ice cream, 'And how about you? What are you up to?'

'I'm at my desk painting stained-glass Christmas cards,' she murmured, her eyes closed so that she could listen to his voice without any visual distractions. 'Why do you ask?'

'I hear that the museum want to see your artwork,' he whispered. 'Congratulations. I would like to help you celebrate.'

It was a good thing she was sitting down, because suddenly all the wind went out of her sails.

'Thing is, if you are like me, you'll probably be working hard at making those pieces the best work you have ever done. And loving it. But you know what they say... All work and no play... So I have a suggestion. And don't panic. It is not another date. Our deal was strictly for a one-off event. Think of this as more of a research trip. And I know how much you love research.'

The bottom sank out of her stomach and she slapped the side of her head.

'Cory Sports sponsor an aqua-therapy programme at a couple of London swimming pools. We've just opened a new class and I'm going to head down to check on how it is doing. Want to come out and play?'

Andy stepped out of the taxi cab into the cool dusky air, and immediately tugged the belt of her navy raincoat a little tighter.

What was the dress code for meeting millionaire CEOs at swimming pools for a research trip? Research into how mad she was to agree to this in the first place. So what if his pitch had been brilliant and the shop loved her proposal. It was the artwork that had swung it, not just the clever marketing ploy.

Casual, Miles had said. What did that mean? Casual by her standards meant loose pants and sweatshirt and fluffy slippers. And Saffie had just laughed her head off when she rang her for advice. No help at all.

And where was she? The cab had dropped her off in front of a small shopping arcade in the middle of a residential area of Victorian and Edwardian houses with a sprinkling of modern flats and bungalows.

No flash glass and stone buildings here. No photographers of paparazzi—just a sign pointing her towards a community gym and pool.

Two minutes later, Andy found her way to the ladies' changing room, drew open the door and instantly reeled back in surprise at the groups of lovely older ladies who were crammed around the lockers, all chatting and laughing and peering into bags and holdalls. But what really struck her was that, irrespective of their age, size and shape, every one of them was wearing a brightly coloured one-piece swimming costume that would not be out of place on some tropical beach. Huge red blossoms, birds of paradise and exotic butterflies clashed with huge banana leaves and gold ribbon trim and swim racer backs.

The room was a riot of colour and life and, try as she might, Andy could not help but laugh out loud in delight and astonishment.

This was the last thing she had expected to find in a small local gym in a residential area of London, but the colour scheme certainly matched the temperature. She had never been in a changing area that was this warm before. Tropical was about right.

'Hey, ladies—any of those swimming costumes left over? They're brilliant!'

'And they pull in the boys,' the nearest lady replied, which set the others off into an explosion of helpless giggling, which was probably not such a good idea for the lady in the wheelchair who had to gasp for breath because she was laughing so much.

Leaving them to their fun, Andy stowed her coat and boots and slipped her feet into a pair of non-slip pool shoes.

Time to find out where Miles had got to.

Andy drew back the swing doors and stepped out onto the tiles. Bright overhead lights reflected back from the water, the light broken by a swimmer doing strong front crawl, length after length. Andy looked up, just in time to see Miles Gibson hauling himself up over the edge of the pool.

Too proud to use the steps at the shallow end.

And the breath seemed to catch in her lungs as she ogled and kept on ogling.

Strong abs. Long muscular legs. Dark hairline going down to his trunks. Spectacular shoulders. She had not expected him to be so fit after months of hospital treatment. Or so gorgeous out of his clothes. Why was she always attracted to the muscular types? She had spent way too much time working in offices if this was what she was missing.

As she watched Miles shook his head back, showering water droplets down over his shoulders and the stunning rippling muscles across his wide back.

Her throat was dry, her palms clammy and walking and talking at the same time were going to be a challenge until he put some clothing on.

Miles Gibson was sex on legs.

Seriously.

Andy broke the spell by sighing in appreciation—way too loudly.

He smiled up at her as she calmly padded across to the poolside bench, but as she passed him his towel his face fell and he instantly dropped the towel over his lap and thighs.

'What? No bikini?' he asked, waggling his eyebrows.

'You should be so lucky,' she replied, 'but, speaking of swimwear, are you responsible for that collection of exotic birds that are waiting to explode out of the ladies' changing area?' She gestured with her head back towards the changing area. 'Because I have to tell you, it certainly brightened up my day.'

His reply was a slow nod and a lazy smile. 'Ladies' night. Cory Sports have spent the last two years developing a full programme of hot-water aqua-therapy classes. Their trainer is on the way but in the meantime the ladies have some fun and the company has some beta testing of its all-ages swimwear. Speaking of which—' and his brows tightened as his gaze scanned her body '—I thought you might have brought a swimming costume? Can't have all of the fun to myself.'

Andy sucked in a breath through her clenched teeth and focused her gaze on the wall murals.

'I was just admiring the pool. Such lovely colours. And warm too.'

'A nice ninety-five degrees. Great for arthritis and rheumatism and a whole raft of other conditions, such as sports injuries. And why are you avoiding my question?'

'I went to a private school which had its own pool. A cold-water swimming pool. The gym teacher thought that icy swimming classes were character forming and invigorating for the pupils.'

'Were they?'

'Of course not. I hated swimming lessons. We all did. I think it put most of us off swimming for life.'

Miles looked at her for a few seconds, his eyebrows high, before giving a small cough.

'Andy. Are you saying that…?'

She nodded. 'Can't swim. Scared of the water. Would you like another towel?'

Andy had only just finished speaking when the door to the changing room opened and an explosion of colour and laughter edged slowly out towards the steps at the shallow end of the pool.

'Scared of the water?' Miles replied, from behind her back. 'I've been teaching people to swim all of my life. That's why I worked this new programme into the schedule. Water confidence. It means working with the ladies one to one but it gets results.'

'Of course it does,' Andy said as she watched the ladies splash about in the warm water. 'Because you want to share your passion. And something tells me that you would be very good at that.' She turned back towards Miles, but took one step too far, colliding with his shoulder, sending his leg slipping on the moist slick floor.

She felt herself falling sideways with him, out of control, just waiting for the crunch as she hit the floor.

Only she didn't hit anything.

Two hands grabbed her waist, and as she moved to push herself back up, his right hand moved instinctively to give her more support. And slid under her loose sweater onto her bare skin.

The effect was electrifying. In a second she was upright, one hand pressed against the muscles of his bare chest, her forehead in contact with his chin and neck, as he pressed her to his body so he could take her weight. She felt the raised stubble on the side of his face, a faint tang of a citrus aftershave and swimming-pool antiseptic and something else. Something essentially masculine. That combination of sweat, tension and musky personal aroma, which was driving cave girls wild thousands of years ago, and was working just fine right now.

She closed her eyes and revelled in the sensation as his hand moved just a few centimetres higher on the skin at her waist. She wanted him to go higher, a lot higher.

Oh, God, this felt so right. So very right.

Neither of them spoke as she pressed herself into his neck, only too aware that his breathing was matching her own heart rate. Racing. Only she had stopped breathing, and her single breath broke the moment. Both of his hands lifted at the same time as she opened her eyes and pushed gently from his body.

And took three steps back, creating some space between them.

It had been a mistake coming here. Seeing Miles like this. A really bad mistake.

Because every cell in her body was screaming for her to give into this attraction and do something mad, like jump onto his lap and kiss him breathless. And where would that leave her?

Nowhere. Alone and discarded. And wouldn't that feel good?

The whole incident had only taken a few seconds but she didn't have the guts to look at him when she eventually spoke.

'That was embarrassing. I almost needed your lifeguarding skills there for a moment.'

'Are you okay?'

His voice was low, caring. Almost whispered. He was breathing as heavily as she was. Andy fought to put together a coherent response. 'I'm fine. Thank you.'

But when Miles stepped forwards, he staggered back slightly and tried to massage his calf muscles into working, but then his knee seized up completely and he had to lean against the bench to relieve the pressure, wincing in pain.

'Cramp?' Andy asked.

'Not exactly,' Miles replied with a sarcastic shrug, then smiled and dropped his shoulders with the gentlest of touches on her arm. 'Sorry. I sometimes forget that the rest of the world doesn't have much interest in my surfing career.'

'Ah, I don't usually read the sports section of the newspaper. But I should imagine that professional sportsmen have a lot of injuries to cope with.' She glanced down at his leg. 'Does it hurt?'

'More than Jason knows. And the painkillers knock me out. So I put up with it.'

He sniffed and hobbled over to the bench. 'And you're right, when you are pushing yourself to the limit, you do get injured. Which makes this—' and he scrubbed even harder at his leg '—even harder to tolerate, because I didn't fall off a board. I got hit by a truck.'

Her jaw dropped. 'Of course. You mentioned it at the museum. How did it happen?'

'I was in a small sports car. It was raining and the truck driver was so drunk he could hardly stand,' he snorted. 'I remember walking out of my girlfriend's beach house on Tenerife into the rain with not a care in the world. And twenty-four hours later I woke up in a city hospital and most of my body was broken.'

Miles stretched out his leg, and began massaging the sinewy calf muscles. 'I was too doped up on painkillers and sedatives to take much in at the time but I recall flashes of my dad's face and people in white coats and words like fractures. Pierced lungs. Hip replacement. Pins. Then they knocked me out again so they could do what they had to do.'

She gasped and stopped breathing for a second. 'What about the other driver—were they…?'

'Cuts and bruises. The drunk was lucky. I wasn't.'

Andy exhaled slowly and blinked at him. 'How did you get through it?'

'I didn't. Good thing my parents understood that yelling at them was only a temporary phase. They were just pleased that I had survived.'

'But you did it. You came out in one piece,' Andy whispered and looked at him.

'Several pieces. And you can still see the joins.'

Andy could not help it. She stared at the puckered red and white skin for several seconds. The scars ran from knee to upper thigh and she could see where the incisions and pins had been, but it was not gory or scary.

It was simply his leg.

'Nice scars.' She nodded, her lips pressed together.

He blinked, looked at his knee, then back at her face. 'Nice scars? Is that it? The girls love my scars. I thought that at the very least you would be impressed and leap into my arms because I am a wounded hero.'

'Over a few leg scars? Please,' she replied in a nonchalant and relaxed voice. 'But your family must have been scared for you.'

'Damn right.'

'Does it affect your swimming?' Andy asked in a completely natural voice with a smile on her lips. Oblivious to the knife she had just slipped up into his heart.

Miles froze, his gaze scanning her face, but saw only genuine concern staring back at him. Not disgust that he was broken and useless, or pity for what his body had been like.

'Not in classes like this, no.'

She sniffed and nodded. 'Good, because, I have to tell you, those ladies are a real handful. You are going to need all of your expert coaching skills to keep the girls in check today.'

Coaching skills?

Miles coughed. And then stilled. She had a point. He had always loved teaching, no matter what age the beginners were. He could do that. Leg or no leg.

The old light switched back on inside him, warmed by the grin on Andy's face as she waved at the ladies.

Time to complete his side of their bargain. 'Speaking of families. Would you like to come back to the Cory Sports building this evening and meet some of my team? Jason is in the mood to cook and he loves having people around. It would be nice to help you celebrate your success at the museum.'

'You want me to come to your apartment?'

Andy's heart was pounding. She would be alone in an apartment with two single men she had only just met. Now that was more than a little scary.

Miles must have heard her thoughts because his next words were, 'Jason's apartment. And don't be scared. My brother has many skills and cooking is one of them. I left him in the kitchen peeling oranges. I think this is a good sign. Plus I've already mentioned your artwork to our website designer, Peter. He'll be there with his wife, Lisa, tonight so there is at least one more creative person in the room. And then there is your umbrella. A sad case. It is missing you terribly.'

He paused and exhaled slowly. 'So what shall I tell Jason? Does he set another place at the table?

'One question. Would I have to do the washing up?'

She heard him chuckle, deep and resonant, and the rich sound filled her head.

'No. All taken care of. Your job will be to enjoy yourself.

Prepare to be positively pampered. I'll even come along and pick you up if you like.'

'Well, in that case, I would be delighted to eat home-cooked food. Thank you. But it would be easier if I took a cab to your office.'

'You got it. Oh—and, Andy.'

'Yes?'

'Just so that you know. I would never stand you up. Never.'

And with that he pushed himself to his feet and strolled over to the cluster of ladies at the shallow end of the pool, who instantly mobbed him like fan girls meeting a pop star. Twenty seconds later they were all laughing like teenagers and splashing in the warm water. Having the time of their lives.

And all the time Andy was sitting on the bench, watching him in the water. Just watching him.

From: Andromeda@ConstellationOfficeServices
To: saffie@saffronthechef
Subject: Dinner with the Gibson Twins
Saffie, you are terrible. Jason might be an excellent cook.

Of course I know that they are millionaires and probably have their food pre-prepared by chefs and supplied in posh microwave dishes, but Miles did say that cooking is Jason's hobby. And, yes, I shall give you a full report of what we ate and how it tasted. And, no, I will not take photographs of the penthouse or the food. Unless I really have to, because otherwise you wouldn't believe me.

This means I am bound to show myself up.

Thanks again for the loan of your posh cashmere.

Wish me luck

Andy the terrified.

'More cheese, Andy? I tried to save you the last slice of the quince membrillo but I was too late—the amazing eating machine here got to it first.'

Jason gestured with the cheese knife towards Miles, who threw his hands up into the air in protest. 'Hey—can I help it if I have a healthy appetite? Anyway, you're one to talk. I only turned my back for two minutes to help Lisa on with her coat and what was left of those fancy chocolates Peter brought had done a magic disappearing act.'

Jason sniffed and flung his head with a dramatic twist. 'Cook's perks.' He pressed his hand to his chest. 'Sweet tooth. I confess. Happy now?' And dodged the napkin that Miles threw at him.

Andy laughed and sat back on the lovely cream leather sofa and patted her stomach. 'Thanks, but I couldn't eat another thing. And don't forget—I have to have that recipe for the pork with ginger and orange. It was the most delicious thing I have ever eaten.'

Jason abandoned his tray and lifted Andy's hand and kissed the back of her knuckles. 'Praise indeed. Thank you, kind lady.' Then he peered at Miles with narrowed eyes. 'See. Did you hear that? Everybody else liked my cooking. According to Peter my menu was inspired... Beat that if you can. Seeing as you can barely use a kettle.'

'Champagne sorbet? Please. That's way too girly. I was expecting at least a chocolate tart or one of those creamy cake things.'

'Don't listen to a word Miles says,' Andy tutted and smiled up at Jason. 'It was a wonderful meal and I feel positively pampered. And very guilty. Are you sure I can't help you with the washing up?'

Jason gestured for her to sit back down with both hands palm down. 'Dishwashers. Marvellous things. You just sit back and relax and try the coffee while this one keeps you company—if you can stand it.'

Then in a flash he had loaded up a tray with the flatware and was off behind the marble slab that separated the kitchen from the dining area of the huge open-plan apartment.

Andy indulged in a secret snigger and raised the tiny espresso cup to her nose and inhaled deeply.

'Oh, that is so wonderful. I love good coffee.'

'Here. Allow me.' Miles got up from the dining table so that he could top up her cup with the fragrant piping-hot brew. 'Jase knows the grower in the West Indies. There are a few specialist shops in London who import the beans but he insists on grinding them to his own specification every time. It takes longer but that's my brother for you. Things have to be just right or it bothers him like mad.'

There was a real sense of pride in that voice, which to Andy sounded as mellow and rich as the chocolate notes in the coffee.

'I noticed. He was so worried that Peter and Liz were going to be late for their babysitter that he sent the limo for them. But of course, I blame you completely for keeping them laughing so late in the evening.'

Miles pointed to the chest of his navy V-necked designer jumper and faked an expression of total innocence. '*Moi?* I cannot think what you could mean.'

'Really?' Andy picked up one of the photo albums from the coffee table. 'So those photos of Peter and Jason hanging off the rigging of an old sailing ship dressed up as pirates just happened to be lying around. Hmm?'

Miles sniggered. 'It took me days to find a parrot which was docile enough to sit on Peter's shoulder. Shame that my mother had fed the poor bird to bursting and not bothered to tell us before we took her out on open water.'

He closed his eyes and sniggered. 'Classic.'

'You were very cruel. I liked Peter. And he was so kind about the party invitation I painted for Elise.'

'No, he wasn't.' Miles shook his head, then sat down on the hard chair facing Andy with his long legs stretched out in front of him. 'Peter does not do kind. He meant it.'

Miles saluted Andy with his water glass. 'He loved your work. It's as simple as that. You have to remember that Peter helped to design the Cory Sports logo based on the Corazon heart theme that you picked up on. It was a genius idea to take the letter C and work in the hearts and Spanish flowers in blue and gold. Genius. And that is not a word that gets used around here very often.'

Miles dug down into his trouser pocket and passed a business card across the coffee table to Andy, who stared at it for a few seconds before picking it up.

'When Peter LeBlanc asks you to call him about buying the exclusive rights to your design—he has already made up his mind. These are his contact details. Have a think about how much you want to charge, then give him a call. He'll be expecting you. And tomorrow would be good.'

Andy opened her mouth to reply, looked down at the card, which she could barely read because her eyes were blurred with tears, then put it on the table and exhaled slowly.

'Tomorrow? This is all a bit fast for me, Miles.'

'We recognise quality workmanship when we see it, Andy. You are a very talented artist and we would like to buy one of your designs. Is that a problem? Aren't you interested in that type of painting any longer?'

'Interested? This is my dream project. I love the illuminated artwork. No—it's not the work. It's me. I am not used to people taking me seriously as an artist. And it has come as rather a shock. First the museum wants to sell my

Christmas card designs and now Peter wants to talk to me about the logo. This has been a very overwhelming week.'

She pressed her finger to her nose and blinked away a sniffle. 'I know that I must sound like a total idiot, but I have been working for a long time to get my artwork off the ground and now everything has come all at once and my poor head is having a hard time coping with the idea that someone has confidence in my work. I am far more used to being ridiculed about my so-called foolish hobby. Sorry.'

Miles sat back in silence, locked his hands behind his head and stretched out his long, long legs so that the muscles in his thighs stretched the fine fabric until it was taut. The expression on his face as he looked at her was so intense that Andy started chewing on her lower lip and shuffling on the slippery leather, her relaxed and happy mood a thing of the past.

She felt that he was weighing her up. Judging her.

It was Miles who broke the tension by flicking through one of the photo albums until he came to a full-page print of the young Miles standing on an upturned plastic crate, grinning from ear to ear at the person holding the camera.

Clutched in his hands was a tiny silver-coloured trophy and he was holding it aloft like an Olympic athlete. Standing on one side of him was a bare-chested Jason in board shorts and, on the other, an older man who looked so much like Miles and Jason that it could only be their father. They had their arms wrapped around Miles's shoulders and their joy leapt out of the photograph and brought a smile to Andy's face.

'I was seventeen. I had just won the Best of Cornwall surfing championship, the sun was shining and I thought life could not get any better. My mother took the photograph, then we walked back along the beach and stopped for fish and chips. And that was when they told me that they were selling everything and moving to Tenerife so that I could train as a professional surfer.'

Miles closed the album with a snap. 'They gave me a chance to show what I could do. And I was so scared that I would let them down, it paralysed me. But I took the risk. And I have never regretted it.'

His gaze dropped to her hands, and he gently turned her right hand over and ran his fingertip along the palm, only too aware that her body seemed to shiver at his touch, and not just from the cold night air.

'You have a long life line. Same as me.'

Then he inhaled slowly and curled her fingers over her palm and held them there.

'Take the chance, Andy. Show us what you are made of. Show us what you can do.'

She hesitated, her breathing fast and hot.

'Is that what you are doing, Miles? Showing everyone what you are made of? It must be hard trying to prove that, even after your accident, you still have the same joy in your work that you had when you were seventeen.'

Miles froze.

The same joy? No. He could never go back to being that same happy teenager with so much to look forward to and so little clue about how much work it was going to take to become the world champion. And stay there.

The seventeen-years-old Miles had been bursting with power and potential and the sheer joy in his sport.

Joy. When was the last time he had truly found joy in what he was doing? Adrenaline rush—yes. Excitement and exhilaration, every time. But joy? No, he had not felt true joy for years. Even before the accident his life had become an endless battle to stay on top of his fitness and competitions and business work.

Little wonder he'd had no time to realise that his so-called girlfriend was more interested in the celebrity circuit than spending time with him.

A dark cloud called disappointment and frustration passed over his heart and he sat back hard in his chair.

When had he lost his joy in the sport?

Miles inhaled slowly, only too aware that Andy was still looking at him, waiting for his reply.

She smiled at him as though she could read his mind, and the warmth of that smile seemed to penetrate his thick skull and blow away the dark clouds, leaving a calm blue-sky day behind.

Strange. He had never thought about it that way until now.

And yet this girl had seen it in him. How did she do that? How did she get under his skin?

An old familiar yearning started deep in his belly and wound its way to other parts of his anatomy.

Attraction. And more.

After Lori he had promised himself that he would stick to casual relationships.

But maybe the cost was too high a price to pay? What happened if he met someone who was more interested in him rather than his celebrity status? How was he going to handle that and risk being rejected again?

Miles straightened his back.

This was one time he was going to walk away from the danger.

He didn't need this. Not now. He could fight it. He had to. Anything else would be too complicated and way too dangerous for both of them.

All he needed was a stand-in date for Saturday night and then he would be out of here and things would be back to normal. That was what he had to focus on.

Whether he wanted it that way or not.

It was Andy who broke the silence.

'Some of us have changed direction so many times I think I am going around in circles most days. Do you ever feel like trying something new?'

He replied with a dismissive snort. 'Never. Cory Sports needs Miles Gibson to be standing on some podium somewhere—the champion kite surfer. King of the surf. That's my job. And I happen to be very good at it.'

'And now you can add expert swimming coach and business mentor to the list. It is a good thing that you are so modest,' Andy replied, and reached for her coffee cup, her eyes not leaving his.

And just like that the air between them bristled with static electricity. It bounced back and forwards, sparking all the way as the silence filled the room. The subtle Spanish background music was gone. Replaced by the sound of their breathing. And the hot crackle of the tension as their eyes locked and stayed locked.

Miles leant forwards so that his whole body was focused on her, eyes bright and smiling.

'Will you at least think about it? Then call Peter when you are ready.'

Then he pushed himself slowly to his feet before she could reply, and was at her side, wrapping his down coat around her shoulders with a low chortle and sliding open the floor-to-ceiling glass patio doors. 'Let's get some air.'

CHAPTER EIGHT

ANDY stepped out onto a long tiled terrace, and what she saw in front of her took her breath away.

The light showers of rain had cleared to leave a star-kissed cool evening. And stretched out, in every direction, was London. Her city. Dressed and lit and bright and shiny and sparking with Christmas decorations and the lights from homes and streets.

It was like something from a movie or a wonderful painting. A moment so special that Andy knew instinctively that she would never forget it.

She grasped hold of the railing and looked out over the city, her heart soaring, all doubt forgotten in the exuberant joy of the view.

It was almost a shock to feel a warm arm wrap the coat closer around her shoulders and she turned sideways to face Miles with a grin and clutched onto the sleeve of his sweater.

'Have you seen this? It's astonishing. I thought the view from the gallery at the museum was spectacular, but this is wonderful. I love it.'

'I know. I can see it on your face.'

Then he turned forwards and came to stand next to her on the balcony, his left hand just touching the outstretched fingers of her right.

'You probably don't realise it, but there are very few people who are totally honest and open about their feelings. But you are one of them. You have a special gift, Andromeda Davies. You aren't afraid to tell people the truth about how you feel. And I envy you that.'

'You. Envy me? What do you mean?' Andy asked, taken aback by the tone in his voice. For the first time since they met, Miles sounded hesitant and unsure, in total contrast to the man who had been gibing with his brother and friends.

'Honesty can make you vulnerable.'

Miles looked down at Andy's fingers and his gaze seemed to lock onto how his fingers could mesh with hers so completely. 'This last year has taught me a few things. There are some things in life you can control, Andy. Some you can't. But I know one thing. I am done with long-term planning. That is out of the window and gone. Because you don't know what is coming your way. You can't. So live for the day. Take the opportunities that come along and enjoy them while you can. That's my new motto.'

Andy looked into his face and remembered to breathe again.

'And how is that working for you?' She smiled.

'Actually not too badly. It means that instead of riding the waves in South America I am here in London enjoying time out with my brother and a lovely lady.'

He held one of Andy's hands. 'I have even found the time to go on an Internet date. Imagine that.'

'Yes. Imagine. Did I say brave earlier? Maybe madcap might be a better expression. I don't have any sports injuries or scars and bruises like that, Miles. Scar-free learning. That's my motto. Maybe that is why I am even more scared than usual. I need that forward planning to make sense of my life and make sure that the bills get paid.'

'No scars and bruises? Yes, you have, you have plenty of scars.'

He pressed two fingers flat onto her chest so they rested above her heart and she could feel the warm pressure of his fingertips through the fine cashmere wool. 'But they are not on the surface like mine are. They are all in here. And they hurt just as bad. Because I think other people pushed you beyond the limit of what you were ready to handle. But here is the thing. When you are competing against the world's best athletes, you soon learn that the only way you can win is to strive to reach your own limits of what you are capable of—not the limits anyone sets.'

'How do you know? What your limits are?'

'You don't. The only way to find out is by testing yourself. You would be astounded at what you are capable of. And if you don't succeed you learn from your mistakes and do what you have to do to get back up and try again until you can prove to yourself that you can do it. And then you keep on doing that over and over again.'

'No matter how many times you fall down and hurt yourself?'

'That's right. You've got it.'

Andy turned slightly away from Miles and looked out towards the horizon, suddenly needing to get some distance, some air between them. What he was describing was so hard, so difficult and so familiar. He could never know how many times she had forced herself to smile after someone let her down, or when she had been ridiculed or humiliated.

Andy blinked back tears and pulled the collar of the warm coat up around her ears while she fought to gain control of her voice. 'Some of us lesser mortals have been knocked down so many times that it is hard to bounce back up again, Miles. Very hard.'

His response was to reach out for her with both of his

long strong arms and draw her into his chest so that her head rested on his shoulder. The warmth of his body encased her in a cocoon of strength and warm cashmere and she was content to cling onto him for a few seconds while the air seeped back into her lungs. Air that smelt of Miles and coffee and biscuits and frost and winter in the city.

'What is it, Andy?' he asked, his mouth somewhere in the vicinity of her hair. 'What does your heart yearn to do and you haven't gone there yet?'

'Me? Oh, I had such great plans when I was a teenager and the whole world seemed to be an open door to whatever I wanted. But then hard reality hit. Six months ago I was working three jobs and most evenings and weekends. Right now I have to think about whether I want to go back to a full-time day job working with men like Nigel, or try and earn enough from my artwork.'

She looked up into his smiling face but stayed inside the warm circle of his arms. 'Nigel is the ex-boyfriend I talked about. Or at least I thought he was my boyfriend. He worked in the same office with those girls you saw in the coffee shop the other evening. There was a lot of competition for clients, so when he asked me to help him work on a major new proposal I was pleased to help.'

Andy smoothed the fine fabric of his sweater as she spoke. 'He played every trick in the book to get me to work for nothing, night after night. The occasional pizza meal out. Drinks. Always promising that we could be a proper couple when the project was approved. Always teasing and telling me how important I was to him.'

Her hands stilled. 'He dumped me the day he got the client account.'

Tears pricked her eyes and she swallowed down the pain to get the words out. 'But do you know the worst part? The girls in the office knew that he was living with the CEO's daughter and that he was just using me to get the work done so he could pass it off as his own. And they didn't tell me. They were having too much fun laughing behind my back. Have you any idea how humiliating that was? I couldn't…' She took a few sharp short breaths before going on. 'I couldn't work there a minute longer. I just couldn't. Do you understand?'

Miles replied by wrapping his long arms around her body in a warm embrace so tender that Andy surrendered to a moment of joy and pressed her head against his chest, inhaling his delicious scent as her body shared his warmth.

His hands made lazy circles on her back in silence for a few minutes until he spoke, the words reverberating inside his chest into her head. 'Better than you think. What did you do then?'

Andy shuffled back from him, laughed in a choked voice and then pressed both hands against his chest as she replied in a broken smile. 'Then I met up with Elise—and, well, you know the rest. I needed that part-time office job until the artwork takes off. Only now it looks like I need to organise myself if I want to sell my designs to you and the museum.'

He grabbed both of her arms as she tried to slip away and looked at her straight in the eyes. 'I agree. Not nearly ambitious enough. Let's start again. And think big. Then bigger. It sounds so good I don't know why you haven't gone into design full-time before now.'

He tilted his head sideways to look at Andy as she moistened her lips, her mouth a straight line.

'Isn't it obvious?' she whispered after several long seconds. 'I'm too scared.'

'Scared of what? Failure? Hell, Jason and I made so many mistakes those first two years we must have been the laughing stock of the business. Good thing we were able to laugh at ourselves and enjoy the journey.'

'How did you do that? How did you laugh when you knew that you had taken a horrible decision which was going to cost you time and money? Because I don't know how to do that.'

'How? Because we felt like we were explorers, charting unknown territory, where every day was a new challenge.' Miles grinned, his face energised, the laughter lines hard in the artificial light flooding out from the dining room. Then he shrugged. 'And we had our parents behind us. Family all the way.'

'Family?' Andy repeated. 'Then you truly were lucky. Because all my family did was to ridicule me and everything I liked to do. I am on my own, Miles. Completely on my own. Can you understand that?'

Miles stood in silence, his gaze locked onto Andy's wide green eyes as she took in a few breaths of the cool night air.

Completely on her own? How was that possible? The hairs on the back of his neck flickered into life at the very thought of being without Jason and his parents and their circle of friends back on Tenerife, and he rubbed his hand over his neck to quieten them down.

They had been his lifeline, his strength and his back-up when times were hard as well as good.

The only people he would accept help from. *Ever.*

'No. I can't imagine being without my parents and family.'

He stepped forward one step and rubbed his hands up and down Andy's arms.

She flashed him a glance intended to make him back off but he ignored it anyhow.

'You talked about your parents at the museum. Have they, er...'

Andy rolled her eyes towards the balcony above their

heads. 'Oh, still very much alive. Still mad as a bag of frogs and still trying to teach English in India. From the letters which turn up every few months they seem to be lurching from crisis to crisis with the occasional frantic phone call in the middle of the night pleading the need for emergency funds to pay for a new roof or replacement parts for some car or other. Practical household skills were not part of the private education in those days. My dad was one of those men who employed tradesmen to wire a plug. Do you get the picture?'

Miles sucked in air through his teeth. 'No. Not really. India. Wow.'

She shook her head and pointed to the balcony. 'I look at this city that I love and think of all of the opportunity that is out there and I fill up with excitement and enthusiasm and I want to do this so badly—and then I think about all of the unknowns and costs and pitfalls and I freeze. And put the plan back in the drawer to think about later.'

'Only there won't be a later. Will there? I am beginning to understand. And I don't blame you for taking the safer option.'

'Do not judge me. We aren't all sporting heroes!'

'I don't expect you to be,' Miles replied, and raised both hands in the air in submission. 'And I'm the last person on this planet who has the right to judge anybody. Don't forget—I have been there and I had my brother and family along for the ride and we still had to work like crazy to get our business started. A one-woman show is going to find it a lot tougher. You need time and money to get your art business off the ground.'

Andy glared at him, narrow lipped, her gaze scanning his face for a few seconds before her shoulders dropped and she sighed out loud. 'I know. And that has always been the problem. But I am sorry for snapping at you. This has been a tough week.'

'No problem. How about a suggestion instead? I know a couple of venture capital guys who have money to invest in new business ideas. All I have to do is make a few phone calls and…what? What now?'

'I don't want to carry any debt. No maxed-out credit cards. No business loans, no venture capital investment. That's how my dad got into so much trouble and there is no way that I am going there. So thank you but no. I might be hard up but I have made some rules for myself.'

Miles inhaled very slowly and watched Andy struggle with her thoughts, her dilemma played out in the tension on her face.

She was as proud as anyone he had ever met. Including himself. Which was quite something.

And just like that the connection he had sensed between them from the moment he had laid eyes on her in that coffee shop kicked up a couple of notches. And the longer he watched her, the stronger that connection became, until he almost felt that it was a practical thing. A wire. Pulling them closer together.

And every warning bell in his body started screaming *Danger* so loudly that in the end he could not ignore it any longer. And this time he was the one who broke the wire and pulled away from her.

She shivered in the cool air, fracturing the moment, and he stepped back and opened the patio doors and guided her inside. And into the luxurious warmth of the apartment.

'No debt,' Miles murmured as he slipped his coat from her shoulders and gestured for her to get comfy on the sofa. 'That's a tough one. Well, you know how much I like a challenge.'

Then his eyes narrowed and a broad smile cracked his

mouth. 'Here is an idea which won't cost you a penny but could be just what you need to get the business up and running.'

He moved onto the back of the sofa and grabbed hold of both of her shoulders so that she could not move an inch as he leant forwards until their noses were almost touching, his eyes locked onto hers.

'You like facts. Here are two. Jason asked me to come over to the London office for a few days so that we can work on the plan for the next product launch. And I didn't argue because my brother is a genius—but you must never tell him I said that.'

Andy took a breath but Miles got there first. 'No talking. But as it happens, I might have an hour or two to spare between physio sessions and meetings.'

Then he relaxed his grip a little and smiled. 'I thought about what you said at the pool today. And you might have a point. I enjoy training. So...how would you like some help with that business plan? A website. Promotions. Marketing. All the things you need to get your artwork out for the world to see.'

She looked back at him, wide eyed. 'Would I have to wear a swimming costume?'

A great wide-mouthed grin illuminated his face as his gaze scanned her body from the heels of her boots to her hair clip, bringing that sparkle back into his eyes. 'Perhaps not. Way too distracting. So. What do you say? Can you spare an hour a day to get some business advice?'

From: Andromeda@ConstellationOfficeServices
To: Saffie@Saffronthechef
Hope your Saturday evening dinner service goes more smoothly this week.
    Thanks again for your offer of your best designer dress

and full kit. And you were right—the red works and there may well be some seriously high-class slutty photos.

Problem is. I am having kittens here. What am I going to do, Saffie? Help!

There are going to be TV cameras and photographers there tonight.

Miles is determined to introduce me to half the room as an illustrator. He has no clue that the first time I mention illuminated fifteenth-century bibles his posh guests will run off screaming or think I am high on hallucinogens.

The last thing I want to do is show him up in any way.

Maybe I can fake the flu? Or chicken pox? That might work. Top athletes hate disease.

Talk again in the morning. If I make it that far. Andy

Andy paced up and down on the bedroom carpet, her hands on her hips, as she moved from her bed to the wardrobe, then back to the bottom of her bed again.

The wardrobe door was open and she blinked at the contents for several minutes before striding purposefully forwards in Saffie's favourite red high-heeled sandals. Her hand stretched out to lift the red chiffon cocktail dress from the hanger, then froze and dropped away. Again.

Her shoulders slumped and she rested her forehead on the waxed oak panel, not caring that she was ruining the make-up that had taken her an hour to put on, wipe off, then put on again in a different way.

Terrified that she was sending out the wrong message. Or was it the right message?

She had been aiming for elegant and attractive, while the girl who stared back at her from the mirror looked more like someone from a low-class burlesque show. Never mind the high-class slutty. She was the low-class slutty.

Reminder to self: find a job with a firm of hairdressers. Or beauticians. Or both.

This wasn't working.

She had been mad to even think that she was ready to go out on a date, with Miles Gibson, millionaire joint owner of Cory Sports. Even if it was for only one evening.

Andy tottered to her bed, fell backwards and let her arms dangle over the sides.

Had what happened with Nigel not taught her anything?

What if she had been right the first time and Miles was a chancer, and she was just about to make herself a laughing stock in exchange for a hot dinner and if she was lucky a glass of the house red?

Andy sniffed. No. That was unfair. Miles was not a cheapskate. He was a very successful businessman and professional sportsman. It would be a very nice dinner in a luxury hotel restaurant owned by one of those chefs who seemed to be on every television channel.

A restaurant where everyone would know that he was a multimillionaire slumming it with the girl who delivered party invitations. And she was fine with that. Better than fine. This was her life and she wasn't ashamed. Far from it.

What she was afraid of was being laughed at. Laughed and scoffed at because she had stepped outside her narrow circle and trusted someone not to use her.

Andy bit down on her inner lip. Deep inside in that secret place where she kept her dreams and most sacred wishes, she wanted to stride into that hotel in these red shoes as the equal of any of the other guests, including Miles. Strong and confident. Like the girl she used to be before life stomped on her confidence and squeezed it out like toothpaste from a tube.

Dratted Miles for reminding her about her other life.

Andy closed her eyes, her throat burning and tears stinging at the sides of her eyes.

She was pathetic.

This amazing, handsome and attentive man had chosen her to be his date for the evening. Which was so amazing that she still couldn't believe it.

Not that she had much time to prepare herself for the big night.

The past few days had passed in a blur of activity and mad work. Miles had not been kidding about how restless he was, but his pacing had slowly got better. He had kept his word and after a few hours going through the Cory Sports systems she had actually started to believe that she had the tools she needed to be a self-employed artist. Peter had set up meetings with their advertising company for next week so she had plenty to think about. But she had done it. She had taken the first baby steps.

And right there, every step of the way, had been Miles.

He had sat on the couch in Reception with his leg on the coffee table holding meetings with suppliers and giving interviews over the telephone—and all the time giving her furtive glances and the kind of not very discreet smiles that made Jason tut and dive back into his office to work on production plans so complex that Andy had taken one glance and left him to it.

So most of the time it had just been the two of them out front. Handling telephone calls and laughing about some newspaper article or sports magazine press clipping over the excellent coffee Jason insisted on making for her. And all the while Miles told her anecdotes about his work and past achievements and how this manufacturer or clothing outlet came to stock their clothing.

Strange how many times a day he found a way to brush against her hand with his, or look over her shoulder at some suddenly vital piece of information on the PC monitor. She had to stop the tickling, of course—that got completely out of hand and she had to scold him about being professional.

A smirk of supressed laughter flicked across Andy's face. *If this was business coaching then she was all for it.*

And maybe it was just as well that she had been kept busy. It had kept her mind away from mulling over all of those intimate moments they had shared since he had walked into that coffee shop. His kisses and touch. His kindness. His quiet compassion. His humour.

A girl could fall for a man like that.

Hell. She was already halfway there.

Then her smile faded. But this evening was more than work—this was about Miles. She would never forgive herself if she messed up the most important event since his accident. And she only had an hour before facing the cameras.

Andy groaned and was just reaching for a pillow to pull over her head when her mobile phone rang on her bedside table.

She stretched out and flipped it open, but stayed lying down.

'Andy Davies.'

'Hey, Andy,' came a voice as smooth and delicious as dark mocha chocolate. 'My folks are having a beach barbecue tonight. I am thinking of making my excuses and jumping on the next flight to Tenerife. Want to elope with me?'

Tenerife? Flight? Elope?

Yes, please. I can be packed and ready in twenty minutes flat.

Deep breath.

'What?' She laughed. 'And miss a chance to hear all of the latest showbiz gossip from Saffie's favourite movie actor firsthand? Perish the thought.'

Andy started fiddling with a strand of hair one handed. 'I never took you for a quitter, Mr Gibson,' she replied with a laugh in her voice. 'Surely you are not going to allow a few reporters to thwart your plans for world domination?'

A manly cough was followed by a low growl and Andy imagined him glowering at the mobile phone. 'You know me so well, Miss Davies. Perhaps I should come over to your place now and you can talk me out of doing a runner?'

'Sorry. No can do. I am nowhere near ready. And I don't want to open the door in my underwear and dressing gown.'

The microsecond the words left her lips Andy winced. Wrong thing to say. *In so many ways.*

'Actually that would probably be the highlight of the evening. I could award points on the amount of lingerie on display and deduct points from the amount of Andy concealed. Sounds like a challenge.'

'And one you will never know,' she added hastily, desperate to change the subject. 'How is Jason's speech getting on?'

'Who? Never heard of him. Now back to this lingerie. Are you at home?'

'Might be,' she replied, not wanting him to have the satisfaction of knowing that she was lying on her bed in her underwear. And the red heels she needed to break in so that she would not fall flat on her face in front of the VIPs. 'Are you?'

'No. I'm still at Jason's place. As you well know. But I have this terrible problem. What to wear? I wonder if you could give me guidance on the matter.'

'Fashion advice? I am a little rusty on gentleman's couture, but I can try. What are you wearing right now?'

She heard his breath catch, and then slapped her hand to her forehead. 'I meant…what suit are you wearing right now?'

'Of course you did,' he growled. 'I am actually sitting

on my bed looking at the three suits I brought with me. But to answer your question?'

Andy pressed the phone to her ear and held her breath.

'Black boxers. Black socks. A knee brace so I can stand for a couple of hours without falling over. The aftershave our Paris perfumers have been working on for Cory but we haven't launched yet. Oh—and a smile. Because I am talking to you.'

Andy bit down on her lower lip as she had a vision of Miles wearing only boxers and socks and the room became remarkably warm all of a sudden. *Stay focused. Stay focused.*

'Ah. You need a dinner jacket for an award ceremony. Do you have one?'

'Two. A midnight blue with pale silk lining. It's cute, trendy and slim fit across the chest. And my old dinner jacket. Black. Red lining. Long line. First suit I ever had made to measure. That takes me back.'

'The black suit,' Andy answered before Miles had finished speaking. 'That's the one.'

'Why?'

'Because I am hopelessly sentimental and I know that when you wear that suit it will remind you that you don't have to prove yourself to anyone. Ever again. You have already been there, many times over.' Then she sniffed. 'And I'm wearing red tonight. Good combo.'

She could almost hear Miles grinning on the other end of the telephone. 'Are you wearing red at this minute?'

Andy glanced down at her less than pristine white strapless bra and Saffie's red French knickers. The red heels were extra slutty and she kicked them off.

'Yes. And no.'

'How much not exactly? Because I am having a vision of red underwear and it is really quite delightful.'

'Is it indeed? Dream on. I am only wearing red French knickers. I mean…I am wearing other clothes but they are not red, and…' She took a breath and sighed out loud. 'And you have the most annoying habit of getting me all flustered. I don't know how you do it. Thank heavens you have already asked me to be your date or I would think that you were trying to chat me up.'

'Red French knickers,' he breathed in a voice of liquid chocolate that warmed her right to the pit of her stomach. 'Oh, Miss Davies. For that I can be dressed and around to your house in about twenty minutes. Get that dressing gown ready.'

'Miles. Stop. Haven't you forgotten something? We have to be on our best behaviour tonight. Remember? My mission shall be to deter other ladies from molesting your fine bod and keeping you company. This is bound to be an arduous task so forget the red underwear. Keep your eyes on the prize.'

'That's what I was doing. Let's make that thirty minutes. I can't wait to see you. Bye for now.'

'Bye.' Her fingers clasped around the phone and closed it, but instead of returning the phone to its charger, she held it to her chest, lay flat on her feather and down duvet and smiled as she waited for her heartbeat to return to something like the normal rate.

Miles Gibson could make her laugh like no other man, and discombobulate her with equal ease. But she dared not tell him. Could not tell him. Letting him know how attracted she was would only lead one way—heartbreak, disaster and unemployment.

One evening. That was their deal. He had kept his side of the bargain. Now it was time for her to keep hers.

Shame it was so hard to remember that fact when he was so close.

Andy clasped the phone harder.

Why shouldn't she enjoy his company for this evening? He had asked her to be his date. And that was precisely what she was going to be. Because they were friends. Good friends. They trusted one another and they could make this work.

Trust. Yes. She did trust him. Tonight Miles Gibson would be her trusted friend who she could rely on not to let her down.

She smiled and slipped off the bed.

She had thirty minutes to get ready for the best party of her life and, what was more, she had every intention of enjoying it. With Miles by her side every step of the way.

CHAPTER NINE

'Hey girl. Ready to rock and roll?'

Andy stepped forwards into his arms and was enfolded in a fragrant cape of fresh citrus and ice-cool testosterone-infused aroma that was all Miles. He held her close for only a second, his lips pressed into her cheek, before he whispered, 'You were right about the red. You look beautiful. These are for you.'

Andy lifted the posy of red roses and sweet freesias to her nose and inhaled deeply, closing her eyes at the intensity of the perfume.

'Thank you. They are beautiful.'

If it was possible, Miles looked even more handsome than she had imagined. He was dressed in a beautiful hand-tailored black dinner suit that highlighted his broad shoulders and slim hips, and a pristine white dress shirt.

He was so tempting and delicious she could have eaten him with a spoon. And skipped the cream.

Instead she looked from the polished black shoes to perfectly tousled glossy hair and gave a quick sigh of appreciation.

And was thrilled to see his cheeks blush.

'My, you do clean up nicely. Can I add a finishing touch?'

She plucked a perfect red rosebud from the posy and

stepped forward so that the front of her black taffeta opera coat was pressed against his chest.

His hands slid behind her back and pulled her closer as she popped the rosebud into the buttonhole of his lapel, slipped the stem into the tiny loop and smoothed down the collar and the front of his jacket with the fingertips of both hands.

'There. Much better.' She smiled and tapped him twice on the chest before trying to step back.

Only Miles had other ideas and held her even tighter around her waist. He tilted his head to one side and ran his smooth cheek up from her jawline to her temple, then her brow, then back to her ear, making her quiver with more than the cold draught that was blowing in through the open door.

'I agree. Much better,' he murmured in a voice that was usually reserved for the bedroom and kissed her so lightly on the lips that she doubted that her lipstick even moved. 'No need to rush.'

He sighed from deep inside and glanced over her shoulder at the staircase. His meaning only too plain. And suddenly the cool draught was not cool enough to calm the thumping heat of Andy's blood.

She swallowed down her overwhelming sense of attraction and pushed it deep inside where she could deal with it later when she was back in her room. Alone.

Take the risk. That was what Miles kept telling her,

Take the risk, Andy. Take the risk and get out there and have the night of your life with this crazy and amazing man who will never know how much you care about him.

She inhaled slowly and turned back to face Miles with a grin on her face.

'I told you that your old suit would be perfect,' she said with a smile in her voice.

'Unlike this shirt,' Miles replied in a choked voice. His chin was high and he had two fingers between the stiff collar of his dress shirt and his throat, trying to create extra space by tugging at the neck. 'Either the collar has shrunk or my neck has got thicker. Possibly both. This is what comes from spending way too much time in offices instead of the beach. Nightmare. I won't last the night at this rate.'

Andy stepped around him and closed her front door, leant closer and whispered into his ear seven clear, crisp words.

'Come upstairs and take your shirt off.'

Miles instantly perked up, his eyes sparkling and only inches away from her face so that she could feel his breath on her cheek. 'I like the way you are thinking but this may not be the best time. Jason will kill me if we don't turn up in the next hour. And what are you doing?'

Andy waved her clutch bag at him, then grabbed his hand and headed for the stairs. 'Like any sensible and organised modern girl, I have a full sewing kit up in my room. I can adjust that top button in a jiffy. Want to follow me?'

'Just lead the way, gorgeous.'

Andy tried to ignore the dark rumblings of innuendo in his voice as Miles positively bounded up the staircase behind her and followed her into her room.

Then stood at the door, frozen and still, as she slipped off her coat.

'Oh, you can come inside. You're quite safe.'

'Shame. But that's not what I am looking at. This is... astonishing.'

'What is?' she asked with a smile and stepped back and turned to follow his gaze.

'I had no idea that you could create something so magical in one room. You've seen Jason's penthouse. Seriously, I had no clue there were so many shades of cream. But this? This is like a rainbow on a dull grey day.'

'It is? I suppose I am so used to it.'

He reached out and grabbed her hand.

'Stand here and try and see what you have created through my eyes.'

Andy took his fingers and Miles stepped back so that his front was pressing against the back of her dress. 'Now. Talk me through each of those posters on the walls. Starting over there.'

He pointed his left arm towards her favourite prints of stained-glass floral scenes and she told him about the great cathedrals she had visited all over London and later Paris with her friend Saffie.

Then the prints of splendid fourteenth-century Royal manuscripts and Renaissance bibles. The tiny gold icon her father had bought in Greece, of course. And then her own work either side of the window, so that she could see the colours in natural daylight.

And the whole time she had been speaking, Miles had dropped his arms to around her waist, his chin resting on the top of her head, but not just listening for politeness. He really listened. Asked questions. Paid attention.

It was only when she moved forwards to show him her latest drawings that she realised that they had been locked together for over ten minutes!

'Oh, no,' she laughed. 'Look at the time. I am so sorry; I could talk for England once I get started.'

Miles stepped up to the desk and took hold of both of her arms and smiled into her face. 'And I could listen to you talk all evening. Look around you, Andy. You love this. And I should be the one apologising to you. When I saw you in the coffee shop last week, in your little grey suit, I wondered if there was any colour in your life.'

He shook his head, looked around her bedroom and inhaled slowly as he smiled warmly. 'I was wrong. Your joy and your colour are all inside this room. And inside your heart.'

His fingertips pressed against the bare skin of her chest above the line of her dress and she could feel the pulse in his warm skin. 'You have the heart of an artist, Andy Davies. And don't you ever forget that.'

And just like that, her treacherous wounded heart gave a skip and a jump and started singing halleluia.

'Do you really think that I am an artist?' she whispered, swallowing down her fears and pain.

'No. I don't think so. I know so.'

His smile widened into a grin that filled her bedroom with more light and joy than any number of halogen lamps, her feet were an inch off the floor and for the first time in too many long years she felt…happy. And it was such a ridiculous and foolish and girly notion that she pressed her hand to her mouth to smother a giggle.

This, of course, only made him grin more.

'Well, thank you, kind sir,' she smirked, 'but all you had to do was ask and I would have moved your button anyway. Now.' She rubbed her hands together. 'We have a party to go to, so down to business. Sit there on my chair and don't move an inch.'

She reached down and unclipped his bow tie so that it hung around his neck.

Miles watched her in silence as her fingers deftly released the top two buttons on his beautifully tailored silk dress shirt. Undressing him.

'Now don't move or I might jab you,' she warned, and bit down on her lower lip as she bent forwards with her scissors to release the fine stitches holding the button in place.

Her fingertips seemed to have minds of their own and

used every opportunity to brush against the fine dark hairs on his chest as she worked. Seconds seemed to take minutes but at last the top button was off and she could sit back and create some air space between them.

His breathing had increased to match hers, and she knew that his gaze hadn't once left her face, which made threading the needle a tad tricky, but she managed it on the third attempt.

By focusing completely on the tiny section of the smooth shirt collar where the button was moving to, Andy managed to hold back from looking into Miles's face. His warm, sensuous chest rose and fell below her hands; his unique scent filled her head with it as she moved her fingers over the lustrous fabric, wishing it were his skin. Each tiny stitch was a triumph of will over temptation so hot and so urgent that if he had grabbed her and thrown her needle and thread out of the window she would have died and gone to heaven.

It was total relief to finally snip off the loop of white thread and create some breathing space between them.

'There you are.' She smiled and busied her hands tidying away the sewing kit. 'I hope it is more comfortable.' She shot one glance at Miles, but he was just sitting there, half turned towards her, watching her with a look that she had never seen before. His hands holding onto the seat, his legs tight together.

Surprise, amusement and what could be admiration or pleasure were all wrapped up inside one single smile.

And something more.

Desire. Hot and spicy and right there, only inches away.

'Thank you,' he breathed in his rich and deliciously smooth voice.

'You are most welcome,' she replied in a strangled voice.

He grinned.

She grinned.

And the world stopped spinning so that they could simply sit grinning at one another. London might be on the other side of the window glass, but at that moment there were only the two of them. United against the world and anything it might throw at them.

Which probably explained why she had no intention of resisting when Miles slid one arm around her waist, tipped her chin up and kissed her on the lips, so tender, so sweet that it took her breath away and brought tears to her eyes.

Her heart was beating so fast she might as well be surfing a huge wave.

'Hey,' she said, with a gentle closed-mouthed smile. 'What was that for?'

Miles pressed two fingers to her warm, moist, soft lips.

'For giving me an insight into a world I knew nothing about,' he replied, and slipped his lips onto the hollow below her ear. 'For trusting me enough to share your dreams.' Andy arched her head back so that his kisses could track down her throat. 'And for turning up to a coffee shop so that I wouldn't be alone.'

He slid back so that he could see her face, and he already missed the way her skin felt, her perfume, the good feeling that came with holding her body in his arms. 'And the fact that you are beautiful and talented and deserve to be pampered on a regular basis. Mustn't forget that one.'

'I am?' she replied in a tiny soft voice, then shrugged and sniffed.

He looked down into Andy's lovely face and saw astonishment and surprise.

And it broke his heart.

After what she had been through in her life, she still had the capacity to care about idiots like him.

The warmth and love in her gaze seemed to radiate into

his body through every inch of his skin until they wrapped around his heart and held it tight. Cocooned and safe.

And he melted.

He hadn't intended to. Or expected to. But it happened all the same.

He didn't know what to do with her response. It was so honest and true and in that moment, in her elegant dress and simple make-up and hair, she looked stunningly beautiful.

And deeply, deeply, desirable.

A deep-seated yearning of naked want started to burn like a raw hot flicker of a flame inside his gut, warming his body in places that he had kept to himself since the accident.

It had been building for days. And working with her in the office had only served to get the coals red-hot and the tinder dry. Just waiting for the spark to ignite them.

Well, here it came.

And instantly he knew. This was a flame that could burn away all of his defences if he let it, leaving him open to all of the pain of rejection.

He should walk away and leave her in this cosy house, with her single bed and her table covered with pens and inks and beautiful designs. Leave her to her safe little world, and well away from the crazy chaos that was his.

Anything else would be too unfair on Andy. He had nothing to offer her but tonight. Long-term relationships were for men who knew who they were and where they wanted to go with their life. Not for men like him.

He rose from the chair, and then clenched his hands into the tiny slim pockets of his dinner-suit trousers, ruining the line and not caring.

'We should be leaving,' he said, only his voice sounded low and way too unconvincing.

She must have thought so, too, because she took a last step and closed the distance between them and pressed the palms of both of her hands flat against the front of his white dinner shirt. He could feel the warmth of her fingertips through the fine fabric as she spread her fingers out in wide arcs and the light perfume enclosed them.

'Don't say any more. I understand. I understand you completely.'

Every muscle in his body tensed as she moved closer and pressed her body against his, one hand reaching in to the small of his back and the other still pressed gently against his shirt. He tried to shift but she shifted with him, her body fitting perfectly against his, her cheek resting on his lapel as though they were dancing to music that only she could hear.

So he did the only thing he could.

He took her left hand from his chest in his right, lifted it high into the air and moved his left arm around her waist and rested it lightly on her hip.

'Did you notice that there will be a dance band at the after-show party? I was hoping you might help me practise a few moves. But with this knee? Don't expect any dips. But could I have the pleasure of this dance, Miss Davies?' he asked in a calm voice.

She stared at him in silence for a second, then slid her right arm from around his waist, flashed him a smile and dived into her clutch bag on the desk next to them and pulled out what looked to Miles like a London bus timetable.

'You are in luck, Mr Gibson. According to my dance card I am free for the next waltz. So yes,' she said, looking into his eyes and holding his gaze. 'You can have the pleasure of this dance. Although I should warn you. The only dancing I do these days is in front of my radio.'

'Forget the waltz.' He smiled and clasped her tighter to his body. 'Did I mention that my mother is Spanish?

Dancing is the national sport. I think a box rhumba might work well.'

'I think you are going to have to teach me that one,' she whispered, but her gaze didn't leave his face, her intense focus making his skin and neck burn.

Miles felt her fingers tighten around his arm over his biceps and his heart rate quickened. His hands moved up to her bare upper arms, her smooth soft skin a delight under his touch.

'Back right, side left, forward left, side right. Like a box.'

His left foot slid backwards, taking her with him, back the sideways, their bodies locked together in a rhythm as old as time.

'Listen to the beat,' he coaxed. 'Slow, quick, quick, slow. Hold that slow step. Lean into it just a bit longer. Do you hear it? Do you hear the beat?'

'I think I do,' Andy replied. But her feet stayed where they were as her hands slid up from his arms onto his neck and stayed there.

She lifted her head and her hair brushed his chin as she pressed tentative kisses onto his collarbone and neck. Her mouth was soft and moist and totally, totally captivating.

With each kiss she stepped closer until her hips beneath her dress were pressed against his and the pressure made him groan.

'Andy,' he muttered, reaching for her shoulders to draw her away. But somehow he was sliding his hands up into her hair instead, holding her head and tilting her face towards him. Then he was kissing her, his tongue in her mouth, her taste surrounding him.

He stroked her tongue with his and traced her lower lip before sucking on it gently. She made a small sound and angled her head to give him more access.

She tasted so sweet, so amazing. So giving.

She gazed at him with eyes filled with concern and regret and sadness as if she was expecting some cutting comment about what a fool she was to invite him to her bedroom— to want to be with him, and only him.

And that look hit him hard.

He did not just want Andy to be his stand-in date for tonight. He wanted to see her again, be with her again. He wanted to know what she looked like when she had just made love. He wanted to find out what gave her pleasure in bed—then make sure that he delivered precisely what the lady ordered.

He went for women who were straightforward. Proud of their gym-and-sports-honed bodies and up front about what they wanted from a relationship. A very short-term relationship.

Which suited him just fine.

Andy was proving him wrong about so many things.

She was as proud and independent as he was. And just as unforgiving with anyone who dared to offer her charity or their pity.

By some fluke, some strange quirk of fate, he had met a woman who truly did understand him more than Lori had ever done. And that was beyond a miracle.

Could he take a chance and show her how special she was? And put his heart on the line at the same time?

He slid a hand down her back to cup her backside, holding her against him as he flexed his hips forward, and one hand still in her hair. She shuddered as he slid his hand in slow circles up from her back to her waist, running his hands up and down her skin, which was like warm silk, so smooth and perfect. He ducked his head and kissed her again, his hands teasing all the while until he was almost holding her upright.

When their lips parted, Andy was panting just as hard

as he was. She looked so beautiful, standing there with her dark hair spilling down her shoulders, her cheeks flushed pink and the most stunning smile on her face.

A wave of hair fell forwards as she rested her head on the front of his shirt and he lifted it back from her forehead and tucked it behind one ear before wrapping his arms around her back and holding her tight against him, his chin resting on the top of her hair.

Eyes closed, they stood locked together until he could feel her heart settle down to a steady beat.

All doubt cast aside. Her heart beat for him, as his heart beat for her.

Andy moved in his arms and he looked down into her face as she smiled up at him with, not just her sweet mouth, but with eyes so bright and fun and joyous that his heart sang just to look at them. And it was as though every good thing that he had ever done had come together into one moment in time.

And his heart melted. Just like that.

For a girl who was not wearing much make-up and did not need any.

For a girl who was just about as different from him and his life as it was possible to be.

And for a girl who had made her tiny bedroom the size of Jason's luggage store into a private art gallery and was willing to share her joy with him. And wanted nothing in return but a dance.

God, he loved her for that… Loved her?

Miles stopped, his body frozen and his mind spinning.

He was falling in love with Andy.

Just when he thought that he had finally worked out how to protect himself from being hurt by a woman.

Think! He had to think. He could not allow his emotions to get the better of him.

If he loved her then he should stop right now, because the last thing Andy needed was a one-night stand that would leave her with nothing but more reasons to doubt her judgement.

This was not what he wanted. He wanted temporary. He wanted live for the day.

'I think we might want to rethink the whole arriving-early-at-the-hotel thing.' She grinned as though she had read his mind.

'Right as always,' he replied, and stroked her cheek with one finger. 'God, you are beautiful. Do you know that?'

Andy blushed from cheek to neck and it was so endearing that he laughed out loud and slid his arms down to her waist and stepped back, even though his body was screaming for him to do something crazy. Like wipe everything off the desk and find out what came next.

He sucked in a breath.

'You are not so bad yourself. I had no idea that sportsmen were such good dancers.' And then she bit down on her lower lip and flashed him a coquettish grin. 'Or did I just get lucky? You are one of a kind, Miles Gibson.'

Lucky? He thought of the long days and nights he had spent training, training, training to the exclusion of everything else in his life, including the girls who had cared about him. Lori had lasted the longest and she'd had her own reasons for putting up with him.

He had sacrificed everything for his sport. *Everything*.

Now as he looked at Andy he thought about what lay ahead and the hard, cold truth of his situation emptied a bucket of ice water over his head.

His hands slid onto her upper arms and locked there. Holding her away from him and the delicious pleasure of her body against his.

'I am not so sure about the lucky bit, Andy. Right now I

am struggling to get back into the mad world of the sports business. Months on tour. Constant pressure. And all the while I feel…I feel as though I have lost everything.'

'No, you haven't,' she said. 'You have not lost everything.'

'Don't you get it?' He took hold of her hand and pressed the knuckles to his lips. 'I don't have a career any more. I have been to ten experts and they are all telling me the same thing. Game over. I am finished. Retired. At thirty-one. Have you any idea how terrifying that is? You deserve better than that, Andy. You deserve someone with a dream and a future they can clasp hold of.'

He lowered her hand and started pacing up and down the bedroom, then looked around and suddenly the walls seemed to be closing in on him, and the ceiling was crushing down on him.

It only took him a minute to skip down the staircase, and fumble with the lock on her front door before lurching out onto the small porch, sucking in the air in one long breath after another. Desperate to be outside under a sky. In the open air.

It took him a few minutes to realise that there was a warm body pressed against his back, her breasts tight against his shirt, her arms around his sides.

He grasped hold of her hands and they stood in silence together for so long that the shiver that ran across his back was more due to cold then apprehension of the unknown.

Andy slid her fingers from between his and he turned around and looked at her, his arms at her waist.

And the look in her eyes almost made him lose it.

He was about to apologise, to explain, but she lifted one finger and pressed it to his lips.

'I know two more things about your future career options. No, actually three,' she corrected herself with a blink and a mini shoulder shrug. 'You don't like confined spaces.' And she flicked her head back inside. 'Office work may not be your strength. I am thinking something sports related.' Then she smiled a closed-mouthed smile and rubbed her hands up and down the goose bumps on his arm. 'Warm climate. You are definitely in need of a warm climate.' And then standing on tiptoe she kissed him on the end of his nose, which made him smile despite his best intentions.

'What about number three? Miss career advisor.'

'Hardly,' she laughed, and then ran her tongue over her lips as though she was nervous.

'Just say it,' he whispered, tipping up her chin towards him. 'Tell me what you are thinking.'

She nodded. 'Okay. Here goes.'

She sucked in a breath and ran the collar of his dinner suit between her fingers. 'The Miles Gibson people will see at the award ceremony this evening is strong and worthy of respect and admiration. You have achieved so much and worked so hard to make your dream of being the best surfer in the world come true.' She paused and smoothed down the shirt, her fingers running in long slow tracks.

Then her fingers stopped moving and she looked up into his face as though she was looking for something. 'But that is not the man who wrote those emails and who came to my museum and loves his brother and is willing to take a risk and give me a job so that I can realise my dream. That Miles is capable of reconnecting to his old friends and making new ones and having fun.'

Andy tilted her head to one side. 'Somewhere along the way to being the best and all that work I think you forgot the fun part. And that funny wild and creative Miles can set new goals and get excited about new things and have the best time of his life. That aqua-therapy session was brilliant! You have so many skills and talents it is dazzling.'

Stretching up onto tiptoe, she kissed him on the lips. 'You. Dazzle me.'

She stepped back and patted him twice on the chest. 'You have to say goodbye to the old you and say hello to the new you. Because the new you is amazing. And surprising and inspiring. And he has shown me that I can make my dreams come true in my own way and I don't have to take second best. Ever again. And I will always be grateful to you for that. Always.'

Then she laughed. 'And now it is time to leave before I embarrass myself even more. And I think the car is waiting,' she squeaked, and moved a step backwards with a smile.

He frowned, nodded just once and said something under his breath along the lines of what he did for his brother, then lifted his head, turned towards the door and presented the crook of his arm for her to latch onto. 'Shall we go to the ball, princess? Your carriage awaits.'

CHAPTER TEN

From: Andromeda@ConstellationOfficeServices
To: Saffie@Saffronthechef

Dear fairy godmother. Am emailing from the back of a limo. And I have to tell you—I could get used to this amount of pampering. I have roses. I have a charming prince and your borrowed red shoes are as hard to walk in as glass slippers. Now all I have to watch out for is the clock chiming midnight.

Totally dreamy. Tell you all about it tomorrow.

Cinders.

ANDY snuggled back against the sumptuous soft leather seats in the back of the limo and gently spread the silk skirt of her red cocktail dress like a fan on either side of her before patting it with the palm of her hand. 'That's better,' she said to herself.

Miles snorted out loud, and then gave a couple of manly coughs into his rolled hand to cover up his laughter.

She play-hit him on the shoulder with her clutch bag.

'Stop it,' she teased, then broke down in her excitement and gave a girly giggle and waggled her bottom from side to side. 'I am having way too much fun.'

Her fingertips fluttered over the smooth fine wood trim. 'I must say that when you pamper a girl, you do it with style. This is definitely a step up from my usual way of getting around.'

'Are you referring to the excellent public transport system in this fine city?' Miles asked while trying to keep his voice calm and serious, but was let down by the telltale crinkling of the left side of his mouth.

She replied by lifting her right leg out high until it almost touched the driver's seat, and twirling her ankle so that the red high-heeled sandal dangled from her toes.

'Regular exercise is essential for the office worker.' She nodded and was about to lower her leg to stop her dress from riding up any higher, but Miles beat her to it.

His warm fingertips clasped around her ankle, his thumbs caressing the back of her foot.

'I'm guessing ballet lessons?'

'Four years,' she whispered from lungs that were too hot to manage a full answer. 'No talent.'

'Worth it. My, you have a lovely ankle, Miss Davies. Good calves too.' He smouldered and ran the palm of his hand the whole length of her leg to the knee, before she grasped hold of those treacherous fingers and lifted them clear of her leg and back to his own.

Only when she was safe of his touch did she lower her leg and tug her skirt down.

'Was that your professional opinion?' she asked in a low casual voice, her gaze firmly fixed on the brightly lit London streets they were gliding down in such quiet and luxurious comfort. Shame that it was in total contrast to the fierce heat burning in her belly from that simple touch of those fingertips on her leg.

'Maybe.' He smiled. 'Maybe not.' And he grinned at her. 'You are looking good, girl. Has to be said.'

Then he turned away, clearly oblivious to the fact that his simple grin filled her heart and her mind with such joy that she wanted to sing and yell and jump up and down on the seat and roll down the window and embarrass herself by shouting out to the whole of London that she was having the best night of her life and Miles Gibson was *her* date!

Her heart was thumping, her throat dry and she was clutching onto her bag for dear life.

Miles was temptation was a capital T.

She wanted to hold his hand and snuggle next to him on the back seat, which was wide enough for some serious semi clad cuddling. *And more.*

Instead she moved one inch closer to the window as they slowed next to the window of a famous London department store. Singing and dancing penguins played on a bright winter scene while Father Christmas flew overhead in his sleigh, packed with gifts, drawn by smiling reindeers.

Miles was going home to Tenerife tomorrow to prepare for a long overseas trip.

And somehow the thought that she would not be seeing him again for weeks, maybe months, was almost too much to think about.

She could send him emails and talk to him on the telephone—if he wanted. *But this was it.* The last evening they would be spending together for a long time. The last time she would be close enough to inhale his fragrance and feel his body close to hers.

He had not promised anything. No long-term commitment. She knew it. *But she could always hope...couldn't she?*

And yet, there was this new idea that kept pushing up. *Live for the moment.* That was what Miles had shown her. *Take the risk Andy. Take the risk, and get out there and have the night of your life with this crazy and amazing man who will never know how much you care about him.*

She inhaled slowly and turned back to face Miles with a grin on her face.

'Don't we make a handsome couple,' she said with a smile in her voice.

His reply was to slide one arm along the back of her seat so that he could tip her chin up and kiss her on the lips, before moving back to grin at her, brimming with self-satisfaction.

'Gorgeous. The press will be far too busy photographing your loveliness to worry about raggedy old me.' He tapped one fingertip on the tip of Andy's nose. 'Dazzler.'

Andy laughed out loud and shook her head. 'Now I know that you have been overdosing on your painkillers. Seriously though,' she added, sitting back, 'is there anyone there tonight who I need to dazzle or watch out for? Because you know that honesty you keep praising?' She sucked in air between her teeth. 'Not always my best feature when I have to be nice to the big cheeses.'

'Relax.' He smiled, and squeezed her hand. 'I do this all the time. The professionals are only interested in the sports personalities and the award winners. There are bound to be a few freelancers who need photos for the gossip pages but they won't bother us. Especially when Lori Wilde is within posing distance. Lori adores this sort of event.'

'Lori Wilde the fashion model?' Andy asked, picking up on the change in his voice and shuffling around so that she could look at him face to face. 'The girl who has that modelling talent show on TV at the moment?'

'The very same. Only when I first met her, Lori was a struggling model waiting for her big break. She was smart, beautiful and ambitious and I talked Jason into using her for our bikini and water-sports ranges. Lori did the rest. We made quite the celebrity couple.'

Couple? Did Miles just say couple?

'Wait a minute. Back up. Are you saying that Lori Wilde was your girlfriend?'

He replied with a relaxed shoulder shrug. 'I thought you knew. We were hard to miss back then. The press loved us. The surfer and the model.'

Miles looked out on the street and nodded slowly. 'We had a spectacular three years. It was Lori who I had left in bed that morning I had the accident. She had a lingerie shoot the next day in New York and I wanted to get some work done before taking her to the airport.'

Three years. Miles had been with one of the most beautiful women in the world for three years!

The bottom fell out of Andy's stomach, leaving a cold emptiness. *What was he doing with her?*

'Three years. That's a long time,' Andy said in a low voice.

'That it is. But we split up after my accident.' He smacked his lips. 'Ironic, isn't it? That I should be meeting her again tonight of all nights.'

'Lori Wilde?' Andy blinked, her brow creased in confusion as her brain struggled to catch up with what he had been saying. 'Lori isn't going to be there tonight, Miles. I went through the guest list this morning with Jason and I would certainly have noticed that name. Are you sure that she was invited?'

'Carlos Ramirez is bringing Lori as his guest. He left me a voicemail message on my personal phone to give me fair warning. Carlos is no fool—he knows that Cory Sports is paying for the award ceremony. He won't do anything to spoil his chances at winning this evening. So don't worry about Lori. She can take care of herself just fine.'

Andy was just about to reply, when the limo slowed, Miles took one glance out of the side window, flashed his signature killer grin and patted her hand.

'Hey, relax. Remember what I said. Just keep smiling, stick by me and you'll be fine. Ready? We're on.'

And before Andy knew what was happening, and could gather her thoughts, the limo pulled slowly to a halt, their driver was at her passenger door and she barely had time to release her seat belt and grab her clutch before Miles took her hand and helped her step out of the car.

To a blaze of flashlights, people screaming and calling his name, over and over again, a crush of bodies and music and colour, which merged into one long blur of over-whelming cacophony.

It was only by physically holding onto Miles as he waved and posed for photographs and forcing her feet to move one step at a time that she survived at all.

As it was, she practically ran through the huge hotel door held open by the liveried doorman.

The red carpet had looked so short when she saw it through the car window, but when she was actually on it? It was a completely different matter.

Leaning deeply against Miles to catch her breath, Andy slumped sideways.

'That. Was. Horrendous,' she gasped between breaths. 'How do you manage to look so relaxed?'

'It's easy.' He smiled. 'You just keep telling yourself that all publicity is good publicity. Cory Sports are paying for this event tonight and the media are going to make money from it. Advertisers, shareholders, everyone in the chain. We need one another.'

Then Miles hugged her closer and whispered in her ear, 'You were amazing. What a star! Thanks.'

'I was a star? Really?' she asked, looking into his grinning face.

A star, he mouthed and pointed at her with a loaded finger. And winked.

And just like that she started to breathe again.

Maybe she could survive this. Even if his gorgeous ex-girlfriend was going to be here. Oh, boy.

One arm around her waist, he turned around and gestured towards a cluster of people gathered at the foot of a long winding staircase. Jason had already seen them and was waggling his fingers at them to come over.

'Shall we go and meet the rest of team? Yes?'

But before Miles could take her hand, a camera crew spotted them and the well-known TV news reporter practically jogged over with his microphone.

'Mr Gibson. Good to see you again, sir. Any chance of a quick interview before the presentation ceremony? I promise you that it will be five minutes at most.'

Miles looked at Andy and shrugged. 'Would you mind? I'll be right here.'

'Not at all,' she replied as though she did this every night of the week. 'Go right ahead.'

Andy stood back and watched him walk away. And within two steps the man she had come to know had gone. Replaced by Miles Gibson, superstar.

She could only stare in amazement as his back and shoulders straightened to fill his dinner jacket to perfection. His chin lifted and he seemed to be taller, slimmer and more elegant than ever before. There was nothing hesitant or undecided in his actions.

Far from it.

His legs strode powerfully forwards to the bank of photographers so that they could get the full benefit of his physique as he gave the interview in a laughing light style, which nobody could ever associate with someone who was in daily pain.

He plunged his left hand inside his trouser pocket,

relaxed and in control, and used his right to wave to the incoming celebrities and, in a few cases, to back-slap a passing sportsman and give him a wink and a joke.

This version of Miles was a revelation. Oh, she had seen a glimpse of the media star that first few minutes when he'd marched into the coffee shop that night, but this was something entirely different.

Miles had missed his true calling. He should have been an actor.

He had put on the costume and now he was playing his part as the king of Cory Sports, master of all he surveyed. Proud, confident and totally in control of what the cameras were recording from this event. He turned from side to side, posing and laughing, the consummate professional.

And he loved it. He loved every second of it.

He wanted the adoration of the media—more than that, he seemed invigorated by it. This was what was missing in his life. This was what he had been used to before the accident.

Oh, Miles.

Little wonder that he had probably forgotten that she was still waiting for him.

And it looked as if he could be holding court for quite some time.

Just for a second Andy sighed with regret, then rolled back her shoulders and turned to find Jason. Only to find that he had already moved on to other guests.

Standing next to Jason was a tall, slim and very handsome man who, judging from the applause and the number of photographers calling out his name, was clearly the star of the show, Carlos Ramirez.

And standing only two feet away from her, patiently waiting for Carlos, was Lori Wilde.

Andy had seen her on television a couple of times in her top-rated modelling talent show, where she seemed to be caring and talented, but in the flesh it was disgustingly obvious that she was one of those tall, very slender women who was so naturally beautiful that it was no surprise that the cameras loved her.

Tonight she was wearing a gold Greek goddess column one-shoulder dress, which was so perfect on her it was ridiculous. Her glossy dark hair was artfully arranged into a chignon, softened by trailing wisps at the front.

For a girl that beautiful the only jewellery she needed was a single platinum and diamond collar and matching bracelet. From her ears dangled diamonds that were probably worth the same as Saffie's house.

She could have been posing for a fashion magazine, and Andy froze. Uncertain about what to do, or say, to this perfect creature who had been Miles's girlfriend for three years.

Take a risk, Andy. Take a risk. These things happen. That was then. This is now. Go for it.

And then Carlos was snatched away by a TV crew and the two of them stood there, only feet apart, giving each other furtive glances, while their men were working.

Oh—this was ridiculous. Andy inhaled deeply, smiled and stuck out her hand.

'Hello there—you must be Lori. Lovely to meet you. I'm Andy.'

'And you—Andy. Is that right? I overheard Jason mention your name, but I was teasing him at the time about who Miles was bringing to the event. What a lovely name. Is that short for Andrea?'

Her voice was warm and expressive and lively and such a contrast to the cool and elegant TV persona that Andy laughed out loud. Lori wasn't cold at all.

'Andromeda. Can you believe it? Parents. You leave them unsupervised for a few years and they come up with a name like Andromeda. But I can cope. It suits my classical bent.'

'Oh! Don't get me started about names. Did Miles tell you that Lori is my stage name? He didn't?'

The stunning brunette looked from side to side, then bent down and whispered something in Andy's ear as discreetly as she could.

Andy glanced back to Lori's face. And her mouth fell open.

'No! Your parents would not be so cruel.'

'They would. Even my Scandinavian friends struggle to pronounce my real name. You can see why I changed it. But not a word. It has to be our little secret.'

Andy tapped the side of her nose twice with her forefinger. 'Not a word.'

A huge round of laughter rang out behind them and both Lori and Andy turned around to watch the red-carpet photographers as Carlos played with a football to amuse the crowd. 'Miles tells me that your boyfriend, Carlos, has been shortlisted for an award. You must be delighted.'

Lori's flawless face glowed with genuine delight that no amount of clever make-up could fake.

'Totally. He works so hard for his success. And he's lovely with it. I'm a lucky girl.'

'I would say that he was the lucky one, Lori.'

Lori turned back to her and, without hesitating, gave Andy a one-armed hug, filling the air around her with a sensational aroma of amazing perfume and elegance and class in the second before she released her. 'What a lovely thing to say. Thanks, Andy. We are both lucky.' And then Lori looked up and her easy warm smile shifted to a look of wariness and concern.

Andy was about to reply when a familiar strong arm wrapped around her waist and drew her closer.

'What was that about being lucky? Talking about me again?'

Andy rolled her eyes and tutted. 'Not everything is about you, Miles. I was just saying how lucky we were to be here tonight. It is a lovely party. Isn't that right, Lori?'

'Absolutely.' The brunette stretched out her hand and Miles accepted it as though it were a poisonous viper. 'Nice to see you again, Miles. You are looking well.'

'Same for you,' he replied and took a firmer hold of Andy. 'I hear that you've been spending time in Rio with Carlos. Great city.'

'Oh, you know what it's like, work, work, wor…k.' Lori's gaze slid down to his leg and Andy could feel the muscles tighten in his arm at her waist. 'Sorry, that was insensitive of me.'

Andy smiled up at Miles, expecting him to make some witty and kind remark, but his face was frozen into a look she had never seen before and would rather not see again. White-lipped, tense and with a fierceness about it that brought the temperature of the already cool reception area down another couple of degrees. The air almost crackled with ice until Andy could not stand it any longer and smiled up at Lori.

'Oh, Miles and Jason never seem to stop working. I have only been in their office a few times but the phone never stops ringing and they seem to be dashing about the place all day.'

Lori's eyebrows defied any suggestion of Botox by creasing together and one corner of her mouth twisted up into a half-smile. 'Oh, I'm sorry, Andy. I thought that you were here as Miles's date. I didn't know that you worked for Cory as well.'

'Andy is one of our consultants,' Miles replied for her in a cold, accusing voice. 'But tonight she is here as my date. Isn't that right, Andy?'

And without waiting for her to reply, he wrapped both arms around her back and whirled her up off her feet and into his arms, twirling her twice and making her laugh. Only then did he stop twirling long enough to kiss her on the mouth in a kiss that would have been magical except that the second before his lips touched hers she smiled into his eyes with delight and what she saw there chilled her to the marrow.

His eyes were open. Only they were not looking at her face.

Miles was staring at Lori Wilde and the bank of photographers behind her back, who were only too happy to get some photos of Miles Gibson kissing one girl while his ex and top model Lori Wilde was only a few feet away. Perfect!

And in that instant she knew.

Miles wanted to see Lori's face when he kissed someone else.

Anyone else.

Miles had not asked her to be his date because he liked her and wanted to be with her.

He simply needed someone to be his date so that he could prove to Lori and the sports press that he was over her. More than that—he wanted to rub it in her face that he was capable of finding another girl after his accident.

Or was that dupe an innocent, lonely girl into thinking that he cared about her so that she would walk through that door this evening?

And in that second she made the connection, any happiness and delight Andy had enjoyed that evening were instantly blown away as though they had never happened. Destroyed. Eliminated.

Her happy memory of their evening so far, corrupted and stained.

He was kissing her for the benefit of the cameras and his ego. As far as Miles was concerned she was just an accessory for the evening.

She had been played. Used. *Again.*

Luckily, she did not have to keep up this game of charades for one second longer, because just as Miles lowered her to the floor Jason appeared at his side and whispered something about heading into the main ceremony. Miles instantly released her to look at his watch and talk timings.

Over his shoulder, Andy watched Lori and Carlos walk slowly along the main ground floor corridor, until the backs of their heads were a blur in the bustling crowd of cameramen, TV reporters and elegantly dressed guests.

'Nicely played, Andy. I might not be able to surf but the prettiest girl in London has just made my evening. And that's the truth…Andy? What are you doing now?' He laughed as she shuffled as far away from him as possible and fastened up her opera coat, her clutch bag waggling under her arm.

'What am I doing?' she said through gritted teeth. 'I'm getting my stuff together because I have just realised that I've forgotten something rather important. Is there another way out of the hotel? Apart from that ridiculous red carpet? I need to get out of here right now.'

And without waiting for Miles to reply, Andy strode back towards the main hotel entrance.

'Through the bar, but what do you mean? Way out?' Miles asked, his brow furrowed in concern. 'I thought that you were having a good time?'

'Oh, I was,' she said, her body turning to face him in jerky, stiff movements.

'Then tell me exactly what it is you have forgotten that is suddenly so important? We are just about to start.'

Andy's fingers balled into fists but when she spoke every word came out burning with fire. 'What have I forgotten? Only this. For a few minutes this week I forgot that I am not prepared to be used by anyone ever again.'

'Used?' Miles looked from side to side and waved at a few of the other guests. 'Andy, lower your voice—you are in the middle of a big public event here. There are cameras. I—'

'No. No. You don't say another word to me. Not now, not ever. You don't get it, do you? You have just admitted it.'

She leant forwards from her waist, her head still, her gaze unblinking. 'You had every intention of using me to make your ex-girlfriend jealous, and make sure that your photograph was on the front page of the gossip magazines tomorrow, and not once—' her voice was shaking now, and she had to take a breath before finishing '—not once did you think about how I would feel. And don't you dare try and deny it, because I won't believe you.'

Closing her eyes through blinding tears she could not fight, Andy forced the words out. 'You didn't invite me out this evening as your friend. You invited me to prove to a lingerie model that you still had some pulling power. Apparently I am just some replaceable girl who you can pick up and put down from the shelf when your ego needs a boost.'

'Andy, no. You don't understand…' Miles moved closer, white-faced, and reached for her arm. But she grabbed her bag and reared away, her feet already heading towards the hotel bar area.

'You are so wrong,' she replied, her voice ice-cold despite the burning in her heart. 'But do you know what hurts the most?' She licked her lips. 'I thought that you were better than that. A lot better.'

And she wrenched her head away and stomped through the crowded cocktail bar, oblivious to the other patrons who were blocking Miles, flung open the side door and was on the pavement before he could catch up.

'Andy. Come back inside. The presentations are about to start.'

Andy slammed the door shut in his face. 'Leave me alone, Miles. I mean it. Because I am not interested in anything you might have to say.'

Her thin-soled red lovely sandals slipped on the wet pavement but she'd turned her back on the man she thought was the centre of her life and strode out into the obscurity and oblivion of crowds of people who thronged the London streets on a Saturday evening.

Miles watched her go for a second, his mind reeling with options.

She was right. So right it shocked him.

He had kissed her for the benefit of Lori and the camera crews, who had lapped it all up. Miles Gibson, stud, was back in town. This was exactly what he had wanted to happen.

But somehow along the way he had managed to fall for the stand-in date. *Big mistake.*

'Andy, wait, please.'

He hobbled down the few steps to the cold pavement as fast as he could, cursing the pain, but to his overwhelming relief her steps slowed before she had gone far.

Andy turned slowly around and looked back at him, her eyes glassy and her face contorted with every kind of emotion that he did not want to see.

She did not speak. She did not need to. It was all there on her face.

'I should have told you about Lori,' he said. 'I knew that she would be coming here tonight with Carlos. But I didn't know how to handle seeing her again. But that's done now. Please—come back inside.' He waved back towards the hotel where cars were still discharging their VIP guests.

'Oh, no, Miles. I have done that little job you wanted me to do. Haven't I? Just the perfect accessory to make your triumph complete.'

The temperature of the blood in his veins seemed to drop several degrees and a chill spread out from deep inside his belly. Speech was impossible.

Andy moved closer, her gaze locked onto his face, scanning, laser sharp. 'All this week I have been asking myself the same question. Why did Jason set you up on that Internet dating site? You don't need help finding a girlfriend—you never have.'

She stopped, just out of arm's reach, and lifted her head before going on. 'I've just worked it out. You didn't want to meet someone different. Oh, no. All you needed was a girl capable of stringing two words together who could stand by your side on one special occasion. This occasion. That's it, isn't it? You wanted a date for tonight so that you could make sure that your photograph made the headlines. And it took one kiss to make it all crystal clear.'

She moved her head slowly from side to side.

'You're pathetic. Do you know that? Everything you have done and told me during this past week has all been for one reason—to charm me into coming here tonight so that you can prove to the media and that lovely girl in there that you are still the womaniser you were and that she was a fool to break up with you.'

Her chin lifted and when she spoke the words resonated

across the cold night air. 'Well, congratulations. Mission accomplished. I hope that you are happy with your work. Sorry I blew it by saying that I worked for you—oh, excuse me. Used to work for you. You should really have given me a script to follow.'

Miles stepped closer, but she backed away as he spoke. 'Andy, give me a chance to explain. Please. Okay, I made a mistake, and I am sorry that you had to find out like that. I should have told you about Lori earlier, but I never wanted you to get hurt. You have to believe that.'

'Believe you? No. I am not listening to another word you have to say. It's over, Miles. Get back inside and do your job. Go. Jason needs you. But Lori doesn't. And that is what really gets you. Isn't it? Lori has moved on and found someone to love while you are still trapped in the past. Tell me I am wrong, Miles.'

She strode forwards, her face rigid with anger, eyes glassy and fixed. 'Tell me I am wrong about Lori.'

'You want to know about Lori. Okay. I'll tell you. Lori didn't just break up with me. She left me. She left me the day I got out of hospital. Because just the sight of my broken, useless body made her feel sick. There. Satisfied now?'

Miles turned away and started pacing up and down the stone pavement. 'The only thing that Lori Wilde felt for me was pity. She felt sorry for me. The minute she saw me in a wheelchair with pins and wires holding my bones together she knew that her fabulous celebrity lifestyle was over. That's why she left. I had stopped being useful to her career any more.'

He glanced back at Andy, who was standing with her arms wrapped around her body, and she looked so vulnerable and fragile he almost slumped down in pain that he had caused her such distress.

'I am sorry, Andy. I am so sorry. This was supposed to be a special evening for you.'

She raised her chin and looked at him with eyes filled with tears, and when she spoke her voice cracked with each word. 'That lovely girl in there cared about you. But you pushed her away. You were the one who told her to go. Weren't you?'

He was thumping his fist into the air. 'After all of those years together she still didn't know me or love me. Lori actually thought that I would be grateful when she offered to stay and take care of me. As if I needed another nurse. I couldn't believe it. So yes, I told her to go and get on with her life and I would get on with mine on my own. And she left. Oh, yes, she couldn't wait to jump on the next plane out.'

'So you drove her away because of your pride. Oh, Miles. Are you still in love with Lori?' Andy's voice was shaking.

'No. Not any more.'

He should have lied. Told her he and Lori were still nuts about each other and she had dumped her current boyfriend the moment she cast eyes on him, walking, talking, polished life and soul of the party just as the old Miles had been before the accident.

But his reply had come out of his mouth without a second of hesitation and as soon as he said the words he knew that they were true.

He had been over Lori for a long time.

Her gaze locked onto his face, with eyes blurred with tears and an expression of the deepest affection and anguish he had ever seen. The emotion in those lovely green eyes rendered him speechless.

'Of course not. There isn't room for anything but your ego. All of this past week I have heard a lot about how you are trying to prove to the sporting world that you are fit and back in the game because you owe it to your family and the business.'

She shook her head slowly from side to side. 'Stop kidding yourself. You are not pushing your body through pain and pretending that everything is okay for the business! You are doing it to prove to yourself that you are still the same man. The champion, the king. Well, congratulations, the press adore you. I only hope it makes you happy.'

Andy stepped forwards so that he could have reached out for her if he'd wanted.

'Everything has come so easily to you, Miles. You have achieved everything you set out to do and more, and instead of celebrating your achievements you put yourself through that little game of charades back there. You have so many remarkable gifts and talents and all you can see is what you cannot do. And do you know what? You didn't just humiliate me just now—*you humiliated yourself.*'

Instinctively he stretched out his arms towards her, but she pushed him away.

'Don't try and contact me. Just. Don't.'

And with that she turned away and he sagged back against the wall and watched the woman he now knew that he was in love with walk away from him. Without looking back. Not knowing that the only person he wanted to adore him was her.

CHAPTER ELEVEN

From: Andromeda@ConstellationIllustrations
To: Saffie@Saffronthechef

Hey busy lady. Hope the Christmas party diners are not driving you too mad. The museum has never been busier with Christmas shoppers fitting in an hour of culture and a coffee break between the stores. Did I tell you that I talked the café owner into stocking that wonderful coffee I had at the Gibsons'? Huge success. I am now high on caffeine and loving it almost as much as my Christmas card sales.

Only two more weeks to go and I can take Christmas off. Bliss.

Madge sends her love. Me too. Andy

'I AM so pleased that you enjoyed the galleries.' Andy smiled into the face of a tiny lady as she popped a splendid book on the porcelain collection into a museum carrier bag. 'But do remember to come back and see us in January,' she added, and nipped out from behind the counter to hand it over in person. 'The new exhibition of ancient Chinese jade promises to be something very special.'

Her last customer of the day gave her a short bow, and Andy was just about to head back to the desk when a stunning and familiar scent wafted towards her from the entrance and she spun around.

And her legs froze to the spot.

'Miles. What…what are you doing here?' she said, her voice thin and high and pathetic as her poor heart tried to cope with the shock of the sight of the tall figure who had strode into the museum shop area. Filling the space with his presence and her mind with exuberant, unexpected and wonderful delight. 'I thought you were in Spain.'

'Hey, girl,' he drawled in that delicious voice that had the power to make her legs turn to jelly. 'I seem to remember that this museum has a great exhibition of illustrated books. Any chance I could have a guided tour?'

'A tour.' She coughed and blinked at his smiling, stunning, amazing face for a few seconds before her brain caught up with his question. 'Oh. I'm sorry. We close in two minutes. You will have to come back…'

But she never got to finish her sentence, because he crossed the few steps that separated them, his gaze fixed on her, wiping out any chance of sensible thought.

Oh, Lord. He looked even more tanned and gorgeous. And smelt better. And every cell in her body screamed out about how much she had longed to see his face. Every day that they had been apart had been a torture.

'I've missed you,' he said with a smile on his lips and in his eyes. 'More than I can say. Any chance that we can get out of here and find somewhere that sells coffee? Because you look good enough to eat.'

Then he walked forwards, pulled her none too gently into his arms, pressed the fingers of one hand into her hair, angled his head and kissed her with every bit of passion and supressed joy that three weeks, two days away from the person you loved could bring. And she kissed him back, matching the touch of his tongue against hers, the hot wetness of his mouth a delicious taster of things to come. She couldn't help it. She had been longing and hoping for this moment to come.

It was Miles who broke the kiss and allowed her to breathe again, and she was just about to go into round two when he grinned and nodded towards the entrance of the museum.

And swung one arm under her legs and the other arm around her back.

Suddenly her legs were swinging in open air.

Because he had picked her up.

And without saying a word, Miles started walking with her kicking in his arms, out of the shop and across the marble paving towards the main door.

Much to the entertainment of the other museum staff and patrons.

Andy squealed out in terror and flung her arms around his neck as she screamed out, 'What are you doing? Put me down right now. I've been comfort eating for the past three weeks. You're going to hurt your leg. Miles!'

His reply was a grin. 'I'm okay. In fact, I am better than okay.'

Andy turned to see her friend the security guard winking at her as he held open the heavy door.

Two minutes later Andy was standing outside in the still bitterly cold December air with her hand pressed against her mouth, trying not to giggle.

'Well, there goes my reputation at the museum,' she chortled. 'How shocking!'

'I agree,' Miles replied and opened up his long warm down coat so that she could step inside. 'Totally scandalous. Although it does give me some hope.'

'Hope?'

'That maybe I can persuade you to forgive me a little.'

She whisked a stray snowflake from his shoulder. 'Will it involve grovelling?' she asked, trying to stay calm.

'Guaranteed. And this is our ride,' he said and gestured with his head towards the Rolls Royce motor car that was parked in the no-parking zone with the engine running. 'Let's go and get that coffee.'

He opened the passenger door and ran one hand down the length of her arm, and the sensuous pleasure of that simple gesture was too much and in an instant she was snuggling next to him on the back seat of the car.

They sat in comfortable silence for a few seconds, both staring straight ahead, until Andy's heart was ready to burst, and at the exact same time that she turned to ask him what he had been doing Miles opened his mouth and said, 'Did you know it was snowing?'

Then they both burst out laughing and, just like that, Andy felt the wonderful connection between them click back into place, the tension gone in a flash.

'You first.' Andy smiled, and pushed at his shoulder. 'Tell me about the past three weeks.'

'Three weeks, two days, and...' Miles glanced down at a watch that had so many dials on the face it must be hard for him to find the time of day, '...twenty-two hours. Which is far too long.'

Andy inhaled a long slow breath as Miles carried on. 'Taking time out with my folks. Enjoying the sunshine. I made an effort and reconnected with old friends who I hadn't seen for years because of the constant travelling, and competing. And I made a few new ones. And along the way I began to realise something so incredible about myself that had somehow got lost in the shuffle that surrounded the accident.'

His voice had sounded low, calm and confident—but there was just enough of a tremble in those last few words to make her turn to face him.

'What was it? What did you find out, Miles?'

He twisted around on the seat, glanced down and clasped his long cool fingers around hers, before smiling into her face.

'That you were right. That I had lost the simple joy of being with people and family and friends and having a barbecue on the beach and watching the sunset. That I could ask for help and people gave it without asking for anything in return. And that has to make me the biggest idiot in the world.'

Apparently there was something fascinating in her hair, and he released one of her hands to gently pop a stray strand behind her ear as he spoke. 'Yesterday morning I stood on the warm sand on my own two feet and felt the sunshine on my shoulders and I felt happier in that moment than I had felt for years.'

Hair safe, he dropped his hand back to take hers, his eyes on hers. 'And then it hit me. I had to say goodbye to the old Miles, so I could say hello to the new Miles. The Miles who enjoys every second of his life with the people he loves. Some clever person told me that and I am here to thank her.'

'Do you miss him? The old Miles?'

'No. But I also know I wouldn't have missed being him for the world. Because he helped to create me and gave me a life of glorious Technicolor detail where I was living on the adrenaline rush and sea and surf. And I am grateful to him for that.'

Andy dropped her shoulders and pressed her lips together before speaking. 'The old Miles wouldn't settle for a black-and-white, sepia-tinted life. But what about the new Miles? What does he want?'

His eyebrows rose high but there was a strength in his reply that lifted her spirit.

'I have a new job. Jason and I took some one-to-one

time away from the office and came up with a small sports-mentoring initiative. We have used our contacts to pull together a small team of professional sportsmen and women who are willing to share their knowledge with the new young talent coming along. The master classes will be held all around the world but the organisation will be based in London, of all places.'

He frowned and blinked in pretend confusion. 'For some reason Jason thinks that I am the right man to run it. How about that?'

'It's a wonderful idea, Miles. You would be an inspiration to so many people. I know that you helped me. More than I can say.'

'Right back at you. You showed me that business is not just about money, it's about making dreams come true.'

'Me? I showed you that?'

He tapped her lightly on the end of her nose and shrugged. 'Look at you. You made a new life for yourself. And you should be proud of being brave enough to take the chance.'

'Brave? Oh, Miles. Nothing could be further from the truth. For most of my life I have been the worst kind of coward.'

Andy slid her fingers from his so that she could rest her hands on his arms.

'I never told you about my dad, did I? No. You see...'

She looked at Miles, suddenly terrified, but what she saw in his face gave her the courage to carry on. 'When my dad lost his job he had a nervous breakdown. A bad one. He even spent time in hospital.'

She paused, her lips pressed tightly together. 'And when he came out he told me that he felt as though the whole world was pressing down on him, crushing him into the floor, harder and harder until all that was left of him was a greasy smear on the pavement. Can you believe that? A man who used to advise financial directors from some of the world's leading institutions thought that he was nothing but a dirty mark other people walked on?'

She shook her head. 'My parents found out the hard way that when the money ran out and the jobs disappeared overnight, that they had nothing to fall back on. We lost everything. So I started to protect myself from things that had not even happened and my world became smaller and smaller instead of bigger.'

Miles reached out for her hands and wrapped them up, safe and warm, giving her the strength to carry on. 'How did you get through that?' he asked in a low voice full of care.

'I did what I had to do. My parents took off overseas. I was out on my own. So I stopped being curious and adventurous. I couldn't take the risk. I think my spirit was withering and crushed inside of me. Until you came along. And you dragged me out of my comfort zone and forced me to re-evaluate what was important. I thought I knew, but I didn't.'

'Me? I did that?'

'I needed help to face my fear and take control—and start living in the future and not keep making decisions out of fear. And I was scared. I felt as though I were about to cross a great chasm with only one of those flimsy rope bridges attached to each side. I was scared to look down and just the thought of it made me feel sick and dizzy because I knew that if I stumbled and fell, this time there would be no getting back up again. This was it. My last chance.'

She smiled up into the handsome face that was staring at her with such delight and astonishment. And she kissed him on the lips.

'So I shocked Elise and walked away from my job and

started work at the museum six days a week. They needed someone to cover the late shift and I was happy to do it. And it means that I have the rest of the day to work on my art and study.'

'Does it make you happy?'

'Yes. It does. *Very happy.* I am never going to make a lot of money but it is enough and I will create something lovely and special and magical that I will be proud of. You helped me to do that, Miles. Thank you.'

His gaze scanned her face for a few seconds.

'I still haven't forgiven myself for what happened. Lori did care about me—she's a great girl. It was never about her—it was always about me. And I'm sorry that you were dragged into that part of my life. It was unfair.'

One of his hands slid out from between hers and his fingertips glided languorously across her forehead and cheek before lingering on the base of her throat and when he spoke, his voice was soft and intimate. 'That's why I am back in London. I want to see you again, Andy. Very much. I want to be with you. But that all depends on you. Tell me now. Do you think we can get past what happened that night and move on, so that we can be together?'

As his fingertip touched her brow and then her cheek Andy could feel the slight trembling in his touch. He meant it. He truly meant it. And her poor lonely heart forgave him right then and there. And forgave her treacherous body for not being able to resist him at the same time.

He was looking at her now, a faint hopeful smile on his lips.

'I won't let you down, Andy. Never again.'

'I know,' she whispered and smiled at him, tears running down her cheeks. 'Otherwise I wouldn't be saying yes. Yes, Miles. Yes.' And then she forgot what she was going to say next because he was hugging her so closely and kissing her breathless. Laughing, crying, and then laughing so much that she did not even notice that the car had stopped.

It was Miles who pulled away first.

'Do you see where we are?' he asked with a lilt in his voice.

Andy tore her gaze from his face as Miles opened the car door and stepped outside.

It was the coffee shop where they had first met for the Internet date.

Miles stretched out his hand and, taking her fingers in his, drew her out of the Rolls Royce car and into the coffee shop.

Only it looked nothing like the place she remembered and she came to a dead stop just inside the door. 'Wow.'

Because there were no customers. No bustle of voices and chatter. Not even baristas.

The harsh white halogens had been switched off, and in their place white pillar candles and candelabra created subtle but warm light.

Spanish music played softly in the background and mountains of fresh flowers in every possible colour combination occupied every corner of the room. Red roses and white freesias spilled out from crystal vases at the centre of each table—but as her eyes acclimatised to the riot of colour and the soft light and shadows her gaze focused on something so familiar she had to stifle a gasp of delight.

The tablecloths had been replaced by white cloths with a single logo—her logo—the one she had designed for Cory Sports, embroidered at the centre in red and blue and gold.

And it looked wonderful.

'Oh, Miles. This is…beautiful,' she whispered.

She looked back, then drew him forwards, clutching his arm as she looked around in disbelief.

'I'm glad you like it. Because this is for you. This is all for you.'

Andy turned around to look into his face. The candlelight caught the snowflakes on his coat and his skin looked golden and warm, as if it had been dusted with gold dust.

'I have an anniversary present for you,' he whispered, and as Andy gazed at him she realised that he was nervous. Which was so new that the final traces of her resentment seemed to melt as fast as the snowflakes. He had done all this for her. And her heart dissolved into mush.

Miles reached into his coat pocket and pulled out a heart-shaped box tied with a wide red ribbon.

'We met for the first time five weeks ago today. And that needs celebrating.'

She smiled to herself and tugged at the bow. A girl could always use more chocolates in her life.

But then she opened the box, and inside was a small velvet jeweller's box nestling in a sea of deep pink fresh rosebuds and white jasmine, the perfume almost overwhelming.

She ran her fingers over the box and the hard knot of loss she had been carrying for weeks dissolved as she realised what he was doing and why.

Andy swallowed down hard and looked into his face. 'Oh, Miles…'

He stepped forwards and as he spoke his gaze locked onto her eyes and held them transfixed.

'Can you forgive me? What happened at the show was all my fault. I am so sorry for letting you down, and you know that I love you so very, very much.'

'You love me? But I am not one of those sleek girls.'

'I don't want a sleek girl. I want you.'

And then he opened the jewel case and presented it to her. And there, nestling in the midnight-blue velvet, was a pink heart-shaped diamond ring. Brilliant cut, gleaming, every surface reflecting back the candlelight. It was magnificent. And the most beautiful thing she had ever seen in her life.

'I want to give you the most precious thing I possess. My heart and my love. This was the nearest thing that came close.'

Andy looked into his face and her eyes filled with tears.

'You are the woman I want to spend the rest of my life with.' And his voice broke. 'If you will take a chance on a madcap ex-surfer who is looking for love. Real love. Ridiculous, inconvenient, consuming, can't-live-without-each-other love that defies logic and interferes with everything in your life—but you cannot live without it. And I think that love is here. With the girl I am looking at right now.'

He hugged her close inside his coat, then closer, chest to chest, his arms wrapped around her body, his forehead pressing against hers. 'Take a chance on me, Andromeda Davies. Take a chance on the greatest adventure of our lives.'

'You want me? Me? Oh, Miles. Yes, yes, a thousand times yes.'

Miles replied with a great whoop and by grabbing her around the waist and swinging her off her feet and into the air, both of them laughing like children. So happy. *So very, very happy.*

Andy stepped into the space between his legs, looped her arms around his neck.

And it was only as her feet hit the ground that she realised that outside the coffee shop window the snowflakes were falling. Thick large flakes. The air was thick with them, transforming the London streets into a winter wonderland of white trees and shrubs and statues.

'Miles. Look. Look.'

She snuggled back against his warm, solid chest, which held a heart as wide as the ocean.

It was truly magical. She was in the arms of the man she loved who loved her back in return. And there was nowhere else in this world that she wanted to be.

Because she had his heart and he had hers.

And all because of a few little white lies.

* * * * *

Snow, sleigh bells and a hint of seduction

Find your perfect Christmas reads at
millsandboon.co.uk/Christmas

MILLS & BOON®

Why shop at millsandboon.co.uk?

Each year, thousands of romance readers find their perfect read at millsandboon.co.uk. That's because we're passionate about bringing you the very best romantic fiction. Here are some of the advantages of shopping at www.millsandboon.co.uk:

* **Get new books first**—you'll be able to buy your favourite books one month before they hit the shops

* **Get exclusive discounts**—you'll also be able to buy our specially created monthly collections, with up to 50% off the RRP

* **Find your favourite authors**—latest news, interviews and new releases for all your favourite authors and series on our website, plus ideas for what to try next

* **Join in**—once you've bought your favourite books, don't forget to register with us to rate, review and join in the discussions

Visit **www.millsandboon.co.uk**
for all this and more today!